Also by Andrea Bartz

THE LOST NIGHT

THE HERD

BALLANTINE BOOKS

NEW YORK

THE HERD

A NOVEL

Andrea Bartz

The Herd is a work of fiction. Names, characters, places, and incidents
are the products of the author's imagination or are used fictitiously.
Any resemblance to actual events, locales, or persons,
living or dead, is entirely coincidental.

Published in the United States by Ballantine Books,
an imprint of Random House, a division of
Penguin Random House LLC, New York.

BALLANTINE and the HOUSE colophon are registered
trademarks of Penguin Random House LLC.

LIBRARY OF CONGRESS CATALOGING-IN-PUBLICATION DATA
Names: Bartz, Andrea, author.
Title: The herd : a novel / Andrea Bartz.
Description: First Edition. | New York : Ballantine Books, [2020]
Identifiers: LCCN 2019038590 (print) | LCCN 2019038591 (ebook) |
ISBN 9781984826367 (hardcover) | ISBN 9781984826374 (ebook)
Subjects: LCSH: Missing persons–Investigation–Fiction. |
GSAFD: Suspense fiction.
Classification: LCC PS3602.A8438 H47 2020 (print) |
LCC PS3602.A8438 (ebook) | DDC 813/.6–dc23
LC record available at https://lccn.loc.gov/2019038590
LC ebook record available at https://lccn.loc.gov/2019038591

Printed in Canada on acid-free paper

randomhousebooks.com

2 4 6 8 9 7 5 3 1

FIRST EDITION

Book design by Dana Leigh Blanchette

For Tom and Cathy

PROLOGUE

The cold crept inside the body's outermost parts first. It turned aqueous cells into something solid, worked its way in millimeter by millimeter. The pert nose. The eyelashes, still coated in thick mascara. The earlobes, studded with delicate silver rings. The fingertips were quick to crystallize, dusty whiteness spreading over the knuckles until the nails, painted black with tiny white stars, stood out like a sore thumb. The blood was briefly sludgy, then solid and stiff, its hard work, zipping oxygen and nutrients and white blood cells around the body, complete.

And the brain—this was a pity. It was an exceptionally good one, a coiled spring packing potential energy, all the grand ideas and glinting insights yet to come. Its tissue froze neuron by neuron, the little synapses that so recently zapped and sparked now just cold, dead space between the cells.

In a way, it was a blessing. They say anything frozen, in theory, could last forever. Beauty may be fleeting, the smooth skin and shiny hair of youth giving way to crinkles and crags, to thin, dingy locks. Taut thighs plumping out or growing weak and scrawny. But not this body. The subzero air surrounding every inch of it assured total preservation. A stopping of time.

It was almost midnight, but the body was bright, bathed in ugly artificial light. A door thudded closed; blackness descended, and the body was left to freeze in peace.

PART I

CHAPTER 1

Katie

MONDAY, DECEMBER 9, 10:48 A.M.

My body tensed before I knew what I was seeing: strobes of red and blue, the universal sign of an emergency. I paused and squinted at the squad car across the street, its lights flashing, eerier for the lack of a siren. I breathed deeply, commanded my chest to relax. Two weeks back in New York City, and despite everyone's warnings, the sounds, the smells, the crush of people and hulking cliffs of steel and glass—none of it bothered me, none of it took any reassimilation. But this was the first manic police light I'd seen, and like Pavlov's bell it'd made every muscle tighten.

I crossed the street and realized the two cops standing bored on the road weren't just blocking my entrance—they appeared to be at the Herd, speaking to a wisp of a woman in an impressively flattering parka. I leaned forward and flashed my widest smile.

"Excuse me, I'm so sorry to interrupt." They flicked their heads my way, annoyed. "It's okay for me to go in?" I pointed at the door behind them.

"Are you a member?" the woman asked.

"I have an appointment with Eleanor." She raised her eyebrows and I sighed. "I'm Hana's sister."

She took a half step back. "Oh, go on up. The Gleam Room's closed but everything else is, uh, business as usual."

I thanked her and hurried out of the cold to wait for the single elevator. *The Gleam Room? What the hell is a Gleam Room?*

On the tenth floor, the doors slid open and I stepped out into a sunlit entryway. I paused, momentarily stunned. I'd seen the floor shortly after Eleanor had first rented it, had even donned a hard hat and closed-toe shoes for a tour shortly before I'd left town, but that hive of dust and drywall and sweaty contractors had little in common with the space before me. It had the girly chicness of a magazine office, but without the clutter or bustle—here everything was calm. Sunlight spilled in from the windows; it was warm but not stuffy, and the air smelled vaguely of plumeria. A woman with glossy French-braid pigtails and molded spectacles smiled at me from behind a marble-fronted desk. On the wall behind her was the now-famous logo: THE HERD, the H-E-R a deep plum, the other letters gray.

She checked me in, had me scribble my finger across an iPad in the wild snarl I counted as my signature, and then she gestured toward the nearest lounge. "Eleanor will get a notification that you're here," she said brightly, touching off a little chirrup in my chest. "Feel free to take a seat."

I thanked her and stepped inside the room, which was ringed with forest-green booths and benches, a few sofas and armchairs clustered at the center. I peeled off my coat and sent a text: "You here?"

I heard Hana before I saw her, her heels clacking along the par-quiet floor. Hana enters any room like Lily Tomlin in an '80s office comedy. "Katie!" she cried, arms wide.

"I take back everything I said," I said into her shoulder. "This place is unreal, Hana. I feel like I'm inside Athena's vagina."

She cracked up and let me go, then took a step back. Evaluating. "That's the Katie I know," she said, tapping my shoulder. "You've been off your game the last couple of weeks. I was beginning to worry Kalamazoo had permanently killed off your sense of humor."

Ah yes, Hana coming in hot with the thinly veiled criticism. "Don't scapegoat Michigan. I've just been getting my bearings." I looked beyond her. "Is Mikki here? Oh, and do you know what's going on this morning? There are cops by the door."

She frowned. "Somebody broke in last night. Spray-painted some obscenities in the Gleam Room."

I held up a finger. "Is that a fancy term for the bathroom? Because I will *not* abide that nomenclature."

She laughed. "It's a beauty room with mirrors. You can hire someone to do your hair or makeup or just use the products there, like, if you have a meeting or audition or date to go to."

A few members had floated by, all perfectly coiffed and clad in stylish, breezy outfits. "Good, 'cause everyone here looks like shit," I remarked.

A woman with a black bun the exact size and shape of a bagel paused behind Hana, leaning in expectantly. Hana noticed her and jumped.

"Katie, this is Aurelia," Hana said. "She's the head member relations coordinator."

She looked younger than me, early-twenties, impossibly chic in a tailored black jumpsuit. A radiant smile, teeth like pearls. "So you're Hana's sister!"

It clicked—she was the woman I'd seen out front. I shook her hand enthusiastically, and she didn't do the annoying double take we often get when people learn we're siblings: the back-and-forth between Hana's thick, dark hair, golden-brown eyes, and dark skin and me, as bland as a cornfield.

"Eleanor mentioned you were coming," she said. "You just moved back, right?"

"She was researching a book in Michigan," Hana jumped in. "She's a journalist."

"Wow! What's the book about?"

I'd been practicing this on the subway ride here: "There's this small technology company there that sort of stumbled into the lucrative world of reality manipulation: fake news, convincing bots, that kind of thing. I wrote a feature about them for *Wired* and now I'm expanding it into a book."

"That's so interesting." Something in her eyes unsettled me, a quivering intensity. "Eleanor and I were just talking about the falsity of the online world, and how everyone's craving real connection. She said—"

"I'm so sorry, but she has an interview!" Hana's teeth gleamed as she sent Aurelia away. When she'd gone, Hana shrugged. "She's sweet, but she'll talk your ear off. I want you focused before your big Herd interview."

"Hopefully Eleanor will go easy on me." I glanced around. "I think people are looking at us. Are you and Mikki basically celebrities?"

Hana rolled her eyes, but I could sense her pride. The Herd employed Hana as its part-time publicist, and Mikki, another of their friends from Harvard, was its freelance graphic designer. More important, the two freelancers were Eleanor's confidantes, part of her tiny inner circle. Now everyone in the room was feigning disinterest in us, too subtle to gaze at Hana head-on; instead they tilted their high cheekbones and typed rapidly into their keyboards.

"Anyway, make yourself at home. I'll find Mikki." She took off, her heels ticking.

I strode after her and peered into the next room, the one that'd just swallowed her up. White bookshelves stretched from corner to corner, the books organized by color. So neatly aligned I wanted to shove one out at an odd angle, fling a few books onto the floor just to see what would happen. Farther in there was a vast, sunny room, and off to the side, a short hallway plastered in hip wallpaper—a pattern of illustrated red lips smirking and smiling and sticking out their tongues. Someone had sealed off the hallway with a strip of Scotch tape, a Post-it in the middle proclaiming CLOSED FOR A MINUTE! The Gleam Room. I wondered again what was scrawled across its walls—what merited the squad car out front.

Then Hana and Mikki burst in from the sunny room, marching out to meet me near the doorway. When she hugged me, Mikki smelled the way I remembered, sweet and a little musky. Winter be damned, she was wearing a crocheted halter top and loose pants covered in an elephant print, her feathered '70s-style hair in crumpled curls, her face bare.

"For fuck's sake, Hana, why didn't you offer to take her coat?" Mikki pulled at the leather jacket slung over my forearm. "C'mon, let me give you the tour and then I want to hear all about Minnesota."

"Michigan."

"Shit. This is how badly I need an update." She grinned, freckles dancing on her cheeks, and spun toward the sunlight at the far end of the space. I'd hoped to see Mikki a couple weeks ago; she'd hosted a big "Misfit Toys Friendsgiving" in her rent-controlled, ramshackle apartment. But when the day had come, I'd been too tired and disoriented to attend.

Hana announced she had to answer some emails and split off as Mikki pointed out a chic café counter along a wall, avocado toast on vintage-looking plates sliding across its marble top: "Coffee is free, but everything else is expensive." She bopped along, smiling serenely, oblivious to the Herders stealing glances at us as we passed.

Mikki's superpower is that she very rarely cares—about anything, really. When I'd announced my book deal on Facebook—my most-liked post to date—she'd commented only to say the CEO of the company I was writing about was sort of hot. At the time, it had stung, but now her cheerful indifference was a relief: one less person pressing me about my research, the months that got bunched up and knotted and ended with ambulances, with sirens chopping the air.

She and I hooked right toward a final set of doors; one led into the bathroom and one was marked MOVE with a faint capital *L* behind the *M*. But it was the third door that Mikki took me through, into a small room with birchwood lockers on one side and clothing racks on the other, holding up a rainbow of coats.

"You can pay for a locker if you want to keep stuff here overnight," Mikki said, plunging a hanger into my jacket's shoulder, "but nobody really steals anything. Just now I left my laptop out on a table." She gestured back into the sun-splashed room, with its blue velvet workstations and glossy acrylic chairs girdling a long, medieval-looking table. "Everyone's so well vetted."

"Except that someone broke in last night, right? A vandal." I followed her back into the brightness. "Aren't people freaked out?"

She leaned in, lowered her voice. "Babe, most people don't know. But it's weird, you need a bunch of different keys to get in. *I* don't even have them all. And the security camera in the elevator, it's motion-activated—no footage from last night." She paused in front of the lipstick wallpaper, the makeshift police tape, then ducked and ran past it like a slapstick ninja. I stifled a giggle and followed.

"Eleanor will be so mad if she sees us," she hissed, leading me into a room and fumbling for the light switch.

"So will my sister," I replied as the lights blinked on. Hundreds of them: vintage-looking bulbs ringing six oval mirrors, a purple stool perched in front of each, the countertop lined with Gleam beauty products. I knew Mikki had done the graphic design on their packaging, jade-green words on a dove-gray background. I was about to reach for a lipstick, as entranced as a magpie spotting something shiny, when movement in the mirror made me turn around.

Mikki was staring at the back wall, her arms crossed. I followed her gaze up to where the striped mauve and white wall met the ceiling: black spray paint, deliberate bubble letters.

UGLY CUNTS

"Someone really sucks at writing positive affirmations," I said after a moment.

Mikki whipped around and smiled. "Some jealous idiot. Probably a dude all enraged that there's five thousand square feet on the surface of the planet he's not allowed to dominate. Maybe someone from the Antiherd."

"'The *Antiherd*'?"

She rolled her eyes. "It's a secret online hate group dedicated to Eleanor and the Herd. Or that's the rumor—I haven't seen the message board. You heard a group of guys tried to sue us for violating antidiscrimination laws earlier this year? Word is that was organized through the Antiherd."

"Gross." But interesting. My journalist antennae went up—there was an article there. Just as quickly, I dismissed the thought: It was a topic Eleanor and Hana would never, ever let me cover. I looked around the room again. "No cameras?"

"None. Ask Hana about that." She flapped her hand. "Eleanor said someone's wallpapering over it tonight. She was so horrified by it she wouldn't even tell me what it said. She *hates* the word."

"What, 'cunt'? Weird they used it, then." I cocked my head. "Actually, I guess it's not that weird. It's the worst thing you can call a woman."

"You can't be here." I jumped and we both turned to see Aurelia, the chatty member relations coordinator, glowering in the doorway. She blanched when she saw Mikki's face. "I mean—the Gleam Room is closed for the day."

"Just needed a little Gleam Cream." Mikki strolled into the hallway.

"Sorry you had to see this," Aurelia said to me as we strode back into the main room. She smoothed the tape onto the wall behind us. "And just let me know if you need anything." I sent her off with a wave.

"Are you hanging out today or just meeting with Eleanor?" Mikki asked.

"I'm planning to stay." I trailed her to the corner where her Mac-Book and bag were spilled across a loveseat's cushions. Her backpack gaped and a whole jumble of shit was slipping out, as if trying to sneak away: tampon, Blow Pop, vape pen, set of X-Acto knives, glue stick, what appeared to be a fun-size can of Mace. "I mean, if Eleanor lets me."

"If I do what?" The throaty voice rang out and I whirled around, wearing a big openmouthed smile. "Katie!" she cried, and wrapped me in a hug. I closed my eyes and felt our necks against each other's, our hair touching, a real hug.

She stepped back, her palms still on my shoulders. "It's so good to see you, my dear. You look fantastic."

"So do you," I replied. And she did, like Entrepreneur Barbie: shiny brown hair in mermaid curls, skin dewy, eyes clear. I looked over Eleanor's shoulder and saw that Hana had returned; both she and Mikki were beaming.

I'd met Eleanor and Mikki when I'd visited Hana at Harvard, back when I was a gangly high schooler in awe of the smart, sassy women my big sister had befriended in the dorms. I flew to Boston every few months, feeling extremely adult as I navigated the airport alone, and they'd always treated me like their collective little sister—movie nights and Ben & Jerry's at first, supervised frat parties when

I was a little older. I'd moved to New York for college, right as Eleanor, gutsy Eleanor, sashayed into Manhattan, Mikki a few months behind her. (Hana, on the other hand, had inexplicably returned to L.A. after graduation, irritating me to no end—but about three years ago, Eleanor had convinced Hana to move to NYC. Now we were all where we were supposed to be.)

Back in 2010, when I myself was a freshman at NYU and my sister and her friends were newly minted Harvard alums, Eleanor had begun luring in investors for her first venture: Gleam, an ethically sourced cosmetics line, back when the natural-beauty industry was still shedding its patchouli-scented skin. Because she's brilliant, Eleanor had done everything right with her fledgling beauty company—founding a crisp, airy lifestyle blog that quickly amassed hundreds of thousands of devotees, investing in pop-ups instead of retail space, creating a public persona that felt personable and real but not oversharey or gauche.

And I was there for all of it. I'd reached out to her, shyly and at Hana's urging, to meet for dinner during my orientation week at NYU. I adored Eleanor but was intimidated, still, and at best I hoped for someone I could keep in my contacts list, a chic "adult" I could call if I got in a jam. Instead, Eleanor became my family—Mikki too. It awed me then, the thrill of getting invites and calls and wine-soaked heart-to-hearts with these magnificent women. We'd Skype Hana together from Eleanor's sofa, gossiping and catching up and feeling as if the warm sunlight on Hana's coast was seeping through the connection and into Eleanor's battered apartment on the Lower East Side. While I studied for midterms and Mikki designed packaging for weird start-ups (a mail-order dog tiara company comes to mind), I'd watched as Eleanor built her beauty brand and grew vast in the public eye, but remained Eleanor, my Eleanor.

"How's your mom doing?" she asked, and Hana stiffened behind her.

"Super well at the moment," I replied. I felt my phone buzz

again and willed myself to ignore it—I had an idea who was on the end of the line. "She's getting her energy back and her scans keep coming back clean. Hana and I are going home to see her for Christmas."

"I'm so glad. I know I've said this already, but it's incredible you were able to be there for her."

I cleared my throat. "I'm glad too. I'm lucky I had that flexibility. And I know it's only been a few weeks, but this time around, New York feels . . . different. *I'm* different."

"Well, it's good to have you back." She smiled and held my gaze, those intense eyes, always able to make you feel like the only person in the room.

Behind her, Hana shifted her weight, stuffing a hand into her pocket. We hadn't talked about it head-on—Hana never was one for discussing our feelings—but I'd assured her multiple times before, during, and after the last year that she shouldn't feel bad about staying in New York during Mom's treatment. Business at her solo PR firm was booming, whereas I'd been unemployed after *Rocket*, the tech news site where I'd been a reporter, had folded. And anyway, Hana's presence at home with Mom would've just stressed both of them out. And so I'd spent pretty much all of 2019 isolated in Michigan, freelancing, working on my book, and driving Mom to and from her treatments.

It'd been a decent time to be a stringer in the Midwest: Politicians were announcing their 2020 runs, the culture wars were heating up, and national papers rooted in the coasts were clamoring for quotes from Middle America, from the "working class," from the "anxiety-filled" white folks in so-called flyover states. Dutifully, I'd attended rallies and conducted interviews and scribbled down quotes and smiled blandly while the crowds railed against my profession. Then I'd tapped out my stories in a trance, only breaking down into sobs after I'd filed my copy. In a way, it felt right; no one expects you to be cheerful when your mother is battling stage-three breast cancer.

"Well, I'm going to steal you away for a bit," Eleanor announced, turning to her friends, "but we'll keep it quick."

My pulse hastened as we headed toward the elevators. I'd had a stress dream the night before in which I'd shown up late and then realized, with mounting panic, that I was still in my childhood bedroom in Kalamazoo, unable to wrench the door open.

"Oh, you should meet Stephanie," Eleanor said. She stopped short and looked around, then led me over to a tall woman in red tuxedo pants and a silky blouse. I recognized her angular jaw and close-cropped hair from her photo on the Herd's website. "Stephanie, this is Katie! Remember I told you Hana's sister was moving back?"

"Of course! So nice to meet you."

"You as well! You're the director of . . . operations, right?" Thank God I'd done my research last night. Eleanor had poached her from WeWork as her first full-time hire.

"That's right, Eleanor's second-in-command." They smiled at each other.

"And it's lucky you caught Stephanie today—after this week she'll be off the grid until the New Year!"

She beamed. "I'm doing yoga teacher training in Goa. It's always been a dream of mine."

"Amazing. Where will you teach?"

"Hopefully here!" She gestured into the space and it clicked: the room marked MOVE was a fitness studio.

"*Definitely* here," Eleanor added. We traded nice-to-meet-yous as Eleanor turned down a small hallway behind the check-in desk, and I gasped at the sight of yet another perfect room: palm-frond wallpaper, spider plants in hanging gold pots, and a seating area with soft white chairs and gold shelving units.

"I hope you have defibrillators all over the place," I said, smacking my chest, "because I don't think my heart can take much more of this. It's *gorgeous*, Eleanor. Every single room. It's even better in real life than it looks on Instagram. Which is almost *never* the case."

"Wow, thank you." She plucked a framed photo off the shelf and handed it to me: Hana, Mikki, and Eleanor with sparkly eyes and skinny arms poking out of spangly going-out tops. It was taken in a dorm room, a crummy, overexposed shot; Mikki and Eleanor looked milk-white in the flash while Hana's skin looked like copper.

"Babies!" I cried.

"I know. Freshman year. The only thing missing from the photo is you."

"Uh, my braces and acne would have ruined the shot." I handed it back to her. "It's incredible that you've all stayed so close. I have friends from college, but not like that."

"I know. We're so lucky." Eleanor placed the frame back on the shelf. Next to it was a stack of leather-bound notebooks and a small knife with a carved handle floating in a stand. The shelf above it held a cute photo of Eleanor and her boyfriend—no, husband now, I'd missed the wedding—on vacation somewhere warm. Mexico, judging by the ornate, embroidered tunic she was wearing, and what looked like a fat margarita in Daniel's hand. Eleanor spoke fluent Spanish and had always loved the country.

She pulled a notebook off her desk and settled across from me. "So when did you actually get back in town?"

"Two weeks ago yesterday."

"After a whole year in Michigan, right?"

"Yeah, about a year." I caught myself picking at a hangnail and folded my hands.

She leaned back, smiled. "Katie Bradley, you're here! You're here and it's all real."

"Yes! I'm sorry it took so long—I should have called when I

landed. It's been crazy with the move and getting back in touch with my editors, and—"

"No, I get it." Her fingers winged up into the *stop* gesture, blue-and-silver nails glinting. "I figured you'd need a little time to adjust. Taking care of your mom and writing a freaking book. Super-woman."

"Oh, please. Look who's talking."

"Everyone thinks they can write a book, but you're actually doing it. Tell me everything."

A pinch in my chest, like tongs squeezing. I rattled off my standard fake-news tech company line.

"So cool. And you already have a publisher."

"Yeah, just—working things out with my agent," I said, mumbling a bit.

Eleanor leaned back in her chair. "We have a few members who work in publishing. People have such varied reasons for joining. Some are here to network, some obviously signed up for the co-working space. But also, we didn't really anticipate this, but about a third of our members have full-time, in-office jobs already. What, why are you laughing?"

I let the stifled giggle bloom into a grin. "You just morphed into Television Eleanor. Teleanor. It was awesome."

Her knuckles found her brow. "God, did I? I'm sorry—I've been doing so much press lately, with the Fort Greene location opening soon. I didn't mean to go all time-share presentation on you."

"No, it's not that! You're just so *on*. Here, I'll feel better if *I* interview *you*." My hand gripped an imaginary microphone and her eyebrows shot up. "Now, Eleanor, I'm surprised to learn that women are signing up for a coworking space without any intention of *co-working* there. Is it really worth spending three hundred dollars a month for the privilege of attending the Herd's after-work programming? I saw that you have panels on Afrofuturism, feminism's global footprint, and how to run for local office."

She scoffed, mock-shocked: "The events calendar is members-only."

"I may have a mole. In my immediate family." We both giggled.

She arranged her face into that perfectly symmetrical smile, the one I knew from profiles of her in *The New York Times*, *The New Yorker*, et al. "It's not just the programming. People call the Herd a club, but we like to call it a community. It's a sacred space designed to make our members' lives more balanced, beautiful, and connected."

"Hell of a line." I nodded approvingly. "For real, though, I got that vibe the moment I walked in. I love how the setup sort of facilitates collaboration." I brought my hands together, tapped the fingertips. "Like, it isn't just a bunch of cubicles for rent. Women seem to come for the other women too."

She kept up the camera-ready facade: "That's exactly right. Wonderful things happen when passionate women and marginalized genders come together."

"'Women and marginalized genders.' God, Michigan really makes you forget how 'liberal elites' talk."

"Only the woke are welcome here." It was clearly a joke, but I felt a ribbon of unease. This past year, as I was falling apart in Kalamazoo, Eleanor, Hana, and Mikki had been here, together, being all progressive—they'd *progressed*. I wished I could go back to 2018 and have a do-over with me here, at the Herd, from the beginning.

Eleanor folded her hands and leaned back. "So how do you see yourself using the Herd?"

My fingers found my necklace. "I'll be working on book stuff, of course," I said. "But I'm also hoping to get back into freelancing—reconnect with old editors and meet some new ones."

"Yeah, you were placing some pretty high-profile pieces, right?"

I was surprised she'd been keeping tabs. I felt my chest puff as I rattled off the publications I'd written for: *Vogue*, *New York Mag*, *People*, *Vanity Fair*, and *Vice*.

"And you wrote that piece on Titan's voice-activated thingy for *The Atlantic*, right?"

"That's right, the Zeus." Wow, she really had been paying attention. My feature on the tech giant's groundbreaking, AI-equipped virtual assistant—and the privacy issues it raised—had been one of my favorite bylines of the year, but it hadn't garnered many page views. "It was a one-off."

"Got it. You still doing any satire? That Steve Jobs piece you wrote for the blog was one of the most-shared things we ran all year."

I grinned. "I *loved* writing for you. But no, not really. Maybe I'll try again." I shrugged. "Networking is a big part of the freelance hustle; it's part of why I'd love to join. But I also . . . I love it here."

She smiled calmly. "We do have to follow the normal procedures for you. There's a waitlist—we don't want to look shady."

I worked hard to keep the hurt off my face. "Yes, I've read some very intense things about the Herd's application process!" There were entire forums dedicated to getting in, picking apart one another's materials in search of a pattern.

"I feel bad about it. The Fort Greene location will let us expand membership—it's huge. But of course the contractors are taking forever." She closed her eyes. "I wish someone would start an all-female construction company. I'd hire the crap out of them. I was on-site in Brooklyn on Friday arguing with the head contractor about the floorboards, and the installer showed up and started talking to him literally right over my head. He's lucky he was wearing a tool belt or I'd have kicked him in the balls."

There was a beat, and what the hell, I went all in.

"Eleanor, I've *missed* you. I've been reading about you everywhere. I can't believe you made all this happen. You're my hero. Emphasis on the H-E-R."

"You know, it's amazing we've put any marketing materials out without your wordsmithery."

"You need me!" I was pushing too hard, a tinge of desperation under my banter, but I couldn't stop. "And though I didn't know it an hour ago, I need this place too. I want to make it my second home until, like, I'm so decrepit they have to wheel me into a retirement community."

"So glad to hear it. It really has all come together, hasn't it? I'm so—" It was the slightest of pauses, the tiniest key change. "I'm so happy."

My sensors went up. They were newly attuned after eleven months of interviewing smiling, close-lipped Midwesterners who viewed me as an uppity outsider. But then Eleanor stretched and grinned and I thought maybe I'd imagined it.

"It will be so great to be able to see you every day," I told her.

"It will, Katie," she said. "It will."

I left Eleanor in her office and skipped through the interconnecting rooms, on the lookout for Mikki and Hana. There was something fizzy in my chest, and I realized with a jolt that this place, this moment, was so annoyingly perfect it looped back into not-annoying. I hadn't had to fight back tears all day. Chris hadn't bubbled up in my mind in almost three hours, a new record. The sadness like a layer of black mold over my brain and ribs—I'd begun to think of it as permanent, the way I'd feel for the rest of my life. Mikki waved me over and I pulled my phone from my purse as I shimmied onto the sofa, then froze. There was a text from Mom: "Good luck today! xoxo"

And four voicemails, all from a New York City number I recognized. I looked at the list: The earliest was forty-two seconds long, and the later ones grew shorter, the last just twelve seconds. I swallowed, feeling my pulse thumping in my neck. Then I reached out and slid my finger across them one by one: delete, delete, delete, delete.

CHAPTER 2

Hana

I watched Katie and Eleanor disappear into Eleanor's office, chatting happily. Katie was wearing leather boots, stained with salt, even though I'd asked her to come in heels. I'd considered texting her a reminder last night, checking if she had any last-minute questions, assuaging the anxiety I thought she might be feeling. But I'd resisted, Mikki's words echoing in my mind: *She's an adult. You're not her mother. You're not responsible for her.* All true, and all things I repeated to myself whenever Katie released a tweetstorm of expletive-riddled jokes or a sudden rant about being a woman in the world. *Your words hold power,* I'd told her once, during a text conversation that quickly devolved into an argument. *Your words shape how people see you.* Things that should be obvious, one would think, to a journalist such as herself.

But she'd shown up at the Herd on time this morning, looking cute if a bit underdressed, and for the first time since she moved back, she looked alert. For weeks she'd blamed exhaustion and seasonal affective disorder, her voice jagged with sleep when I called her at eleven, noon, sometimes one. It seemed clear something else was bothering her—I had my money on heartbreak—but hadn't asked.

Katie's move—what an odd day. She'd found a roommate through friends, a fellow NYU alum with an open room in Bed-Stuy. For a year, while Katie was in Michigan, her furniture had sat in a moving pod somewhere in Queens. When she unpacked it last month, furniture sliding out like pieces of a 3-D puzzle, her eyes remained wide, her mouth a small o. As if U-Pack had bundled up and handed over someone else's life.

She hadn't invited me back, so I didn't know how unpacking had gone. But I'd had her over several times, ostensibly to catch up but in practice to eat dinner while watching a movie, my cat, Cosmo, curled in a furry ball between us. Katie hadn't said much about Kalamazoo, about those last few weeks when she fell radio silent before announcing her return, but I was trying not to press her. I wanted things to be different, better, this time around, and Katie didn't respond well to nagging.

Katie would love the Herd, was already impressed—I could tell. She'd been ready to roll her eyes, but the way her face lit up as she walked through . . . it was vindicating, I'll admit.

Next to me, Mikki pulled a massive nubby cardigan from her backpack and swung it over her shoulders. She looked so cozy in her billowy pants and blanketlike sweater; I felt the squeeze of faux-leather leggings against my own waist.

"So this is the first time Eleanor and Katie have seen each other?" she asked. "Since she got back, I mean."

"Yeah, first time." Too bad—maybe if they'd seen each other sooner, somewhere private, Eleanor could have asked Katie the inevitable *How's your mom?* without me cringing and blushing three feet away. It wasn't Eleanor's fault, it was kind of her to ask . . . well, that was the problem: The fault was all mine. I'm the older sister, the one with means and, as a freelance publicist, a flexible work schedule—the obvious candidate for moving back home. And yet I'd put it off, panicked at the prospect of having to spend all that time with Mom. I'd cried with relief and shame when Katie announced she would be the one to move to Michigan.

I cleared my throat. "I guess she needed a little time to get her bearings."

"Well, and Eleanor's become a bigger deal since Katie moved away. Maybe she felt intimidated."

"Maybe."

I'm the one who studied psychology, but Mikki (BA in visual arts) was a keen observer too. It's what makes her such a good artist, most likely: She can people-watch, drawn in by the smallest details and spinning them into larger narratives. The gaudy engagement ring peeking out from a frayed jacket cuff. The gold-link watch, sagging on a skinny wrist. And yet she often misses things the rest of the world can't shut up about: a meme that breaks the Internet, a major piece of news.

Eleanor and Mikki were roommates in the dorm freshman year—random roommates, and randomly just two doors down from me, because the Fates are kind like that sometimes. Eleanor and I met during move-in day, smiling at each other across a thrumming certainty that *yes, we would be friends.* Eleanor quickly grew close with Mikki, an arty yet unpretentious hipster from Asheville and the first in her family to attend college. Orientation week, when other freshmen were wandering the campus in massive frightened globs, we were already a trio.

A burst of high, chattering voices from the corner; a gaggle of women had come upon the pair they were looking for, hugs and exclamations all around. I recognized a few of them: They were starting a nonprofit to aid disaster relief efforts with phone-tree technology. Around them, other Herders flashed their chins in the group's direction, moving like a school of fish.

"I can't wait for the Fort Greene location to open," Mikki said. "It's such a zoo in here."

"I miss being able to sit outside. You were the last one who could stand it."

"I know—but I had the entire roof to myself. I was shivering and typing with fingerless gloves, some real *Mr. Popper's Penguins* shit." She mimed it, waggling her fingers. The closing of the Herd's rooftop garden had felt like a small death. Winters always hit me hard, the frost seeping into my lungs and camping there as something like sorrow, a sweeping melancholia no pricy therapeutic lamp could counter. It's one of the reasons I'd moved to L.A. after graduation. Though not the most pressing one—the incident I'd smashed into the tiniest corner of my mind.

Mikki pulled a vape pen from her backpack and took a hit.

"Didn't Eleanor already yell at you for that?"

She smirked. "It's CBD. I need constant calming. And c'mon, you know we can do whatever we want here." Mikki's favorite pastime is making me uncomfortable. "Hey, you staying for Monday Mocktails? It's the bartender from Bamboo tonight."

"That new tiki bar in SoHo?" I tilted my head. "I'm surprised Eleanor didn't write it off as, like, cultural appropriation."

"I guess when *New York Mag* devotes three pages to your cocktails, you get a free pass. I think they bill themselves as 'Pacific kitsch' or something."

"Figures." I drummed my nails on my computer. "I have a client meeting at four, so I'll have to miss this one. You should ask Katie, though. It'd be good for her to start making friends here."

"You shouldn't worry about her." She nodded toward the other rooms, toward Eleanor's office, past the Gleam Room I'd ducked into this morning when no one was looking: UGLY CUNTS.

"She's got friends in high places."

———

"Hana!"

I was zooming toward the elevators, answering an email on my phone as I walked, when I heard the holler. I looked back and saw Eleanor leaning out of her office door, hinging at the waist so only her head and shoulders popped out, like someone in a goofy sitcom. She was forcing a smile, but her eyes gave her away.

I walked over. "What can I do for you?"

"Have a seat." She leaned back, as if it were my job to begin the conversation. My phone lit up and I turned it over on my lap.

"So how'd it go with Katie?" I said brightly.

"She is *such* a rising star. It's so cool to see."

"I know, I'm so proud of her."

She clasped her hands. "You know I love Katie."

"I sense a 'but.'"

"I'd love your opinion. If you have time."

"Of course." Three thirty-six, my phone had read—if I didn't get out of here soon, I'd be late for my meeting. Eleanor did this sometimes—snapping into professional mode even when it was just Mikki and me. It was necessary, the reason we could be both best friends and coworkers without anyone ripping anyone's head off. But that didn't make it less annoying.

Her eyes floated to the right, like she was choosing her words carefully. "I'm not entirely convinced she's someone we'd normally take," she finally said. "She's brilliant, obviously. But she's young."

I dipped my chin. "Eleanor, your head member relations coordinator can barely purchase alcohol."

"Okay, immature. We're so selective here, and it's really a . . . a discreet bunch. Katie can be a little rash on social media, an over-sharer, I think sometimes she speaks without thinking. . . ."

I sighed. Eleanor wasn't wrong, of course, but I wasn't sure what she wanted from me.

"Hana, you know we have some extremely high-profile members here. And part of what they love about the Herd is that it's private — it's a haven where they're out of the public eye."

My eyes rolled before I could stop myself. "C'mon, Eleanor, you know Katie's a sensitive, conscientious person. And anyway, I'm not the person you should be talking to. Katie's twenty-seven; I'm not her keeper."

"I understand, and I wasn't implying that." I knew Eleanor's poker face well enough to recognize irritation swelling underneath the serene expression — irritation matching my own. "I just thought you might have some insight into how she'd be in this environment. Especially given all your work with A-list clients. I just want everyone to feel comfortable." Her palms bobbed in front of her chest as she spoke, as if she were juggling invisible knives.

"Well, I appreciate that," I lied. I began to gather my things, slipped my phone back into my purse. "I think Katie would be a wonderful addition to the Herd community and I hope, based on her own merits, you feel the same. Look, I am so sorry but I have a meeting on Fourteenth Street at four. Is there anything else you need? Anything for the event next week?"

"No, we're fine there, thank you."

We smiled at each other. Another point of contention: Eleanor had asked me to plan an event for the following Tuesday, essentially a press briefing around an exciting announcement, but she hadn't told me what the damn announcement would be.

"Anyway, thanks for letting me grab you." She swept a lock of hair off her cheek. "I love your dress, by the way."

"Thanks!" I chirped, and I waited until I was almost at the elevators to let my smile drop into a scowl.

I gripped the knife tighter and squinted at the flesh before me, sitting in a puddle of pink-red juice. The recipe for stuffed chicken breasts hadn't sounded too complicated, but now, in my small kitchen, I realized just how much detail was missing.

"How's it going with the spinach?" I called.

"I think good?" Her voice curved into a question mark. "Hopefully this is small enough. The recipe just says 'chopped fresh spinach.'"

I turned to inspect the recipe card on my kitchen island, keeping my hands up like a surgeon. "I think it needs to be finer."

"*You* need to be finer," she murmured. She squinted at the card. "You don't think this looks like that?"

"I'm sure it's fine. Want to start on the onions?"

I made a terrible head chef, but Katie kept on doggedly relying on me for kitchen management. For years, we'd both assumed we disliked cooking, likely because our mother hated it. When she'd come across a cooking show, she'd shake the remote at the screen and holler, "You're watching somebody do a chore!"

But Katie had, unexpectedly, returned from Michigan with a new goal on her lips: She wanted to learn to cook. And I could see the obvious downsides of my nightly take-out habit. So here we were, in my fully equipped kitchen, hunching over a meal kit.

When the dish came out of the oven, though, we both stared in quiet horror.

"We've made a terrible mistake," Katie whispered. Cheese and spinach had spilled out everywhere, burning in peaks and ridges, and the "stuffed" chicken breasts had curled closed like irritated clamshells.

I couldn't help it—I let out a laugh, then stifled it into the dishtowel still clutched in my hand. Katie snickered, too, and then we were both laughing uncontrollably, doubling over in my kitchen. Cosmo wandered in, sat down just long enough to fling up a leg and groom himself, then padded out, prompting another wave of hysterics.

I swiped the instructions off the island, wiping my eyes to read it.

"We were supposed to keep it shut with toothpicks!" I gasped between giggles.

"You skipped the chicken sutures?" she choked back, then composed herself. She let out one of those high, happy sighs people make to seal their laughter, as if already reminiscing about it. "I guess we won't be getting board-certified in fowl surgery."

I erupted into laughter again and she joined me, face red. I felt something in my ribs and froze the moment long enough to identify it, before it could slip away: It was the first time since she'd moved back that I'd seen Katie being Katie.

After we'd eaten the mess, Katie suggested we take a walk. She'd done this a few times, and I hadn't quite figured out why: whether this was something she did in Michigan, carving up the loneliness with long, patient strolls, or whether she perhaps was trying to reorient herself to New York, a city that had changed so much in even the eleven months she'd been away. I liked our walks—they reminded me of afternoons in Kalamazoo spent exercising our doofy yellow lab. When I was in junior high and Katie in elementary school, we'd circled the neighborhood, Kobe bounding ahead as I confidently imparted to Katie everything she needed to know about popularity and makeup and boys and fashion, topics I barely understood myself.

We ventured out into the cold, our breath forming little clouds in the streetlamps' glow. I directed us off of my street, lined with boutiques and cafés closing up for the night, and onto a residential one, where townhouses with tasteful holiday decorations unspooled down either side.

"Mom says hi," Katie said, stashing her phone in her pocket. "I texted her a photo of tonight's *fowl* play."

I snorted. "It looked like something Mom would've made."

"Only it tasted better." We walked quietly on and I waited to see if she'd say more about Mom, blunder further into the tension. When she didn't, I changed the topic: "So how was Mocktails?" We'd spent most of dinner discussing her interview. From what I could tell, Katie had no idea that Eleanor wasn't sure Katie was Herd material.

"All anyone could talk about was the vandalism," she said. "If they were trying to keep it a secret, they failed. Why didn't they just have someone come in and cover it up right away?"

"I said the same thing. But Eleanor always insists on using her friend for repair jobs. And he can't come until after hours."

Katie tugged her cap down. "I'm just offended that I couldn't re-contour my cheekbones at three in the afternoon. What kind of hellhole tears women from their Gleam Cream like *Sophie's Choice?*" I gave her a shove and she stumbled to the side, grinning. "Seriously, though, I think she should leave it up. Call it art. Cunts are awesome—they birth tiny humans. You say tagging, I say tag-line."

"Eleanor hates that word. It's not the first time some misogynist dude has come after her, but—I could tell it bugged her. She usually has a pretty thick skin."

We exchanged an identical *that sucks* look: nose scrunched, lips downturned. We don't share an iota of genetic material—myself a mélange of Middle Eastern, Eastern European, and South Asian, per an expensive DNA testing kit I'd ordered in college, and Katie an Aryan dream—but everyone comments on how alike our mannerisms are.

"'Come after her'? What happened?"

I sighed. "There are idiots who crop up if you're a public figure, especially a woman, *especially* a woman trying to fight the patriarchy by creating an empowering space for other women." We turned right, past a jumble of trash bags and old office chairs, piled like a sculpture. "She doesn't talk about it, the same way movie stars don't talk about their stalkers. The worst thing you can do is give an attention-seeker attention. But she's a huge deal. People are kind of obsessed with her. And she gets, you know. Death threats and stuff."

"Really?" Katie turned to me, her eyes like two moons.

"Of course." We'd reached a little community garden with a Christmas tree in the middle, studded with blue lights. I paused at the gate and she headed inside. "I mean, there are a lot of angry men in the world," I added, following her in. "But Eleanor won't let them scare her into shutting up."

Katie didn't reply; instead she marched up to the base of the tree and stared, her elfin face and big eyes washed in cobalt. "A lot," she said softly.

"What?" I joined her, dead grass crunching under my feet.

"There are a lot of angry men." She turned to me. "In the world."

I tilted my head, watching her closely, and then a clang rang out behind us; Katie recoiled as if struck, and I turned to see the metal fence banging closed. We hurried back and found it hadn't locked, had just swung in the wind. Katie stepped out onto the sidewalk as I tried to push the gate back open behind us.

"You okay?" I asked when we'd begun moving again.

"Of course. I'm just—Mikki said you guys don't know how the tagger got in. And he didn't, like, trash the place or anything, he just left that one message. It's weird, right?"

"Super weird. But it's not anything to stress about. Eleanor said today they're going to beef up security. Cameras at the entrances and all that."

She slipped off her beanie and tucked it into her pocket. "Oh, Mikki said to ask you why there wasn't already a camera in the Gleam Room?"

I raised my eyebrows. "Would *you* want footage of you using the Gleam Room?"

"In the other rooms, then?"

I shrugged. "When we were designing the space, I pointed out that studies show that women are less productive and feel less comfortable in offices with security cameras. Especially with this kind of clientele—what if somebody hacked in and got footage of, like, Myla Robin spilling a pitaya bowl on herself?"

"What the hell is a pitaya bowl?"

"Oh, Katie. You've missed so much." I patted her shoulder.

"They had to be studying coed workplaces, though, right? The researchers." She stepped over a cigarette butt. "Even if the study was about women feeling, you know, under a microscope, I doubt it applies to the Herd. It's one place where you're free from the male gaze."

"But I think it's conditioned—an automatic response to being watched all our lives," I said. "Anyway, it wasn't my hill to die on. I just thought it seemed relevant, and then later Eleanor decided that the only camera they were installing would be the one in the elevator."

A motorcycle came tearing around the corner, and Katie jumped.

"You okay?" I slid my arm across her shoulders. "What is it—sensory overload after Kalamazoo?"

She turned to me slowly, then swung her head away. "I'm fine."

We were almost back to my apartment, our footfalls synchronized, when Katie dug in her pocket and pulled out her phone. I took a couple more steps before I noticed she wasn't next to me, then turned and saw her frozen on the sidewalk, brow furrowed.

"What's up?" I called.

Her eyes slid over the screen a few more times before she looked up. "It's nothing. Hey, I'm gonna—"

We both saw it, a yellow cab approaching with its roof light on. She stuck an arm out—confidently, I thought, like a seasoned New Yorker—and it wheezed to a stop.

"I'll see you tomorrow!" she cried, pressing me into a quick hug and then scuttling into the back. I watched through the window to see if she'd wave, but her eyes were back on her cell.

My own phone buzzed as I reached my front door, and I pulled it out to see a text from Katie: "Left my laptop at your apt. Can you bring it to herd tomorrow?"

Katie was always forgetting her things. Not *losing* them, per se, because she always got them back—luck followed her like a scent. She texted again: "Sorry I took off so suddenly. xo"

I noticed all at once how cold my nose and fingertips had grown, and I fished for my keys in my purse.

"Hi, Hana!" the doorman called as I passed. "Slow down, you have a package!"

"Great, thanks!" I skidded to a stop at his desk. He'd mumbled when he introduced himself months ago, and I'd said *pardon?* twice but still couldn't catch it, and now I can never ask. He has an unfair advantage; every time I pick up a delivery, he gets a glimpse of my name on the address label, the woman in 4C.

I checked Instagram as he fumbled in the package room and saw that Katie had posted a photo from Mocktails: her, Mikki, and Eleanor, holding up drinks topped with flowers and cherries and tiny paper umbrellas. The old insecurity blared on: how perfect they all looked together, how strangers sometimes asked if they were sisters. Katie had grown close with them the very moment I left for the West Coast in 2010, and though that was my call, though I'd *encouraged* them all to hang out without me, though earlier today Eleanor was considering not letting Katie into the Herd—I felt a pinprick of fear that they would replace me now that she was back.

My phone pulsed in my palm as I rode the elevator. A Face-Time—no video, just audio—from Eleanor. *What?*

"Hello?" I asked, but the elevator was like a tomb, reducing her voice to staticky clicks. I pawed at the Call Back button as I plodded down the hall.

"Hana?" she said, and I paused in front of my door. Her voice sounded strange—pinched, almost.

"I'm here. What's up?"

"Can you come to my apartment?"

I froze, my key in midair. "Right now?"

"Yes."

"Is everything okay?"

The phone line sizzled for two seconds, three. "Just get here."

Two beeps, and she was gone.

CHAPTER 3

Katie

There were three keys on the fob Samantha, my new roommate, had given me—one for the deadbolt, one for the door, and one I kept meaning to ask her about—and this evening, none of them fit. I futzed and fumbled, jabbing at the keyhole like an awkward teen during his first sexual encounter, until finally the door clicked open. Then I froze, the text replaying in my mind, before pushing it open.

I'm at your apartment. I'm not leaving until we talk.

I stepped inside, holding my breath, and then exhaled when I spotted Samantha washing dishes in the sink. Maybe she'd left.

"Hi!" a voice called from the living room. I swung my head and spotted my literary agent on the couch, her fingers wrapped around her phone.

"Hey, Erin," I said as casually as possible.

I dropped my keys on the counter and fucking Samantha finally looked up from the rushing faucet and grinned. "Katie, your friend's here!"

"I see that!" I forced a smile and Samantha went back to scrubbing.

Erin started to rise and I crossed to the sofa to hug her. The black muck had settled all over my brain and chest again, this time with a splash of panic. "It's good to see you, lady," I said.

"Likewise. I was starting to think you were still in Michigan."

Something shot through me, an unpleasant geyser. "Erin, I'm really, really sorry I've been MIA. I've been so crazed with the move—"

"You're probably wondering how I found you," she cut in. I opened my mouth, closed it. "Josh mentioned you were subletting from someone in his sister's year. I asked for the address." She rubbed at her wrist. "I hope that's not creepy. I've been sitting here for a while thinking about it, and I decided my text was actually pretty creepy."

"No, it's—I understand. Should we . . . ?" I looked over my shoulder, where Samantha was washing silverware with the furious concentration of a frat guy playing flip cup. "Let's maybe talk in my room." Erin nodded and followed me in; I offered her the small chair in the corner, bordered with boxes, and sat on my crumpled duvet.

She took a deep breath. "Katie, I know this isn't super professional of me. I'm sorry if I'm overstepping, but . . . I'm worried about you. I don't know what the fuck happened in Michigan or why you're not answering my calls, but we need to talk."

Hot tears filled my eyes. Since I got back, everyone had been so curious, so interested, so jealous of my fancy book deal and research sabbatical, I'd barely admitted even to myself how broken I felt.

"Katie, talk to me. Nothing good is gonna come from avoiding me. I'll just keep clinging. Like a . . . flea."

I laughed and wiped my eyes.

"No, a leech, because girl, I don't get paid until you do," she continued. "Agents are real bloodsuckers, you know?"

I laughed again and allowed her to hug me. We'd been friends since junior year, when we'd randomly chosen seats next to each other in a massive Russian Lit seminar. When she was finally promoted from an assistant to a true literary agent two years ago, I was one of her very first clients. And when my article on Northern Sky Labs had blown up, she'd helped me pull together a proposal, and she'd convinced a bright young editor at a prestigious publisher to offer me a book contract. I owed her so much, and I hated fucking her over.

"You're gonna kill me," I announced, hunching like a pill bug.

"I'm not." She patted my knee. "Let me guess: You don't think you can write the book."

I nodded, tears trailing down my cheeks.

"Everyone feels that way when all they have is a pile of reporting and a deadline and a scary blank page. We can figure this out. What do you need, transcription services? A research assistant?"

"That's not it," I said. "I know it sounds like writer's block or whatever, but it's not. I can't write *this* book."

Her eyes flashed, but she squeezed them closed and said soothingly, "Tell me what you need, Katie. We're in this together."

"I need to cancel this book."

"But why?"

Strobing lights: red, blue, red, blue. "I just need you to trust me. I can't do it. I'll pay back the advance." I stole a glance at her. "I'm so sorry."

She shook her head. "I don't understand. Between the proposal and research, you've sunk a *year* into this. And now you just want to throw it away? Why? Did something happen there?"

I saw myself pulling over on the fifty-minute drive from Kalamazoo to Iron River, resting my head against the steering wheel and sobbing. "I just can't." I shook my head, sniffling. "I can't, I can't, I can't."

"You're being childish, frankly." I watched her morph into the bad cop, trying a new tack. "You signed a contract, Katie. This could be very, very bad for your career. What publisher wants to work with someone who gets a book deal, cashes the check, and then pulls out?"

"I know," I said, my voice bloating up into a wail. "I just . . . please."

"Is there a different angle I can go back to them with? Something more general . . . weird start-ups in the Midwest? The Rust Belt meets Silicon Valley? 'Rust Valley'—ooh, that's kind of a good title."

I considered it, then felt another blast of nausea. "No."

"Katie, what the hell? You're making this huge decision and you won't even tell me why."

It flashed before me: the flickering lights, darting through the woods. Then the wail of a siren, rumbling between the trees. I shook my head again, and she lifted her chin and closed her eyes. "I can't believe this is happening. You know *I'm* still trying to establish myself as an agent too."

"I know," I whispered.

"You were my first sale. I really advocated for you."

"I'm sorry."

I peeked up and saw she was blinking back tears too.

"What do we do now?" I said.

She threw her hands out. "Unless you have another brilliant fucking book to write instead, we go back and tell them you're pulling out. And we pay back the advance." Her palms settled on her stomach. "I think I'm gonna be sick."

My mind hurtled after it like a drowning person spotting a hole in the ice: *another brilliant fucking book to write instead*. I bit my lip, sifting through the articles I'd written over the last few years. Tired-eyed Trump supporters who'd voted for Obama eight years earlier, hooking their hopes on the promise of change. Weary poll workers who'd tottered out of retirement to check in registered voters, less interested in the democratic process than the $9.50-per-hour paycheck. Ruddy-nosed men at local rallies, wearing misogynist T-shirts and spitting as they spoke: "You're too pretty to be a part of the fake media. You're actually fuckable."

UGLY CUNTS on the beautiful pinstripe paper, my reporter spider sense tingling at the sight.

There are a lot of angry men in the world.

Hana had said it, just an hour ago. And just before that—

I said it without thinking, the idea booming out of me like a cannonball.

"Eleanor Walsh."

Erin raised an eyebrow. "The Herd founder?"

"And beauty magnate. She's fascinating, right? And incredibly private."

She's a huge deal. People are kind of obsessed with her. Hana had said that too.

Erin propped her elbows on her knees. "What about her?"

"I know her well. Since high school. I'm joining the Herd—I signed the paperwork today." An exaggeration, but only a small, convenient one.

She cocked her head. "What are you saying?" Her eyes grew wide. "An authorized biography of Eleanor Walsh? Would she let you do that?"

"Maybe more of, like, an oral history of the Herd?" I tilted forward, buoyed by her interest. "I could talk to Eleanor and everyone else involved in its creation. People are enchanted by her. And it. There are forums online that strategize about getting in and make guesses about her personal life based on her Instagrams and stuff. And some people *hate* Eleanor and the Herd." I balled my hands into fists. "There's an online community called the Antiherd. And apparently angry dudes send her death threats and stuff. Oh, and today there was graffiti on the wall in one of the rooms that said 'ugly cunts.' No one knows who broke in to do it, or how. I could do a part memoir, part investigation, part unauthorized oral history starting with this weird hateful tagging on my very first day—I can try to figure out who did it and trace the Herd's history back to its creation. It could be super of-the-minute."

Erin was nodding, slowly at first, then with fervor. "I could sell that, Katie," she announced. "I could sell the shit out of that. But are you sure you want it to be unauthorized? I mean, I'll take juicy over sanitized and PR-friendly any day, but we also don't want you to suddenly get, like, a cease-and-desist."

"Good point. We should slow down." Guilt plunged through me. The last thing I wanted was to piss off Eleanor . . . or Hana, or Mikki, or anyone, really. But the way Erin was looking at me, the excitement in her eyes—this was my shot, the escape route out of the mess I'd made. And I couldn't ask Eleanor now, on my first damn day as a Herder. Er, applicant.

"Let me do some poking around," I said. "I've only been there one day—I'll do some observing and background reporting and I'll start thinking about how to organize it."

"I like the idea of looking into these threats against her," Erin said. "Like, what happens when you're so beloved by women that men hate you, maybe even want to kill you?"

I nodded, remembering with a harpoon of shame how Hana had described Eleanor's calculated dismissal of her haters. She'd said the worst thing you can give an attention-seeker is attention, and here I was, about to throw a floodlight on the haters. Hana and Eleanor would come to understand, wouldn't they? I was desperate. "She's very buttoned-up, so I want to approach this carefully." *Teleanor*—that's the only side she showed the media. For this to work, I'd have to bust beneath the shiny veneer.

"Would it help to say there's interest from a major publisher? Because I can call Faith tomorrow. Off the record, of course."

"Maybe. As long as it's totally, totally off the record." Faith, the editor who'd offered on my book proposal, scared me. The idea of Erin enthusiastically steering her away from the reality-manipulation book (working title: *Infopocalypse*) eased my panic, even as this new guilt rushed in. "I'll do some research and, when I have a better sense of what I want to do, I'll talk to my sister. She does their PR and she's best friends with Eleanor, so she'll know how to handle it." She'd know how to sell this to Eleanor as an opportunity, not an affront. She had to. Eleanor was kind and good and understanding.

This has to work.

"Perfect," Erin said, sitting up. "Well, good thing I stalked you. I left you, like, three voicemails today, Katie."

"Four," I replied, rising to see her out.

Once she'd left I rummaged around for a notebook, determined to act before the obnoxious angel over my shoulder could whisper it aloud: *This is a terrible idea.*

Unmasking the Herd, we could call it. Or just *Inside the Herd*—that was better. Or *Unmasking Eleanor*? I found a pen and pressed a half-used notebook open, rifling for an empty page.

But it was a notebook from Michigan, interview notes and jotted-down details, and my mind swung to the subtleties I'd been cataloging in secret: Chris's thick, unruly eyebrows, the spatter of freckles, fingertips skimming over my neck, my waist, the back of my knee. Then a scene change: the bright cymbal crash of humiliation when the EMTs had burst into the room. I felt a wail rise up through me and fought it, my knuckles pressed against my lips. No. I had to get to work.

I Googled Eleanor and began printing out profiles that'd been written about her—a big one in *The New Yorker*, breathtakingly sexist, and frothier ones on *Goop*, *Time*, *Cosmopolitan*, *The Cut*. Mikki and Hana occasionally appeared in the photos with her, which was a little odd, since neither was a full-time employee. To their benefit: Hana had no interest in dropping her other clients, and free-spirited Mikki couldn't be tied down—she was an artist, dammit, not a forty-hour-a-week packaging designer. Yet Eleanor always made it clear they were her work wives and closest confidantes, three corners of a power triangle. The living embodiment of what she'd said in our interview this morning: "Wonderful things happen when passionate women and marginalized genders come together."

With any luck, those wonderful things would extend to the nosy journalist, the oral historian eager to get it right. I gathered my printouts in a manila folder, and hope billowed in me for the first time in months.

CHAPTER 4

Hana

Just get here. Eleanor's voice, tinny over the phone, echoed in my ears as I headed to her apartment. She was commanding, bombastic, larger-than-life—but never a drama queen. She was calm and controlled, knowing the power in composure. So whatever had her summoning me to her place well after business hours must have her thoroughly rattled.

I hadn't been over to her apartment in a few weeks, and as I climbed the steps of the orange-brick West Village townhouse, I was struck anew with how beautiful it was. Steep-roofed and skinny with a tasteful wreath on the door, eucalyptus branches and bright bursts of berries. She slid open the door and ushered me in. She looked cross.

The inside was even more perfect than usual, thanks to a fat pine bough in the vestibule, the slash of green bouncing back and forth between the mirrored closet doors and floor mirror there. Eleanor was good at everything—a casually excellent interior designer, personal stylist, makeup artist, businesswoman . . .

She collapsed onto a sofa; on the coffee table, her laptop gleamed.

"So what's going on?" I pulled my coat off.

Eleanor sighed. "Someone stole my phone."

"I'm sorry." I waited for more, then frowned. "Did—did you call the police?"

"It disappeared—I don't even know exactly when. Sometime during the day. I took the subway to the Fort Greene site this afternoon, so it could have been then."

So that's why she'd FaceTimed me, presumably from her MacBook. But . . . why had I just taken an $11 Lyft here?

I nodded patiently. "That sucks, I'm sorry. I assume you tried Find My iPhone?"

"Of course. It was turned off right away."

"So that's why you think it was stolen?"

"No. *This* is why I think it was stolen." She pushed her laptop in my direction and I squinted at the screen: There it was again, UGLY CUNTS. I scrolled through four photos of the defacement she'd found this morning, then—

"What is this?" The same two words sprayed in similar bubble letters, this time orange, across a sheet of nailed-down drywall. Then another picture of the words scrawled across graphic wallpaper, a pattern of illustrated hand mirrors and combs.

"It's the other two locations," she said, rubbing her eyes. "The first few photos, I took them this morning to show the police. But I hadn't sent them to anyone yet—they were just on my phone. And the other two are in Fort Greene and San Francisco. Someone hit our other sites last night. Coordinated attacks."

Goosebumps rippled up my arms and neck. This felt personal—for as long as I'd known Eleanor, her hatred for that particular profanity had bordered on maniacal. A few months back, one of her favorite contributors to the *Gleam On* blog had pitched an essay on "reclaiming the C-word," and Eleanor had dismissed it with unprecedented vehemence.

"You should've told me," I said. "Did everyone at the San Francisco Herd see it?"

She shook her head. "We were lucky—the head member relations coordinator went in early and spotted it before they opened. She sent photos and called me right away. It was on fabric wallpaper, so I had her rip it down before they even opened. The police weren't happy about that, but . . . I mean, I am." Eleanor tugged at the sleeve of her sweater.

"And in Fort Greene?"

"The lead contractor found it this morning. He sent me photos and then just painted over it."

"Okay." I looked back at the screen. "So what does this have to do with your phone?"

She pointed at her laptop. "That's an email from Joanna. My friend at *The Gaze*."

"This is making less and less sense, the more you tell me. What's going on?"

"Okay. Whoever stole my phone found these photos on it and sent them all to *The Gaze*. Anonymously, of course—they have all those secure drop boxes set up. Anyway, *The Gaze* is planning to run them, and my friend Joanna gave me a heads-up as, like, a courtesy." She slipped a gray pillow in front of her stomach. "She was trying to call me all day because she didn't want a paper trail of her snitching on her employer. Really wish I had my phone."

It clicked: She'd called me because she needed her publicist. "Got it. Well, we can talk about ways to mitigate the damage, but I don't think this is going to be a big story. We can write a statement for your blog and put it on the Herd's site: 'This proves that, now more than ever, women need spaces like only we can provide, you know you're doing it right when you're pissing people off,' that kind of thing." I shrugged. "People might sort of love it. That discrimination lawsuit just made those men look whiny and pathetic. Gave us a huge surge in applications."

She shook her head. "I need it not to run."

I let out a surprised laugh. "I'm sorry, what?"

"The Herd can't have bad press right now," Eleanor said. "The big announcement next week? This just looks too bad. It shows we can't keep criminals out of our coworking spaces, for one thing." She futzed with the clasp of her earring. "And also, just associating us with the C-word. In bubble letters. The timing could not be more terrible."

"Sweetie, there's never a great time for a hit piece." I crossed my ankles. "This announcement—you're supposed to fill me in by Friday so I have time to prep the press release. I think you're gonna have to tell me early."

"I can't. Legally, I can't tell anyone."

I rolled my eyes. "I mean, I won't *tell* anyone you told me today. I'm a freaking publicist, I'm a vault of sellable secrets."

"Let's just stay focused on how we can kill this story." Eleanor's eyes were pleading. "Joanna said it's scheduled to go live at eleven."

I chewed my lip. "Was it a contractor who did it in Fort Greene? Who even has access to the site?"

"It's a construction site—*anyone* can access it." She composed herself. "The police are investigating; I'm not asking you to crack the case. The *Gaze* article is the immediate issue here."

I nodded, thinking. "Tell me about the announcement. Off the record. I think I know how to make this go away."

Eleanor stared at the floor for a moment, then sighed. "Titan Industries is acquiring the Herd." She smiled. "It's an industry first. It'll be huge for the company—for all of us. The biggest technology company in the world is buying us out but still letting us run the company. Oh, the resources we'll have access to, and the ways we'll be able to expand globally . . ." She trailed off and looked at me expectantly.

I blinked at her. "Wow. When did you decide this?"

"They first approached me in the spring."

Why didn't you tell me? formed in my throat, and I swallowed it. "Does Mikki know?"

"No one does." She flapped her hand. "Legality."

I looked away, nodded slowly. "Well, we can use this. It's big."

"Unprecedented. Front-page-of-the-*Times* big."

"Front page of the Business section," I corrected her. I pushed the laptop back across the coffee table. "We're gonna give *The Gaze* an exclusive on Tuesday's announcement. They'll break the news the moment the event begins. They might want a twenty-four-hour exclusive, which everyone else in the media will hate. Other journalists might refuse to come."

She nodded. "That's fine. I just can't let the Herd take a beating before Tuesday's announcement."

"And I have carte blanche to barter with anything I can? Exclusive interviews, maybe future Q&A's, even personal photos? Eleanor, before she was a star?"

This was a litmus test—even I had barely seen any childhood photos of her, and I'd been to her parents' house countless times. She scrunched her nose. "Yes. But don't lead with that."

"Obviously. Okay, I need the number of your friend there." I pulled my phone out of my purse. "And I'm charging you time and a half now."

Such is the curse of crisis PR: If you're good at your job, no one knows you intervened. I'm like a goalie, unsung unless I really screw up. It took every persuasion technique in the book to convince Joanna, a nervous-sounding woman with a bell-like voice, to bring my offer to her editor, but then she agreed, as I knew she would, and at 10:43 p.m. Monday evening, I put the deal in writing.

"There you go," I called to Cosmo, who was splayed indecently on the rug near my feet. "All taken care of." I reached for his furry haunches and he flopped like a fish.

The *Gaze* interview would go well, because all interviews with Eleanor went well. She was the kind of client publicists dreamed about: eloquent, beautiful, speaking in tight sound bites and giving every camera the just-right pose and smile. Only a handful of us saw how it exhausted her sometimes, how her face dimmed like an extinguished candle once her back was turned. We understood it, sympathized—what woman, dabbing a layer of pleasantness onto every interaction and sprinkling exclamation points into emails to remain eminently palatable, wouldn't? But I didn't envy Eleanor this part of the job.

Cosmo arched himself into a crescent shape, stretching his velvety legs, and I stood to find a cat toy to dangle his way. I had to admit: convincing Joanna, calmly listening and mirroring like a skilled hostage negotiator as I nudged the conversation onto its track . . . it was a rush. And Eleanor's big announcement next week—the media would eat it up. I did wonder how the Herd community would react. Resources were great, but there was something cozy about being privately owned.

As I bobbed a ball of feathers in Cosmo's face, I thought back to that moment in 2012, when I'd flown in from L.A. to help out with Gleam's launch. The three of us had huddled in Mikki's Greenpoint apartment, the one she lives in still: a rent-controlled one-bedroom in a crumbling prewar building, all its hard angles softened by dozens of coats of cheap white paint. How our fingers hovered over our laptops, the press release and website and social media announcements all cued up and copyedited and practically vibrating inside. Once Eleanor gave us the signal, Gleam would be *real*. Eleanor's very first company, a beauty brand that would change all of our lives. We lifted our chins and looked at one another, eyes sparkling—too young to feel any doubts marbling the excitement. To think about everything that might go wrong. That already had.

Go, Eleanor whispered. Our hands swooped. Gleam was alive, it was out there. A thrilling second, two. Then Eleanor spoke again, her voice thick with awe: *It's done*.

For a moment, we beamed. Then Mikki hit Play on a Skrillex song, tinny on her computer's speakers, and soon we were all on our feet, dancing in her living room, the world our shimmery, pearl-filled oyster.

CHAPTER 5

Katie

Pain—the kind of deep hurt that wafts into your whole body, sets your teeth on edge, makes everything tremble and fold in around the source of it.

"And five . . . and four . . . keep your hips square, don't let that right hip pop! And three . . . keep going . . ."

I'm no mathematician, but we'd completed about fourteen heel-raises since the perky instructor called out five. Stephanie, the beautiful yogini, was just ahead of me, moving like a dancer, and next to me Mikki was glistening prettily, her wild hair gathered in a silver scrunchie. I looked back down at my mat and sweat funneled off the end of my nose, two drops, three.

The Herd offered Workout Wednesdays, something I hadn't known about since Hana never went. (Thursdays also had a designated event, Cultivation Thursdays, when women gathered at lunchtime to share updates on their passion projects and side hustles. *Are the first four letters of* that *always purple too?* I'd cracked, the first time Hana mentioned it.)

I still hadn't been offered a membership at the Herd. Not that it bothered me or anything.

Mikki had invited me here when she heard that Sabine, her favorite krav-maga-barre-fusion instructor, was leading this week's class. I'd gleaned that I'd need to choose an exercise to fit in at the Herd, the way board-game players claim a color: Eleanor was a runner. Hana did Reformer Pilates in a eucalyptus-scented studio. And Mikki had signed on for this hellaciousness.

"I know you can get lower! The only one holding you back is you!" Sabine called. Mentally, I wove a complex tapestry of obscenities as we completed another set of microscopic push-ups. And then it was over. I collapsed onto my back and lay there, sweat puddling in my eyes, blood beating through my ears.

"You all right?" Mikki appeared above me, dabbing a towel along her slightly damp hairline. "I felt dead after my first time too."

"I think that was outlawed by the Geneva conventions." My chest heaved. "I'm being waterboarded by my own sweat."

I followed her back out the door marked MOVE and into the bathroom. A small line of women stood waiting for the two shower stalls at the end. A few had stripped and were hanging out in towels; one had wrapped hers around her waist, casually topless. Mikki had completed the class in an improbable kelly-green unitard that hit mid-thigh, and now she rolled the top down, a towel dangling over her small breasts like a scarf.

Back at Harvard, Mikki had been the outrageous one, grinning mischievously as she sloshed Captain Morgan into my Diet Coke. She was free-spirited and kooky, crowing about her sexual exploits and cheerfully explaining lewd terms to me as I sat on the floor, saucer-eyed. (*I was so disappointed to learn I don't enjoy eating pussy—I mean, I love oysters* is a Mikki quote still tattooed on my cerebrum.) She'd drummed up my first fake ID and she never shaved her legs or underarms, which had struck high school me as incredibly cool and daring. She'd of course mellowed since then—now she had that carefree artist vibe, the kind that made you insecure in your own uptightness. Everything she did had a certain effortlessness, someone serenely and unself-consciously dancing in the forest in a mumblecore movie.

Now as she fluffed at the nape of her neck, I saw that her armpit was smooth and hairless. This made me sad for some reason. Like The Man had won.

"I do see the appeal of learning self-defense," I said, patting a towel across my collarbone. "I took a one-day seminar in college, but obviously none of it stuck. I'd have to be like, '*Hold still, sir—if you're holding the knife there, I need to use* this *hand to push it away while my knee goes here. . . . '*" I acted it out, the awkward shuffling.

"Yeah, you really have to just do it over and over until it's second nature. That's why I like it: It makes me feel like I don't have to take any shit. If someone tried to mess with me, I wouldn't need to think—my body would just act."

Hana had mentioned once that Mikki had been abused as a kid—her drunk dad had knocked around his wife and children whenever he was in a mood. Mikki never discussed it; she talked as if her life began as soon as she got out of North Carolina. It made her extra-impressive now, this badass artist thriving in NYC.

"Anyway. What are you working on today?" Mikki leaned into the mirror and picked out an eye booger.

"Just sending out about four thousand emails," I replied. I'd crept in on Tuesday, still cruising with my temporary guest pass, nervous that Eleanor and Hana and everyone would take one look at me and shout, "Traitor! Banned for life! Booooo!" à la the osteoporotic old woman in *The Princess Bride*. But somehow, improbably, everyone had treated me normally, continuing on without knowledge that I harbored secret hopes of writing about them. If anything, on

Tuesday Hana and Eleanor seemed to have sort of forgotten about me—distracted, blustering by without looking up much—but the relief far outweighed the vague rinse of feeling left out. "What about you?"

"I'm talking to a gallery in Bushwick about doing a show," she replied. "Only collages, no sculptures. So I'm working on an artist's statement today. Actually, would you be willing to look at it later? I'm not much of a writer."

"Of course! And I'd love to see your collages sometime. When I left you were still mostly doing those metal sculptures."

"Yeah, soldering. But I think the collages are my best work, to be honest. Each one has a lot of meaning for me. I've been doing these large-scale works and then taking photos of them and working *those* into my collages."

"Large-scale? Like, slinging paint onto huge canvases?"

"Sort of. And then I cut the photos into these weird, intricate shapes with an X-Acto knife. I really hope I get the show. It's frustrating: I've worked so hard, but people only know me for boring graphic design shit." She looked away. "Nobody takes my actual art seriously and that's all I want to do."

I was about to reply, surprised by the sudden candor, when a woman moving toward an open shower slipped in a puddle, her arms flailing. Mikki lunged forward and caught the woman's forearm in both hands as her own towel crumpled to the floor.

The woman righted herself and burst out laughing. "You just saved my life," she said, giving Mikki a half-hug, perky little exposed boobs and all. The woman hopped into the shower, and Mikki gathered up her things, grinning.

She caught my eye and cocked her head toward the Gleam Room. "That's the thing about these ugly cunts," she said. "When you fall, we'll catch you."

———

For a coworking space, the Herd didn't make working easy—the communal tables were too high, the individual workstations too low, more fun than functional. I drained my coffee and set it on the little marble table I'd pulled up to my knees. It was my fifth day of working at the Herd, my first Friday. I'd thought maybe it would be emptier today, freelancers tapping out for the weekend early, but it was more packed than ever, the sound level higher, giggles and squawks boinging off the snake plants and salt lamps.

And it was dark out; frost fringed the windows, which were now hazy mirrors. On Fridays the Herd closed at five. Eleanor said this was to ensure a healthy work-life balance for employees, which made negative sense when the Herd was open on weekends, albeit with limited hours and a skeleton crew.

"I'm gonna get moving," Hana announced. "You staying here until close?" She looked especially pretty today, with her dark curls pulled into a pile and careful eyeliner framing her umber eyes. People are always commenting on her striking features. Meanwhile, the guy I lost my virginity to in college once told me, *You kind of look like a ferret . . . but, like, a cute ferret.* Not even a hot ferret. I continued to hook up with him for an additional three weeks.

"I don't know." I brought my hand to my crown and cracked my neck. "The Wi-Fi's still being dodgy. I've been trying to send these photos for, like, an hour."

She squinted at my screen. "It only seems to stop working when *you're* on the network. They're resetting the router tonight."

"I know, I'm Wi-Fi Kryptonite." I closed my laptop. "We're on for tomorrow, right?"

"Of course." It was an annual tradition: We'd start under the massive snowflake improbably suspended above Fifth Avenue and then make our way past other showstopping decorations. I'd made up my mind that I'd broach the topic of the book with her then. Research was going well—I was in touch with the plaintiff behind the discrimination lawsuit and he seemed sufficiently unaware of my disdain for him, and I'd joined some online fan forums that'd bought into the whole Herd cult of personality. And in a stroke of luck, Eleanor had scheduled a glitzy and mysterious event for Tuesday, with reporters and influencers and B to B+ celebrities spangling the guest list, all with the promise of a big surprise announcement. Whatever the announcement was, it was sure to bring a flurry of new attention to Eleanor. Mentioning my book pitch to Hana— softly, carefully, *This is just a little idea I had; it'd be done so lovingly and totally with her approval*—felt like a natural next step, a gate I could hop over on the way to unicorns and rainbows and people in the publishing world not hating me.

"All right, I'm making moves." Hana grabbed her purse and gave me a half-hug goodbye. I tapped at my computer, prepared to shut it down—at long last, the damn photos had uploaded. Aurelia, the Herd's member relations coordinator, breezed through, flicking off lights, and I promised I'd be out as soon as I finished one thing and bade Eleanor goodbye. Aurelia had darkened the other rooms—the library and the sunroom, as I now knew they were called—and it wasn't until her elevator door thudded closed that I realized how expansive and eerie the Herd was at night.

The light from the elevator's floor indicator flickered, casting dim shadows along the entryway; wind pressed against the windows, and a single hanging pothos plant swayed. I leaned way over in my seat—Eleanor's door was open a crack. I watched, waiting for movement.

Farther in, something crashed. I let out a clipped scream. Eleanor jetted out of her office, her head whipping back and forth, then spotted me.

"Did you just yell? What's going on?"

"I heard something. Between a crack and a thud." I pointed into the darkness of the two adjoining rooms, and she stepped behind the front desk; suddenly all the lights blared on anew, leaving us squinting.

"Maybe something just fell off a bookshelf. Or a window ledge." She grabbed my arm and strode forward, ignoring my mousy fear.

We searched beneath the bookshelves, behind them, the shelves themselves; all the ledges along the wide glass windows and every table, big and small. Nothing was out of place.

"I bet a bird flew into the window," she said finally, but she seemed less certain.

"Can we check back there?" I asked.

She frowned at me, opened her mouth to answer, and then our heads snapped toward the entryway: a single phone was ringing, louder and louder.

"Shit." She clattered off toward the front desk and I dashed after her, my heart thumping.

"What?"

"I forgot he's coming tonight," she replied as she reached the front desk and lifted the vintage-looking phone there. "This is Eleanor."

She listened for a moment, nodding, then said, "Right, the router. Actually"—she looked up—"Katie, the Wi-Fi hasn't been working for you, right? What's that?" She leaned away, listening again. "Oh, perfect. I'll buzz you in." She replaced the handset and felt for a button under the desk. Then she dropped into the chair there, forgetting, it seemed, the confused and antsy hamster of a woman standing over her.

"Ted's coming up—did you ever meet him? When you visited us at Harvard?"

"I don't think so. His name's familiar though."

"We've been friends since we were born. He's our handyman. And good with IT stuff too."

I let out a bark of laughter. "I thought the best man for the job is a woman!"

Her shoulders tensed, and instantly I regretted it.

"There are amazing women in every field of IT, obviously, but I haven't had the energy to seek out and hire one when Ted is so great. Low-hanging fruit, you know?"

"Low-hanging fruit, huh?" We'd both missed the sough of the elevator doors sweeping open, and now a man stood just outside them, tall and lanky with a baseball cap set at a jaunty angle. He smiled through a thick brown beard. "Tell me how you really feel, Eleanor."

"Just bragging about my one and only secret male employee!" She trotted over and he pulled her into a big bear hug. So big, in fact, I'd be waggling my eyebrows were she not a married woman.

"She's referring to my manual labor services, by the way. I'm not an escort."

"Hey, *manual labor*'s just a connotation away from *hand job*," I blurted out, then blushed hot pink. *Shut. The fuck. Up, Katie Bradley.*

Eleanor's brow levitated from puzzled to surprised while Ted burst out laughing—a big, booming guffaw.

"Can I hug you too?" He crossed the room and wrapped his arms around me. It felt like hugging an old friend. He smelled like fabric softener and cedar.

"Ted, Katie; Katie, Ted," Eleanor called. "She's writing a book about a weird backwoods tech company, and you do weird backwoods tech stuff, so you'll get along just fine."

She reiterated the router issue and cheerfully he set about fixing it, murmuring things about firmware and caching and packet overload, which also sounded at least a little dirty. In a dramatic climax, we all gathered around my laptop as I toggled Wi-Fi off and on (*please don't let anything embarrassing be visible on my screen*), and then we cheered when CNN.com appeared in my browser.

"Should we get a drink to celebrate?" I asked. Ted said he

couldn't, though he really wished he could, holding my gaze as he answered.

Eleanor checked the time. "I could do a quick drink," she announced. "Daniel and I have dinner reservations at seven-thirty, but just around the corner. Actually, there's a bar in the front—let's go there."

In the dim bar, Eleanor expertly commandeered two stools. The hook placement under the bar meant I had to straddle my laptop bag, and the chair's dimensions were a poor fit, the lower dowel too high for my heels. I flopped around as Eleanor sat like a damn queen, smiling from her throne until the bartender approached. She ordered Prosecco and I followed suit, and they arrived in pretty coupe glasses.

"To your triumphant return to New York!" she called. She held my eyes as we clinked glasses, which is of course how you're supposed to toast, but while meeting her gaze I sloshed bubbly onto her knee.

"It's fine, it's fine." She giggled, snatching napkins from a stack.

"Well, now I'm definitely not getting into the Herd," I joked.

She looked up from her lap and made sort of an empathy pout. "I'm sorry! I hate that you're still coming in as a guest. I've been so bad about processing paperwork this week—I've got that event on Tuesday. You're coming, right?"

"Of course! We're all dying to hear the news. No hints?"

She cocked a pretty eyebrow. "I'm sworn to secrecy."

"Verbal nondisclosure agreement? Press embargo? I'm good at keeping secrets, you know."

She laughed. "I would if I could. But it's good news for everyone." She pushed her hair over her shoulder and changed the subject: "Hey, I'm glad we finally got some one-on-one time. How's your mom doing? If you want to talk about it, that is."

Normally I didn't, but the fact that Eleanor cared, her earnest eyes—they bubbled in my chest like the Prosecco. "Yeah, she's doing well, so it's much easier to talk about now."

"I'm glad. Hana didn't say much, but I could tell she was really torn up about it."

"Really?"

"Of course."

"She hasn't talked to me about it. You know she doesn't get along with our mom. They're like oil and water."

When had I first noticed it? Second or third grade, maybe, right around the time you realize your parents aren't actually superheroes. The way Hana and Mom would both stiffen when they were in a room together; their shoulders would rise as if attached to balloons, and they'd grow snippy, avoiding eye contact. They didn't fight, certainly didn't scream—anger was not allowed in our house—but young as I was, I picked up on the charged air. It confused me, in fact: Mom was nice and fun with me, as was Hana, and yet together they morphed into sparking live wires.

"Anyway, how are your folks?" I asked. I'd met them once or twice while Eleanor was in college, and they were the kind of parents everyone adores—gregarious, kind, welcoming, funny. One of many reasons I was sad I couldn't attend her wedding: I'd missed my chance to see them.

"Oh, Gary and Karen are as ridiculous as ever. My dad retired in September, so they're getting used to both being at home. They're talking about buying a trailer and driving around to a bunch of national parks. I told 'em I can't see it."

"Gary and Karen in a *trailer*?" They were both silver-haired and well kempt—WASPy, but Catholic. "They need to bring a documentary crew."

"Right?" She giggled. "But don't worry, it's a luxury trailer. They bought a pickup truck so they can pull it. No, I'm serious." She shook her head, grinning. "They were like, 'We thought we'd be okay with this smaller model, but then we went to a car show and

realized we'd need the four-hundred-square-foot one to be comfortable.' It's bigger than my first apartment. Remember, on Ludlow?"

"With the stray cat on the fire escape and the heaters that sounded
like a drum solo? Do I *ever*."

We'd had so many good times in that apartment—our mouths
bruised with boxed red wine, Mikki and Eleanor confidently advis-
ing me on how to ask out the cute guy in my stats class. There was
the night a bird had flown through the open window, leading to
much shrieking and flapping of towels, and another when Mikki,
insistent that Trader Joe's two-buck chuck wasn't as awful as Eleanor believed, had set up a blind taste test, complete with classical
music and a classy array of cheeses. (Eleanor had sniffed out the
cheap stuff instantly.)

"We were so dumb," she remarked. "Who was that friend of
yours you were in love with? And we'd spend all night texting with
him, pretending it was just you?"

"That's right—Devin! I saw he's engaged now. He moved back to
Chicago." I watched the strings of bubbles in my glass shimmer like
tiny pearl necklaces.

"You were so much cooler than him." She took another delicate
sip. "Have you started dating now that you're back? You on all the
apps?"

I froze and thought back to just a couple months ago—the giddy
state when my brain wasn't my own, when every sight or sound or
conversation funneled my thoughts back to Chris. *Chris would find
this hilarious. Chris has a crazy story about four-wheelers.* The glori-
ous addiction, the pink flashes of desire. And now, the pain in my
chest like a sickness.

*Chris will never, ever speak to you again. Chris is the reason you
know how ambulance lights look carved up through winding country
roads.*

"I don't really have time to date right now," I said, like every single single person in history.

"I totally get that. And you have way more interesting stuff going on than worrying about stupid boys."

"For sure." *Like my secret book proposal.* There was something I'd been meaning to find out and I finally gave up on nailing a natural segue: "Hey, can I ask you something?"

"What's up?"

"I'm not sure how to phrase this." I rested the glass on my knee. "So in Michigan, I wrote a couple op-eds based on what I was seeing at rallies and stuff. And, like . . . as a female tech reporter, I'm used to sexist bullshit. But the level of vitriol . . . the effort people would put into finding ways to contact me, to tell me what an ugly bitch I am—it stunned me. Obviously I was just blocking people like crazy, but it was hard—there's still emotional labor in seeing that hateful shit, you know?"

Eleanor was nodding while hitting me with her most earnest, empathetic face. I paused and she set her hand on mine.

"I'm just wondering how you deal with that. I got a tiny slice of it for, like, twenty-four hours the two times I wrote editorials. But you must deal with it nonstop, right?"

She nodded, looked away. "It's hard because there's no model out there for what to do. It's this incredibly psychologically damaging thing, and yet we're not supposed to talk about it because that might lead to more trolling, so most people have no idea."

"It's like when guys are so bewildered when you tell them you feel afraid walking alone at night."

"Exactly." She sighed. "It's hard. You do get a thicker skin over time, and I know some other female CEOs who can commiserate—we have a WhatsApp group. But mostly you just do your best to ignore it. Sometimes I fantasize about throwing a spotlight on it, though. Posting all the awful stuff I get. Or even having this big event where we try to show men what it's like, the lived experience—" Her phone jolted on the bar and she glanced at it.

"Sorry. Daniel's on his way."

"Yes! I'm excited to see him." I tried to steer the bus back around. "An event to show men what it's really like—that's a wild idea."

"I know. Except I think it'd end in bloodshed." She smirked. "If guys had to deal with the shit we put up with every day—"

"Excuse me, I'm sorry to bother you." Two women stood before us shyly, both with blond highlights as evenly spaced as rows of wheat. The taller one giggled self-consciously. "Are you . . . you aren't Eleanor Walsh, are you?"

Eleanor smiled magnificently, magnanimously, all her Teleanor charm aimed like a tractor beam at these strangers. "I am! It's nice to meet you!"

"Jocelyn. And this is Nicole." They shook Eleanor's hand gleefully. "We're visiting from Missouri, and we were having an argument over there about whether or not it was actually you! We're both big fans of Gleam."

"How sweet of you to say hi! And this is Katie Bradley, she's an incredibly talented journalist and soon-to-be author." I kept a grin plastered on my face, ready for this diversion to end so we could return to real life. *Did this happen often?*

"This is our first time in New York," Jocelyn went on. "We've been on the lookout for celebrities."

"I saw you on the *Today* show," the other said. Nicole. "Talking about your women's club? You were great."

"Thank you so much! Hey, if you're still in town this weekend, you should definitely stop by the Herd and see what it's all about. Here's my card—just give the front desk a call and let them know I sent you."

They squealed and squawked and asked me to take a photo of them, Eleanor, as always, looking luminous and superhuman among the mortals. They thanked her and scurried off, eyes shining.

"That was so nice of you!" I said, my voice somewhere between impressed and alarmed.

She drained her Prosecco. "There are rumbles that the Herd is too elitist—snob vibes. These damn thinkpieces keep coming out about how we're a 'flash point for debates over feminism and power.'" She gave it air quotes, rolled her eyes. "I want it to be approachable. They seemed harmless, and now they'll go back and tell everyone in the South how great it is."

"The Midwest."

"Right." She frowned, then shrugged. "But it's a fine line. Obviously I don't want strangers coming in and sneaking photos of our high-profile clients. Hey speaking of, I wanted to ask you—"

A man swooped in from behind me and bent close, got in her face. I jumped but then she smiled and kissed him back: Daniel. I felt an unexpected clap of jealousy toward him, that he had Eleanor's attention, her love. He was a hospital administrator—I wasn't sure what that entailed because my brain checked out, spread out a beach towel and sipped a piña colada every time he tried to tell me—and they'd met at a party the year before I'd moved to Kalamazoo. He was handsome enough, and friendly, though nowhere near Eleanor's stratosphere, from what I could tell. When she'd texted to tell me she was engaged, it'd felt like fake news, a dispatch from another reality: I was hunting for paper towels to clean vomit from the bathroom floor, where Mom hadn't made it in time. Eleanor had invited me to the engagement party, but I didn't want to leave Mom alone (Hana accused me of being a martyr), and then I'd been in the thick of book reporting during the actual wedding a few months later. (Leave it to Eleanor to throw together a beautiful wedding in six months flat—one documented in *People*, naturally.)

He turned to me and smiled. Cuter than I remembered—better dressed, like maybe Eleanor's taste had rubbed off on him. He was tall with sharp cheekbones and a thick swoop of black hair.

"Daniel, you remember—" Eleanor began, but Daniel had already stuck out his hand to introduce himself. "You know Katie!" she scolded, and he lost at least half my goodwill on the spot.

"I'm Hana's little sister, we met right when you two started dating, no, no, it's fine!" I kept a big smile on my face as he blushed and shifted the handshake into a sterile hug.

"I'm sorry, Eleanor told me Hana's sister was moving back, but I didn't—you guys don't look alike at all!" Eleanor grabbed his bicep; she looked mortified.

The whole scene was going badly enough that I leaned in: "We don't? Most people think we're twins." I kept my face earnest as he flicked his eyes back and forth between Eleanor and me.

"For Christ's sake, she's fucking with you," Eleanor snorted, and he laughed uncertainly.

I waved my arms. "She's adopted! It's not a secret! You're good!"

Once we'd stopped giggling, Eleanor asked him if the table was ready. He nodded and awkwardly asked if I'd like to join them, but I said no. He still looked shaken as I hugged them goodbye, and I gave a final wave as the hostess led them into the dining room. They looked good together, pretty and put-together. It wasn't a great call, making him uncomfortable—now he might be more guarded around me, less forthcoming if I got around to interviewing him for the book. *But . . . c'mon. He deserved it.*

CHAPTER 6

Hana

When I spotted Katie at a southern entrance to Central Park, tugging on thick fingerless gloves, I felt a swell of pride: my bold baby sister, blending in with all the New Yorkers around her. Often she irritated me (and the feeling occasionally teetered into resentment), but today there was nothing but affection. She saw me and waved; she had the universally agreed-upon prettiness of a Pixar princess—a wavy bob, big eyes, a pert little nose, and a good, sharp chin.

It'd been surprisingly fun having her at the Herd all week. In the period leading up to her interview, I'd worried that she'd be distracting and childish, violating the Herd's tacit rules about noise levels and profanity, but so far my fears were unfounded. Like a new, eager coworker, she'd sought me out every morning, cheerfully dropping her bags nearby before skipping off to hang her coat. She was meeting other women, too, a development I observed like a proud mother hen: chatting with coders and designers and small-business owners seated next to her, shyly asking for their email or Instagram handle toward the end of the day. She still seemed tense, but newly focused. She was vague about what she was working on, but I didn't press; I remembered from my own move to New York how getting things rolling felt less like an A-to-B and more like a million small to-dos.

She hurried across the street and gave me a quick hug, then patted her pockets. "I either left my hat at home or on the subway."

"That tracks," I teased.

She shrugged and pointed to the massive snowflake strung over Fifty-seventh Street. "How big do you think it is?" As I reached for my phone to find the answer, she spoke again: "We have to guess! *Price Is Right* rules."

She waited for me to go first ("eighteen feet across") and then guessed nineteen, a very Katie thing to do, then hopped in excitement as I dramatically read out the actual dimensions: twenty-eight feet tall and twenty-three feet wide.

She whistled, turning back to its twinkling lights. "I wouldn't want to drive a convertible under that." She stuffed her hands into her pockets. "Hey, do you know Eleanor's friend Ted?"

I frowned. "Yeah, he's an old family friend of hers. Why do you ask?"

"I met him yesterday. He came in to fix the Wi-Fi."

I nodded. She dipped her head and looked up at me, catching my downturned eyes.

"What's his deal?" she asked.

"Oh, he's fine. He went to BU and sometimes he'd come to parties with us and stuff." I shrugged. "He's just . . . I could never figure him out."

We'd reached Bergdorf Goodman, where clusters of bundled-up

people peered into the windows. This year's theme was the Gilded Age, and this display showed a miniature Gatsby mansion during a winter soiree, with fat red sashes and intricate wreaths hanging from its facade. Katie stepped closer and spread her gloved hands against the glass.

"Beautiful, isn't it?" I sidled up next to her.

"Gorgeous. I always loved this book. Hey, remember my friend Holly Janssen? From growing up? She just moved into a house like that in East Grand Rapids." She nodded toward the window. "Her husband's family owns a bunch of breweries or something. All my friends from high school are, like, buying McMansions and having babies."

Much to my relief, she'd dropped the topic of Ted. Katie's observant, good at sensing signs of tension.

"That's the great thing about New York—if you get pregnant, *you're* the weird one." I stopped in front of the next display. It had something to do with the transcontinental railroad: small train cars cruising down a track, the sides cut open to reveal elegant interiors.

"Is it weird that Eleanor's married?" Katie asked. A gaggle of teenagers arrived, reaching over us to photograph the window. "Do you feel less close?"

"She's pretty good about making time for her friends. It helps that she's my client."

Katie's eyes trailed the miniature train. "And Daniel doesn't have any cool friends to set you up with?"

Dating, relationships, marriage—always a delicate topic for Katie and me. Though she was currently single, I knew it wouldn't be long before that changed; Katie attracted men everywhere she went, dudes delighted by her brash tongue and delicate features. Meanwhile, I'd been cycling on and off of dating sites for the better part of a decade. "Intimidating" was the word guys often used—each time a small corkscrew to the heart, screwed further in as I scrambled to make myself softer, kinder, more feminine and palatable. Although some found another fun way to make me not a real person: "You're so exotic-looking," or "What's your background?" or "No, I mean where are you *from?*" or the real kayo: "What *are* you?"

"Sadly, no," I said. "Like every other straight male I know, Daniel says that all his friends are either married or 'jackasses.' His word."

"Nine million New Yorkers and not one worth dating."

She said it playfully, but I groaned. "If you go on the apps, you'll see how much time and labor it takes to go on a single date—it's just not where I'm focusing my energy."

"You know I don't care at all whether you're seeing someone or not." She squeezed my shoulder and we moved on to the next window. "More sister time for me."

It was a sore spot: A few weeks back, when Mikki and I were chasing Mocktails with cocktails at a happy hour down the street, Mikki had tipsily admitted that Eleanor had remarked that I was single simply because I was too picky. *But I defended you! I said you're just waiting for the right guy!* Mikki had burbled, slurping the last of her third margarita. I'd changed the subject, but her words stung.

"It feels good, right? Being back in the same city," I said. We approached the corner, where a woman shook a bell over a Salvation Army bucket. "I mean, I missed you when I was in L.A. and you were at NYU. But with you in Michigan this past year—it made me realize how much more fun New York is with you here."

"I still don't understand why you moved to L.A." She dug in her bag and dropped a few coins into the pail. "When you graduated and I was about to move here. I feel like I ask you this every few years and I still don't get it. Eleanor and Mikki were here, too, and it seemed all set. And then out of nowhere, at the last minute . . ."

This was *not* where I wanted the conversation to go. The night I never talked about—the one I flew three thousand miles to get away from, because I couldn't travel back in time, couldn't undo what I'd done. My heart sped and I shook my head. "I didn't think I was ready for New York. I had more growing to do. But hey, we're both here now."

"I know, and now I can basically be your annoying coworker who talks to you all day." She drummed her fingers together like a self-satisfied villain. "I can't wait until I'm a real member without my weekly guest pass."

I looked down. Eleanor hadn't mentioned the status of Katie's application since her weird ambush on Monday, but she had given me an odd look when I'd asked how the investigation into the defacement was going: *The police said whomever sent the photos might be accustomed to working with the press.* That time I couldn't hide my eye roll; unless Katie had pilfered Eleanor's phone, determined to screw over her powerful friend and ruin the best thing she had going for her, she wasn't the anonymous tipster. Obviously.

"I can't wait until they make it official either!" I said. "I'm sure it'll happen soon. Eleanor's just busy getting ready for Tuesday."

"She said the same thing last night." She held her phone out and gestured for me to join her for a selfie; we beamed at the screen. "Hey, do you know what Tuesday's announcement is gonna be?"

"I can't say. What's the rumor mill reporting?"

"Just speculation. A big new partnership or something. Opening a location abroad, like the Cave just did. Aurelia said *The Gaze* is getting an exclusive?"

"It's true! Not my first choice, but." I fished a water bottle out of my bag and unscrewed the cap.

"So why them?"

I took a long sip, buying time. "Eleanor's friends with a reporter there," I said. "Joanna Chen. She just wanted it to be there." I sniffed the air. "Ooh, I smell a Nuts 4 Nuts cart. Should we get some?"

She shook her head. "They smell better than they taste. You said it's Joanna Chen?" She paused, like she was committing it to memory. "I'm gonna ask Eleanor about it on Monday. That just seems so strange." I peered at her, frowning, and she spoke quickly: "Since *The Gaze* is kinda mean. But also I've been meaning to make a contact there. So maybe if they're friends, she can introduce me at the event." She threw a sideways glance at me. "What?"

We paused in front of Tiffany's, the diamonds in the window twinkling like stars. "Katie, just be careful."

She shook her head. "I thought networking was, like, a huge part of the Herd experience."

"It is, and that's great." Suddenly the holiday lights clinging to the building lit up, blinking through tall ovals and then outward in graceful arcs. "It's just not a great time to give Eleanor the impression you're looking for a scoop or whatever. She's sort of . . . private, as much as she can be."

"We call that *media-unfriendly*," she said. We moseyed over toward the next display. "That's why I was curious about the *Gaze* exclusive. That's all."

"You're not going to try to write about anything that happens at the Herd, are you?"

She didn't stop walking, but I thought I saw her shoulders hike up. *We have some extremely . . . high-profile members here*, Eleanor had said, clearing her throat.

"What are you talking about?" Katie said finally.

"It would just be . . . weird. A conflict of interest. I tell you stuff in confidence, and I'm their freaking publicist. You don't want to jeopardize anything."

"I know that. I'm not stupid, Hana." She leaned toward a window. Her annoyance alarmed me. I'd expected surprise, shock at the whole idea, *that literally didn't even cross my mind.* Yet here we were, speaking tensely over $26,000 sapphire-studded Tiffany watches.

"I know you're not. And you should think of me as a resource as you're getting your freelance stuff back off the ground. I know a lot of people." It had begun to snow, tiny flakes swirling like dandelion fluff. We'd picked the last warmish day for our excursion; tomorrow, temperatures were expected to plummet and stay in the single digits for a week or more. "You don't have to be, you know . . . too proud to ask for help."

"Oh my God, Hana. When did this become the Katie Bradley intervention special?" She turned on her heels and headed down the street.

"I'm sorry. Let's drop it. I know you're doing great." We walked in silence for a while, then approached a bulge of people in front of Radio City Music Hall; the marquee promised the Rockettes' Christmas Spectacular, long lines of perfect legs kicking in heels. Katie curled around a corner and the sidewalk opened up.

I cleared my throat. "Look, I'm sorry. I know you'd never sell secrets to *Page Six* or whatever. I'm just being a paranoid publicist." I saw my out: "Because of the big announcement."

"I get it. No worries." She steered us over to a cart and ordered two hot chocolates. "For everything you've done for me," she said, tapping her Styrofoam cup against mine. We crossed the last block between us and the Rockefeller Tree. It was outrageously tall, and together we stood looking up at it, flanked by other people, feeling big and alone and surrounded and small.

The room felt crackly and bright. There was the buzz of any Herd event: all these smart, ambitious women milling about in stylish outfits, forgoing the four million other things New York had to offer that Tuesday evening. They loved the Herd, detected its specialness, tweeted things like, "If you think it's not for you bc it's too bougie/white/annoying/whatever, please come be my plus-one and see for yourself how inclusive and supportive and wonderful it really is."

The crowd was mostly media plus a few VIPs, and they churned around the space: a private room at Hielo, a tapas restaurant off the lobby of a hotel. It was early; the announcement was scheduled for 8 p.m. and the *Gaze* interview with Joanna was at 7:30, but already, a little after 7, people were filing in, photographers checking the light and staking out the best vantage points. I hadn't seen Eleanor all day, which just added to the mystery. Yesterday she'd warned she'd probably work from home ahead of the event—likely so she could get a blowout and makeup application at her leisure—but I was eager for her to sashay in.

"Are you close?" I texted. I'd emailed her this morning with a room reservation for her interview, and she'd responded with a thumbs-up. Nothing since, though I imagined she was busy with last-minute preparations.

I spotted Mikki making her way toward me in a peacock-print jumpsuit with billowing sleeves; a photographer stopped her by the door, and she cocked her hip and grinned. Her smile crumpled as she rushed over.

"You look great," I told her. "Everything okay?"

"Have you seen Eleanor?"

I shook my head. "I take it you haven't either?"

"Ted told her to get here by six forty-five for the sound check. He just texted to ask if I'd seen her, but nobody has."

"Did you call her?" I lifted my phone to my ear.

"Obviously."

"She was home today. I'm sure she's just stuck in traffic." I turned a bit as Eleanor's voice kicked in, but it was just her voicemail.

A petite woman with swingy black hair tapped me on the shoulder. "Hana, right?"

I recognized her from my earlier Googling. "Joanna. So great to meet you."

She shook my hand limply. "I thought I'd see Eleanor out working the crowd. Are you keeping her tucked away before our chat?"

I smiled and checked my phone again; less than twenty minutes until their scheduled interview.

"I'll escort you upstairs in just a few. I got us a conference room. Have you met Mikki? She's responsible for the Herd's aesthetic."

I excused myself, dialing the Herd's front desk. "She didn't come in today," the girl said, confused. "Wasn't she working from home?"

I bit my lip. "Can you find the name of her usual hair and makeup person? It's Annika or Anya or something. Check if she saw her today."

Eleanor was inconsistent about that kind of thing, sometimes hiring professionals, sometimes prettifying herself—she was, after all, a beauty tycoon. And she'd chosen not to have an assistant, someone tasked with handling her calendar, with knowing her whereabouts. It was one of her Eleanorian quirks.

I looked around; Ted was fumbling with a tripod as the crowd swirled around him. I texted Katie and then saw her making her way over from the bar, clutching a glass of red wine. I pulled Mikki away again and shuffled us into a small hallway meant for servers.

"Has anybody heard from Eleanor?"

Everyone looked at one another.

"She must be on her way here, right?" Katie finished her glass of wine.

"Has anyone talked to her?" I pressed.

Katie made a combo laugh-scoff. "Breathe, Hana. If everyone reacted this way every time I was twenty minutes late . . ."

"It's just not like her. Who heard from her last?"

"I think I got an email from her this morning," Mikki offered, pulling out her phone. One by one, we all checked. "An email at ten fifty-four. She just said, 'Let's discuss tomorrow.'"

"She texted me right before one. Just said, 'Okay,'" I added.

"I haven't heard from her, but"—Katie shrugged—"she was busy preparing for tonight, right?"

"What do you think happened? Was she in an accident?" Mikki said what I'd been thinking, the only reasonable explanation I could come up with. Why hadn't anyone contacted one of us? Didn't she have ID on her? Had it *just* happened—oh God, was she mangled, critical, barely recognizable as Eleanor?

My phone rang and I almost laughed at my histrionics—that had to be Eleanor, sprinting down Sixth Avenue after getting caught in traffic . . .

But it was the Herd's front desk. "I just talked to Aria. Eleanor had a four o'clock appointment but didn't show. Didn't cancel it either."

"Okay. Where was it supposed to be? The appointment?"

"Eleanor's apartment. Aria said it's happened a couple times before, where Eleanor changes her plans and forgets to cancel, and she still pays the full amount plus the cancellation fee, so Aria wasn't too concerned."

"So she rang the doorbell and no one answered?"

"Right, that's what she said."

I thanked her and relayed the update. Again, my mind whipped up an image: Eleanor's body crumpled on her kitchen floor, blue from choking on a grape or bloodied from a sudden fall or perfect-looking, normal, the outside hiding the hemorrhage streaking blood across her brain . . .

"Okay, so she said Eleanor's been flaky before." Katie crossed her arms, still determinedly unconcerned.

"Who has Daniel's number?" Mikki asked.

I whipped up a finger, then turned on the speaker as I dialed.

"Hello? Hana?"

"Daniel, I'm with Mikki. Is Eleanor with you?"

"What? No, I'm on my way to Hielo right now. From work." A siren wailed in the background. "It hasn't started yet, has it?"

"Did you talk to Eleanor today?" Katie broke in. Silence, so she added, "This is Katie."

"No, I was planning to see her at the event."

"Do you know where she is?" I said.

"She isn't with you?" Like it was dawning on him: "Wait, where is she then?"

"Daniel, can you track her phone?" Katie asked. "Like, with location services?"

"That won't work," I cut in. "She told me last week she wasn't going to turn on location services on her new one. Better to maintain her privacy, and she pointed out that it didn't do her any good with the last phone."

Katie looked confused and Mikki said, "Huh?" right as Daniel said, "How do we find her then?"

Shoot—Katie and Mikki hadn't heard about the stolen phone and subsequent photo debacle. I pretended I hadn't heard them. "Have the cab take you home—see if she's left a note or anything. Let us know."

I could feel the night careening out of my control, black ice beneath the tires. I kept seeing it: Eleanor's body by the side of the road. "Her *Gaze* interview is supposed to start, like, now," I announced.

Mikki frowned. "We should cancel it, right?"

I squeezed my eyes closed. *What Would Eleanor Do?* "The timing is—we need to make the announcement now because we're already so close to the end of the year. Something with stocks, the trading calendar."

Mikki squared her shoulders. "Hana, I swear to God, if you don't tell us what the hell this announcement is all about—"

"Titan is acquiring the Herd." I took in their blank stares and sighed. "It's huge news. Unprecedented. The world's largest technology company is buying the Herd."

Two seconds, three. Katie frowned. "Wait, what? Eleanor's giving up the company?"

"No, she's retaining control. But it'll mean we can grow and expand in mind-blowing ways. We can—"

"Hana, stop." Mikki flung out her palm. "We don't know where Eleanor is. This isn't—this doesn't matter at all."

"I'm just trying to think. It does matter to her, I know it does." I chewed on my lip. "She said that with filing laws, we need to announce today in order to have enough trading days before the end of the year. It's already down to the wire, and she's very concerned about bad press." UGLY CUNTS, the graffiti I'd miraculously kept hidden from the news vultures. "She won't be happy if the *New York Times*' headline is, like, 'Herd Cancels Buzzed-About Event Minutes Before It Starts.'"

"You know what also won't look good?" Katie snapped. "'Herd Founder Goes MIA; Organization Holds Event Anyway.'" Mikki nodded and pointed at her, jabbing her hand in agreement.

They stared at me, two kids begging their mom to make it all okay. Eleanor wouldn't miss this for the world. But . . . but Eleanor had to be okay. I took a deep breath and pulled myself together, an inward sweep.

"I'm sure Eleanor's fine," I said, my voice a tick lower. It was what everyone wanted—reassurance it'd all work out somehow. "But you're right. We can't make the announcement until we know where she is."

Joanna Chen was calling me again. She wouldn't be happy.

"Okay. I need to cancel the interview. And recall the press release, which is scheduled to go out in twenty minutes. And make an announcement to everyone who came out tonight. Oh, lord." A headache materialized, a little spear behind my right eyeball.

"Can we help?" Mikki asked, and Katie nodded eagerly.

Ugh, if only. "Thanks, but I've got this. Maybe you guys could see if the events coordinator heard from her. It's the bald guy in a suit." They marched off and I followed. In the dining room, Joanna looked annoyed, and I snapped into professional mode.

I delivered the bad news to her first, apologizing profusely as the blood drained from her face. Then I was a squirrel paralyzed in the middle of the street as I jerked toward my laptop to recall the press release and the podium to disappoint the jumpy masses here. Finally I took off for the front of the room, fumbling with the microphone until Ted came to the rescue, and blurted it out, my composure fraying: "Eleanor sincerely apologizes but due to a family emergency, we're postponing this evening's announcement. A press alert will *not* be issued at eight p.m., but I promise to keep you personally apprised once we have more information." Confusion and annoyance ruffled through the crowd. Mikki and Katie were watching me from the corner of the room, their faces a dead giveaway that something was wrong. I smiled. "Again, we're so sorry, but we have the space until ten so please enjoy the food and drinks until then. Thank you."

I bolted for the elevators, bleating apologies at those who tried to stop me, and skidded into the conference room I'd reserved for Eleanor and Joanna's interview. Ignoring my jolting phone, I tapped away at my laptop, until — 7:58, with two whole minutes to spare, I sat back. The press release wouldn't be sent out.

I glanced at my phone. "Ted and events manager know nothing," Mikki had texted. "Still no word from E?"

I was beginning to text her back when another message came through, this one from Eleanor's husband: "Just got home. Eleanor's not here."

Shit. I rubbed a knuckle against the bridge of my nose, tears for the first time prickling my eyes. If she wasn't home . . . where the hell was she?

I started to reply, then saw he was typing again. His text appeared and I had to read it several times before it had meaning.

My insides turned to ice and my hands began to shake.

Daniel said: "Something's wrong. She hasn't been home at all."

CHAPTER 7

Katie

At first I'd thought everyone was overreacting, the way they did with the Gleam Room graffiti: imagining menace in something childish and at least a little hilarious. But now that we'd collated our data points—Eleanor's cryptic texts, her missed beauty appointment, the fact that no one, not even her husband, had heard from her—I was beginning to worry too. This wasn't like Eleanor. She allayed stress, never caused it. She'd seemed normal at Mocktails last night, hadn't she? Relaxed and charming as ever.

I'd almost skipped Mocktails—I'd almost headed home in defeat. My stomach clenched at the memory now . . . had I somehow endangered Eleanor, summoned one of her haters back into her life? Monday afternoon, I was alone in a booth at a diner in my neighborhood, one with cracked, greasy menus and cracked, greasy tabletops and pots of bad coffee burbling behind the counter. I'd chosen it because I wanted to meet my interview subject in public, for obvious reasons, but that meant choosing somewhere I knew no Herder would see me.

But Carl Berkowski, the surprisingly affable-seeming man who'd led the charge behind *Berkowski v. The Herd, Inc.* (and who was almost certainly a member of the Antiherd), hadn't shown. Around 3:30, I'd checked my phone for the fourth time in as many minutes; after a half hour of waiting and no response to emails and texts, I decided to throw in the towel.

This was supposed to be my first real interview since Erin had talked her way into my living room, since I'd blurted out Eleanor's name like I was screaming a password, *Open Sesame*, a way out of the mess I'd made. I was relieved to pour my efforts into something other than *Infopocalypse*, but Hana's out-of-left-field warning to not even *think* about writing about the Herd . . . it had me shook.

But I couldn't stop now. I'd promised Erin a progress report by midweek, once the Herd's big announcement was splashed across front pages all over the world, wide web and otherwise. I'd figured I'd have some yarns to show her by then, some interesting backstory and colorful characters. Like this men's rights dude, Carl. Of course his name was Carl.

But Carl had stood me up, freed up my Monday. I'd slapped down my laptop's screen and signaled for the check. I got on the C train daydreaming about the Herd's airy beauty. My second Monday Mocktails was spectacular; the bartender was from the Elm Grove, known for their creative use of tinctures and fermented teas and drinking vinegars, and at one point I'd looked out at the crowd, all these cool women being kind to one another, and I thought: *No wonder you wish you could be a part of this, Carl.*

And now Eleanor was . . . gone. My brain kept bumping up against it, a Roomba stuck in a corner. Half the crowd had dispersed after

Hana's disturbingly poised announcement. Ted, confused, had stopped by with his gear in a little rolly bag to tell us he was heading out.

"She's okay, though, right?" he kept asking, and Mikki and I nodded blankly. Now she and I were hiding in a corner, with me blocking her from the room lest anyone approach her with questions. This bothered me, which was fully absurd. That Mikki was a celebrity and I was a face in a crowd.

A text from Hana: "Where are you guys?" As if now that one person was unaccounted for, she was eager to keep track of her other kiddos, a mom at the pool doing a desperate headcount. Then another: "Meet me back in the hallway."

We watched as Hana clattered toward us, heels higher than ever, ankles confident on their stilts, chest and core and muscly shoulders all sculpted into defiance.

"I think we should go over to her apartment," she announced.

"Is she there?" Mikki called, her voice birdlike with hope.

Hana shook her head. "Daniel's there now. He said it doesn't look like she's been home all day. The last time he's sure he saw her was yesterday morning."

"What?" I leaned back against the wall. "Where has he been?"

"He said he worked late yesterday. Spent the night in his office." Three sets of eyebrows spiked in unison.

"So he's fucking somebody else." Mikki said it flatly, like someone reading off a lame fortune cookie.

"Who knows. But if he doesn't even know what he's looking for at the apartment, we should get there."

"Should we call the cops?" I asked, fiddling with a purse strap.

"Daniel said he was about to. We can call on the way too. I just feel like we need to go. Right now."

"What about the . . . the event?" Mikki's voice was small, high up in her skull.

Hana stared like she'd spoken in Dutch. "What?"

"All this." She gestured toward the dining room. "We just leave?"

Hana shrugged. "Aurelia's here somewhere. If someone has a problem with us checking on our friend, they can go fuck themselves."

Hana rarely cursed—it sounded wrong, like a parent using slang. Mikki and I nodded weakly.

"Daniel doesn't know we're coming," Hana said. "Let's head out."

Our driver trundled down Seventh Avenue, jamming at the brakes as if every car in front of him were a surprise, and Hana, normally patient, kept letting out frustrated sighs. After a few minutes she gasped and looked around wildly, then called Aurelia and asked her to grab a tote bag Hana had left behind the bar.

"There's a bunch of folders inside, right?" she asked, then exhaled. "Good. Just bring it tomorrow."

Hana hung up and then called Eleanor's parents in Beverly, Massachusetts, who had no idea why Hana was calling or where Eleanor might be. She called 911 while Mikki and I listened uncomfortably; the dispatcher said they'd review this afternoon's ambulance and arrest (!) records before sending detectives to Eleanor's address. Outside the window, street signs slowly counted us down: Sixteenth Street, Fifteenth, Fourteenth. Fear was fanning out inside of me, working outward from my gut.

"Do you still think Eleanor is okay?" Mikki asked.

"She has to be. She *has* to be." Hana hung her head. "Eleanor is *somewhere*. We just don't know where yet."

The driver jerked to a stop and turned on his hazards, and we listened to their metronomic clacking: tick-tock, tick-tock, tick-tock. Together, we gazed out at Eleanor and Daniel's townhouse. The curtains were drawn across the bay window, with a strip of yellow light leaking through. They'd bought the place shortly before their wedding, and while it probably looked charming on normal evenings, tonight it was all angles and peaks, a haunted house.

Hana rang the doorbell, which echoed inside, and then we stood, listening as car horns and engines and distant bass lines made the air around us quiver. A hand appeared in the bay window and ripped the curtain aside. Mikki jumped.

Daniel cupped his hands over his brow and leaned into the window, squinting, and Hana waved. The front door swung open, moving ominously. The city soundtrack seemed to crescendo as Daniel stood before us, all six-foot-three of him, his thick black hair and tailored suit and boyish face all equally rumpled.

He caught the door with one foot and stepped forward with the other, and instinctively I reared back—but it was to unfurl his wingspan to Hana, curling her into a hug. She stepped past him and Mikki and I hugged him in turn, a receiving line. The realization that I knew almost nothing about this guy resurfaced like something bobbing up from the bottom of a lake.

We stood in the vestibule, mirrored closet doors everywhere and the walls around them painted in stripes of gold and white. One closet door faced a floor mirror, so there were a million versions of the four of us, unbuttoning coats and yanking off gloves as Daniel lurched around, hanging things up. The silvery mirror world, the endless identical lines of us shooting out in every direction, sent a shiver up my scalp. *Maybe Eleanor's lost in here*, my brain shot out.

"So you don't have any updates," Hana prompted, leading us into the living room and sitting. "You haven't heard from Eleanor."

He shook his head. His brown eyes looked glassy. "Not a thing. I didn't hear from her once today, but I didn't think that was weird. I hadn't contacted her either, so."

"Is it normal for you guys to go a whole night and day without talking?" I asked. This was my area of expertise, not Hana's, I reminded myself—no matter how in-charge she seemed. I was the beat reporter here, trained in the subtle art of whittling away bullshit to get to the crystalline truth underneath.

He nodded. "Pretty normal. I mean, we text at some point most days, but I knew she was busy getting ready for her big event tonight, and she knew I was . . . busy too. With work." His eyes darted back and forth between us, too fast.

"Where were you?" I said, at the exact same time Hana prompted: "What made you think she didn't come home?" He looked overwhelmed, and Hana repeated herself.

He focused on her. "Eleanor's predictable. She leaves her dishes from breakfast in the sink and then loads them into the dishwasher after work. She made oatmeal yesterday and didn't eat much of it—I commented on it before I left for work. When I got home a little while ago, the oatmeal was still sitting out." He pointed to the open kitchen, and again the question blared like something on a marquee: *Where were* you?

"And she'd picked out an outfit for the event," he went on. "But it's still in her closet." He gestured toward the staircase that led upstairs—directly into their big sunny bedroom, and beyond it, the study.

"Daniel, where were you last night?" Mikki leaned forward, her elbows on her knees. "You can tell us the truth."

He blushed. "I told you, I slept in my office."

"Bullshit." Mikki crossed her arms. "We all know that's code for having an affair."

"It's not like that!" Daniel looked like he might cry. "I would never—I love Eleanor."

"The cops are on their way, right?" Mikki went on. "We're going to tell them. They'll ask where you were."

"No, she . . . it was her idea."

"What?" Hana's face was frozen in alarm.

"It's . . ." His body language changed; he'd made a decision. "Fine, I'll show you. Hang on." He stood and galloped up the stairs, his footsteps echoing. After a second, I rose and sprinted after him. Hana and Mikki followed.

He crouched in the study, long legs bent at an absurd angle, and fumbled to fit a key in the bottom drawer of Eleanor's desk. Finally he yanked the drawer out noisily, fished around in it, and then held out a sheet of yellow paper, an edge ruffled where it'd been ripped from a notebook.

"Here," he said. "It's all in here."

I darted over and snatched it from him, and Mikki and Hana crowded around my shoulders, reading. It was Eleanor's loopy handwriting, instantly recognizable:

RULES:

- *24-hour warning before dates*

- *Ask permission before spending night → no contact until 3pm following day*

- *No one we both know*

- *Transparency re: married/experimenting only*

- *NEVER discuss EG/Gleam/Herd*

- *Sex only/no emotional affair*

- *SAFE SEX/regular testing*

- *Biweekly check-ins/prioritize HONESTY*

Signed: Eleanor Walsh 10/25/19

Daniel Kim 10/25/19

"Jesus Christ," Hana said.

Mikki looked up, shaking her head. "You two had an open marriage?"

"It was her idea." He clutched his hands to his stomach and hunched over like he might throw up. "It was the first time I even met up with anyone else."

Mikki crossed her arms. "You guys have only been married, like, six months."

"And she's the love of my life. That's why I had to say yes. She said that . . . something about the wedding, the permanence. I guess it made her feel trapped. The thought that we'd spend the next sixty years with only each other . . . and you know how she dated a few women. She was really hung up on not ever . . . doing that again." His cheeks reddened again and he cleared his throat, coughed. Hana and I exchanged a puzzled glance, but Mikki nodded.

"She never seriously dated a woman," Hana said, like she could prove him wrong.

"Well, no." He ran a hand over his hair, leaving it with new crazy tufts. "But this is . . . this is sex."

"She was involved with a couple once," Mikki offered, nodding our way. "For a month or two. I remember that."

No one had explicitly told me this, but it all jibed with my image of uber-progressive Eleanor. "So you went straight to seeing other people?" I crossed my arms. "Why not go to sex parties together? Or have a threesome?"

"Katie, stop—we're getting off-track." Hana gave her head a horselike shake. "This contract. You both signed it. So she's been sleeping with other people, and so have you?"

"Last night was the first time for me," Daniel said again. I shot Hana a look: *Do we believe him?*

"And you don't know who she was seeing?" I said.

Daniel shook his head. "She wasn't doing it that often. Three times since we signed this."

It was so very Eleanor to have drawn up a tidy contract. "You're going to have to think long and hard about exactly when she had these hookups, and what you know about who she was with," I said. Also on-brand: covering her tracks with the neatness of a cat.

"You think someone she met is responsible for her disappearance?" Daniel's head whipped around, his hair bobbing.

"Well, it doesn't look great. That she had secret lovers." Mikki leaned against the bookcase.

If this were a noir, we'd have a new deck of possible motives: Eleanor had run off with someone new. Or she'd met up with a bad seed, someone who'd kidnapped her or worse. Or we could look at the flip side, ignore Daniel's insistence that none of this was his idea: Perhaps Daniel had fallen in love with someone else and decided to dispose of his wife. Or a new lover had fallen for Daniel and opted to eliminate the inconvenient spouse. Or nobody had fallen in love with anyone, but Daniel had set his sights on this new single life, convinced his wife to open up their marriage so he'd have her permission in her own goddamn handwriting . . .

"So you were with someone last night," Hana prompted.

He nodded. "I worked late, then met her at a bar in her neighborhood. I thought it would be awkward to, you know, come home first, see Eleanor, and then take off again. And then—not talking the next morning, that was her idea, because neither of us wants to know details. She wanted it to be completely separate." He whipped his hands out, away from each other. "It was just a woman I was talking to online. I'd never met up with her before. It was just sex."

"The cops are gonna look into your alibi," Hana said.

"I know." He nodded. "Everyone in the world is about to know about my sex life. I don't give a shit. I just want Eleanor back."

The doorbell chimed, echoing up the stairs, and we all turned in the direction of the front door. Daniel loped out into the bedroom and the others followed.

My eyes fell on the drawer, still gaping open like a question mark.

Moving quickly, I kneeled and plunged my hand inside. Financial documents: I didn't have time to read them, but I whipped my phone out and snapped photos of the pages, one by one. A pad of Post-it notes was in the drawer, too, unmarked, and I peeled off the top quarter-inch of sheets and shoved them in a pocket before strolling back downstairs.

They were seated awkwardly around the living room, a pair of cops, a man and a woman, on the sofa, Daniel and Mikki in armchairs. The policeman appeared to be copying down details from Daniel's driver's license. Hana stood a few feet behind Mikki, her whole body curved toward her phone.

"The news about Titan got out," Mikki murmured, nodding in Hana's direction.

"What? I thought Hana pulled the press release back?" I whispered. I pulled out my phone; Joanna Chen's article was at the top of *The Gaze*'s homepage, flame emojis indicating it was surging in traffic, and already twenty-seven comments clung to the bottom. It clicked: the tote bag full of press kits Hana had stashed behind the bar and then forgotten. Had a nosy reporter found it?

"And you are?" the policewoman said, craning her neck to see where I'd come from.

"Katie Bradley." I pointed at Hana. "Her sister. And also one of Eleanor's best friends."

"I'm Detective Ratliff. This is Detective Herrera."

"Are there more of you?" The male cop—Herrera, apparently— had wide arms, a thick trunk, and a New York accent to match: *Are thair mora you?*

"No, sorry. I—I got distracted on my way downstairs because people started texting me about this article that just went up. About the Herd." I unlocked my phone, held it out. "It mentions Eleanor."

Ratliff—pretty with full lips and wide-set eyes—plucked it out of my hand and scanned it.

"This is about the event Eleanor didn't show up for. The news wasn't supposed to get out tonight, though. It's what our friend is dealing with—she's their publicist." Mikki jerked her head in Hana's direction, then met my eyes. "They've never heard of the Herd." We held each other's gaze for a moment, keeping our faces neutral. Blink, blink.

Ratliff held out my phone and looked away theatrically. "You just got a new text."

It was from Mom: "Just saw the big news abt the herd!!! Very interesting choice to join Titan." A moment later, a second text: "Tell Hana to call me sometime. xo"

Hana walked back over and leaned against Mikki's armchair, apologizing. She looked like she might puke. I mouthed *You okay?* And she gave a small, unconvincing nod.

"All right, do I have your attention?" Ratliff seemed more bored than annoyed. We all nodded rabidly.

"Right now we're trying to assess the level of risk for the missing person. Ms. . . . Walsh. That depends on a number of factors, and it helps us determine if we need to start investigating now or if we should wait a few days before taking further action." She pulled a pen out of a pocket, clicked it. "Most people who are reported missing show up within forty-eight hours. So if she's not immediately at risk, we'll take that into account."

"Of course she's at risk," Daniel blurted out. "She vanished into thin air. She had an event tonight. Something must have happened."

"We're considering all possibilities," she replied mechanically, handing the folded yellow sheet to her partner. The polyamory contract. *She thinks Eleanor just bolted.*

"Officer, we know her extremely well," Hana said. "This is completely out of character."

"Is she on medication?" Ratliff replied. She was flipping through a small notebook to find a clean page.

"What?" Daniel asked.

"If she requires medication or treatment, that's an important factor in assessing the level of risk." She looked at Daniel expectantly, as if the rest of us weren't there.

"Um . . . I don't know, birth control, antidepressants, she takes something for her allergies but that might just be in the fall and spring. Her medication's in a drawer on the nightstand—I can go get it." He started to rise, but the cop shook her head. Herrera shifted his feet, impatiently, like a horse kicking at the dirt.

"Has she ever been involved in a missing-persons case before?" she continued.

Daniel swung his head wildly. "Never."

I glanced over at Hana—had she and Mikki exchanged a look, or were my eyes playing tricks on me?

"Okay." Ratliff made a note. "Let's keep thinking. You mentioned this business announcement tonight. Is there anyone who'd benefit from it not going through? Or who'd want her out of the way?"

We all frowned. "We only just learned about it," Hana finally said. "So I don't know who, on our end, would have an opinion either way. I guess you should check with Titan."

Ratliff nodded. "Is there anyone else we should keep in mind? Ex-boyfriends?"

"Eleanor didn't really date anyone seriously between her high school boyfriend—she dated him the last year of college too—and Daniel." Hana nodded toward him and he jumped. The high school boyfriend she'd briefly gotten back together with—I hadn't met him, but I vaguely remembered him from photos. Blond and handsome, floating somewhere in that surfer/stoner/ski-bum continuum.

"And the high school sweetheart, they're not in touch?"

"I guess a little. He doesn't live here." Hana kept tilting her head as her thoughts tumbled out. "Actually, we talked to his brother tonight. He was at the event."

"I'm sorry, what?" Ratliff shook her head. "The brother of her ex was at the event this evening?"

"What are you talking about?" I prompted.

"He was there," Mikki replied, frowning like it was obvious. "His brother is Ted."

Ratliff copied down our contact information and handed us her business cards. She had a few more things to discuss with Daniel, she said, looking at us pointedly until we rose and headed for the front door. Hana was slowest to leave, handing Ratliff her own card as Mikki and I suited up for the cold. Outside, I opened my mouth to rehash everything that had transpired—the open relationship, what we thought those two cops were thinking—but then Mikki burst into tears, and when Hana hugged her she began to cry, too, and I almost wanted to join them, but the pressure behind my eye-balls was panic, not tears. Then Hana's car was there, Mikki's right behind it, and I was alone on the cold front stoop, the strangeness of the night spilling down the steps in front of me. I watched it, seep-ing into the street like billows from a fog machine, and suddenly knew what to do.

On the car ride home, I scrolled through my contacts, praying I still had the number. With a spritz of relief, I saw it was there, and I sent an encrypted message before I could think too hard about it: "I'm back in town and need you. Call me ASAP."

As the car rolled along Delancey Street, I felt the old familiar pull, like a scratch, like a black hole centered somewhere in my lower torso: *Figure it out.* It was the feeling I got whenever an editor sicced me on something, had me sniff at the confusing pieces so I could pick up the scent and take off running.

My phone buzzed in my palm and I read a text from Erin: "Just saw announcement abt titan acquiring the herd. CRAZY!! Idk if you racked up serious karma or sold your soul to the devil or what but as your agent I am HERE FOR IT. I'm sure you're celebrating/reporting like crazy rn but call me when you can to discuss."

Of course Erin, too, had seen the headlines. Poor Hana—my sister *never* messes up, and now someone else had screwed her over. She gets so worked up, a balloon on the verge of bursting, when things don't go according to plan. And then she acts irritated that she has to deal with it, but also doesn't trust anyone else to help.

At least news of Eleanor's *disappearance* hadn't broken yet. I pulled up my photos, swiping through and confirming my surreptitious photocopies from Eleanor's desk were indeed readable. I ran my fingers over the sticky notes in my bag. Somewhere in my chest, my resolve took shape and hardened, like clay in a kiln.

"Erin, you have no idea. I'll call you in 30," I texted back, then rested my head against the backseat and gazed out the window. Manhattan's barbed outline flickered in the dark as the car thundered over the bridge and into Brooklyn.

PART II

CHAPTER 8

BIG NEWS I COULDN'T BE MORE THRILLED TO SHARE

By Eleanor Walsh *Published to* Gleam On *Dec 6, 2017*

Good morning, <u>Gleam Team</u>! I woke up with a huge smile on my face because I couldn't wait to tell you the secret I've been keeping for the better part of a year. My beloved publicist, <u>Hana</u>, encouraged me to share it first in a huge media outlet, but I was adamant: I wanted to share it here on the blog. You lovelies have been with me since Day One, you're my inspiration, and you're what makes running Gleam <u>a dream come true</u>.

First, a story from my childhood. I went to junior high outside Boston, and every summer, a week before the start of the school year, the entire school took over a huge "Adventure

Camp" about an hour from our hometown. It was a two-night outing to encourage bonding, team-building, and problem-solving with activities like a ropes course, Capture the Flag, rock climbing, and more. Sounds fun, right?

WRONG. Lovelies, I dreaded Adventure Camp *literally all summer*. Every time I thought about it, I felt like I'd swallowed a bag of rocks. Nothing especially terrible ever happened to me there, but I felt so nervous and judged and miserable in the months leading up to it and definitely during it. My ENTIRE goal was to get through it without doing anything embarrassing or having anyone laugh at me or even *think* something mean about me. You know how crazy that is, trying to control what other people think?!

Anyway, I made it through those two outings intact (obviously!) and pushed Adventure Camp to the back of my mind. Then, a few years ago, a friend mentioned that her niece was about to head off to Adventure Camp. She said her niece, who was nine, genuinely loved going every year. She sent me a link to an article about the program, and lovelies, my jaw *hit the floor*.

This Adventure Camp? All girls. On the surface, it looked a lot like the one I'd attended: ropes courses, archery, boating, you name it. But the program was based on research about how girls can build resilience. High-achieving girls, the article said, are often super-stressed out and terrified of failure. The camp actually throws them into (safe!) stress-inducing situations and equips them with the tools to come out stronger.

As I read, I kept thinking: WHY was my experience so different from these girls'? The answer was both totally obvious and a little shocking: My Adventure Camp was coed. I don't need a mountain of studies to show you that many women are more comfortable, more creative, more relaxed, more able to think big and let loose when they're in a space with all women (although there are <u>researchers looking into this very topic</u>). I wondered: What would an all-girl Adventure Camp for adults look like?

And then I had my second lightbulb moment. When Gleam was getting off the ground, our scrappy little team couldn't afford our own office space, so we rented some desks in a coworking space. It was a huge help, but every one I looked into was owned by men with a majority-male C-suite. One night, I was lying in bed when I thought, "Wait . . . what if . . ."

That's right, Gleam Team: I am SO excited to announce that we're starting the world's first coworking space and community exclusively for people who identify as female. We're calling it THE **HERD**, both because that's what you are—my team, my flock, my people—and because it's all about **HER**. We're crossing our T's and dotting our I's on an amazing location in NYC now. I'll share more news soon, but I wanted you lovelies to be the very first to know.

XX,
Eleanor

CHAPTER 9

———————

Hana

Someone was coming up the hallway as I walked down it, a twenty-something woman pulling a dachshund on a leash, and they both regarded me curiously as I passed. I imagined my dripping nose, my bloodshot eyes, the black tracks ribboning my cheeks. I'd cried the whole car ride home from Eleanor's place, and when I finally made it to my apartment, I took just a few steps in before sliding out of my heels and lowering myself to the ground. Leaning against the kitchen island, I breathed deeply, pulling myself together like someone sweeping crumbs into a pile.

Frame by frame, I went over it in my head: When had Joanna stolen the press release? She'd been furious when I'd told her the interview wouldn't happen; she kept repeating, *We killed a story for you,* as if last week the *Gaze* team had brought the graffiti photos out back and executed them with a firing squad. *Ugh.* I had promised her the exclusive, and in my harried state I'd assumed she'd accept my apology and await further updates.

What a mess. Aurelia had counted and confirmed only one press release was missing, and Joanna had broken the news first; a few reporters who'd been at Hielo had tried to confirm the embargo was lifted, but of course, once other outlets started running the story, there was a mad dash for clicks, shares, eyeballs.

Cosmo emerged from the dark hallway, his tail flicking. Of course, my brain was hurtling after Joanna Chen because it couldn't face tonight's much larger Terrible Thing. Eleanor was not one to sabotage her own event. Her own *company.* I could tell myself she had, for some bewildering reason, bounced without warning or explanation, but I knew it was bullshit.

First things first: I fished my phone out of my pocket, ignoring all the new-message alerts, and performed the same series of searches I did every few months—Google, then a handful of apps, the series of memorized usernames, tapping on tagged locations to be sure. Nowhere near NYC. I set my phone down and exhaled.

My gaze fell on my bag, crumpled on the floor just inside the door. I blinked at it and got the eerie sensation that the object inside was staring back at me. Waiting quietly, like a grenade with the pin yanked out.

I crawled over to it and sat, pulling the satchel onto my lap. It had all happened so quickly. The doorbell had chimed, and everyone had tumbled downstairs after it. Alone in the room, I'd let instincts take over—lunging over to Eleanor's bed, to the side I assumed was hers thanks to the presence of La Mer hand cream and a worn bell hooks book. I slipped my hand under the white duvet, feeling dirty, feeling an instant urge to apologize to the bed for reaching inside. I forced my hand into the crease between the box spring and the mattress and felt it: a crisp corner, stiffness where only softness belonged. My whole arm had buzzed as I ripped the object out and flung it into my bag just as my phone began to ring, and I'd answered while pummeling down the stairs, grateful for the excuse for my tardiness.

Now, heart pounding, I turned the envelope over in my hands: nothing on the outside, the edges a little worn from use. I slid a finger under the flap and then paused.

Eleanor and I had been talking about chores, the household chores we hate. How long ago had that been? Two months, maybe three? It'd been a conversation like any other, banal thoughts rolling around like marbles on a tray when we crossed paths at the Herd's café. I'd mentioned I was debating hiring a cleaning lady, and she'd told me about her own hire but used the much more gender-neutral term "housekeeper," which touched off a jolt of embarrassment. She'd reported that she loved hers but had to ask her to stop folding the laundry because Eleanor liked doing it herself, which I found downright nuts. I'd pointed out I'd love a housekeeper (yes, a housekeeper) to make the bed after laundry day, a step I dreaded, and Eleanor had grinned. *I asked her not to strip the bed or make it, either, but that's just because I store my secrets there.* Her eyes sparkled. *It's where I kept my diary growing up, so my mom wouldn't find it. Old habits die hard, I guess.* I'd giggled and bantered back that that was a perk of living alone—my secrets lived almost out in the open, the gratitude journal and expensive vibrator chilling in an unlocked drawer to the right of my bed.

I'd forgotten about it altogether until we ran upstairs tonight, my and Mikki's and Katie's feet a stampede on the wooden stairs, and saw Daniel crouched in front of Eleanor's desk, feeding a key into a locked drawer. So this was a hiding place, a shared one, for secrets between the two of them, but back in the bedroom . . .

I flicked the envelope open. Inside was a Post-it stuck to a scrap of computer paper, torn from a corner. Both papers had strings of numbers written on them: 527434340100 on the purple Post-it,

8914512191 on the scrap. They were in the same handwriting—
block numbers, not Eleanor's.

I tapped them out on my fingers and noticed that while the first
was too long, the second might be a phone number. I tried it: a jazzy
little riff, then, "Your call cannot be completed as dialed." I Googled
both numbers; no hits.

Passwords? I pulled out my wallet and confirmed that both strings
of numbers were too short to be credit card or bank account numbers. Again, I tapped my fingers against my lap as I recited my Social Security number—also nine. What the hell were these, and
why were they tucked in an envelope in Eleanor's bed? I couldn't
believe I'd taken these. Thank God no one had noticed in the hub-
bub.

I stood clumsily and made my way into the living room. Cosmo
watched me from the back of the couch, his front paws curled underneath him. I flopped down and pulled him onto my stomach; he
thought about it for a second, then knotted himself into a circle.
Texts and email alerts kept rattling my phone against the hardwood
floor twenty feet away.

Had Ratliff and Herrera contacted Cameron yet? It was strange
to picture them calling him; he felt like someone from another lifetime, a world that didn't Venn-diagram with ours. It'd all been rather
sweet: Eleanor's childhood home was down the street from Ted and
Cameron's, and while Ted and Eleanor had been friends practically
since birth, in high school she'd begun dating Cameron—one year
older and still living at home while he went to community college.
She'd implied his decision not to head farther afield for school was
about wanting to be near her—and so he hadn't been pleased when,
the summer before her freshman year at Harvard, she told him it
was time to see other people.

A week or two into freshman year, as we ate late-night pizza and
talked breathlessly about our (nearly nonexistent) sex lives, Mikki
and I had forced Eleanor to show us photos of her high-school-

boyfriend-slash-recent-ex. We were not particularly surprised to see
that he was hot, with bright-blue eyes and Rumi quotes tattooed on
his arms and the tousled hair of a wannabe surfer.

Cameron's photos, in fact, left us overly excited to meet his little
brother, Ted. But we quickly discovered the younger Corrigan was
gawky and thin, all elbows and ears and 20,000 leagues below Eleanor. Ted was just starting at Boston University, and he would occasionally take the bus over to Harvard. It was pretty obvious that Ted
had a puppy-dog crush on Eleanor, but they both ignored it and got
along spectacularly as old friends. He brought us greasy boxes from
Union Square Donuts (a.m.) or pizza from Pinocchio's (p.m.) and
made us all smile with his unintimidating goofiness. Still, Cameron
remained a mystery to Mikki and me.

When, during sophomore year, Ted mentioned he was meeting
Cameron in town for a party, we persuaded Eleanor it was a good
idea for us to go with him. Mainly I just wanted to see Cameron in
the flesh, this mythical older man, Eleanor's capital-F first. We'd
trekked to Allston-Brighton in our cutest outfits, prepared to dazzle,
but Cameron had been there with his then-girlfriend, almost theatrically ignoring us.

But the party itself was epic: slick tables set up for beer pong and
flip cup and something called chandelier, an ice luge, different
music in different rooms, shots we swallowed with teenage abandon. That night, Mikki had gone home with a hot musician who,
she later told us, played her a violin concerto at five in the morning.
(*It was beautiful but so* loud, she recounted.) I'd fallen asleep on a
sofa at the tail end of the house party, and Ted and Eleanor had
decided to leave me behind. I'd woken to Cameron gently shaking
my shoulder, and I can still remember the sheepishness, the sharp
hangover, the little moon of spit where the pillow met the corner of
my lips. I'd left with a quiet crush on Cameron, one I never mentioned to the gang.

In the ensuing years at Harvard, we almost never saw Cameron after that; Ted sometimes mentioned him, how he had his own apartment in Salem now, how he was doing fine. Then, senior year, we'd all returned from our exciting summers—internships in New York and Los Angeles, Mikki's eight-week design intensive in Milan—and Eleanor had announced that she and Cameron were dating again. They'd reconnected while she was living at home, she said. There was still a lot of passion there. That was probably when Cameron peaked, before the cascade of bad turns that landed him in rehab.

And Ted—well, Ted had turned and triumphantly marched off to the beat of his own drum. He'd filled out, now with thick, hairy arms and a thick, hairy beard, and discovered he had a knack for *making*, anything from a custom liquor cabinet to a custom video game to twenty-four tiny custom mechanisms that stretched to simulate breathing—a local artist had hired him to insert them in dolls that looked like sleeping babies, dolls the man placed around Boston to get a rise out of unsuspecting people. It sounded very avant-garde to me at the time.

But still, there was also something about Ted I didn't like. Or didn't get, maybe. He was doing pretty well now, kicking around NYC. Far and away the more successful of the two brothers.

I should call Ted. Had the cops contacted him already? Or maybe they weren't concerned at all. Maybe they figured Eleanor was a newlywed entrepreneur with a failing marriage and an Atlas-esque sphere of pressure pushing down on her, and she'd be back in a few days once she'd sorted things out. *Is that what I'd assume, if the AWOL woman were a stranger and not my best friend?*

With a sigh, I pushed Cosmo away and rolled off the side of the couch. I grabbed my phone and triaged the texts, emails, and missed calls from journalists and friends. Their excitement shot out of the screen, like the little bubbles that hit your nose from a full glass of Champagne. These people had no idea that everything was wrong, bad, scary, nonsensical. Several articles used the same photo of Eleanor, Mikki, and me from the last Herd announcement. It was a favorite of Eleanor's—we all looked good. Sometimes it struck me, though, how convenient it was for Eleanor to have a non-white face in her inner circle. A deep prickle of insecurity, a question of whether on some level, perhaps subconsciously, Eleanor had been strategic in befriending me, practiced as she was at curating her appearance. . . .

Then Mikki's name appeared. I took a deep breath and answered it.

"How are you doing?" I asked.

"I'm freaking out. Aren't you?"

"Obviously." I sighed. "The stuff about her wanting to see other people—it's weird she didn't mention it." Sure, she'd stopped discussing her sex life in lurid detail once she and Daniel got serious, but this was . . . *big*.

"Yeah. Guess she's good at keeping secrets."

"I guess." *Aren't we all, Mikki?*

"Do they think it has to do with the vandalism?" she said. "That was practically a threat."

"I don't know. I mentioned it to the detectives on the way out." The stolen phone too. Eleanor hadn't wanted anyone to know about it—not even Mikki.

"Right. They seemed so eager to help." She sighed. "What do you think, Hana? What happened?"

"I have no idea. I just know she had big plans for this week, this month—next year, clearly. She and I have a postmortem scheduled for first thing tomorrow morning, for God's sake." *Postmortem*: I'd always called it that, a chance to dissect and learn from the previous day's event or campaign launch. This was the first time it sounded morbid.

"I know." We were both quiet for a moment. "Have you tried to reach Stephanie?"

God, Eleanor's number two had left Saturday to do yoga on a

beach in India—she hadn't even crossed my mind. "Not yet. She said she'd only have Wi-Fi a few hours a day. She'll probably see the articles and think Eleanor really did have a family emergency."

"Right, okay," Mikki said. "And has Titan reached out to you?"

"Yeah, they're in my inbox somewhere. I'm going to keep them in the dark, obviously. Buy some time." I figured we had a decent shot at keeping Eleanor's AWOL status under wraps if she showed up in the next few hours. Which she had to. She *had* to.

"You've got it under control?"

"I'll handle it. The press release nightmare too." I felt a flare of annoyance: How nice it must be for Mikki, for everyone, to sit back and trust that I'd take care of it. Mikki had this blinky obliviousness that automatically absolved her of responsibility. It made people want to take care of her. This was not something we had in common. And Katie, too, could just plow through life like a toddler, glancing wondrously at messes she'd made in her determined scramble to get ahead . . .

Speaking of messes: "Have you talked to Ted?" I asked.

"No. He texted all of us, did you see that? I'm sure he's worried."

"Maybe he'll have some ideas of how to find her. They're still close." I'd always found Eleanor and Ted's continued friendship a little confounding—he was sweet, sure, but what did they have in common other than some shared playground memories? But that meant I didn't have a clear inventory of what she told him, the personal baubles that passed between them. "I'm going to call him."

"Okay." A few charged seconds and I could feel us both listening, waiting, wondering if the other would say it. My pulse rushed up into my ears, faster and faster, a runaway train bumping over the tracks.

But she didn't mention it.

"I'll keep you posted," I said finally, and hung up.

I tried Ted, left a pleading voicemail. Exhaustion hit me suddenly, like a weighted blanket tossed over me. But when I finally slid into bed, my mind whirred. Twice I took my phone off airplane mode, but Ted hadn't replied. I took an inventory of my latest inter-actions with Eleanor: a text at 12:54, just "okay." An email last night at 7:02: I'd had some last-minute questions on the logistics of the acquisition, and she'd answered in her usual calm manner.

Inspired, I emailed Mikki and Katie and asked them to provide the same info in a shared document—when they'd last seen and heard from Eleanor. Mikki had gotten texts from Eleanor at 10:42 a.m. and 3:03 p.m. today. Katie had left Eleanor at Mocktails at 6:28 p.m. ("per Lyft receipt"). Mocktails ended at 7.

Someone was calling me, a number that wasn't in my contacts, and it took me a full two rings to realize it was Ted.

"Thanks for calling me back."

"No prob. Did you find Eleanor?"

"No, she's still missing. Katie, Mikki, and I went over to her apartment, but she wasn't there either. We talked to some detectives—they might try to contact you too."

"Huh." He thought this over. "I sent her a bunch of texts after I left Hielo, but she hasn't responded. Do they think something hap-pened to her?"

"We're not sure." I took a deep breath, in and out. "They asked about exes. Have you heard from Cameron?"

"Cameron? He wouldn't know anything. Him and Eleanor don't really keep in touch."

"When did you talk to him last?"

"Let's see . . . I was home for Thanksgiving and we haven't talked since then."

"Is he living there, still?"

"That's right."

"How did he seem?" *Still clean?* I almost blurted out.

Ted chuckled uncomfortably. "He seemed normal. Hana, what's Cam got to do with any of this? I'm sure he doesn't even know El-eanor's missing yet. No one really does, right?"

"You're right. The cops asked about exes and I'm just . . . I wish I knew who to talk to." I mashed a hand against my eye. "I'm so worried. The night of a big, important event—it's an especially terrible time to disappear."

"Is there ever a good time?"

"I guess." One night earlier, and we'd be alarmed she left just before the announcement. One day later, and we'd be shocked she vanished on the heels of her exciting news.

A beat. "I'm sure Eleanor's fine, Hana. She's a smart girl. And very private. If she had to get away for a minute, she may not want us to know the reason."

Woman, I thought. *She's a smart woman.*

"You know, everyone says that: She's so private, she's so guarded, look at her running a lifestyle blog but hardly ever sharing anything about her own life." I stood and crossed to the kitchen, fumbled in the cabinet for a water glass. "People think they're opposite poles: You can be all TMI and post a million no-makeup selfies, or you can be like Eleanor and only post about your professional life. But it's not any different. Eleanor doesn't have *more* secrets than the woman who posts four hundred times a day. She just invests less time in hiding them."

A long silence. "I like that she's private," he said, because he didn't get it, not at all. "She just does cool shit and lets her work speak for itself."

"That's one way to think of it." I took a sip of water. "Anyway, I'm gonna call your brother."

"Good luck with that."

I dialed anew, listening to the rings without much hope. After a few, a cheerful robot lady told me that this user has a voicemail that has not been set up yet, goodbye.

I was out of things to do and that meant I had to face it again: Eleanor missing, Eleanor gone without a trace, Eleanor most likely, most rationally, most reasonably dead in a ditch somewhere, because why else wouldn't she have contacted us? Cosmo stood and leapt off the bed, annoyed by my shaking breaths.

I was about to switch off my phone when Mikki texted: "I've been thinking about this a lot."

No. No. No. No.

I tensed my shoulders, squinted my eyes, bracing as her second text came through.

She wrote: "I think we need to tell them."

CHAPTER 10

═══════════

Katie

Eleanor. I kept going over the last time I'd seen her the night before. I'd just drained my mocktail, a purply thing called the Botanist, and I was eager to get home and jot down some details from my experience: the music, the energy, the member I'd met who was the first nonbinary model to grace the cover of *Vogue*. A general loveliness I wanted to capture. I'd glanced over at Eleanor and debated grabbing her arm to say good night, but she'd been Eleanoring hard, working the room, and so I'd slipped into the elevator and told myself I'd see her in the morning.

But I hadn't seen her since then—what if I never would? There was still a small part of me clinging to the idea that she had, inexplicably, skipped town. But Eleanor's career was everything; she wouldn't destroy it. And her friends were a close second, and leaving would be a betrayal of sorts, with all of us panicking in her wake.

But no, I *had* to believe that that was the case, because the alternatives were awful: kidnapped, taken, drugged, maybe hurt, possibly even . . .

I leaned back against my pillows. My phone was still on my lap, headphones tossed on top. My call with Erin had been almost an out-of-body experience. Though sworn to secrecy, she was thrilled. (*Agent-client privilege*, she kept saying, as if that were a real thing.) She was trying to hide it, trying to make sympathetic noises and ask appropriately kind questions, but I could sense it. I was freaking out on the phone, attempting to keep my voice steady, but in an odd, horrible way, her excitement had been the tiniest bit infectious. I was worried sick but also thrumming, like an amp that's just been switched on, emitting a hollow buzz.

Perhaps because now I could *do* something, I could help. The cops were unimpressed, unenthused, unmotivated: Now that they knew Eleanor and her husband weren't monogamous, they likely thought she'd absconded voluntarily. Adrenaline shot through my limbs, and with it a desire to figure it out, to know, to pound at the door or the wall or the muscly chest of whomever knew the truth: What happened to Eleanor?

Ted. He was the low-hanging fruit, as Eleanor had said, presciently. We'd chatted earlier tonight at the presentation—him smiling as he untangled cords and unpacked equipment—but only for a minute before Hana had texted in a tizzy. He'd given me his card on Friday, as we were leaving the Herd, and now I found it in a heap of receipts on my desk:

DIFY, LLC

THEODORE CORRIGAN
FOUNDER

Coder // Maker // Custom Fabricator

You spelled "defy" wrong, I'd announced in the elevator, because saying mean shit is my love language.

It stands for Do It For You. Like, in contrast to DIY. It made sense at the time. He'd probably been forced to explain it hundreds of times, but still he smiled easily. He had these luminous gray eyes, beaming out under wide brown eyebrows—

Focus, Katie.

"Hello?"

"It's Katie."

"Any updates on Eleanor?"

"No, nothing."

"I don't know why anyone thinks I know anything." He sounded defensive. "Hana called me too. I'm as worried and clueless as you guys are."

"They asked about exes. I had no idea you're Cameron's brother."

"Yeah." There was a flatness in his voice. Finally: "You know him?"

"No, we never crossed paths. And after they split, Eleanor barely mentioned him. Do you know why they broke up?"

"Which time?"

"Both, I guess."

"Well, first time she was leaving for Harvard." He sort of chuckled. "Second time, she was moving to New York. I don't know the details, but you can connect the dots."

"You didn't know anything about their relationship? Aren't you two good friends?"

"Eleanor and me? Yeah, for sure." He cleared his throat. "But she didn't talk to me about dating. Especially not about dating my brother. And Cameron and me, we've never been close. Anyway, I don't think the two of them have talked in years. Not for any bad reason, just 'cause they grew apart or whatever. He's up in Beverly."

"Huh." I centered my voice between agreement and skepticism and then waited, but he stayed silent. "When did you see her last?"

"When I came in to reset the router. And met you. Friday, right?" I assented. "I was supposed to do an audio check at Hielo tonight and then—well, obviously."

"Do you know when you last heard from her? Email or text or anything?"

"Hang on." A little fumbling. "Eleanor texted me around noon. I was confirming when I should be at the restaurant, and she just sent a thumbs-up."

"And before that? The last time she said anything substantive?"

"Let me check."

It wasn't unusual for Eleanor to be terse in messages—with great power comes great ability to send one-word texts and dumb acronyms and emails that lack any sign of proofreading (or, at times, of coherence whatsoever).

"I asked her about AV needs yesterday and she sent a couple sentences back. I'll forward it to you—what's your email?"

I supplied it, then gave an awkward laugh. "So I guess you didn't hang on to my business card as carefully as I did yours."

"Nah, I know exactly where it is. Actually"—he chuckled self-consciously—"I was gonna hit you up and see if you wanted to get a drink sometime. But now . . . yeah." I understood: Now that Eleanor was missing, now that we were mid-crisis, it seemed obscene to plan a first date. Still, something in me sat up like a meerkat at the news he'd planned to ask me out.

"I got the forward," I announced. "I should let you go."

"If I can help with anything, lemme know," he replied. "I'm good with tech shit, so maybe I can help."

"Thanks. I worked as a tech reporter, so I'm no Luddite, but I might take you up on that."

I pulled my laptop cord from my bag and stooped to plug it in behind my nightstand. I spotted the flash of purple Post-its and set them on the table. In the light, there was definitely something legible in relief, and I grabbed a pencil, shaded carefully. In Eleanor's wild loops was what appeared to be gibberish:

ACA 1010 CUU ESEGYM

Was it a code? Google was no help. I took a photo of the shaded note, cranked up the contrast, and printed it out, followed by my snapshots of Eleanor's bank statements, then slid everything into a folder.

Keep going, Katie, keep going. I quickly checked her social feeds: Eleanor hadn't posted to Facebook in a few days, and she hadn't liked anyone else's photos or updates since yesterday morning. Her last personal update—about as personal as she got on Instagram— was of a rubber plant drinking in the sunlight, a slash of snow visible on the window behind it. She'd captioned it "Calm before the storm," likely because it went up on Monday at 8:18 a.m., before the start of a bustling week.

It rose through me without warning: a plume of anxiety, neon and strong. *Eleanor could be dead.* My chest tightened and I felt a swoop of dizziness, but I gripped the sides of my desk and fought it. *Breathe in. Breathe out. Focus.*

I returned to my email and saw that Hana was gathering data on our latest contact with Eleanor. No one had seen her, it seemed, since last night's Mocktails, and everyone was pretty sure they'd left before her. I squinted, again scanning my memories for anything unusual as the crowd clinked glasses and admired the Elm Grove's pretty floral-patterned trays and napkins. *Normal, normal, normal.*

New cameras had gone in sometime last week, Hana had said, so we should be able to check exactly when Eleanor had left. She was typically one of the last people to head out, especially the night be- fore a work-from-home day. I drummed my fingers on the edge of the laptop, then pushed it aside and found my notebook:

❏ *Access security cameras (Ted?)*

❏ *Security cameras at street level? On Eleanor's street?*

❏ *General background checks on E + D: financial trouble? New lawsuits, arrests?*

❏ *Open relationship: Who had Eleanor met up with?*

❏ *Confirm Daniel's alibi last night/today: date (app/site?) + work*

❏ *UGLY CUNTS vandal: related? Leads?*

❏ *Where are E's laptop + phone?*

I leaned back and tapped the pen against my lips. This was helping, a narrow egress for my worry. Something was bothering me from earlier today, prickling at me like stinging nettle. I wound the night backward in my memory, back across the bridge to Eleanor's apartment, then inside Hana's Lyft, and then Hielo, its back hallway, in all the servers' way. Here the feeling intensified, desperate as a charades player when your guess is *so close*. Hana cinching in the huddle, Daniel on speakerphone . . .

I caught it, *snap*: Hana had said something about location services—how Eleanor hadn't turned hers on, how last week it hadn't done her any good. Eleanor had shown up with a new phone case last week, a robin's-egg blue that matched her new Herd-branded background, one of Mikki's designs—and I'd hazily filed this away as a detail for my book proposal ("so chic, she changes cases the way most of us change handbags"). *Was it actually a new* phone? *Had she lost (or ditched) the old one for some reason?*

My call to Hana went straight to voicemail, so I dragged my laptop back onto my knees and looked over my list. The spray-painting bandit intrigued me most, but I wasn't sure how to chase him down.

Daniel, then—what did any of us know about him, really, from before he meandered into Eleanor's life? What other skeletons were in
his closet? And where was he last night?

I sent him a friend request on Facebook and, in the meantime,
clicked through his profile photos. Most were of him and Eleanor,
but one fit the bill: selfie, his game face encircled in a navy hoodie,
his beloved Yankees splashed across his chest. I dragged it into a
search engine, then—

Bingo. Scouring the Internet, Google had found this exact same
photo on Click, an online dating site. I made a throwaway profile,
limited all my filters, searched for terms I'd seen in Google's pre-
view, and—

"Gotcha," I murmured aloud.

Three photos, the hoodie one cropped so it was from the nose
down, a vacation photo centered on his blue tank top and surprisingly chiseled arms, and then—I felt myself blush—an admittedly
hot topless selfie from the chin down. *Hello there, 82menace.*

My heart raced as I scanned through the usual profile words
(*running, CrossFit, travel, foodie . . .*). I was desperate for any clue,
anything that would point me to Eleanor, panicked at the thought
that just as we were reconnecting, I could lose her for good. My
hands went cold when I got to the end:

**You should message me if: You're patient, chill, and okay
with the fact that I have no idea what I'm doing, lol. My
wife (MoreFracturedLight) is the most incredible partner
in the world and we're making this up as we go along.**

I had never before clicked a link with such ferocity. MoreFracturedLight's profile was less complete than Daniel's, with only one
image of her from behind, wearing a floral dress somewhere
sunny—but that dark ripply hair, the hourglass frame, this was defi-

nitely her. Anonymous enough that no one could prove it, though. She'd filled out just one section, the most barebones of profiles:

Self-summary: Exploring my options in a newly open relationship. I write back rarely; patience, please.

I whimpered aloud; here I thought I'd found a lead, but it was just another dead end. A sudden electronic chirrup made me jump—I had a new message on Click, from a headless figure showing off his decent abs over some low-slung sweatpants in a dirty bathroom mirror: "So your the mysterious type lol." *God. A woman needs neither photos nor words to attract creepers here—just a female designation.* I sent both Daniel's and Eleanor's profiles to my printer and listened to it screeching away, the sheets skittering onto the floor as the machine spat them past the tray. I stapled them and slipped them in the folder.

My phone buzzed on my bed.

"Calling you in 20." Fatima, finally responding to the text I'd sent from my car ride home. A little space opened up in my chest.

I'd first met Fatima when I was on-staff at *Rocket* (moment of silence), when the scrappy tech website not only existed but even had the funds to bring people in for workshops. Fatima had led a brief master class on "digital investigation techniques," and she was fabulous and fierce, with her blue-green hair and shit-kicking boots. The next day I'd invited her to coffee, and over lattes she revealed that she's a fairly talented hacker-for-hire. We hadn't talked in years, but I felt galvanized by her quick reply.

And she *had* taught her student well; while awaiting her call, I combed through some criminal databases, moving quickly to keep ahead of the hysteria smoldering in my chest. Nothing for Eleanor; a DUI for Daniel in June 2002, which put him in . . . college, if my calculations were correct. Neither one showed up in sex-offender registries, thank God. I checked a police report database: nothing for Daniel, but in October, Eleanor had reported her passport and wallet stolen. I couldn't see the details of the incident report, but it didn't ID it as a mugging or break-in—just a theft. To the printer with all of it.

Most of Eleanor's hits in the public-record database were unsurprising: trademarking Gleam and the Herd, that kind of thing. But my search resurfaced court records I'd been looking at just days ago to track down the angry Antiherd mob who'd brought a suit against the Herd. I shivered; in just twenty-four hours, Carl Berkowski had gone from an annoying potential source to something much more sinister. *A potential abductor?*

My phone exploded with sound; I jumped so high, I practically bonked my head on the ceiling.

"Fatima?"

"'Sup." It was a statement, not a question.

My voice shook as I skidded past our normal pleasantries. "Look, I can't really explain, but I'm going through some shit and I need you to look into something for me. And it has to be secret."

"Like everything I do. What's up?"

"A friend of mine just went missing," I said, "tonight. I'm trying to find her."

"Oh, shit. I'm sorry. But, okay, I'm here to help."

I quickly brought her up to speed. "I feel like looking at their inboxes would tell me a lot. I know that's not . . . entirely legal."

"What are their email addresses?" Fatima prompted. Her lack of hesitation steeled me. I shared them and she was quiet for a minute. "Nope, two-step verification on both. Not gonna happen."

If only hacking were as easy as it looked on TV: Hack into location services, hack into police records, hack into anything as if cyberwalls and VPNs and security measures were little white baby gates to be snapped open or stepped over.

"What about browsing history?" I asked.

"Do you have her Wi-Fi info?"

"At her apartment? No." An idea blossomed: "Is there a way to see what she was doing at the Herd?"

"Just her? Hmm. If you were physically there, I could have you log into the router. Problem is, it'd include data on *everyone's* devices."

"I could narrow it down by time—she's usually the last person there."

"Ooh, that's all I need. Might take some guesswork to get into the router, though."

I smiled. "I can ask the guy who set it up." I jotted down her instructions and set a time for her to come by the Herd.

"Anything else you want me to look into between now and then?"

I rested my chin in my hand. "Eleanor and her husband both have Click profiles," I announced. "I'd like to see their messages. I'm trying to figure out who Eleanor was seeing, and who Daniel was with last night."

"That should be doable." She paused. "And Katie, I'm so, so sorry. I'm sure she'll turn up, but I'll do everything in my power to help."

I fell asleep praying I'd wake to happy news: *Everything's fine, they found her and she's A-OK, it's actually a hilarious story, come on in and she'll tell us all about it.* My heart battered around in my ribs as I pulled my phone off the nightstand, but . . .

Crickets.

I showed up at the Herd around eleven and spotted Mikki and her things scattered across a sofa. She was wearing high-top sneakers and velvet leggings under a huge sweatshirt and drinking an iced coffee the size of Montana. "Nothing?" I said, in lieu of a greeting.

"Nothing." She gave me a halfhearted hug. "How are you doing?"

"Broken. Miserable. Sick with worry."

She nodded. "I used up half my CBD pen trying to fall asleep last night."

I sighed. "Where's Hana?"

"She said something came up. Told me to tell you that."

"Huh." For some reason, this felt like an affront.

"I can see not wanting to be here with Eleanor gone. Since we're not supposed to"—her eyes widened and she lowered her voice—"since we're supposed to keep it on the DL."

I dragged an acrylic chair over. "Has anyone checked Eleanor's office?"

She groaned. "Aurelia said it's locked. I suggested smashing the glass, but nobody seemed into that."

"Does Eleanor usually lock her door?" I asked.

"I think so. Definitely after the whole vandal break-in situation."

"Good point." I tapped her knee. "Hey, I forgot to return the question. How are you doing?"

"I'm just worried," she said with a shrug. "And I hate having to act like it's business as usual. I'm supposed to have a gallery visit this afternoon."

"For the collages?" She nodded and I wrinkled my nose in sympathy. "I'm sure you can reschedule."

"I will. But it's not like anything's happening here anyway. With the investigation or whatever. Nobody's heard anything from the cops."

I thought back to my checklist. "Can we review the security footage from Monday?"

"You're not gonna believe this." She leaned forward. "You know how they just got new cameras? Well, they're in the middle of switching over systems or something, so the cameras didn't record."

"You've got to be fucking kidding me."

"I know. Aurelia had a long call with the technician this morning. She was so frustrated, she burst into tears." She shook her head.

"Poor thing is in over her head. Aurelia's basically a glorified assistant, but with Eleanor MIA and Stephanie in fucking Goa, she's somehow in charge."

"Hold on. You said she had a call with the technician? Was it Ted—did he install the new cameras?" Seemed odd he wouldn't have mentioned it.

"No, a private firm." She sighed. "They installed the new cameras last week but then there was some issue with the router not recognizing them. The guy told Aurelia it was just bad luck."

"'Bad luck'? That it just randomly stops working the night Eleanor goes missing?" I felt a stab of fear. Maybe someone needed that footage deleted. Maybe something really did happen to her. Maybe this was real.

An issue with the router—Ted had been here to reset it Friday, *packet overload*. I texted and asked if he could walk me through his reset, adding that it might help us track down Eleanor, and he replied in seconds, noting that he'd be in the neighborhood later if I wanted to meet up. My phone jolted as I was still typing, and I stared in confusion at the text for a few minutes before the pieces snapped into place.

The sights and smells and sounds around me, women and clatters and chatter and colorful fabric, sunlight from the windows and upholstery the color of jewels—all of it faded away, the world on a dimmer switch, everything reduced to a meaningless gray blob around the outskirts of this text.

It was from Carl. My scheduled but noticeably absent coffee date from Monday. Carl Berkowski, men's rights activist, plaintiff in the doomed case of *Berkowski v. The Herd, Inc.* Known enemy of Eleanor Walsh. He'd chosen now, right now, to finally answer my texts and calls.

Ice pitched through my stomach as I reread it, over and over.

It said: "So it seems Eleanor's out of commission, hmm?"

CHAPTER 11

Hana

I dreamed about the numbers I'd found in Eleanor's bed: They had something to do with money, and Daniel was using them in lieu of cash to pay Eleanor's ransom. I woke up and willed the dream's details to stick so that I could comb through them later in search of baubles of insight, but then I grabbed my phone and saw Mikki's text still at the top: *I think we need to tell them.* Terror lurched through me again, so tense and taut that Cosmo sensed it and vaulted off the bed. Last night I'd sent back one word right away: *No.* Now I deleted the whole exchange and tended to my other alerts, and the dream slipped away like something sinking into a quarry.

I'd failed to set an alarm and it was somehow almost eleven. I called Daniel as I was drinking coffee, still unsure if I should go into the Herd.

"How are you doing? Hanging in there?" I swiped at a drip sliding slowly down the mug.

"Okay. I'm just . . . at my desk."

"At the hospital?" I let out a surprised laugh, tried to turn it into a throat-clearing. "You went into work?" That explained his low, sheepish tone.

"I did. I don't . . . I'm out of PTO days for the year."

"Jeez. I'm sorry. You didn't want to just tell them you have a family emergency?"

"We're not . . ." His voice got even lower. "Since we're not saying anything. The cops, last night. They said to just maintain my normal routine. And I—I have a bunch of meetings today."

"Huh." His behavior was so strange, I almost felt embarrassed for him: *Your wife goes missing and you're thinking about PTO days?* Carrying on like nothing had happened—Christ, was that the behavior of an innocent man? I didn't have a spouse, but if he went missing, I wouldn't give a shit about my stock of personal days—I just wouldn't show up. "Is there anything I can do?"

"No, it's okay. I'll just be here all day." A beat. "Uh, thanks, though."

"Of course. So no updates from the detectives?"

"Nothing. They went through the apartment last night, pawed through all our stuff. Didn't seem to find anything interesting, though."

An idea crystallized, a better plan for my day. "Let me know if you need anything, okay? Anytime, day or night."

He thanked me and hung up.

I thought about inviting Mikki along, since, after all, she faced the exact same stakes as me. But she was probably at the Herd right now, likely with Katie, and after her text last night, the last thing I needed was another chink in her resolve. Instead I let her know I wouldn't be coming to the Herd today. Then, pushing through the fug of my worry for Eleanor, a heady sadness that billowed like incense, I got dressed and headed out.

A few whiskery clouds bristled the edges of the sky, the sun over us almost taunting in its coldness. The streets were nearly empty— even at lunch hour, no one wanted to venture out into the Arctic afternoon. I checked my phone: a wind chill of -6 degrees. Aurelia had touched base from the Herd, letting me know Ratliff had just arrived, and this soothed me—no cops would be knocking at Eleanor's door anytime soon.

Her street looked different in the light: a tree-lined road of row houses, their stoops spilling outside like the graham-cracker paths leading into gingerbread houses. I'd always thought of this block as warm and fairy tale–like, but today a crust of bruised-looking snow capped the curbs, and the trees, spindly and stark, raked at one another angrily. I climbed the stoop and froze—what if Eleanor never walked out of this door again? My mind skipped ahead to funerals, black dresses and hot tears, Daniel tearily putting a For Sale sign out front. But the cold had found me: My nose prickled, my fingers stung, so I fumbled with my spare key and shoved the door closed behind me.

I had no clear idea why I was there, what key or keyhole I was looking for or even whether I'd know when I found it. But maybe Eleanor had left behind another clue, possibly tucked deeper under her mattress, that'd give these random numbers meaning.

Or perhaps there was something in her apartment that I had to be sure nobody could find.

I'd only been here without Eleanor once or twice, when I'd walked over from the Herd to water her plants while she and Daniel were away. Alone in her huge townhouse, I'd always felt the vague, faraway urge to poke around—the same distant impulse I'd felt as a teenage babysitter, feeling grown-up and saintly as I resisted. The house was empty, the cops long gone. Finally, I could give in.

I left my coat in a heap in the foyer and climbed upstairs, then practically flipped the mattress confirming there wasn't anything else under there. Her nightstand drew my eyes—Daniel had said she kept pills in the drawer, right? Antidepressants? I pulled it open but if there had been anything in there before, it was gone now. On top of the nightstand was the bell hooks book (very on-brand) with a Books Are Magic bookmark two-thirds of the way through (ditto). I thumbed through the pages for notes but found nothing.

In the dresser, I found myself groping through lingerie. I blanched with embarrassment before moving on to the other two drawers: nothing out of the ordinary. I stepped back and surveyed the bedroom, my chest throbbing, my thoughts a wail: *Where are you, Eleanor?*

In the en suite bathroom, I poked at the makeup bag yawning open on a shelf. Lots of Gleam products—she practiced what she preached. Several products from the Nimbus collection, "designed to flatter all skin tones and types." The Nimbus launch had bothered me for several reasons: First, that we needed a POC add-on to begin with—it was lame that Gleam's initial products, in particular its highlighter and eye shadows, didn't work especially well on darker skin. Second, that journalists expected me to join Eleanor for interviews and photos about the line, as if my face gave the effort authenticity. One reporter, a bearded dude from *Fortune,* even asked about my "ethnic heritage." It's especially fun to speak on behalf of all women of color when you're barely in touch with your own brown-ness.

Eleanor's mirror snapped open when I pushed it, and I stared into her medicine cabinet, the rainbow of products there: toothpaste and cotton balls, facial bleach and pimple patches and antiaging eye cream, plus moist flushable towelettes and vaginal itch cream under the sink. All normal things around which I'd always felt a cloud of shame, and here they were in Eleanor's bathroom, almost out in the open but for the soft click of a cabinet or mirror.

Eleanor was a human, like the rest of us, carefully curating the lac-
quered shell we all admired. Eleanor was . . . really missing.

A rush of impropriety and I slammed everything closed. Tears
stung my eyes as I made my way into the office. There, my gaze fell
on the built-in bookshelf, a custom, complicated mass of oak slabs
and copper tubing. A thick book with silver and gold letters on a
blue spine looked familiar and I took a step toward it when—

The doorbell chimed, reverberating through the mirrored foyer.
I froze, like I'd been caught. The detectives, they were back, and I'd
be in trouble.

No, that didn't make sense; they knew Daniel wasn't home today.
Amazon delivery guy? I padded back through the bedroom and
peered out the window.

There he was, in a shiny down coat and sweatpants. He still had
sparkly blue eyes and that angular jaw, now bristled with a five
o'clock shadow.

Before I knew what I was doing, I'd trotted down the steps and
swung open the front door. Cameron took a step back, his eyes
wide.

"You heard what happened?" I asked. He squinted and I reached
for my heart. "Hana, Eleanor's friend. Remember me?"

I'd only seen him a handful of times over the last decade; he was
at Eleanor's wedding, and I couldn't decide whether that was odd or
not, and once or twice we'd all hung out while he was in town visiting Ted. He'd remained in Boston when he and Eleanor had broken up right around our graduation, which was also when his life
had taken a nosedive. While I was out in L.A., Cameron had flown
to Arizona and checked himself into a treatment center for opioid
addiction. Afterward, he defaulted on the sprawling condo he'd
bought in pricy Beacon Hill and, at his parents' urging, moved into
the renovated cottage in their backyard. Years later, he was working
again and looked, with his long blond waves and clear eyes, nothing
like a junkie.

"This is Eleanor's place, right?" he said in his chill, pothead drone.

I nodded. "I . . . just came to pick something up." I swallowed. "But Daniel doesn't know I'm here."

"Daniel, right." He nodded, holding my gaze, then looked over my shoulder. "So can I come in?"

"Right! Sorry." I held the door and he pushed past me, coldness wafting off him, and I realized I'd just invited him into someone else's home. He unzipped his coat and sauntered into the living room, then plopped down on the sofa.

"I tried calling you last night," I said.

"You have my number?"

I raised my eyebrows. "You have Eleanor's address?"

"Ted gave it to me."

"Funny. He gave me your number."

"Huh." He leaned his elbows on his thighs and ran his hand over his chin. I'd settled into an armchair across from him and began to laugh.

"What?" His lips curled into an involuntary half-smile.

"Sorry, I just—we're casually lounging in Eleanor's living room, and I keep fighting the urge to offer you something to drink. It's . . . oh my God. Eleanor." The laughter careened into something darker and more hysterical—a mask for my grief. I took a deep breath. "What are you doing here? Did you just get in?"

"Yeah, I talked to the detectives this morning and then got in my car and drove down. I wanna help. Will there be search parties?"

"I don't know—no one's organized anything yet. They haven't announced it publicly." I leaned forward. "Are you staying with Ted?"

"Probably. Or maybe a hotel. I hadn't thought that far."

"Okay." He hadn't answered the obvious question, so I gestured around: "And what are you doing . . . here?"

"I thought Daniel would be home. Where is he?"

"He's at work." I shook my head. "Why did you want to see him?"

"To offer my help. Tell him I'm sorry." His jaw muscles bulged like he was biting down.

The hair on my neck and scalp prickled—something was off. Well, everything was off, but especially Cameron's presence here. "You didn't think to call him?"

"I don't have Daniel's number. Ted doesn't either." He leaned back, draped an arm along the sofa's back. "So no news yet?"

"Not yet. They searched here last night."

"Did they."

I shrugged. "Supposedly they're working *very* hard to track her down."

"Supposedly?"

"To me, they seemed pretty convinced she left of her own accord."

"Why would they think that?"

I thought about it, but couldn't see a reason to hold back: "He and Eleanor had just opened up their marriage."

His sandy-blond eyebrows shot up near his hairline. "Shit. Do you think she took off?"

"No. She's always put her career first—she wouldn't run away because of a broken heart. And anyway, Daniel claims it was her idea."

"Yeah. Well, it worries me because Eleanor's got enemies." He pointed at the wall and I wasn't sure what he was referring to—the fireplace? The stockings hung by the chimney with care? "She comes up all the time in the news. She's a public figure."

The TV, mounted on the exposed brick. "Do strangers who hate her count as enemies?"

"You know what I mean."

"So you think someone did something to her?"

"Dunno. Could also mean she had to get away."

"What makes you think that, though? I can't see her running away from all the good stuff she has going for her."

"I didn't tell the cops." He brought his hands to his jaw, ran a knuckle over his mouth. "When they called? But she called me out of the blue, maybe three months ago." He folded his fingers under his chin. "She asked if I knew anyone who could forge a passport. I don't know what she had in mind, but I keep thinking about it. Why would she be messing with that kind of shit?"

My mouth gaped open, an oval of shock. "Why didn't you tell the cops? It could help them. And who did you send her to?"

The look he shot me stung like a whip. "I didn't tell them 'cause I don't need them thinking I'm a perp. I told Eleanor I don't know anyone. I'm not part of some vast criminal network, you know."

I felt embarrassed, then indignant—Eleanor's no idiot, and *she'd* thought Cameron could help. "Sorry. I'm just so shocked to hear that. I think of Eleanor as, you know, an upstanding, law-abiding citizen."

"Most of the time," he muttered.

I turned to him sharply—*no, he must just mean the fake passport.* I shook my head. "Have you talked to Gary and Karen?"

"Sure. I checked in with them. They gave me the idea to come down." He turned on Eleanor's father's thick Boston accent: "'You let me know if you think we should get in the cah and head down theh.'"

Eleanor's parents had been in Mikki's and my lives fairly regularly during college, taking us out to dinner near campus or having us all up for the weekend. Though I didn't know the details, I had the impression Gary and Karen were like surrogate parents to Ted and Cameron too. They were almost comically nice, the kind of people who send a thank-you card for your thank-you gift. I thought of them and felt a surge of warmth and pity—Gary, a baseball cap–wearing real-estate developer and community magnate with a bald head and loads of energy, and Karen, a retired nurse with her crisp slacks and silver bob. Being with them was always soothing, my first true glimpse into how an unsplintered family could feel. They, too, must be praying she'd run off on her own and was safe and fine. It was a strange thing to hope for.

"Cameron, you've known Eleanor longer than I have," I said. "To me, this isn't like her at all. Has she ever done anything like this?"

"Nah." He thought, then shrugged. "Actually, I guess her parents would say yes. When she was still in high school, if her parents were pissing her off she'd come stay with me. Or she'd crash with her friends—Mrs. Walsh would call me in a panic. Eleanor was, you know. So young."

I laugh-scoffed. "I mean, we all were. In high school."

"But she was especially—you know she skipped two grades, right?"

"She did?" Did I know that? It felt new.

"She skipped seventh and eighth grade," he said, frowning. "She was two years below Ted, at first. So she was *twelve* when she started at that Catholic high school." He cleared his throat. "We didn't date till her senior year, obviously. When she was sixteen. But I figured you guys knew, at least, even if she didn't make a big thing of it."

I tilted my head. "So she's actually thirty right now?"

"Uh . . . three years younger than me, so yeah."

"Huh." I leaned back. It was a small discrepancy, but a weird one: Why keep this from us all these years? Had Eleanor hid it in the first few years of college and then felt she couldn't come clean? We all had fake IDs from freshman year on, good ones, so it wouldn't have been hard to quietly slip that out of her wallet even throughout senior year. But all this time, all these articles about Gleam and the Herd and, well, *her*, all extolling the accomplishments of a woman of a certain age—our age.

"You think that's relevant?" he asked.

"No. It's just weird." I cracked my knuckles. "I think if something bad happened to Eleanor, we owe it to her to try to help."

"And that's what you're trying to do?"

"I am. Same as you."

"No one's demanded ransom, no contact at all?"

I winced. "Nope."

"Well, the last time I heard from her was when she was asking about a forged ID. Before that, we hadn't talked since her wedding. Seriously, no one's suspicious of her husband?"

Had Daniel done something to Eleanor? The thought made my stomach roil; he'd always seemed to dote on her, but his behavior today, business as usual, was nothing if not bizarre. I felt an odd instinct to ask Eleanor what she thought about it, followed by a rinse of despair. "Daniel seems genuinely worried and eager to have her back," I said. "I'm curious to hear what he's learned from the cops."

"Keep me posted, if you wouldn't mind."

I stared at him. I hated this feeling: so much subtext, but I couldn't figure out what any of it meant. I gave him Daniel's number and mine, and then we both stood, the air between us cold and staticky. "So you're sticking around?" he asked. Faux casual, like he thought I was up to something sketchy.

"For now. I guess I'll walk you out."

We dawdled at the door as he pulled his coat back on. Finally he caught my eye and gave a cool-guy nod. "You know, even under such shitty circumstances, it's good to see you, Hana."

I froze. Seeing him out of Eleanor's apartment—what the hell was I doing, standing here as if I were *Talented Mr. Ripley*-ing her life? I gave a little wave and pressed the door closed behind him.

For a moment I watched him from the window. Why had he come? Why, really? I was pretty sure he and Daniel had never been alone in a room before, and it was hard to imagine them exchanging bro-y sympathy. *Was he actually convinced of Daniel's guilt, here to intimidate the man he'd deemed responsible?* It hadn't really crossed my mind before, but of course Cameron could still be in love with Eleanor. So many people were.

I trudged back upstairs, desperation bulging inside me—this trip couldn't be for nothing; I had to find *something*. I returned to the bookshelf and surveyed it, hands on hips. So many feminist memoirs and essay collections, spanning all the waves. Some domestic noir, a fat run of *Calvin and Hobbes* books, an entire row of *Jane* magazines. The blue cover that'd caught my eye earlier: *Frida*, a hefty tome she'd brought home from a Frida Kahlo exhibit at the Brooklyn Museum earlier this year. I pulled it out and flipped through the glossy pages. She'd always worshiped Frida, had been a fan since her parents took her to the Blue House museum in Mexico City when she was a little girl. I replaced the book, imagining I could feel Eleanor's fingerprints on it, little echoes of her attention pressed into the pages.

I locked the door behind me and felt the cold envelop my outsides: pressing hard on my nose, eyeballs, ears. My visit had been a bust, and this unleashed a new torrent of hopelessness. I was out of ideas, and with every passing hour, that candle flame of hope, the desperate belief that Eleanor was fine, dwindled. The app had said my car was two minutes away, but as I watched, bouncing on the balls of my feet, the driver took a wrong turn and the wait time jumped to six minutes.

Kalamazoo had winters like this, bell-clear and frigid. Katie had loved playing outside when we were kids, even when temperatures were in the single digits, and one winter we'd dragged a bunch of lawn furniture into a clearing in the woods behind our house, then sculpted the snow that fell on them into a kind of roof. Wearing long johns and snowsuits, we'd sit for hours in the series of protected ovals and rectangles underneath, and I'd boss Katie around as she fixed snow slides and tunnels. Katie must be wondering where I was. I should text her.

At home I hesitated in the living room, phone in hand—I should check in with Mikki, I should try to contact Stephanie in her fancy beach hut in Goa. I should call Mom; Katie had sent me a screenshot of Mom telling her to tell me to call her, a literal game of telephone. But Mom would inevitably find a way to make me feel even worse. Even when something positive had happened and I'd rushed to Mom for approval, she'd found a way to twist it. When I got into Harvard: "Well there goes the cottage in Escanaba we were saving up for." When I got scholarships and took on my own debt: "You better hope you find a good enough job when you graduate to stay on top of that." Going to her with good news was foolish; calling her with bad news was unthinkable.

Instead I went to my call list and tapped on one from last night.

"Hello?" He sounded suspicious.

"Gary? It's Hana."

"Hana! I thought you were one of those damn telemahketers." More quietly: "Karen, it's Hana!"

Some fumbling and clicking, then Karen's voice: "Hana, hello!" She attempted to sound cheery, but I could tell it was forced. Then, suddenly tense: "What is it, do you have bad news?"

"Not at all! I'm just calling to see how you're doing." I sank into the couch. "I know I was pretty frantic on the phone last night."

"We're just waiting to hear anything," Karen said. "You know, trying to stay positive. We feel so out of the loop about what's going on down there."

"We talked to Daniel last night, he gave us a call," Gary said. There was a quaver in his voice, though he was trying so hard to sound like his usual jolly self. "Asked if we'd heard anything, obviously, and we asked him the same. The whole thing is bizarre. We're just telling ourselves, I don't know—she must've decided to get away for a few days."

"They said her laptop, phone, wallet, she took all that with her," Karen added, almost manically. "So she had to have left by choice—right?"

I wasn't sure what to say.

"I can't bring myself to imagine the worst-case scenario." Her voice lowered to almost a whisper. "I just can't."

"Of course. I'm sure the detectives have got it under control. They assured us they'd take this seriously."

"We got a call from that detective last night. Ratcliff."

"Ratliff," Karen corrected.

"Just wanted to know when we'd last heard from Eleanor. We decided it was Thanksgiving. Hard to believe it's been that long, but, you know—you blink, and it's almost Christmas."

"I know, I've been meaning to call home for too long too." I gazed up at the ceiling; there was a small moon near the wall—*a water spot?* "How did Eleanor seem, back then?"

"Oh, fine, just normal," Gary said. "She spent Thanksgiving with Daniel's family, so she called that day to just chat. Said they were having a nice time in Peekskill. Daniel had a cold, and apparently her mother-in-law had burned the turkey."

"And we went over plans for Christmas—she and Daniel are coming up on the twenty-third. It should be cozy, just the four of us."

Their use of present tense, their dogged confidence that she'd be there in one week—it unnerved me. Did they have some reason to think Eleanor was safe, off taking care of something but about to reappear?

"Are you heading home to Minnesota?" Karen asked.

"Er—Michigan, yes. My sister and I are flying that same day, the twenty-third." I cleared my throat. "I'm sure you guys will have a nice holiday."

"Eleanor is fine," Karen cut in, her voice a squeak. I winced, brought my hand to my collarbone. "She has to be."

Gary let out what I think was an uncomfortable laugh, but it sounded more like a sob, and he cleared his throat to cover it. "What my wife means is that of course we're worried sick. We hung up the phone with Daniel last night, and we looked at each other and swore—*swore*—we'd be strong. How else could—what else could we—?" He trailed off.

"Eleanor is *fine*," she said again. "And we feel even better knowing you're helping look for her."

"Of course. Daniel, Mikki, Cameron—everyone's eager to do whatever we can." I waited for them to jump in about Cameron, how he was down here helping out, but they didn't take the bait. *I ran into Cameron today* was almost out of my throat when I realized it would be strange to say I was poking around Eleanor's personal effects on my own, for reasons mysterious even to me. "It's really too bad Daniel wasn't home Monday night, right?" Surely he hadn't told them about his, er, extracurricular activities?

"Horrible. Some luck, spending the night in your office *that* night, of all nights." Gary seemed grateful for the change of subject. "But you know Daniel. A workaholic, just like our Eleanor."

I pulled at the toe of my sock. "Did Daniel say anything else?"

"Oh, the detectives had just left and so he kinda filled us in," he replied. "Have you seen him today? I'm worried about him."

"No, but I called him this morning. He was back at work."

"See? What'd I tell ya. A workaholic."

"It's true," I said. More silence. All these people, normally so skilled in the art of conversation, fumbling around for the right thing to say. "Well, I'm sure he'll keep you posted, but I just wanted to check in. Call me if you need anything, okay? I'm happy to be your eyes and ears down here."

"Thanks so much, sweetheart," Karen said, and Gary echoed her. "We'll do that."

———

Work consumed the afternoon, a welcome distraction from my own maudlin imagination, an endless reel that made my stomach wrench: Eleanor locked in a basement, Eleanor chained up in a fallout shelter, Eleanor bound in the back of a speeding truck. I played Whac-A-Mole with journalists seeking updates and had about forty ninety-second-long calls with Stephanie in India, the reception ducking and weaving like Cosmo when I try to get him into his carrier. She was trying to move up her flight, but holiday bookings left her with few options. She was fine with leaving Aurelia, the head member relations coordinator, in charge until her return.

Finally I slammed my laptop closed and tossed my phone onto the rug. Eleanor's bookshelf . . . I kept seeing it, the rainbow of spines, colors and words, matte and glossy. The royal-blue hardcover with the gold and silver lettering. I pictured myself pulling it out, flipping through. Her fingerprints on the pages smudging under mine.

The idea bloomed in my skull as if someone else had whispered it to me. My lips popped open, mouthed the words, *Oh my God.*

I lunged for my phone, Googled two words and two numbers. The split second between hitting Enter and seeing my results fattened and stretched, and then words swamped the screen. The ones at the top told me everything I needed to know.

Of course. *Of course.* It was so obvious I let out a little laughing scream. I brought my hand to my forehead, alarmed by how stupid I'd been.

I wasn't sure whom to call first, so I sent a group text to Katie and Mikki: "Guys, I think I know where Eleanor is."

CHAPTER 12

Katie

I dropped my phone, theatrically, like a mime demonstrating shock. It slid off my knee and clattered to the floor, bounced once before settling.

Mikki looked alarmed: "Everything okay?"

I grabbed it and reread the text: *So it seems Eleanor's out of commission, hmm?*

"What is it?" Mikki prompted again.

My fingers and jaw had gone cold, as if someone had propped open the door to the rooftop above us. I looked into her eyes and decided it was safe to share.

"Please don't tell Hana," I said, "or anyone, okay? But I've been—I was thinking about pitching an article about the Herd, a business profile timed to the Fort Greene location opening." A ham-fisted lie, but it'd do. "And I reached out to the guy who filed that stupid discrimination suit earlier this year, since I thought it was relevant—talking to the people who basically show why the Herd needs to exist, right?"

Mikki nodded.

"We didn't even end up talking—he flaked on our interview. But he just sent me this." I handed her my phone and she gasped.

"How does he know this?"

I shook my head. "He could just mean that she wasn't at the event last night—'family emergency'—and she hasn't been on social or anything since then. He's probably mildly obsessed with her."

"Do you think he's a stalker?"

"No idea. In my research, I didn't see a restraining order or anything." I flipped the phone's volume button on and off. "Did anyone mention him to the cops? Like, as a possible enemy? He has—bad blood, certainly."

"Motive." Mikki frowned. "I don't think anyone did. The lawsuit went nowhere. But you should probably let that detective know." She reached for her bag. "Do you still have her card?"

I left Ratliff a voicemail, then texted Carl back: "What do you mean?" No response.

And not much time to worry about it, because around noon, Fatima arrived. I scurried to the front desk, where her jaw was shuddering from the continued cold snap; it felt appropriate somehow, the outside providing that same teeth-chattering discomfort I felt whenever I thought of Eleanor's absence. Again, I pushed down the anxiety like someone sitting on an overstuffed suitcase to zip it: *I can solve this.*

I settled Fatima into a corner sofa and set my laptop on the cushion between us. The whole thing felt a bit like sorcery: Fatima typed an IP address into my browser and entered the router info Ted had provided, and then the screen flooded with ugly raw data.

Fatima gestured with a flourish: "This is it. It's way less than I thought there'd be. Apparently it only has the history going back to . . ." She squinted at the screen. "The thirteenth. What is that, Friday?"

"Yeah, Friday night. They just reset the router." I frowned, remembering. "There were only three of us here that night, and Eleanor was the last one using it."

She scrolled, clicked, then pointed. "That's her, then. I'll pull it into its own file."

"You're a wizard."

"I prefer 'goddess.'" She handed the laptop back over. "I gotta bounce, but I should have those Click profiles for you soon." She slung her bag over her shoulder and nodded toward my screen. "Hope you find something helpful in there. And, you know. I'm praying for your friend." I thanked her and waved, the kind words reigniting the alarm I'd been suppressing.

I looked back at the words and numbers swimming across my screen. *Eleanor.* AKA IP address 95.246.174.28. On Friday night, before we left to drink Prosecco, Eleanor was on Gmail for a few minutes. I almost dismissed this, then remembered that I'd seen the email client on her work computer: Outlook, her domain @theherd.com. I, for one, had no record of a Gmail account belonging to Eleanor.

She was back in the office on Saturday, the last warmish day before the cold descended, while Hana and I were out looking at window displays and arguing over whether or not I'd sell secrets like some shady back-alley salesman. Eleanor had read the *Times*, clicked around on *The Gaze*, looked at Twitter, and somehow spent just three minutes on an inordinate number of views of White Plains, New York, in Google Maps. She passed a few minutes online banking at HSBC, which I almost disregarded—*but wait, she banked with Chase.*

I was pulling out my folder with printouts of her bank statements when Detective Ratliff called. I told her about my sudden, creepy text from Carl, carefully repeating the line about my surreptitious article research. She asked for a screenshot and my copy of the court filing.

I tugged at my earlobe. "If you question him, then he'll know she's really missing, right?"

"I can't imagine we'll tell him. Right now we think it's best to not release any information to the public. But we'll follow up on this and get in touch with Mr. . . . Berkowski if we feel it necessary."

"Okay. Thanks for your time." *Why does* thank you *so often throw on a suit and stand in for* fuck you?

I hung up and wandered over to the snack bar. I ordered an artichoke hummus platter, then gazed at the beige mush and realized I had never been less hungry. As I pushed cucumbers around on my plate, I looked again at the Chase bank statements. There were an awful lot of ATM withdrawals, come to think of it. Not easy to spot—they were at different locations, round numbers with the fee tacked on, $123.50 from a Duane Reade in Hell's Kitchen and $182 from a restaurant in DUMBO. Three or four times a week, another wad of cash withdrawn—and of course, Eleanor was a cashless Millennial, whipping out cards or paying for a round with her phone. *Why was she squirreling away wads of bills?*

"Katie."

I jumped and my head shot up. Aurelia, the glossy-haired member relations coordinator, was standing over me, her hands stuffed into her pockets.

"Aurelia. Hi." I closed the file folder, all casual.

"There's a detective here. Ratliff." She jerked her head toward the front desk. "She's going to look through Eleanor's office. She said we can watch as long as we don't touch anything. Hana . . ." She shrugged. "She suggested I have you there. What with your investigative journalist instincts and everything."

Hana had interacted with Aurelia today, but not me? "Of course."

Ratliff said hello stoically; I couldn't tell if she realized we'd talked on the phone less than an hour earlier. She stepped inside

Eleanor's now-unlocked office while the three of us—Mikki, too—clustered in the door. The room, with its rectangle of sun and bursts of happy green, somehow seemed sinister now. The chairs in the corner looked mocking in their emptiness; the spider plants seemed to sag.

It was neat—impeccably so. Eleanor's broad computer monitor sat on the desk, taunting us. Ratliff snapped on gloves and moved to turn it on, but Mikki mumbled something about how it wouldn't do anything without a computer hooked up to it; sure enough, the screen blinked to life, then coldly demanded an input.

From then on, it was exactly as excruciating as standing motionless as a TSA employee attempts to repack your bag. I pointed to Eleanor's small golden trash can and said something about checking it. Ratliff ignored me and fumbled with the pashmina and sweater draped on the coat rack, checking pockets. Then she tugged at the mint-green file cabinet rolled under the desk and thumbed through hanging index folders.

"I know she keeps Herd applications in there," Aurelia called. "And stuff related to the Fort Greene site." Ratliff nodded, then pulled out large clear bags and loaded the folders inside.

"Uh, some of those are original documents," Mikki said. "Permits and stuff."

"You can have them back once we know they're not pertinent," Ratliff replied without looking up. My stomach twisted—the invasion of Eleanor's personal space felt creepy and wrong. Ratliff was rifling casually, as if the owner wouldn't be back, as if these were a dead woman's things. At the shelving units, she picked up the first leather notebook on the stack and flipped through it—empty, I guessed, because she set it back. Same with the three below it.

"Didn't Eleanor carry around a notebook?" I asked.

"I think she kept it in her purse," Mikki said, crossing her arms. "We still don't know what happened to her purse or laptop."

"That's what we hoped to find here," Ratliff cut in. She ran a finger across the glass shelf. "When was the cleaner last here?"

"Monday night," Aurelia replied. "Probably around five. She couldn't clean yesterday because it was locked, obviously."

Ratliff nodded and then leaned forward, inspecting the little knife. "And can anyone tell me about this?"

"I've asked her about it before—the handle is so beautiful." Mikki pressed a hand against the doorframe. "She brought it back from Mexico City at some point. She's had it for a long time—since she started Gleam, at least."

Ratliff loaded the blade and its holder into an evidence bag as well. Finally, she fished in the trash can and bagged two tiny receipts (*ATM withdrawals? Credit card slips from delis?*) and a subway card. She stuck her hands on her knees and stood. "Is there anything else you think I should see here?"

We looked at each other blankly.

"Is there anything else you *want* to see?" Aurelia finally asked.

Ratliff shook her head. "You have my number if you think of anything." We bumbled out of the doorway and accompanied her out.

Aurelia floated back to the front desk, and Mikki and I exchanged a look. "What the hell kind of search was that?" I demanded.

"She barely even looked around," Mikki said. She turned and marched back toward Eleanor's office. "If she won't look properly, I will."

I hurried after her and closed us inside. "Do you know what you're looking for?"

Mikki was already cross-legged in front of the shelves, yanking at books that lined the bottom two rows. "No idea," she replied.

The door swung open and Aurelia appeared. Without a word, she plopped down next to Mikki, who was shaking books by the covers so the pages lolled.

"What did she want to talk to you about?" Mikki asked.

I looked around in confusion, but Aurelia answered: "She had questions about the acquisition. Who would benefit, if anyone was against it, that kind of thing. I was pretty useless—I didn't know about it till this week either."

Ratliff must have shown up earlier than I'd thought, chatting with Aurelia before conducting her half-assed search. It shook me that Ratliff could've walked right by Fatima and me.

"And could you think of anything?" Mikki asked.

"Not really. I wish Hana were here, she knows more than I do. The detective asked for files on all our members. Oh, and everyone working on the Fort Greene site."

I pulled at the backs of the framed photos, the one of Mikki, Eleanor, and Hana as big-eyed, thick-banged eighteen-year-olds, plus the one of Daniel and Eleanor vacationing together. Nothing written on the back of either.

"Have either of you been to the construction site?" I said. "Maybe there was a creepy contractor."

Aurelia shook her head, but Mikki looked up. "I've gone a couple times, to sign off on changes with the design," she said. "But I don't remember anyone leering or anything. I mean, it's construction workers. They're just tired and trying to do their jobs."

"Eleanor's really picky about who we work with—I know because I was in charge of getting bids." Aurelia leaned back on her hands. "The contractors we went with are expensive but super professional. She didn't want to hire anyone who'd do anything, you know. Below board."

"Undocumented workers, that kind of thing?" I said.

"Yeah. Or even just cutting corners, forging ahead without the right permits or whatever. She kept saying we wouldn't survive a scandal. I guess 'cause of the acquisition."

Mikki flung herself into an armchair. "Speaking of scandals, did they ever figure out who was calling us ugly cunts?"

"The detectives know about it, but no progress, no."

Suddenly a phone buzzed, and for a brief, wild moment I thought it was Eleanor's, hidden here in her office, and it would solve everything and prove she was okay. My heart took off, but then I realized the phone was mine, vibrating inside my bag on Eleanor's desk.

Fatima. "It's for a story," I told them, my get-out-of-jail-free card. "I gotta take this."

But of course, when I called her back a minute later, Fatima didn't pick up. I texted her and then tried Hana again: It was strange enough being here without Eleanor, and it wasn't like Hana to blow me off. Where had everyone gone? Suddenly the frustration surged up like nausea and I found my cheeks dripping with tears.

I needed distraction, needed to keep digging. I thought of Ted, who this morning had mentioned meeting for food, and sent him a text: "I'm wrapping here—what's your plan?" He suggested a burrito place nearby, and though I couldn't imagine eating a fucking burrito at the moment, I'd do anything to get out of here, away from Eleanor's once-perfect and now-rumpled things.

I glared at those I passed in the street, well-dressed and good-looking even under their thick winter layers—lucky bystanders, people who didn't know or care that Eleanor was someplace she shouldn't be. That my writing career was fucked, that there was a bloodstain somewhere in Michigan where a Chris-shaped hole had been cut from my chest. I gulped in the frigid air and hurried over to Eighth Avenue.

I spotted Ted through the fogged-up windows and felt my spirits lift. He wore a down vest over a plaid shirt, all mountain man-y. We hugged hello, a little awkwardly, and when he ordered a margarita, I did the same. I sucked at it when it appeared, eager for the softening, the way tequila sanded down the rough edges.

"So how're you holding up?" he asked. Chips arrived, the oily deep-fried variety, and he plunged one into salsa.

"I'm okay. I'm trying to keep busy—makes me feel like I'm doing something." I pulled a napkin from the little dispenser.

"I hear that. I just keep getting stuck on . . . we were all high-fiving over your computer on Friday. A few days ago. Where could she have gone?"

"She didn't seem like someone with any plans to leave." I sighed. "How often do you normally see her?"

He shrugged. "Every few weeks. When she needs something at the Herd, usually. I saw her twice last week, with that spray paint in the bathroom."

"It's the Gleam Room, Ted," I said, with mock seriousness, and he raised his palms.

My phone, facedown on the placemat, buzzed a few times in a row, and I flipped it over. *Dammit—automated texts from a political campaign.* "Sorry. I haven't heard from Hana all day and it's kinda freaking me out. It's not like her."

"Do you want to try calling her now?"

"No, it's fine. Sometimes she . . ." I plonked my elbows on the table. "Sometimes she gets stressed out, and it's like I'm the only one she can . . . *punish* is too strong a word. Take it out on?" I cocked my head. "She uses up a lot of energy trying to seem to-gether. All cheerful and easygoing and all that. But she's actually so tightly wound, sometimes I worry she's going to, I don't know, im-plode into a little diamond or something." I squeezed my fists to demonstrate.

Our burritos arrived, fat rolls in red baskets.

Ted slopped sour cream onto his plate. "Oh, for sure. Does she think she's hiding it?" He chuckled and even though I'd brought it up, I felt a flare of irritation: *I* could criticize Hana, but he couldn't.

I thought back to Hana's and my walk down Fifth Avenue, how her eyes had flashed at the mention of Ted. I made my voice light: "Be honest, do you two have bad blood? She was weird when I asked about you." I smiled conspiratorially. "I smell unresolved sexual tension."

"Oh God, no." He tossed his head. "Er, I mean, not that she's not—she's great! But that's definitely not it."

"You're sure?" I raised an eyebrow and gave my margarita a sip.

"Positive. All I meant was—" He took a breath. "I knew all of them in college. Harvard girls are no joke. And even of the three of them, she was the serious one. Super driven, super focused, like she had something to prove. You can . . ." He waved at the air in front of him. "I'm not crazy, right? She comes across as determined as shit."

I stared at him for a second. Did he really not see why she had to work eleven times as hard as her white friends? How she didn't have the luxury of screwing up? But then I shrugged. "She gets shit done, so I can't blame her for being controlling. When you're dependable, everyone depends on you."

"Which is fine, if you can do it without the martyr complex." I took a tiny bite in lieu of answering. The mix of salt and fat and spice made my stomach churn. "Anyway, I hear you, man," he went on. "Siblings are the worst."

I swallowed. "Does Cameron treat you like you're childish and incompetent?"

He laugh-snorted. "He's still living at home and playing video games all day, so he wouldn't have much of a case."

My antennae went up—I'd heard very little about this Cameron fellow. "Was he always sort of a slacker?"

"You could say that. He was hot shit in high school. Tons of friends, really good snowboarder. Just kinda effortlessly popular, you know?"

I nodded. "Then what?"

"He didn't really try in school. Part of his whole cool-guy thing. I was lucky—I was a huge nerd. Robotics club and everything."

I set my fork down. "So he had, what? A failure to launch?"

"He did fine at the community college for a while. Then halfway through he sorta suddenly announced he wasn't going to finish. My parents were furious. Mr. Walsh got him a job at his company; they were always close, they bonded over sports and shit. But then a few years later, Cameron managed to fuck that up too." He stopped short and stuffed the rest of his burrito into his mouth, a gargantuan bite. I waited approximately four hundred minutes as he struggled to chew, then realized he wasn't going to go on.

"That must've been rough. For the whole family."

With effort, he swallowed. "Yeah, I didn't mean to start airing out all my family shit."

"All families are fucked, right?" He nodded, wiped at his mouth with a napkin. So I went on: "Hana and my mom can't stand each other. They can't even be in the same room without fighting. They're like . . . you know those little fighting crabs?" I pummeled the air up near my chin. "So then my mom got diagnosed with cancer, and when I moved home to help her, Hana was supposed to stay for a couple weeks—she made it two days. I think she considers it her most obvious personal failing and she hates when anyone brings it up." I was being cruel now, the words like fire, but I couldn't stop. "Meanwhile, my dad left us when I was ten, just got fed up with Mom always criticizing him and didn't come home one day, and Hana saw her opening and moved out to L.A. to live with him." I paused, took a gulp of water. It felt oddly good, prattling on about my own minor difficulties as if everything were normal, as if Eleanor were a few blocks away, hard at work inside her beautiful outfit and office and company and life.

"Whoa," Ted said. "But you and Hana are pretty close now, right?"

"We get along." I shrugged. "I don't know if we'd be this close if I wasn't separately friends with Eleanor and Mikki." I didn't know I was thinking it until I said it, and then it was out, hovering in the air between us, somewhere over the basket of hot-sauce bottles. Scrambling, I tried to pierce it with a joke: "Did I say that out loud?"

He leaned back and smiled. "You don't need to worry," he said. "This is a safe space."

"Oh, good. What the Herd is to women, Benny's Burritos is to family drama."

"That's right. And speaking of the Herd, I looked into what you sent me about the new surveillance system. It's kinda complex." He blathered on about video compression and DVRs and digital streaming. "My best guess is that us resetting the router kicked the new cameras off the network. Which sucks."

"Damn."

"I know. Hey, were you able to get into the router?"

"Yeah, thanks again for that info." I leaned forward. "When I called yesterday, you said you and Eleanor are pretty close, right?"

He shrugged. "We've known each other our whole lives, yeah."

I pulled the folder from my bag. "Okay, don't tell anyone. But I found some stuff about Eleanor that—well, I'm not sure what to make of it." I plucked out a sheet. "White Plains, New York. Does she have any connections there?"

He sipped his margarita thoughtfully. "That's in Westchester, right? Nothing comes to mind."

"Right. Okay, do you know what bank she uses?" He raised his eyebrows and I pressed: "I don't know, did she ever make you stop at an ATM with her?"

He shook his head. "Sorry. I feel like this is a quiz and I'm failing."

"It's okay. I'm just looking for clues." I flipped to the Chase bank statements, where I'd highlighted all the withdrawals. "I think she was hoarding cash. Can you think of anything she said, or—"

"Is that Daniel?" I was tilting the bank printout toward me and Ted slid out the page underneath. It was Daniel's Click profile. "Wait, what the fuck?"

I sucked on my teeth. "Yeeeeahhh. He told us about this right away, and the cops—Eleanor had, uh, opened up their marriage.

She was actually on the site too." I flipped around the second print-out and he reared back in his chair.

"Are you serious? Was she meeting up with random dudes? Why is this not—isn't this a huge lead?"

He was so worked up, so quickly. "I'm trying to figure that out. Daniel said it was her idea. And not . . . not just for meeting dudes."

Ted missed it—his eyes slid over the page, reading. "Do the cops know you're doing your own investigation?"

I shook my head and tucked the pages back into the file. "Like I said, it's keeping me busy so I don't sit around all day worrying."

"Your book's not keeping you busy? I want to hear more about it."

I crunched at my plastic water cup. "I didn't tell Eleanor this," I said, "but I'm not even sure I can write that book. It's a long story."

"What happened?"

"It just ended up being . . . kind of a shitshow." The shriek of sirens. The spastic light splitting into red and blue. Skin sweaty under my palms as I willed the heart underneath to beat.

"I'm definitely missing something."

"I really don't want to talk about it." My words splatted onto the table between us and Ted looked down, like a chastised dog. I cleared my throat and tried to sound pleasant: "But I'd love to hear more about the weird tech stuff you're working on. What's the kook-iest thing you've had to design?"

As we were splitting the bill, Ted nodded at my bag again. "Can I get a copy of the stuff in that file?" he said. "Maybe I'll notice some-thing you didn't."

"You can take this. I have everything backed up."

"You sure?" He was already slipping the folder into his backpack. "Thanks. I'm just . . . I'm worried. Nobody seems that freaked out; Cameron was like, 'Whatever, she's a sensation-seeker, she probably just got bored with her life and moved on.'" He put on a surfer drawl, bobbling his head. "But I dunno. She's a public figure now. Between this and that stupid graffiti I had to wallpaper over—it doesn't sit right."

"I know. I feel the same way." I smiled sadly. "It makes me feel a tiny bit better that we're both on the case."

"And you know what, hopefully Cam's right." He reached for his coat. "We'll get a call any minute that they found her, like, boarding a flight to Fiji from LAX."

Something fluttered, a shadow lurching across my skull. "Say that again."

"What, that I hope she's on her way to Fiji?"

It was gone. We hugged on the sidewalk and parted ways. I had a missed call from Fatima and a text that I should call her in an hour. On the subway ride home, I read the Wikipedia entry on White Plains, still a dead end—*why had she been looking it up on a map?* It played a pivotal role in the Revolutionary War, I learned, and was the birthplace of a certain Mark Zuckerberg. My eyebrows lifted: White Plains was also home to a small international airport, a nerve center for private jets and sleek chartered planes.

Fatima started chattering the second she picked up the phone: "I still haven't gotten into the dude's account," she said, "but More-FracturedLight? You won't believe this. She was only talking to one person: a woman in Mexico. About *moving* there. She called it her, quote, 'go-to mental escape hatch,' said she'd always dreamed of starting over there."

It was so obvious, it was like I'd been nosing around the idea without allowing myself to think it. The relief was intense, a deep bath I plunged into: *Eleanor is alive.*

"And you think she actually went there? That's different from a . . . a mental escape hatch." *That's outrageous*, I wanted to say. But it wasn't, of course. The secret bank account and email, the cash withdrawals. The airstrip thirty-five miles north of here.

"I don't know, dude. Read it yourself. It starts out pretty harmless, just kinda flirtatious, but then it's clear Eleanor has really done her research, talking about these small cities and asking this woman—the other woman's British, I think—how she made it work. Then suddenly, like a week ago, she asks if they can talk offline. And all their messages were deleted, I found them in a temp folder. That's a pretty big coincidence, right?"

My phone buzzed, but I kept it pressed against my ear. I stared hard at the ceiling, feeling this new information whorling around my skull. *Could Eleanor really do it? Leave it all—leave us all—behind for a new, secret life over the border? To illegally slip down there, hope, absurdly, that no one would notice or look for her . . . ?*

"What cities did she mention?" I asked, sitting up on my bed. Fatima spelled them out and I typed them into separate tabs, and Google helpfully tossed some flight paths at the top of my search results.

Oh God. ESE, Ensenada Airport. GYM, Guaymas International Airport. I scrambled for the shaded Post-it on my desk, and now it felt obvious:

ACA 1010 CUU ESEGYM

Acapulco. Cancun. Ensenada, then Guaymas. She was researching flights.

"Send me everything you've got," I told Fatima. "I need to figure out what plane went from White Plains, New York, to a Mexican airport sometime after Monday Mocktails."

"Monday what now?"

"Never mind. But thank you. Are you able to tell me anything about the woman she was messaging with?"

"No dice. Whoever it was shut down her account between their last exchange and now, so there's just nothing to go on."

"Bummer." *This mystery woman—she knew where Eleanor was, didn't she?*

"I'll keep working on the other profile you sent me, the guy's."

"Maybe hold off—I don't need to check his alibi if Eleanor really did walk off on her own."

"You got it. And also . . . I'm sorry? Er, I guess congratulations that she's okay?"

"I don't know how to feel either." My stomach was contracting as if I'd swallowed something spiky. "But thanks."

I hung up and then saw Hana's group text: *Guys, I think I know where Eleanor is.* I couldn't call her fast enough, my fingers slipping over the commands.

"Katie. I'm so sorry I wasn't around today. But I think I figured it out."

"She's in Mexico."

A long silence.

"How did you—"

"Hana, I've been trying to find her too. Did you find out about the Click messages?"

"The what?"

A confused beat, and then she told me about her calls first with Cameron, then with Eleanor's sweet parents. I never thought of Hana as much of a digger, but I was impressed she followed her instincts. She was good at the psychology bit.

"Cameron talking about the forger was obviously a huge red flag," she went on. "Like, did she find another way to procure a fake passport?"

"Makes sense to me." I was intermittently taking notes and doodling in a notebook.

"When we were all in their little home office last night, I noticed her Frida Kahlo book on the shelf, and tonight it just snapped into place. I looked again at the numbers I'd spotted sitting, er, out on the desk as Daniel was showing us that weird contract—one looked like a phone number but didn't connect, and the other was two digits longer. So I Googled the first two digits of the longer number with the words 'country code.' Mexico. The two numbers were for burner phones."

"Smart." I'd looked hard at that desk too. When had Hana snatched up some random phone numbers? And why would they be sitting out where Daniel could see them?

"What about you? What'd you—hang on, Mikki's calling."

A few beeps, the usual swirl of *you-theres* and *hellos*.

"So where is she? Is she okay?" Mikki sounded frantic.

"We think she's okay," Hana said. "She left voluntarily. Moved to Mexico."

"Oh, thank God." A crazed laugh. Then: "What the fuck?"

"She's been planning it for a while," Hana noted. "I'm . . . so relieved, and yet so furious?" She said it curiously, like she was neither of those things.

"I'm so glad she's okay, oh my God," Mikki said. "But why would she—especially when the Herd—" Her voice cracked, like it was stuck at the top of her lungs.

"I guess maybe things weren't as good as they seemed?" Hana said.

"That cunt!" Mikki sounded amazed. "That fucking brilliant, horrible cunt. Do we know for sure she's down there?"

"I hope so, because it would mean she's alive and fine," I broke in. A surprised silence, like they'd forgotten I was there.

"Katie, you were about to tell me what made you think she was in Mexico," Hana prompted.

I quickly assessed: There was no reason to mention Fatima, or the bank records, or my meeting with Ted, or anything other than the smoking gun, really. "She was figuring out how to ditch her identity and move to a town called Guayabitos. Described her plans to a stranger online."

A stunned silence.

"Well, you probably should have led with that," Hana said.

"I *just* found this out. She—"

"Who was she talking to?" Mikki interrupted.

"A stranger on Click," I said. "She had a profile, and it wasn't too hard to reset the password and access it." I gave them the Cliffs-Notes version, implying I'd worked alone.

"I really, really want you to be right," Mikki said carefully, "but also . . . goddammit, Eleanor. That bitch didn't even say goodbye. And she left behind her two companies without warning or any plan to keep them going? That . . . that doesn't sound like her."

"I guess this is a PR nightmare," I said. I didn't mean to sound flippant, but.

"Not to mention . . . hurtful? That she just thought it was fine to abandon us one night?" Mikki's voice rose to a scratch. "I can't believe it. Those smug-ass cops were right."

"What do we do now?" Hana asked, always the mom, always the planner.

"I guess tell the detectives?" I said after a moment. "Will they still look for her if she left voluntarily?"

"I don't think so," Hana said slowly. "If she has debts here, her creditors can come after her. And if she's in the country illegally, that's Mexico's issue."

I let out something between a laugh and a groan. "I just can't believe this. It's *Eleanor* we're talking about. Would she . . . could she really do this?"

No one spoke. The static on the phone line seemed to swell.

"I know it's shocking, but I think it's true," Hana said. "She's so intelligent and strong-willed and . . . can't you kind of see it?"

Give it a few days, maybe weeks, and Eleanor would reappear at the Herd, her swishy hair glistening, a smile molding her cheekbones, the wildest story on her berry-colored lips—

"I don't really know what else to say." The voice was rickety and it took me a moment to decide it was Mikki, not Hana. "Actually, I gotta go. I think I'm gonna throw up."

Hana and I tried to jump in with something sympathetic, but when the kindness cleared we realized she was already gone.

"Well, I guess I'll call Ratliff," Hana finally said.

"Has anyone told Daniel?" I asked. "Or her parents?"

"I think we should leave that to the police. I'll call Ratliff now and just say this is what we think happened. Her parents might have contacts down there. People who can look for her. They were always taking her there growing up."

We ran out of things to say, like it was the awkward end of a Q&A session, and I hung up, jealous of Hana with her assigned tasks. I still had things I could do—chasing down the White Plains airport, rereading the messages from Eleanor's new British friend in search of overlooked clues—but suddenly I was tired, my bones turning to lead. I felt the tears brewing and let the weird combo of relief, anger, exhaustion, and self-pity swirl: *Eleanor's alive and safe. Eleanor left you, a week after you came back into her life.* I let myself cry, felt the cold tears collect in my ears. At one point Samantha, my roommate, knocked softly on the door, but I ignored her and she went away.

Thursday was cold, as cold as all the days before and all the days yet to come. I thought about staying home, keeping the curtains drawn, but instead pulled on my puffy coat and took the subway into the city. At first I thought the others hadn't come, but finally Aurelia, all-seeing eye of the front desk (basically Sauron), pointed at the wall behind her. "They're in Eleanor's office."

They'd closed the door, which meant I wasn't welcome. But: Fuck it. I knocked once, twice, three times.

The hushed tones ceased.

"Who is it?" Hana called.

"It's me."

Dark figures moved behind the frosted glass, and then Hana

pulled the door open. Hana was crying; Mikki's face was contorted into . . . confusion? Concern?

"What is it?" I said.

Mikki tapped at her phone and handed it to me. As she did, I realized the look in her eyes was outrage, exasperation, wrath.

I had to blink a few times to put all the pieces together.

An email. To Mikki and Hana, their personal emails. From Eleanor, her Herd account. From the nineteenth—today—at 9:56 a.m. local time—less than fifteen minutes ago. It was short, like most of her emails. The brevity of a powerful woman who doesn't need to impress anyone.

> **I'm so sorry, my lovelies, for all the worry and pain I'm sure I've put you through. I'm fine and safe and no longer in the country. I can't explain why, but I need you to trust me: I'm happy, and I won't be coming back. I trust you to tell all the right people and to continue all the amazing things we've begun together. xoxoxo**

My ears buzzed, a staticky crackle, like when you rest your head at bubble level in a bath. My vision softened around the edges, but I breathed hard and thoughts began streaming back in, a trickle at first and then all at once.

"So she only sent this to you two. No one else."

Hana swallowed. "As far as we know."

"Not Daniel? Not her parents?" *Not me?*

Hana shook her head. "I texted Daniel and Gary, just said, 'How are you?' They both said they were okay. I can't imagine they've gotten this."

I handed the phone back to Mikki. "Did we trace the email back? The IP address? We can figure out where—"

"She doesn't want to be found." Hana stopped staring at the

ground and looked at me, her eyes shiny with tears. "She's done with us. Even if we found her. She's gone."

"No." I darted my eyes between them. "No, we have to try. This doesn't make sense. She can't—she wouldn't—" A swooping sensation climbed up my lungs and out of my mouth as a curdled sob. Hana crossed the three feet between us and wrapped me in her arms.

"Something's wrong," I said, shaking my head. "She always signs off with XX, right? And it's cute, because it's kisses but also the female chromosomes? And this is—"

"Katie, stop," Mikki said. I felt Hana's chin turn toward her. "This is it. She's a fucking lunatic and this is how she's ending it." She began to cry, too, but they were fury tears, annoyance brought to a boil.

We stayed there for a while, Mikki pacing and cursing, Hana crying wetly, me shaking in Hana's arms. Finally Hana swiped at her cheeks and somehow pulled herself into organizing mode, and she and Mikki made a plan. Their questions floated over my head like speech bubbles in a cartoon, and for once I was grateful that I was a hanger-on, a little kid in this adult situation. I heard snatches about press statements, a story that would resonate, legal counsel, grief groups.

"Okay." Hana mashed her hands together. "Let's go then."

I stayed behind for a minute, collecting myself, then paused at the threshold between the sunroom and the library. I let my gaze soften until the women around me were just a beautiful blur. A phone rang; two Herders giggled loudly, their laughs like pretty sparklers.

My eyes focused again on a figure in the corner, near the coatroom—wide shoulders hunched, her neck drooping. Hana. I blinked and hurried over to her, tapped her arm. We stared at each other.

"I'm gonna go home," she announced, with the same zoned-out

drone you use at the end of the night, when you realize you're too drunk and no longer having a good time.

"Okay."

"I just . . . can't be here right now." She rifled through the coat rack, thrusting sleeves aside. "Do you want to come with me?"

She stared at the coats, not meeting my eyes, which I took to mean she didn't want me to.

"I'm gonna stay. Make sure Mikki's okay."

She nodded and then pulled me into another hug. "Call me if you need anything."

"I will," I said. But I knew I wouldn't.

I wandered home shortly after, past the Cultivation Thursday crew convening near the front desk. I glared at the women there: nodding, laughter, notes in pretty notebooks and forks scraping on creamy green plates. Things were falling apart, but to them, it was business as usual.

I slept late on Friday, then woke to a string of texts from Erin. My little chipmunk of a literary agent was eager for an update on my book proposal, eager for anything new on Eleanor. She didn't know yet—nobody knew. Ninety-nine percent of the world thought Eleanor was waylaid by a family emergency, Erin and a handful of others thought she was genuinely missing, and just a few of us—one-third of one-billionth of the population—knew the bizarre truth. Thoughts of Chris came clanging back to the surface. My heart had just begun to scab over, now that I'd put seven hundred miles between myself and Michigan, the awful night when it all went wrong. Now the wound opened back up and mingled with how much I missed Eleanor: a shimmering ache radiating outward from my chest.

The Herd had a hushed, curious energy. By now—with Eleanor three days gone—everyone was keenly aware of her absence, and the Herd's fresh Instagrams (still posted regularly by one of the

member relations coordinators) had hundreds of comments clinging to the bottom, all vague and cheerful vows of support for Eleanor and her "family emergency." Each made me feel something
between faint and sick.

Hana's eyes had that focused glint, her body stiffened with determination. She was putting the final touches on a press release before sending it to the Herd's lawyer for approval. Yesterday's paralysis,
it turned out, hadn't lasted long. Hana always behaved this way
under pressure: She became maniacally efficient, a robot plowing
through its tasks until she'd suddenly break down into tears that
seemed like a surprise even to her. It freaked me out—the automa-
ton eyes, her manic typing, as if Eleanor hadn't just thrown a grenade into our lives.

I swung Hana's screen my way and scanned: The press release
was a soft, twirling spin on the truth, a carefully worded claim that
due to "continuing family circumstances," Eleanor was permanently stepping down from her posts at Gleam and the Herd, and
asking everyone to respect her privacy during this difficult time.

"Family circumstances?" I repeated, pointing.

She shrugged. "It sounds better than 'personal reasons' but
means the same thing. Isn't everyone a member of their own family?"

I looked at her, astonished.

Mikki appeared and slid onto a seat at the communal table we'd
commandeered. "I can't believe you got so many people to agree to
not talk about it." She looked at me and clarified: "Daniel, Cameron, Ted, Eleanor's parents—they're all staying mum."

"To be fair, I don't think her folks are able to form coherent sentences right now." Hana sighed. "But it's true, they're all signing
NDAs. I think everyone saw the logic of keeping this quiet so they
have an actual shot at grieving in peace. Can you imagine if it was
on the news?" She held an imaginary mic under her chin, her voice
bubbling up with a newscaster's shocked emphasis: "Bizarre news is

rocking the small but powerful world of commercial feminism today. Following an announcement that the Herd will be acquired by internet giant Titan, its founder has *cleared* out her bank account and *run* off . . . to Mexico!"

A stunned silence. "You do a really good newscaster," I said finally.

"Have you been practicing that?" Mikki looked uncomfortable.

Hana rolled her eyes. "It's my job to think about the worst-case scenario, okay? The Herd is still my client, and believe it or not, I still care about this place."

"Aw." I patted her hand. "This place cares about you too."

"Glad somebody does." She lifted her screen again. "Not to mention I have other clients. Whom I've been basically ignoring for a week."

"I know what you mean. I missed a meeting with a super-important gallery owner."

"Aw. For the collages?" Mikki nodded. I was screwed, too, but I couldn't share why. I hadn't replied to Erin. My hunch was that she'd try to convince me to keep pursuing Eleanor, to perhaps even travel to Mexico in defiance of Eleanor's blow-off, a thought that made my stomach knot almost as badly as the idea of dusting off my notes from Michigan and writing *Infopocalypse*.

"I just really miss her," I said finally.

Aurelia bustled out at one point, giving me a sharp nod hello and then announcing she would be canceling Monday Mocktails. The hired bartender was from a buzzy Japanese bar, and the Herders seemed disappointed as she spread the word. But I was relieved, knowing I wouldn't have to look up in the darkened afternoon to see throngs of cheerful women sipping virgin lychee mojitos.

Mikki invited Hana and me to dinner at her apartment in Greenpoint: "All carbs, probably Italian, and we're watching *Project Run-*

way in lieu of talking, obviously." Hana and I both liked the sound of that, and as the sun plunged lower and lower I tied up loose ends: confirming Fatima wouldn't tell anyone what she'd seen on Click (*Bitch I break laws for a living lol you have nothing to worry about*); drafting an email for Erin explaining this new book idea wouldn't work out either. But discomfort buzzed in me whenever my mouse hovered over the Send button. Maybe I wasn't ready to call it quits? Maybe I needed someone to tell me this was worth pursuing, now more than ever?

Mikki and I grew antsy as the crowd thinned, murmuring on their way out about the canceled Mocktails and the denial of their God-given right to tangerine-ginger fizzes. Hana pretended not to notice our fidgeting as she typed madly at her computer.

"Sorry, guys, I'm just racing to get this news alert out before the end of the day," she eventually said, her eyes swinging up. "God, I never thought this was an announcement I'd be planning."

The Herd's official closing time neared and then rolled past. Aurelia popped over, blinking in the light.

"You guys heading out soon?" she said with as much friendliness as she could muster.

"We can lock up," Hana said, her face bluish from her laptop's glow.

"And we'll be out of here soon," I added on behalf of all of us, because I felt tired and ungenerous and eager to get the fuck out of there. Aurelia said good night and I herded us into the coatroom and plucked my puffer from a hanger. We were looping scarves and tugging on hats when a sudden round of gunfire made us freeze.

It started again. Not gunfire—drums, a drum line. Snares and bass, now a cymbal crash. Hana, Mikki, and I grabbed our things and hustled out of the coatroom and into the sunroom, pressing up against the windows. On the street below, we could just make out a troupe of drummers, their marching-band uniforms decorated to look like nutcrackers. One of them blew a whistle and then they broke into their most elaborate cadence yet, their arms a blur, the plumes on their cylindrical hats bobbing, and the half-circle of spectators shook their shoulders to the beat and lifted their phones high, recording. In the windows of the buildings around us, silhouettes appeared. I pulled my phone from my purse and held it to the glass, but all I could see was our reflections.

"Can we somehow turn the lights off in here?" Hana asked, tapping at her screen.

"The switches are all the way at the front desk," I said.

The drum corps was marching in time to the music now, forming shapes visible only from above: a starburst, a cross, a triangle—no, a Christmas tree.

"This is so cool. I'm gonna see if I can get it from the roof." Hana turned toward the staircase, tucked back by the coatroom and fitness studio.

Ten floors below, a percussionist whaling away on a triangle dropped the instrument, whipped off his hat, and launched into a confident back handspring. The crowd went wild, their screams and whoops reaching up through the glass. I leaned my head against the window, feeling its coldness on the space between my brows, on the third eye.

"Are you okay?"

I turned to Mikki and saw that she was looking behind her. At first she just sounded confused, but when she repeated herself, her voice tightened up into concern: "Hana, what's wrong?"

I spun around and saw Hana at the far end of the room. She'd dropped to her knees and her chest was heaving so hard, we could see it from here. Not just see it—*hear* it, a rasping *hee-hah, hee-hah*.

"Hana?" I called, more quietly than I intended. *Go to her,* my brain shot out, but my feet were glued to the floor.

"What's going on?" Mikki took one small, scared step forward. "Are you okay?"

Hana opened her mouth but what came out was a strangled

mewl. She kept lifting her finger to the ceiling and gaping her mouth like a fish.

The spell broke and I rushed to her, dropping onto my own knees and sliding the last couple feet between us. Outside the drum line did a frantic crescendo, echoing around the buildings, boomeranging booms. I grabbed her shoulders. "Hana, what is it?"

She looked at me, her eyes widening.

"Eleanor," she said, her voice hysterical. "She's on the roof."

PART III

CHAPTER 13

===

PLEASE STOP SAYING YOU SUFFER
FROM IMPOSTOR SYNDROME

By Hana Bradley   *Published to* Gleam On *April 10, 2019*

Hi, Gleam Team! Hana here—publicist for Gleam and the Herd. In PR, I'm lucky to work with ambitious, accomplished, hardworking people who inspire others . . . much like yourselves! And you'd probably be shocked to hear that many of the women I work with come to me with a confession. They lean in and say it softly, like they're letting me in on an awful secret: *I feel like a fraud. I have no idea what I'm doing and I'm not sure I deserve to be where I am.* That's right: These incredible, inspiring people are diagnosing themselves with Impostor Syndrome.

It's a term we hear a lot these days, and it seems to perfectly suit that secret, shameful feeling many of us experience. But it's nothing new; Impostor Syndrome actually came from a scientific paper published by two female psychologists in 1978. They theorized, based on their own anecdotal research, that young women were vulnerable to "impostor phenomenon," or feeling like an "intellectual phony." The researchers observed that, despite "outstanding academic and professional accomplishments," many women think they're really not too bright and that they've fooled anyone who thinks otherwise.

They published the study, and the news went . . . nowhere. That's because follow-up studies couldn't link impostor phenomenon with gender or, specifically, with high-achieving women. And in 1993, one of the original researchers retracted her theory, admitting that the "syndrome" they'd originally identified actually applied to—wait for it—*80 percent* of the population. Old, young, male, female, anything in-between— almost all of us have these feelings.

And that should've been the end of it: *Whoops, sorry, #notathing.* But no. The term took on a life of its own—you've almost definitely heard a friend invoke it after nabbing a promotion, and maybe you've used it yourself. I have a huge problem with this debunked pop psychology term: It implies that occasionally doubting yourself is a *pathology*, when really, it's just a part of the human experience. (Uh, maybe we should be worrying about the weirdos who *don't* occasionally wonder if they're as great as others seem to think they are?)

Feeling like you don't know what the F you're doing shouldn't trigger shame. It means you're challenging yourself—stretching, learning, and growing. And that's something to be proud of.

This article was adapted from Bradley's presentation at the Herd on April 9.

CHAPTER 14

Hana

I couldn't stop shaking.

Someone had given me a blanket, and at first I thought vaguely that it must have been from the paramedics, the ones who magically produce them to wrap around shivering children during an action movie's denouement. Then I realized: No paramedics had arrived, because Eleanor was clearly dead. Instead, medical examiners bustled by, different uniforms, same stern looks. And then I realized I was rubbing my fingers over the thick knit of this particular blanket, swipes of gray and black, and concluded that it was probably something someone had grabbed from Eleanor's office in the ensuing pandemonium.

Eleanor was dead.

It kept grabbing at my chest, an echo of the pain, the way a burn on your skin stings over and over again. Last week, I would've given anything to have my answers, to just *know*. Now I wanted to climb back into that uncertainty, when Eleanor was maybe, possibly, probably still alive.

It'd crossed my mind that she might be dead, of course. Killed in some tragic accident orchestrated by the Fates. Spinning their yarns, tying off Eleanor's with a crisp knot like whomever knitted this blanket. That'd been one of my favorite classes in school, Psychological Theory of Folklore and Mythology. Early, elaborate attempts at understanding human behavior.

But who could make sense of this? I pictured her coat, the crescent of blood black against the collar. And when I got closer, the jagged line against her white neck where a scarf should be.

Katie slung her arm around me and briskly rubbed my back.

"Is it cold?" I asked her. "They should shut the door to the stairwell."

"It's not cold," she said, leaning more of her body into me. "I think you're in shock."

"I'm not in shock." My teeth chattered. "I'm just cold."

A police officer approached. He was young, his face round and clean-shaven. My eyes floated to the gun on his hip. He kept addressing Mikki and Katie instead of me, and the two of them probably assumed it was because I was shaken and shaking, but I wasn't so sure. They don't know what it's like to be the one cops eye suspiciously, their tone just one degree off.

"When we're done here, I'll need all of you to come to the station to make a quick statement," he said.

"How much longer will it be?" Mikki called out. She was slumped on a blue sofa.

"Maybe an hour?"

Mikki's lip popped into a pout. "Okay."

I felt Katie looking at me. She turned back to the officer. "I don't think Hana should be forced to stay here," she said. "There's a deli right on the corner. Could we wait down there?"

He hesitated, and she gestured toward me. "I'm worried about my sister. Sitting here isn't helping. I mean, we're obviously not a flight risk."

Not a flight risk. Unlike Eleanor, a week ago. Had she really intended to leave, or was that a weird cover-up orchestrated by her killer? Or had she been trying to escape because she knew she was in danger? *Someone killed Eleanor*—my jaw took off clacking again and I wrapped the throw tighter around my shoulders.

"Let me check." He clomped away, shoulders hunched, moving like an awkward teenage boy.

A little sob escaped from Mikki. *Sad*, that's how I was supposed to feel, right? Or maybe afraid, freaked out by the horror show directly above our heads. Instead I felt . . . numb, maybe. Removed. Up on the roof, I'd felt fear as I crept toward what I first mistook for a forgotten boot, and now I could recall the jagged panic that'd gripped me when I spotted a second, but then my memory closed in around just one more sight—the stiff skin of a mannequin, a dark half-moon at the top of her coat, brownish in the roof's sallow light. Next thing I knew, I was on my knees in the sunroom with Mikki and Katie staring at me. Like an audience, like theatergoers looking up at me onstage.

"Sorry. They said we gotta keep you here." The cop spoke as he was still scurrying back. Mikki whimpered. "Oh, and don't—alert anyone. Or touch anything. Just stay here, okay?"

For a while, we all stared into the distance. It was like I'd strapped on a heavy breastplate, making it difficult to breathe. I was the only one not crying, and this struck me as unfair: They hadn't gone up on the roof. They hadn't seen the gash in Eleanor's neck. Instead they'd stayed warm here in the sunroom, staring at me.

At first, they'd been confused—they thought maybe Eleanor was alive up there. Once I'd set them straight, Katie had yelled out, *No one goes up there—we're calling 911*. We'd huddled on the floor as the sirens grew louder; each new whoop had made her jump.

The cops congratulated us on not messing with the crime scene. Which I liked. I like when authority figures say "good job."

A little shout and some shuffling, and two men rolled Eleanor out in a body bag spread across a gurney. Mikki stifled a wail. They huffed directions as they navigated the tight corners, and I stared at the black sack, something blazing in my belly like an ember. The score along Eleanor's neck. The darkness leaking from it, soaking the top of her coat. Someone had *taken* her, someone who had no right.

I thought of the Fates again, the three of them, sisters who carried torches, whips, and cups of venom to punish wrongdoers on Earth. Relentlessly pursuing murderers, torturing them until they were driven mad. Monstrous, smelly hags with snakes in their hair and bat wings on their backs.

Wait, not Fates. Those were Furies.

The interview room was nicer than I'd expected. Years of TV-watching had primed me for a blank, bare-bones box, a table between us with a ring meant for affixing handcuffs. But this pretty much looked like the meeting rooms I'd rented for sit-downs with my own PR clients. Cream walls, a decent-sized window, rolling chairs, that smooth, generic table.

Still, my heart banged in my chest. Pounding like the big bass drum that'd jolted me up to the roof in the first place. Detective Ratliff appeared and shook my hand warmly.

"Ms. Bradley, I'm so sorry for your loss." She pulled out a seat across from mine. I was glad it was her. Detective Herrera, the little ham hock of a man who'd shown up at Eleanor's the night she went missing, gave me bad vibes—something in the cock of his hip, the confident set of his shoulders. He reminded me of the Cambridge cop who'd wandered over when, senior year, a bouncer with white dreadlocks had refused to believe my driver's license was real. Mikki and Eleanor had made a scene, jabbing their fingers in his face as tears coated my eyes, until the officer had intervened and snatched the ID from the bouncer's hand. Mikki and Eleanor had been so relieved—finally, an authority figure to set things straight—and their faces crumpled as the cop snorted, *This is obviously fake* and folded my (state-issued) Michigan driver's license in his fist.

"We appreciate your giving a statement tonight," Ratliff said. "I know this must be difficult for you."

"Well, anything to help you figure out who did this." A little honk escaped my lips and I cleared my throat to cover it. "Has anyone contacted her parents?"

"We left messages for them. We have someone driving up to their home now."

"Good. They're going to be just . . . devastated."

She nodded, shot me a sympathetic look. "We're doing everything we can. Now, can you walk me through what happened, starting with when you decided to go up to the roof?"

I recounted it, careful to get the details right, to mention anything that might be useful, always eager to please. Back in the Herd's sunroom: Katie and Mikki pressed against the glass, gazing at the street below as I beelined for the stairs.

"I got to the roof and my first thought was how cold it was," I continued. "I started making my way to the edge—it's kind of a maze of different sections, which are, like, seating areas when it's open in the summer. Now all the furniture is in piles." I saw it again: chair- and cushion- and table-shaped lumps haphazardly stacked against little barricades. How I'd hustled by, the clamor of the drummers echoing off nearby buildings, when something made me stop and glance back.

"I looked at one of the piles and at first, my thought was, 'Why did someone leave a shoe up here?' It was kinda sticking out, a boot. And then I realized there were two. So I got a little closer to try and look, and I saw—I realized—"

Something in my throat squeezed and bobbed. I pushed out a deep breath. "I got closer and realized it was a body. For a second I was like, 'Is a homeless person squatting on the roof?' But it's way too cold for that. So I took a few steps around the pile of lawn furniture, and she was there, in this little space between the pile and the partition. I already had my phone out so I turned on the light, and I could see—"

"Where were you standing?"

I blinked. "Right at her feet. I basically shined the flashlight up along her body." I indicated a sweep over my own torso.

"And you didn't touch her."

"I didn't touch anything. As soon as I got to her coat I think I knew, although I hadn't consciously processed it yet. And then I got to her face and it was—there was no mistaking it." My voice wobbled but I breathed again, controlled it. "Her eyes were closed and her skin was so white—it looked like, I don't know, a dummy that was designed to look like her, or a wax figure or something. And then I realized there was sort of a gash across part of her neck." I waved my nails alongside my throat. "At first I thought it was a choker? And then I spotted this big stain along the top of her collar. Right underneath it. In the darkness it just looked black, but that's when I ran back downstairs." I could still feel the fumbling panic, my feet skittering backward over the wooden slats as my lizard brain hit the air horn: *Get away, get away, get away.*

Ratliff nodded. "Did you notice anything else unusual up there?"

"I'm not up there much in the winter. No one is. There's a sign saying the door is alarmed, but we discovered early on that nothing happens if you push it. But this is the first time I've been up there since maybe October." My thoughts were popping out of me in the wrong order, swirling nonsensically.

"So . . . you're saying you wouldn't have noticed if anything else was disturbed."

"Right. But I didn't touch anything. You guys saw the exact same roof I did."

"Okay. The crime scene investigators are doing a thorough job."

I frowned. "Will they be looking through the entire coworking space?" When we'd left, the Herd was still crawling with forensic experts measuring and swabbing and photographing.

She raised an eyebrow. "I imagine so. It's unlikely the body was dropped there from somewhere else." My eyes widened and she shook her head. "Sorry—that was callous."

"No, it's okay. I'm just realizing we'll have to close the space to-morrow." Another thought unfurled: I was still the Herd's publicist. Would I be tasked with breaking this news? "Will you guys be mak-ing an announcement? Holding a press conference?" It was like all my knowledge of public relations had leaked out with my snot and tears: How did police briefings come to be?

"Our media relations department will handle that," she replied. "In conjunction with the family. You don't have to worry about it."

"Okay. Thanks." Ratliff didn't say anything else, so I went on: "It'll be big news, right? Because she's a public figure?"

She hesitated. "It's likely we'll have to keep the local media ap-prised of the investigation, yeah. But we'll wait until the timing's right."

I stared at the scratched tabletop, then looked up at her. "What are you going to do? To catch this person?"

"Detective Herrera and I will be following up on all leads. We take every homicide investigation seriously."

"Just like you take every missing-persons case seriously." I raised my eyebrows.

"We'll be taking into account everything we learned about Ms. Walsh over the last week. The stolen phone, the defacement, the planned escape to Mexico—we'll be poring over everything for leads."

The email . . . from Mexico. "You must be able to track down whoever sent that email yesterday. That had to be her killer, right? She must have been long dead by then."

She folded her hands on the table. "We'll wait for an autopsy before we try to place the time of death. But at first glance, my medical examiner—" She hesitated. "They aren't sure if they'll be able to pinpoint it. Because of the weather. It's like a deep freeze."

Like a chest freezer. I thought of the hulking one in our basement in Kalamazoo, how Katie and I would run down there, feet pattering, to choose a flavor of pizza or ice cream. Eleanor, frozen in time like a gallon of rocky road.

Something clunked in my brain. "But we can look at what she was wearing, right? See if it's what she wore to the Herd that Monday?" The thought chugged along. I was so tired. "Daniel was pretty sure she didn't come home that night. Which would mean someone else faked those emails and texts from her the next day. You guys should look into *that*."

"We'll be exploring all leads," she said again. She jumped and then glanced down at her phone. "Unless there's anything else you need to tell me, we're gonna let you get home and get some sleep." She paused and I fought to keep my expression neutral. There was one other thing, a massive one, but I'd already confirmed this wasn't about *that*.

I managed a bland smile. "Will I need to come back in?"

"Not sure yet. Will you be available?"

I sighed. "I'm flying home on the twenty-third. For Christmas."

"That should be fine, as long as you remain accessible."

Didn't realize I needed your permission, I wanted to say. Instead: "Just let me know how I can be helpful."

Katie was asleep in the waiting room, cheek in palm, elbow on an armrest. I felt a crackle of annoyance that Mikki had left her here.

But it was late and I probably wouldn't have waited for anyone other than my sister either. I woke her and we blurrily figured out that her subway wasn't running; I was about to order her her own Lyft when she asked if she could stay with me.

At home I set her up on the couch, carrying pillows out from the linen closet even as she crashed her head onto the decorative mole-skin cushions there. I collapsed into bed, my door left open a crack, as always, for Cosmo. I was asleep within minutes and then woke, swimming only halfway toward the surface, from pressure on the bed. Not Cosmo—Katie climbed in next to me, then curled away. We're not a touchy family; we hug hello and goodbye and say "I love you" when we think of it, always with a wide globe of personal space. I was almost nervous as I reached out and rubbed her back. Without turning, she curled an arm across her chest and touched my fingers near her side, held them there and then gave a little pat. I rolled away then and together, we fell asleep.

I woke and lay in bed for a moment with my eyes closed. Then it all came rushing in, like someone had turned on a cold tap: Katie next to me, Ratliff in the station, and, with a dizzying lurch, Eleanor, Eleanor frozen like a venison steak, Eleanor's neck with its rimy crust of blood.

My stomach seized and I rolled over, clutching it, wishing wildly I could back up into my dreamland, where none of this was reality. A few feet away, Katie snored softly. Trying not to disturb the covers, I slid my legs out and padded down the hall.

I was just squeezing toothpaste onto my brush when, in the mirror, something moved behind me. I jumped and whirled around: Katie was thumping down the hall, holding my phone out in front of her.

"Daniel keeps calling you," she announced, her brows knitted.

I set the toothbrush on the sink and took the phone from her.

"Thanks," I said, pushing the door closed. She didn't move, her eyebrows now reaching for the sky, so I basically shut the door in her face.

"Hana?!" he yelped, before I could hear a single ring.

I kept my voice low, pictured Katie with her ear pressed against the door. "What's up?"

"Get here now," he said. "I don't—I don't know what to do."

"Are you in danger? Should I call 911?"

"No police. You don't want police." He sounded terrified, unhinged.

"*I* don't want police?"

"It's about—Hana, it's about what happened in 2010."

It hit me like a force, like a fire hose, shot at all of me all at once. My ears rang and I clutched the side of the bathtub. *How on earth did he know? What had he found?*

"Listen to me very carefully." I curled away from the door, my voice just above a whisper and so cold, so bloodless, it scared even me. "I'll be there in ten minutes. Don't contact anyone else. *No one else.* Do you understand?"

Another gaping silence and the air itself seemed to lean in.

"Get here," Daniel said, and then he was gone.

CHAPTER 15

Katie

SATURDAY, DECEMBER 21, 8:10 A.M.

Hana flung the door open and stood centered in the frame. The sconce lights on either side of her mirror glowed behind her so she was silhouetted, an outline of Athena preparing for battle.

"I have to go," she announced.

I was lingering in the hall, all casual. As if my ear hadn't been one with the door a second earlier.

"What'd Daniel say?"

"I'm heading over there now."

"Why, what'd he say?"

She sighed and her shoulders slumped. "He's freaking out. Threatening to kill himself." I waited, and she went on: "I guess he started drinking and didn't go to sleep all night, and now he's, like, out of his mind and consumed by grief. I don't actually think he's going to try anything, but he's freaking out."

"So it's a cry for help?"

"Sure sounded like it."

"But why did he call you?"

Hana tipped her head back, closed her eyes. "My thoughts exactly. God, I don't need this."

She pushed past me, down the hallway, and I called after her: "Doesn't he have any other friends?"

"Not that many, honestly." She made it to her bedroom and threw open the closet. "He got out of a ten-year relationship right before he met Eleanor. At the wedding he had one guy, a friend from high school, as his best man, but that's it." She hooked on a bra, stepped into a pair of underwear.

"So why not call that dude?"

"I don't know. Maybe he's unavailable. Maybe Daniel doesn't want to talk to someone who barely knew Eleanor." She yanked a turtleneck over her head.

"Did he try calling Mikki too? I'm just trying to understand why—"

"Katie." Hana stared at me for a second before unfolding her jeans with a flick. She had tears in her eyes, and a spear of guilt went through me. "I don't know what you want me to say. He just called me, repeatedly, begging me to come over."

She turned away and yanked her curls into a bun. She looped the elastic, then whisked her knuckles across her eyes.

"I'm sorry," I said. Then: "Let me know if you need anything."

Tossing things into her purse, she pretended not to hear me.

The slam of the front door seemed extra-loud and final, somehow, like the clang of a gavel or the bang of a book's heavy back cover. I leaned against the kitchen island, statue-still, until Cosmo padded over and rubbed against the hem of my pajama pants.

I dropped to my knees to scoop him up, and as I did something rushed up through me, something sharp and bright, and then it hit my throat and came out as a moan. I hugged Cosmo to my chest and he hung limply as my head and hands filled with crackly static and my heart beat so fast I thought it'd burst, juddering as if it wanted to shoot out from my chest. I gasped with the wild, unself-conscious panic of a toddler mid-meltdown.

Finally I found my breath again, blinked hard until the static lifted. "Eleanor," I murmured, dropping my nose to the top of Cosmo's head. He twisted his neck, blinked at me. "Poor Eleanor." Cosmo wriggled free and sauntered off toward the hallway. I managed to leave Mom a voicemail, my voice quavering as I asked her to call me back.

I stacked the pillows I'd left on the sofa and attempted to fold the fluffy duvet. In the doorway, Cosmo watched me with his grasshopper-green eyes. As I headed for the bathroom, I paused outside Hana's bedroom, and my eyes fell on the scrap of paper on her bureau. The note she'd mentioned, the numbers scribbled on top. It definitely hadn't been on Eleanor's big desk as Daniel unlocked the drawer below.

Another memory, an echo of dialogue that I'd tucked away for later: Tuesday night, while the three of us were still panicking in the hallway of a tapas restaurant, Mikki had said, *Who has Daniel's number?* and Hana had raised her hand and dialed confidently. Why did Hana even have him in her contacts? A thought like a whisper: *What else are you lying about, Hana?*

I showered, torturing myself with a mental montage of beautiful, sparkling Eleanor and all the smiles she'd never shoot out. As shampoo foamed against my scalp I realized a suspect had been taking shape underneath it, a heady suspicion I could investigate on my own. Quickly, a plan stitched itself together in my mind. It was steadying, giving the grief and desperate exasperation something to cling to, like handrails in a shower stall.

Outside, the air was a little warmer, the sky silvery and swollen — probably around freezing, but it was a relief after all those stark, icy-blue days. I checked the weather forecast and groaned: a "wintry

mix" was headed our way, and headlines despaired over the probable upending of holiday travel plans.

For now, at least, our Monday flight was still on time. I pictured
the three of us in Kalamazoo, eating off the nice china in Mom's
dining room. It'd be an especially awful meal: Hana creepily pretending everything was fine, me scrabbling at my mounting anxiety,
Mom complaining about what bad company we were being while
subtly, expertly excoriating all of Hana's life choices. If Mom didn't
call me back soon, she'd probably hear about Eleanor's death on the
news.

As would my agent, Erin. This time I'd be ready for her; in fact,
I'd get ahead of it. I'd been close to calling the whole thing off: Last
week, I couldn't imagine defying Eleanor's wishes, telling the world
how she'd parachuted out of her perfect-seeming life. Implying
judgment, sending the news vultures and TV and podcast crews
scuttling after her to Guayabitos, in search of her casa. I couldn't do
that to her. But now? Now I was a snapping hound dog on a leash,
more determined than ever. Eleanor deserved justice. On the subway, I emailed Erin, concluding with a promise, a vow, ripped from
the parlance of bad action movies: "I'm not going to stop until I find
the motherfucker who did this."

At home, I pulled up my research file on Carl Berkowski, a
Known Enemy of Eleanor. I remembered he was an engineer at
Hopscotch, a stupid app that lets you check into a business to unlock discounts and freebies there. And I knew from my time as a
tech reporter that start-ups expect every goddamn employee to use
their product with the fervent devotion of a Scientologist. Bingo:
Sixteen minutes ago, Carl had checked in at Ghost Cafe in the Financial District. I skidded off toward the subway, backtracked when
I realized I'd left my phone on my desk, and then headed into Manhattan.

It was a packed little coffee shop, people chatting eagerly or gazing wide-eyed at their laptops, as if trying to prove to themselves that

the din was energizing, not distracting. I spotted Carl at a table in the back: short brown hair, glasses, sloping chin, gray hoodie. Big Bluetooth headphones like my own. I pulled mine down to rest around my neck, tapped at my phone, and steeled myself, mentally raising a sword in the air and bellowing *For Eleanor!* Then I took the seat across from him.

He stared over the top of his laptop. "Uhhh . . ."

"Katie Bradley." I thrust out a hand. "We were supposed to have a coffee last week? I was hoping we could—"

"What are you doing here?" He leaned in, his eyes shooting around, attracting far more attention than I had.

"I just thought maybe we could have that coffee now."

"I could report you."

"For being in a coffee shop?"

"For stalking me." He slammed his laptop shut. "How did you find me?"

I blinked at him for a moment. Had he literally never considered the practical implications of his employer's product? Oh, to be a white man in the world. "You checked in on Hopscotch. I just want to talk."

"Why?"

Eleanor surged back into my brain, thwacking me with grief. "Why'd you stand me up?"

"*I* stood *you* up?"

"Yeah, I—I waited, like, a half hour, tried texting and calling, and you never showed." A note of confusion crept into my voice.

"Oh, that's rich. Nice try. We said we'd meet at four; when I got out of the Lincoln Tunnel I had a couple confused texts from you, and the diner was empty. I was *livid*. Really great use of my one day off, so thanks for that."

"No, we said—" My voice faltered and I got that feeling, hot and cold at once, indignant but also maybe he was right and I'd messed up. *Didn't we have it in writing?*

Dramatically, he sighed. "So now you're following me . . . why?"

I squared my shoulders. "You texted me about Eleanor last week."

"That's right—thanks for sending that detective my way. That made me *super* eager to text you back."

"What'd you tell them?"

"Why would I talk to you? I didn't even *have* to talk to her." He crossed his arms. "I hate cops. Second time in two weeks the cops are asking me about Eleanor Walsh."

I frowned. "Second time?"

"Yeah, after they called about—" He stopped himself, cocked an eyebrow. "I mean, I'm not the only person on the planet who doesn't like her. You can't automatically assume that any inconvenience in her perfect life traces back to me."

I shook my head, still stuck. "What other inconvenience? Why did they contact you before that?" The week before last—that was right when I first set foot in the Herd . . . "Was it about the graffiti?"

"Graffiti? Do I look like a vandalizer to you?"

Vandal, I corrected him, silently. He smirked—he was enjoying this, having something over me.

Then the penny dropped. "It was about her phone."

"The allegedly stolen phone, yeah. Which, if she can't keep track of her shit, that's not my problem. Where is Eleanor, by the way? Still hiding out from the messes she's made of her two companies?"

Messes? Gleam and the Herd were both turning huge profits and bopping around the top of best-places-to-work roundups. "What's your problem with her, really?" He started to groan and I barreled over him: "No, I'm serious. What has she done to make you mad?"

"What she did was illegal. Barring a demographic from a public space—that's some 'whites-only' shit." With every ounce of self-control, I leaned forward and nodded, and he went on: "She's such a smug little bitch. She gets everything she wants without even trying. And she's devoted her life to dangling that in everyone's faces."

"How so?"

His palms winged upward. "Are you serious? Her blog, her companies—her whole brand is basically: No Boys Allowed."

I gazed at him. I thought of what I had to say next and sadness billowed in me, threatened to burst out from behind my face. Swallowing, I flipped over the only card I had: "Eleanor's dead, Carl."

Three tiny movements, all at once: Shock whipped across his face, he leaned back as if to distance himself from me, and his hand shot to the back of his neck, settling on the overgrown tufts there. "Shit," he finally said. "Dead how?"

A teakettle-like shriek as the barista steamed milk. "How about this: I'll tell you something if you tell me something."

"Oh God." The eye roll returned.

"How did you find out she was missing? When you texted me last week, I mean?"

"I have my ways."

"Illicit ways?"

"What, are you going to turn me in to the police for observing that she was supposed to speak at a highly publicized event and . . . didn't? Oh right, you already did." He sneered. "Anyway, my turn. What happened to her?"

"She was killed." My stomach squeezed and I let it rush out: "Someone slit her throat." I wanted to watch his reaction but I couldn't; I felt lightheaded and tipped my head forward.

"Fuck." He sounded uncomfortable. "I'm sorry."

I inhaled wetly. "Is that going to end up on the Antiherd? If it does get out, I'll know it was you."

"I don't know what you're talking about."

"I think you do." I hunched forward again. "I want access to the group."

"No way. Not gonna happen." He leaned back. "Look, I'm sorry about your friend, but . . . if you were friends with Eleanor, why would I help you?"

"Just a second." I slid my phone out of my back pocket, then turned up the volume.

The voice leaking out of my iPhone was tinny and shrill: ". . . got out of the Lincoln Tunnel I had a couple confused texts from you, and the diner was empty. I was *livid*. Really great use of . . ."

His eyes bugged. "You were recording me?"

I touched the headphones still resting on my neck. "They make great built-in microphones these days. The sad thing is that in real life, unlike in movies, I can't hit one button and have it play back the most damning sound bite. But I'm sure you remember it. 'Smug little bitch,' et cetera."

He was beside himself. "But . . . but that's illegal!"

"It's not. And you should calm down—people are beginning to stare. Hey, your offices are down here, right? Rebecca Rosenthal?"

At the sound of the CEO's name, his face turned coral-red, his ears like two plums. "This is stupid," he announced. "You don't have the balls."

"I also have nothing to lose. Unlike you. With your job." I leaned forward. "I won't post in the Antiherd. I won't take screenshots or share anything. I just—"

"So you're playing kid detective? Just let the grown-ups do their job."

A *fuck-you* rose up through me but I bit it back, rearranged my face into a blinky earnestness. "Carl." I tapped his forearm and he recoiled. "You're right. I know it's stupid. I don't want to get anyone in trouble. And I really don't want the cops to know I'm looking into this on my own. I just want to figure out who . . . who hurt my friend." My voice wobbled and again, he reared away from me.

"Twenty-four hours," he finally said. "I'll give you twenty-four hours if you delete that audio file right now, in front of me. And then you fuck off forever."

———

At home I flung open my laptop and logged into my new, male, fake Facebook account (*Fakebook!*), and then felt a surge of adrenaline as the notification appeared: *You've been invited to join the Antiherd.* I wasn't sure what I was looking for, but I started with last Tuesday, the day we reported her missing. Some useless general hate speech, things that turned my stomach, reminded me of the panicked feeling I got while reporting from rallies in Michigan. I crossed to the kitchen and pulled out a seltzer, breathing hard, then forced myself to keep reading.

A few minutes later, I hit gold: A dude with a police scanner had posted about the 911 call from her address (which, creepily, said user knew by heart); the "possible ten-fifty-seven" had led to much gleeful speculation that her sad, whipped husband probably skipped town to get away from her. Gavin K commented that maybe the bitch had seen the light and killed herself, and someone else—Ron A—replied that that was unlikely when she'd just announced she was going to make herself even richer: He'd linked an article about the Titan acquisition, which had gone up just a minute before.

I clicked on Ron's name and scrolled through his most recent posts and comments; he hadn't uploaded a profile photo, so it was pretty clear this guy had a secret account for his hate speech. (*More Fakebook!*) My heart seized up when I saw a photo he'd posted to the Antiherd a few weeks back: a faded shot of a female teenager . . . no, a child, maybe twelve or thirteen but struggling to look older in the awkward getup of circa-Y2K—flared jeans, platform sandals, budding boobs under a corseted crop top. The face was unmistakably Eleanor's: pretty even then, but rounder, her eyebrows thinner, her skinny arms a deep tan. Above and below the photo were strips of diagonal grayish lines, zigzagging into short columns, and I realized they were the gluey backing of an old-school photo album; someone, somewhere, had cracked open a dusty old album and snapped this picture of a photo inside.

It was presented without comment, but other users had quickly jumped in: "Born a whore," "A cock-teasing bitch even then," "lol people probably hid from her on the playground." How had anyone gotten their hands on this? The original photo—someone had snapped it, developed it, stuck it lovingly on a cardstock page and smoothed clear plastic on top. The only place where you could find similar pictures of Hana and me was in our mother's living room, in the musty albums in our bookshelf. Maybe Eleanor's parents kept something similar in their house. Who would've had access to it, what visitors or neighbors or . . . ?

Neighbors. The kids next door. I looked at the fake username again. Ron was typically short for Ronald, of course, but could it also be the tail end of Cameron?

Goosebumps rose on my arms as I scraped back through everything I'd learned about him: Ted's older brother, Eleanor's boyfriend both of her senior years, high school and then college. I searched for his Facebook profile—the non-fake version—and clicked through his photos. He gave the vague impression of a once-hot guy who'd lost his mojo and then felt bewildered by his dwindling prospects. His profile photo was of him in a Patriots T-shirt, his face painted, making a tribal yell in front of the open back of an SUV, all set up for a tailgate.

Outside, the snow was like a silvery mist filling the empty space around fire hydrants, trees, grimacing pedestrians. The thought was as hazy as the light: *What if Cameron* did *hate Eleanor?* He lived in another state, of course, but he knew people here . . . and he might have friends in this disgusting online community. What if he'd found someone to help him, or vice versa? The bubble letters from my first day at the Herd flashed before me: UGLY CUNTS.

I was still reading through jabbering vitriol, none of it useful and all of it jabbing at my gag reflex, when Erin texted: "Call me now." Another text from my roommate, and then, as I was unlocking my phone to read her entire message, ones from Mikki and Ted. The calls and messages came like the snow had this afternoon—a few errant flakes, then steadier, and then suddenly a storm.

With shaking hands, I opened the *New York Times* homepage, and there it was at the top: *Eleanor Walsh, Lifestyle Guru and Feminist Entrepreneur, Dies at 30.*

Isn't she thirty-two? I thought numbly. Another text from Erin: "You're going to kill me."

CHAPTER 16

=====

Hana

I stared out the window as my cab sped toward Daniel and Eleanor's apartment. *Just Daniel's now* — the thought was a bubble of sadness. Trash levitated and spun in the wind before smacking back into the sidewalk. The streets were already emptying as people headed home for the holidays.

What could Daniel possibly have gotten his hands on? *It's about what happened in 2010*, he'd said, his voice almost a shriek; and *you don't want police*. The driver braked hard in front of the townhouse, and I pushed the car door open against the wind. My third visit this week — much more frequent than when Eleanor was alive. Something deflated in my chest as I looked at her home's dark bay window, its empty stoop. On Tuesday night, I'd charged inside with the then-absurd notion that something had happened to her, something bad. On Wednesday, I'd come back to browse, fumbling around for some guidance, a clue. Some reassurance that our secret was still safe. Now Eleanor was dead and Daniel knew about 2010. For a shimmering second, I thought I would vomit.

I marched up the steps and rang the doorbell. A wreath was thawing out from the week's deep freeze. The door swung open and a puff of warm air floated past me. Daniel looked awful: hair greasy and unwashed, skin sallow, eyes swollen. Both gaunt and puffy, somehow.

"Daniel, hey. I'm glad you called me."

He closed the door behind me and I gave him a long hug. Before this week, I'd never seen him be anything other than cheerful and removed, a polite conversationalist at parties and events but what Mikki had called *a tough nut to crack*. Now misery wafted off of him in waves.

"I wasn't sure what else to do," he said. "I mean, your name was on it."

"On what?" His eyes bugged, and I gave a brave little smile and gestured toward the living room. "Should we sit down?" We were still in the disorienting entryway of mirrors.

He gazed over, like he was working out what the words meant, then nodded. "I'll go grab it."

I pulled my coat off as I made my way into the living room. I had that rushing feeling, the sense that something irreversible was about to happen. Daniel clattered down from the second floor, his steps staccato, then presented me with a sheet of printer paper. It was creased in thirds, like it'd arrived in an envelope. I took it from him and blinked:

RE: MAY 7, 2010
DATE DUE: 12/31/19
JINNY HURST
ELEANOR WALSH
HANA BRADLEY
MIKKI DANZIGER

Then strings of numbers—a payment amount, network cost, and account number. I looked up at Daniel, frowning.

"It's about ten thousand dollars," he said. "In Bitcoin. I think it's blackmail Eleanor was paying anonymously."

I gasped. "Where did this come from?"

"It was in our mailbox." He swept his hand toward the front door. "I hadn't checked it in a week, with everything going on. But then I went back through our bank statements. There were withdrawals, odd numbers from our different accounts, adding up to about ten thousand dollars a quarter. Going back a year."

"Jeez." I frowned. "Did you look at the postmark?"

"Yeah, it was sent Wednesday. From Nashville, of all places."

Wednesday—*after* she went missing. The sender believed Eleanor was still around and able to pay.

I held the paper aloft. "Could this be why Eleanor was trying to get away? If she couldn't go to the police, I guess that'd be a reason to try and disappear. Although, I don't know. Forty thousand dollars a year is a lot of money, but not something she couldn't keep up with."

"Hana, what's this about?"

I ignored him, reread it again.

"My first instinct was to call the police. Have them dust for fingerprints, investigate the cryptocurrency account." He swallowed. "But my second, stronger instinct was to talk to you first. Because I don't know what this means." He pointed at the sheet quavering in my hand. "I don't know what Eleanor did."

I took a deep breath. The image of her flashed in front of me: eyes closed, nose flour-white, a wide, black smear along her collar. A few sharp sobs juddered out, and I sniffed. "I don't understand either, Daniel," I said. "Eleanor didn't do anything."

"Who's Jinny Hurst?"

I shook my head, tears slipping from my eyes.

"I looked her up, Hana." He was breathing deeply, as if fighting down the impulse to take a swing. "I know who she is. So what the fuck is her name doing on this list, with Eleanor? With *you?*"

"I don't know her!" I wiped at my cheeks. "I only met her once. Right before she disappeared. We bought drugs from her one time—she was a dealer. I don't even remember who had her number. I only saw her the one time."

We sat together for a beat, the only sound the distant hum of traffic, car horns and rumbling trucks, their drivers barreling through today like any other day. Suddenly Daniel snatched the sheet from me. "Then what the fuck is this?"

"I don't know! I have no idea." My eyes filled with tears. "Here's what happened: Right before graduation, the three of us were hanging out at Eleanor's apartment one night. That Friday. The date on the sheet." I flicked my chin toward the paper. "Eleanor had . . . she'd tried mushrooms at a party the weekend before, and Mikki and I admitted we'd never done it. It was just this stupid idea—safe space, a bonding moment or whatever. Eleanor had gotten this woman's number at the party, so we had her pop over and we bought some stuff off her." I sniffed, wiped my nose. "But she went missing that night. They never found her. We were pretty freaked out when we saw it on the news a couple days later, but of course we had no idea what happened to her . . . and we weren't going to be like, 'Hi, we met her while breaking the law.' Nothing happened. I haven't thought about it in years. But none of us had anything to do with that."

Daniel kept shaking his head. "I can't . . . why would somebody send this? And why would she *pay* it?"

"I don't know. If you Googled Jinny, I'm sure you saw she's from Tennessee, originally—where the postmark's from. The only thing I can think is . . . Was there something else Eleanor never told us?"

Daniel's lips shook like he was either trying to speak or trying not to cry. Probably both. "We should tell the police. Right? This has gotta be our best lead."

"It sure seems like it. God, this is wild." I took the sheet and re-read it. "I just wanna make sure . . ." I hesitated and my eyes filled with tears again.

"What is it?"

A little laugh. "Ugh, always the PR girl. So, Eleanor's a public figure. I don't want to see her name dragged through the mud—for your sake, not to mention Karen and Gary. Oh God. She couldn't have had anything to do with this woman's disappearance, right?"

He just kept shaking his head. He let out a horsey noise and dropped his brow into his hands.

"Do you want me to talk to Mikki?" I said.

He stood and walked out of the room. For a confused second, I thought he was ending the conversation, but then I heard the rush of liquid against glass and he reappeared with two waters.

"Hana, I'd give anything to know who killed her. This could help."

"I would too." I grabbed a glass. "But you said this came *after* she disappeared, yes? I know it's upsetting, but . . . that means whoever sent this has no idea Eleanor's gone."

He sat and looked away, his chin trembling. "I don't know, Hana. I can't think straight."

"How about this: I'll ask Mikki if this means anything to her—maybe she knows something I don't." I set my glass down and leaned forward. "We'll get through this, Daniel. I know how much you love Eleanor, and you know I feel the same way."

He balled his hands against his eyes and nodded. "If she did something . . . bad, I don't wanna know. I don't want to live out the rest of my life thinking that about her."

"Okay. Okay. Let's just . . . get through today. They're gonna make an announcement soon, and I think the best thing to do is just batten down the hatches. Okay?" I sat up and spoke softly: "You know to just hang up if journalists get your number, right? And you should close all your curtains. They might set up out front."

"I know. I'm not talking to anyone. I learned that a week ago when I basically had a gag order until they checked out my alibi."

"So they did clear you."

"Yeah, they talked to . . . the woman I was with. From Click. And I showed them the messages." He looked away. "Talk about fucked-up timing."

It popped out before I could think it through: "Well, unless Eleanor knew you were going to be gone that night."

He rubbed his forehead. "And had chosen it as her night to fuck off to Mexico? Yeah, the cops mentioned that too. But the big announcement at Hielo. She seemed so excited. I don't know."

Your wife, I thought, *was extremely skilled at keeping things from you. From all of us.*

"Have the cops told you anything new?"

His eyes vaulted up and to the left. "Not a lot," he admitted. "Last night they said it probably happened Monday night, based on what she was wearing."

So after Mocktails. "At the Herd, then?"

"Yeah. They aren't sure where in the building, though. There wasn't enough . . . enough blood on the roof for it to have been there, so she was probably moved." He cleared his throat, his voice shooting out in a loud clap. "If whoever did it couldn't get her out, it was his best option because of the cold: no smell. The problem is that nobody knew the Herd was a crime scene—the entire office, I mean, the whole floor—so it's all been compromised. The janitor's been through a bunch of times since then, so finding clues or whatever is unlikely."

"Shit." I frowned. "Are they going to test for DNA?"

"I don't know. It hasn't even been twenty-four hours. They want to search here again." His voice cracked.

Jesus. They could be over any minute.

"If you're okay, I think I'll get going." I pulled my coat on. Daniel didn't move, his jaw resting in his palm, his eyes staring into the distance. "Let me know if you need anything. Memorial service, dealing with journalists—you name it. And obviously, don't talk to anyone." I finished zipping my coat and paused. "Basically, don't trust anyone."

I blinked into the late-morning sun and descended the subway steps. As I rumbled home, my brain hazed in and out of coherence. I kept picturing the slash I'd seen on Eleanor's throat, a casual diagonal, like a finger mindlessly dragged across a fogged-up window. The murder weapon—no one had said anything about the murder weapon. My mind kept returning to the little knife she kept in her office. The only sharp object I could think of when I mentally wandered through the Herd.

I cried for a bit, my chest seizing with a fresh wave of horror. The other people in the subway car, two teenagers and an elderly woman, averted their eyes. Then another break in the fog: Those freaking surveillance cameras. Useless thanks to the router reset. *Could someone from the internet provider try to recover the data? No, it wasn't a technician from the company who came—it was Ted.*

Ted.

The subway squealed to a stop; the doors clanged open and people trotted in and out.

Ted, who watched his beautiful best friend, the literal girl next door, date his brother and then go on to fame and fortune while he continued splitting a house in Bay Ridge with three roommates.

Ted, one of a very few non-members who had easy access to the Herd. To Eleanor's office, to the knife on her shelf. I pinched the bridge of my nose. I'd always thought of Ted as sort of uncomplicated and hapless, the one guy who'd do anything for Eleanor. His devotion to her had bordered on unnerving, but in a way, I'd almost envied it—wondered, privately, what it must be like to have a man worship you like that. No way he could've . . . ?

At home, I checked my email and had only a few, which meant the news about Eleanor hadn't hit the papers yet. Way out in India,

Stephanie relayed that she was still trying to catch a flight back; the coming storm made rebookings a nightmare. I pictured her on the beach in Goa, coconut in hand, wondering if the Herd was hers for the taking when she got back. Aurelia had emailed to relay that, per the ongoing investigation, the Herd would be closed until further notice ("through the end of the year at minimum") and could I please disseminate this news? Not even one day, *one day*, to mourn the loss of my best friend, her supervisor. The thought of writing a media alert, one carefully crafted and bristling with low-stakes bad news, made me want to sink to the floor and stay there until January.

In the living room's floor-to-ceiling windows, snowflakes bopped in the breeze. The impending "snurricane." Those who weren't traveling for the holidays would be treated to a white Christmas. The rest of us were screwed.

I was still poking away at the press release, willing my brain to focus, when my video intercom shrieked. Two figures, standing shoulder to shoulder and towering over the sweet nameless doorman.

"Ms. Bradley, you have two . . . guests?"

"Who is it?"

A beat. "They say they're detectives."

I glanced around—the apartment was still a mess, my coat and umbrella slung on the floor, sheets and pillows on the sofa where I'd set up Katie for the night. My pulse picked up its tempo, but I couldn't say no, couldn't send them away without arousing suspicion.

"Send them up," I replied.

"Ms. Bradley, how are you?" Ratliff called as I opened the door. Behind her Herrera was stout and tense, like a closed fist.

I shook their hands, then murmured, "Thank you for coming," like a host at a dinner party. *What?*

"We know you were at the precinct until quite late last night,"

Ratliff said. "But time is of the essence, so now that you've had a little time to process, we hoped to go over everything again."

"Of course." They followed me into the living room and hovered as I moved the pillow and duvet from the sofa to the hallway. I felt their eyes on me, watching, judging.

"Didn't realize you had guests," Herrera remarked.

"Just my sister. She stayed here last night." It was a little odd she hadn't checked in, come to think of it—earlier, she'd been *very* interested in my trip to Daniel's. "Can I get you two anything?"

"No thanks." Ratliff pulled a notebook from a pocket and opened it with a flick. "So as you know, we were just in the process of closing the investigation. Based on the email you and your friends had gotten."

I nodded. "It looked like Eleanor had left town. Moved to Mexico. But now it seems pretty clear someone staged that to, to throw us off their trail or whatever. Whoever sent those texts and emails from her account is the obvious smoking gun, no?"

Ratliff's face revealed nothing. Her eyes could be catlike, intelligent but expressionless. "We've determined those texts and emails were sent from Ms. Walsh's phone," she said. "From the vicinity of her apartment."

I frowned. "You're sure they were from her brand-new phone? Not the stolen one? 'Cause if someone just logged into her iCloud from the old one . . ."

"The new one. Purchased the week before."

"Okay." I watched Cosmo amble into the room and sit, his tail swishing. "Well, if it was the vicinity of her apartment, it was also the vicinity of the Herd. They're within a few blocks of each other."

"That's correct. Unfortunately, we've only narrowed it down to a cell tower's range. Location services were turned off."

Herrera leaned forward. "You're sure you haven't seen her new phone anywhere?"

"What, just lying around? No. Obviously the killer took it with him." I opened my palms. "So either he stuck around the neighborhood the next morning, or he made it look like he did. Even I know how to use VPNs."

Ratliff made a note. "Backing up, can you tell us exactly what you were doing the evening of Monday, December sixteenth?"

I felt a prickle of fear. "I was here. Getting everything ready for the announcement. Sometimes I have trouble focusing at the Herd, so I went home midday."

"Directly home?" she said.

"Yes. I had lunch here." I swallowed. "I was in all night."

"And the front desk could confirm that? I saw they have CCTV."

"I think so. Actually, wait." I shook my head. "If I was coming from the subway, I'd take the side entrance. Gets me inside faster when it's super cold. But they'd have footage of me leaving the next morning."

They had me repeat some things I'd already shared: How I knew Eleanor, my role at the Herd, how Eleanor had seemed these last few months, what I thought about Daniel. The last one was the hardest: How does anyone feel when their spectacular best friend partners with someone who is . . . fine? He was *fine*, inoffensive and sweet, appropriately head-over-heels for Eleanor (I'd thought), and good in all the checklist ways a best friend watches closely: He respected her independence, wasn't intimidated by her success, made a passable effort to be chummy with her friends, check, check, check. He wasn't as incredible as Eleanor, but then again, who was? He had an unglamorous yet stable job as a hospital administrator and vague interests in running and nice foodie restaurants and CrossFit. Right now he was on my Nice list for calling me instead of the detectives upon finding that blackmail note. Today's one-on-one conversation was the longest Daniel and I had ever had, I realized. Hopefully he hadn't mentioned it to the cops.

"He always seemed like a great guy," I wrapped up. "Eleanor was really ready to meet someone—she even set a deadline and said she was going to manifest a partner by whatever date. And then they seemed happy together. Our gang is kind of a . . . girls' club, we don't often bring our partners around when we're together, but he's, you know. Good people."

Ratliff glanced down at her notepad. "Okay. Let's talk about anyone you think might have had a problem with Ms. Walsh, a grudge against her."

Involuntarily, my eyes flicked onto my coat, with the blackmail note shoved deep in a pocket. Picturing it shot my chest with coldness, fresh as mint. Had someone from Jinny's family gotten it in their head that Eleanor was responsible for Jinny's death? But of course I couldn't bring it up.

"The graffiti," I said. "I mentioned it again last night. Someone broke into all the Herd sites, spray-painted profanities on the wall, and later stole her phone. I'm sure you have this somewhere."

"We're still looking into that," Herrera said.

"Well, thank you." I sighed and looked around the room. "Who else? She has internet trolls saying terrible things to her all the time, of course. I think there are even dedicated message boards. But nothing lately, no stalkers or threats or anything." Except the blackmail letter, which was a kind of threat, I supposed. "I'm also curious if the Titan acquisition will go through with Eleanor gone. I'm not really clear on who was supposed to benefit from it, other than Eleanor. I forget her lawyer's name, but Aurelia—she's sort of the number three, I know you talked to her—she should be able to connect you."

"That's very helpful. Thanks."

"Anyone else?" Herrera prompted.

"The one thing is—" I faltered, fell silent.

"What is it?" He leaned forward.

I sighed. "I don't even think it's worth bringing up."

"Sometimes the tiniest details or even intuitions turn out to be helpful," Ratliff said.

"Okay. It's probably nothing, but . . . her friend Ted, his name's probably come up, right? Ted Corrigan." I swallowed; suddenly my heart was thrashing around in my rib cage like a baby bird. "I just keep thinking about how much access he had to the Herd. More than any other man I can think of. He was Eleanor's go-to handyman-slash-IT-guy, so he was in there maybe a few times a month. After hours."

I scratched at my eyebrow. "He came in a few days before she went missing to reset the router. And I guess they now think that's what kicked the new cameras offline. Which seems like a big coincidence, right?"

"Are you saying you think he shut down the cameras in anticipation of attacking her?" Herrera set a fist on his hip.

"No, that's—now that you say it, that's ridiculous. I know Ted; he wouldn't hurt a fly." I shrugged. "I was just thinking . . . I don't know, he always seemed to carry a torch for her. And you know how in the news, you're always hearing about these guys who go berserk after a woman romantically rejects them? I just . . . I wonder if she rebuffed him at some point."

"Do you know for a fact that she rejected him?" Ratliff asked. "Was there an incident?"

"No, nothing like that. Forget I said anything." Guilt whooshed up through me. *Why had I sicced them on Ted?*

"We'll look into it," Ratliff said. "Now I need you to do something difficult. Can you walk me through last night again, from the moment you went up onto the roof?"

I sighed, exhaustion and gloom filling me up from the inside, from my bones, but I squeezed my eyes shut and repeated it, frame by frame. When I got to the part about seeing the gash in her neck, Herrera jumped in.

"You saw a line cut along her neck?"

"Yeah, a line. At least, I think it was a line." My brain cued it up, an image projected on a massive screen, and I felt a wild pitch of nausea and despair. "She keeps a knife in her office, you know."

"We're still looking for the murder weapon," Herrera replied, and then he tapped near his Adam's apple. "See, it's actually less of a slash and more of a stab. We're still waiting for the coroner's report, but on sight he thought it looked less like a knife or scissors and more like a scalpel." He punched his fist toward his neck.

"A scalpel," I repeated. "Why would anyone have . . ." I froze. I knew exactly one person who worked in a medical center—a bustling, sprawling spot with stockrooms around every bend. I'd sat on his couch and sipped his water this very morning.

"Something *like* a scalpel," Ratliff explained. "And scalpels are easy to get your hands on—you can pick one up at the Rite Aid down the street, believe it or not. But for someone to have been carrying it . . ."

"That would mean it was premeditated. You think someone went there to murder Eleanor." My voice had swooped into hollow amazement, like I should punctuate it with a whistle.

"We're still—"

"Exploring all possibilities, I know, I know," I finished.

"Ms. Bradley, is there anything else you think we should know?"

I thought about it. "Maybe someone was bitter about not getting in? The Herd gets way more applicants than they have spots for. And women were really rabid about it, there were online forums about trying to get in and stuff. Maybe you'll find something there." I clicked my tongue. "Eleanor pissed a lot of people off. Just by being fabulous, by being an ally and a champion. And she was so calm about it, so brave. Took it all in stride. Never asked for . . . for support." My voice cracked and I inhaled sharply.

"There are counselors available if you'd like to speak to someone," Ratliff said. She was starting to gather her things. "Thanks again for your time. We'll see ourselves out." But still, I rose and ushered them to the door. I pointed them back in the direction of the elevators and wished them happy holidays. When I looked back, the snow outside had thickened.

My phone had more missed calls and texts than I could fathom. Mikki's fought its way to the top: "CALL ME NOW."

"Someone leaked the news about Eleanor to the press," she said, her voice pinched with fury. "Eleanor's parents hadn't even had a chance to tell their friends yet."

She directed me toward the *Gaze* article ("EXCLUSIVE") that'd broken the news an hour ago, written by a reporter whose byline I didn't recognize; it had very little information, the cause and time of death missing, but it did have the date and location of the discovery of her body. A whole wave of other articles had come out rehashing the same sparse details, and a showy obituary was on the homepage of *The New York Times*. I fought down a groundswell of nausea as Mikki's righteous anger chopped itself up into profanities.

"Okay. Okay. I'll call my contact at *The Gaze*," I said soothingly. "I'll figure out who did this. It could just be a crooked cop, someone trading secrets for cash." I flopped back on the couch and glanced out the window, where a curtain of snow had smeared away the outside. Would every Christmas from here on out be haunted by visions of this one—Mikki's disembodied sobs, Katie sniffling on the bed next to me, Eleanor's boots poking out from behind the lounge chair, toes up like they belonged to someone admiring the night sky?

Katie was calling.

"Did you see the alert?"

The urgency in her voice poked at me—so unlike the milky sadness I'd just settled into.

"About Eleanor? I'm trying to figure out who leaked it."

A beat. "I was talking about our flight. They just canceled it."

"Shit."

"What should we do?"

"Call the airline. Both of us."

For seventy-five minutes I paced my apartment, intermittently tidying up and then crashing onto seats to stare out the window. I hated the hold music for a while, then got into it, nodding along involuntarily, and then circled back to hating it again. When I finally reached someone, the news wasn't good.

"So we're missing Christmas," Katie wheezed into the phone.

"I mean, Christmas is occurring regardless," I replied. "But I feel bad we're not going to see Mom."

"Me too. Plus I wanted to get away and curl up in my own bed and block everything out for a while. And now we can't."

There was something fluttering in me, mothlike: I was relieved. Not having to interact with Mom, to deal with her bright, fake laughter and needling criticism, not having to sit around a tree and sip cocoa and listen to old hymns while Eleanor's unsolved death hung over us—there was something appealing about it, a bottle uncorked.

"I'm disappointed too," I said, "but what can we do? At least we're stuck here together."

"I guess." Katie's misery was contagious. "Well, I'll call Mom and let her know. She's probably been watching the flight and already knows."

That stung, deep in my torso. "Tell her I'll call her tomorrow. And that we'll talk on Christmas, obviously."

"Tell her yourself," she snapped—then three beeps, and she was gone. Outside, the snow churned and throbbed against the window, like something trapped in a glass cage and trying to get out.

Suddenly I realized what I was forgetting, the to-do that had been flickering in the back of my brain all day. It blared inside me, cranked up my pulse. On shaking legs, I walked over to the coat closet and pulled out the blackmail note, popping out the crease and swiveling my wrists to smooth it. I read it over one more time, although by now I could recite it by heart. The same page had been showing up in my own mailbox for a full year now.

With practiced hands, I ripped it in two and rolled the first into a tight cigarette. I crossed the kitchen and turned the stove on, four even clicks and then the *boorrsshh* of a blue flame.

As I had with three blackmail notes before it, identical but for the deadline at the top and the name on the envelopes they arrived in, I burned its halves one after the other. The ashes swirled like snow before coming to rest on the steel below.

CHAPTER 17

═══

Katie

I was grateful for the flight cancellation, in a way; for the ninety minutes I was dealing with it, groaning and texting and falsely thinking each intermittent "please stay on the line" was a human about to help, I didn't have to think about what my agent, Erin, had told me earlier in the afternoon. Because I *couldn't* think about it, couldn't face it, the sixty-foot tsunami about to come crashing down all over me. Mentally I stuck it on my to-do list: Solve problem, save my own ass.

I called Mom, who picked up this time. I told her about Eleanor, my voice fracturing into sobs as I tried to answer her questions, and she kept repeating, "My poor baby, my poor baby." Then I told her about our canceled flight, and she was as composed and soothing and deeply, deeply sad as I imagined she would be. She clearly already knew about the cancellation but feigned surprise, a long three-note moan between "awww" and "ohhhh."

We were wrapping up when Hana called again.

"So I just got off the phone with Eleanor's parents," she said. "You've met them, right?"

"Yeah, once or twice."

"Well, I called to help them write their statement for the media now that some jackass leaked the news about Eleanor." A puff of shame went through me. "And I kinda can't believe this, but they invited us up to their house for Christmas. They have nonrefundable Amtrak tickets for Monday—for Eleanor and Daniel, but I guess he's spending it with his family now. And when I said our flight was canceled, they insisted we come up."

"They want us to take their dead daughter's tickets?" I said. "That's the most morbid thing I've ever heard."

Hana let out a little *oof*, like I'd wounded her.

"Sorry. I don't mean to . . . but don't you think it's weird?"

"I mean, I can see them not wanting to be alone in that big house on Christmas Day. They're really warm people. They were always so nice to Mikki and me. And I guess Ted and Cameron's parents kinda sucked, so they were like surrogate parents to them too." She cleared her throat.

"Wouldn't we be . . . imposing? Don't they want to grieve privately right now?"

"I said the same thing. Asked over and over. They really want us to come, Katie. Mikki, too, assuming she can't get to Asheville. They're calling her now."

We would go, obviously. This felt like a freebie: a perfect chance to see Cameron in the flesh, maybe even scour his and the Walshes' home for a photo album with navy herringbone glue on each page. And, though Hana still had no idea I'd been talking to Ted, it wouldn't be hard to sneak off and see him. But I knew she had to feel it was her call, so I said, "I don't know, Hana. Maybe we should use the next couple of days to process instead of tiptoeing around and being polite guests, you know?"

She sighed. "I just want to feel like I'm . . . in a *home*, not my sad, sterile little apartment." I hesitated and she added, "You'll *love* them."

"Even forty-eight hours after they found out their daughter's been murdered?"

"Okay, they won't be at their cheeriest. But we can keep 'em company, maybe even help out around the house for a few days. They don't have other kids."

"You're sure it's a good idea."

"I have no idea if it's a good idea, Katie." There was a tremor in her voice and it sliced through me. "But I know I want to go."

I swallowed. "What time is our train?"

Penn Station was miserable any day of the year, a Dante-esque cacophony of burnt coffee and pee smells and bad signage. On this particular Monday morning, it was worse than ever, since, with all flights grounded, trains were one of the only means for escaping the city. The masses were crabby and high-strung, unsure if they'd make it home in time. The scene reminded me of rallies in Michigan, where I endured jeers and boos on my break from nursing my sick mother. This hellhole was almost *satisfying* in its terribleness: an external match for my emotional interior, which in turn resembled Munch's painting *The Scream*.

In the Amtrak waiting area, Hana was jealously guarding two seats, tucked between a pile of shrieking toddlers and a dude in a baseball cap loudly braying into his phone. Two wrestling kids tumbled onto my foot as I picked my way through.

"*Oooh, heaven is a place on Earth,*" I sang, jazzily sweeping my arm out. Hana glanced up and it was clear she'd been crying; I collapsed into the seat next to her. "Hi. I got us cinnamon-sugar pretzels. Self-care."

"Thanks." She gave me a side-hug. "How are you doing today?"

"Well, you know." We'd both spent Sunday alone in our beds, binge-watching the same Netflix show and texting occasional commentary, ignoring the torrent of calls and emails from journalists seeking comment on Eleanor's untimely death. She nodded and plucked open her greasy bag, then chewed thoughtfully.

We rushed down to the train the second the track was announced, arms and hips and children and suitcases buffeting us about as we Tetrised our luggage onto the rack and plonked into seats. I yanked on my headphones as we emerged from under the station and into a gray-white wonderland, the air still swollen with snow. There was something sad but soothing about our pilgrimage to Beverly. There, I wouldn't have to worry about Mom and Hana snapping at each other. There, we wouldn't need to act cheery or try to put into words who Eleanor was or what she meant to us. It was like a multiday memorial, a walking wake. Remembering Eleanor: The Experience.

"Hey, I meant to ask: What happened with Daniel on Saturday?" I said as we pulled away from a stop. "Was he okay?"

"Yeah, he just needed someone to sit and cry with him. Said he was numb when the cops told him the news Friday night, and then he didn't sleep, so by the morning he was a wreck. But he was okay by the time I left." Outside the window, an occasional sight pierced the white: a flicker of tree trunk, the flash of a red house. "What'd you do after I left?"

I thought back; she had no way of knowing I'd paid Carl a visit at Ghost Cafe. "Pretty much the same—I sat around and cried. Only with Cosmo, instead of Daniel."

She regarded me for a second, then nodded. She got out her earbuds, prepared to seal off the conversation.

"Did you ever call Mom?" I asked.

"Ugh, I completely forgot. I will soon. How's she doing?"

"Okay."

We both went back to staring at the woolly world outside.

A few hours into the ride, Hana's phone rang. She'd been dozing and I watched as she startled, then stared at the screen. I didn't catch the name, but she answered in a low voice.

She listened, hunched over, piping up with the occasional, "I'm sorry, what?" and "Can you repeat that?" and "Are you sure?" The female voice on the other end of the line was fucking livid, and Hana turned to shoot me a barbed stare before standing and walking off toward the end of the car. It was the shocked, betrayed look a dog aims at you when you've pretended to have a treat and then opened your empty fist. My heart plummeted. It was over. As Erin had warned. *Hana knew.*

I sat there, bathed in that cold, rushing feeling. My teeth began to chatter and I wished there were an escape hatch, somewhere I could run and hide. Finally, Hana returned and sat down carefully, staring straight ahead.

"That was Aurelia," she said, her voice soft and terrifying. "Katie, please tell me. That you did not tell your publisher. That you'd write a tell-all exposé about Eleanor."

My jaw was chittering too hard for me to open it and speak. Slowly, slowly, she turned to look at me.

"Tell me it's not true."

"I didn't call it a tell-all exposé," I said with the voice of a five-year-old. She made me repeat myself and I knew I was fucked.

"Let me get this straight," she said, lifting her eyebrows. "You told your editor you'd write a book about Eleanor." I nodded. "And you didn't ask for permission or come talk to me about it." Nodded again. "And so you were secretly reporting out this book for a proposal, knowing full well Eleanor hadn't and probably wouldn't sign off on it." I started to protest and she went on: "No, don't even. Because I also know that you've been feeding your agent confidential information, and that—no, listen to me—that is the reason news of her death was leaked. Which fucked up the investigation and has made the NYPD furious. *That's* what you've done."

I knew I should apologize, should roll over and show my belly, but defensiveness barreled out first: "Okay, I had nothing to do with the leak. I told my agent everything we discussed was in confidence and she messed up, *she* let it slip to a coworker, who apparently passed it on. And I one-hundred-percent planned to talk to you—and, and Eleanor, originally—when the time was right. I hadn't even started a proposal yet. I was just trying to see if I could report this out instead of my other book idea because that didn't work out. But this was just deep background, and obviously that was before she went missing, and I would never—"

"Just *stop*!" Hana shot both palms out and I recoiled, like she'd hit me. "Katie, stop. You're not talking your way out of this. You're not—actually, you're doing exactly what you always do, using my connections and then making a mess of them and then trusting that ol' Hana's going to be here to clean it up for you."

My jaw dropped. "What are you talking about? You kept—"

Someone shushed us, fiercely, and we both whipped our chins over to an elderly man across the aisle.

I lowered my voice. "You kept trying to hook me up with your fancy-ass contacts, and you know what? I didn't take a single meeting. I didn't take you up on a single goddamn thing, because I knew you would do this, you'd lord it over me and continue to tell yourself and everyone else that I can't do shit without you, that I'm this useless little kid who can't take care of herself—"

"Can you? I mean, look at yourself. You get all this money to write this amazing book, and what do you do? You throw it away. And what do you mean that other idea 'didn't work out'?"

"It's not—I wasn't trying to—"

"And anyway, my God, I am *so sorry* for trying to help you. For trying to get you into the Herd when there are hundreds of women dying to get in." This was disorienting, this was churning around in a dangerous riptide, which way was up, who was *this* Hana? It wasn't like my sister to be cruel, to go for the throat.

"Hana, I—"

"You ride on my coattails and then you're shocked, *shocked*, when shit blows up in your face. Well, guess what, this bomb managed to take a bunch of us out with it too. I hope you're happy, Katie. Even I can't swoop in and fix this."

"I ride on your coattails?" I tapped furiously at my collarbone. "I force you to deal with the real shit? Answer me this: Who the fuck moved to Michigan when Mom got her diagnosis?" I sat up straighter. "Who ran off to California with Dad and left her ten-year-old sister behind the *second* shit got tough? You think you're the one who has to deal with real problems? You know what, fuck you. I know I'm supposed to be grateful that you *deigned* to let me into your life at Harvard, just like you've *deigned* to help get me into the Herd. But guess what: Mikki and Eleanor liked me too. They wanted to be my friends and you hated that." I leaned my face close to hers. "I'm sorry to break it to you, but I'm not just your fuckup, piece-of-shit little sister. I'm a real person, and honestly? People seem to like me better than you."

The train thundered along its track, jolting suddenly and sending both of our shoulders swaying. But she kept her eyes on me and, after a second, my insides did something complicated. I'd thought it would make me feel better, winning the fight, landing a true burn. Instead I just felt sick.

"Well, that escalated quickly," I said feebly. The second that followed contained this whole shimmering alternate timeline where Hana cracked a smile and pulled me into a hug and said something smart and soothing about how stressed we both were, how racked with grief, and let's try it again and find a way forward.

The vision faded as the intercom crackled: "South Station, South Station, this is the last and final stop, all passengers must depart."

"If you're so independent," Hana hissed, "find somewhere else to stay tonight." Then she stood and reached over me, yanking down her suitcase with such ferociousness, it almost clocked me in the head.

The snow was lighter here, and actually pretty, an idyllic scene like those porcelain winter villages old ladies set up in their living rooms. Orange-brick churches with spindly spires and immaculate parks and fat streetlamps all stamped with quivering towers of snow. I admired it with a kind of Dickensian sullenness, feeling unwanted and pitiful as I stood behind Hana, looking out over the parking lot. She'd huffed off of the train and out of the terminal without so much as a look back, and I'd trailed her here, darting around people and tripping over suitcases to keep up. Now she was sighing impatiently and calling someone over and over, presumably Mikki, who'd gotten into town a few hours ago and was supposed to pick us up. Hana flung her arm in the air—"I'm waving, can you see me?" and finally I tapped her arm and pointed toward Mikki on the opposite end of the pickup zone. Hana spotted her and took off.

Usually Angry Hana was exasperated and lively, rolling her eyes and muttering, *You've got to be kidding me.* This was worse. Quieter, more controlled. We finally, mercifully, all made it inside the car, and Mikki and Hana chatted in the front: This was the Walshes' car, yeah it was nice of them to invite us, they seemed to be doing okay, keeping it together. Hana ignored me so completely, so aggressively, that Mikki followed suit.

I tried to find a hotel for the night, halfheartedly, but since it was Christmas Eve Eve, most places were fully booked or astronomically expensive. Hopefully the house would be big enough for Hana and me to avoid each other inside. And she'd have to be nice to me in front of the Walshes, I figured. The last thing she'd subject them to was our own familial strife.

I texted Ted: "You with your fam this evening?"

Warmth spilled across my torso as I saw he was typing right back. "Glad you're coming. Heading over to the Walshes' now to snow-blow their driveway."

Knee-jerk, my brain whipped up a joke (*Does this make you the blowjob guy?*), and then I felt a sickening punch. *Eleanor is dead. None of your stupid wisecracks matter.*

We rolled through the eerie white streets as Christmas jazz leaked from the speakers. A few final turns and Mikki turned into a driveway. Here it was, the Walshes' grand eighteenth-century home, now squatting on the corner of a street with smaller, newer Colonial houses spreading out in all directions. It was like something out of a novel: a perfectly symmetrical mustard-yellow Georgian with an odd stubby roof, orderly white trim, and huge, stark shutters flanking the seeming millions of windows. A portico stuck out over the front door like a snout, and beneath it Ted was clearing off the front porch. Everything was frosted in a dollop of snow.

As Mikki killed the engine and we gathered our things, I went over my mental checklist: tracking down the photo album. Meeting Cameron, perhaps asking a few pointed questions about his feelings toward Eleanor, his activity on secret Facebook groups. Seeing Ted, getting one of his long, healing hugs. Hana may be furious and the book might be fucked, but those were feelings I pushed down the road, onto the snow-covered lanes that stretched to the left and right of us.

CHAPTER 18

Hana

I could feel Katie smiling in the backseat, I could feel it without looking, as if the corners of her mouth were disturbing the air inside the car, shaking up the molecules. I was so angry the anger was blinding, something I had to keep blinking through, like a blindfold somehow yanked on from beneath my skin. We passed the Corrigans' white mansion, and while the columned home was dark, light spilled out from the cottage in the backyard. Cameron's domain, the old carriage house. A half block down, we pulled into the Walshes' driveway, snow crackling under the tires, and Ted stopped snow-blowing and waved cheerily. Ted, the reason the Herd lacked security-cam footage from Monday, December 16. I hated him in that moment.

Gary and Karen appeared in the door: "Come in, we can't have you freezing to death out there." We stamped our boots on the welcome mat and hoisted our suitcases into the foyer. I breathed deeply—a faint cedar smell, that woody tang of historic homes.

Pleasantries were even more awful than expected: The Walshes had crinkled bags under their eyes, sadness wafting off them in waves, and yet they welcomed us bravely, took our coats, offered us cider. They'd set out sandwich fixings in the kitchen, but none of us ate anything. In my torso, I felt a deep, internal ache, more like exhaustion than hunger.

Gary and Karen had pulled out the sofa in the den for Katie and made it up with plaid sheets and a triangle-pattern quilt, and the sight of it made me want to weep. Their perfunctory kindness blasted through me, a grenade. They left us alone to "freshen up" and Katie turned and said something about hotels being sold out tonight, and I stalked upstairs without letting her finish. I rolled my bag into Eleanor's room—they'd placed me here and Mikki in the guest room, which only felt creepy now that I was alone among Eleanor's things.

This was where we'd hung out when visiting from college, sprawling across her bed or on the floor. I could almost see the three of us, our younger, silkier, frothier selves. Once, fascinated by these close new friends whose pasts were a mystery, we'd all described what we were like in high school. Mikki had been an arty kid, choosing her outfits from the thrift store at first out of necessity and then with determined weirdness. And though she didn't use the word, it wasn't hard to ascertain that Eleanor had been popular. At the time I'd felt even more thrilled that they wanted to be friends with me: straight-A, straitlaced, teacher's pet Hana, now in with the A-listers.

Nearly a decade had passed since graduation, but the room was untouched. I felt like someone entering a museum exhibit as I moseyed up to the bed, smoothing a palm over the cloud-print comforter. Framed posters studded the teal walls: a Miro print she'd purchased at a museum store, a woodcut pattern that was probably a sheet of expensive wrapping paper, an unofficial movie poster for

Pan's Labyrinth, pink and black and eerie. I flopped onto the bed and cried, an indulgent, sobbing, sniveling cry with long wet sniffs powering huge, braying cries.

The holidays always made me feel sad. Ninety-nine percent of the year, I could be happy with my life, with everything I'd built for myself: the close friends who served as my surrogate family, the career I loved and clients who adored me, the quiet thrill of competence and action and determination and, of course, external validation: *You did good.* And then the holidays rolled around and with them, a torrent of pictures and updates and hashtag-*grateful* (somehow less basic than #blessed), shiny happy people with their beloved families, writing odes and 'gramming pies. And something about all the Rockwellian joy split something open, a crack through which envy flowed, a little girl crying up at the sky and realizing life's not fair. *I want that.* I wanted a mom who actually wanted to see me. A dad who made special cheese dips and built fires on Christmas Eve, not a man I'd stopped calling years ago only to realize he didn't care, wasn't about to pick up his end of the relationship. I knew these were Champagne problems, peanuts compared to the family strife millions of others felt. But every year, around this time, I'd look around at the wreaths and pies and blinking holiday lights and ask into the starry heavens, my own "Silent Night": *Why these parents, why this, why me?*

But at least I'd had Katie. Even when we were thousands of miles apart on a holiday, I knew I could reach out, squeeze her hand under the metaphorical table. She had the same shitty dad, one even more distant to her than he was to me, and while she and Mom were closer, she saw it, understood how Mom pushed me away like the opposite end of a magnet.

And then this year, my makeshift, chosen, surrogate family had whiffed away like a candle flame. Eleanor with a hole in her neck. Katie with her secret project, just inches behind my back. It was so hurtful, it still felt unfathomable. And then to whip it around on *me?* I realized why that move felt so familiar: It was right out of Mom's playbook.

I was an idiot. I'd stupidly thought being here would be nice: This loving couple, unlike the parents I'd grown up with, scooping us in as if we were their foundlings. This grand home, with its multiple family/living/recreation rooms—it was like a life-size dollhouse, unlike the small ranch we'd all lived in before high school, and then the two-bedroom apartment Dad rented in Culver City.

Oh, Culver City. What a bold move that'd been, in retrospect: announcing, adultlike, that I was leaving Kalamazoo and joining Dad in California. He and Mom had been fighting for months, for years, and then one night, as Mom was scooping out the casserole and complaining that he was late for dinner, he called to say he was in a hotel in Wheaton, heading west and never coming back. I was fourteen years old and gutted by the two months that passed without him. I told everyone it was just because Mom and I had never gotten along; Dad was laid-back and lax, the kind of "cool" parent all teens want. Plus, as I admitted only in my angsty middle school diary, Mom seemed to resent my presence, though it was entirely her own fault: She and Dad had adopted me when I was two, shortly after a series of miscarriages and dismayed acceptance that they'd never be biological parents. Two years later, Katie had been their miracle, their dream come true. And I was the odd-looking child inconveniencing them.

Of course, Dad wasn't any more interested in parenting than Mom was. He set me up on the daybed in his new apartment—I never got a real bed, never thought to ask—and continued on with his adult life, finding a job and dating new women and leaving me to fend for myself. How lucky for him, for both my parents, that I was smart and determined, that I got myself into Harvard no thanks to them. When he'd driven me to LAX for my flight to Boston, my suitcases almost bursting in the trunk, he'd turned up the baseball game on the radio in lieu of talking. I'd spent the entire drive—plus the six-hour flight—panicked about how I'd get myself from Logan International to my dorm.

But then, like a dummy, I'd thought things would be different after I graduated. I was an adult now, too, not someone he was expected to care for—not that he'd done much of that. That summer, I moved across the country at the last minute, ostensibly for a job at a tiny PR agency but in reality because I needed to run, needed to put as much land between Massachusetts and myself as possible. Then the loneliness really descended, like a heavy velvet drape: Eleanor, Mikki, and Katie having fun in New York City, and me miserably staring out at the Pacific. When Eleanor had begged me to move to New York and help her start the Herd six years later, I'd wept with relief.

I padded into the hallway and knocked on the guestroom door; inside, Mikki was crumpled on the bed, on top of the quilt.

"Hey," I said.

"We need to go to the police," she replied. "About the Bitcoin."

I sat on the edge of the bed and swallowed.

Eleanor had called Mikki into her office the day she got the first blackmail letter a year ago; mine and Mikki's had arrived that same morning, so we were all caught in the same hellish conundrum. In low voices, we'd debated; Mikki admitted that Jinny's mother, still a high school teacher in Tennessee, had just been looking at her on LinkedIn. It might be her, we reasoned, the one person to whom Jinny had mentioned her whereabouts, now pushing us to turn ourselves in or at least make her life a little easier. The one person still searching for Jinny.

Mikki had suggested coming clean, giving the poor woman some closure, but Eleanor had shut that down. "I'll pay for yours if you can't afford it," she'd hissed, and Mikki had blushed. Again, Eleanor had sealed off the incident, cauterized it on the spot: *We never, ever speak of this again.* And we hadn't. And it had been working out fine, unless this woman—or someone she knew—had made their way to New York with Eleanor in their crosshairs.

"I don't think we should," I said. "But here's the thing: Daniel got one of the letters. Meant for Eleanor."

"*Fuck.*" Mikki tugged a pillow over her face.

"But he doesn't want to know anything about it, about what Eleanor did. I didn't tell him we've been getting them too. He let me take the letter, said the last thing he wants is to sully his memory of her. So it's still okay."

Mikki hugged the pillow to her chest. "I looked the mom up," she finally said. "Definitely looked like she hasn't been anywhere near New York this month. Or ever."

"I did the same thing." The minute I'd gotten home from Daniel's apartment, before I'd even opened the envelope I'd yanked from Eleanor's bed, I'd tracked Celia Hurst on all her feeds and apps. She always tagged a location or checked into spots on Hopscotch throughout her day, and certainly it appeared she was going about her life in Bristol, Tennessee. An alarming thought hit me and I shoved it away: *What irony that'd be, if she'd collected our money and used it to fund her trip to the Big Apple—to fund Eleanor's murder.* "We're gonna get through this. There's nothing tying us to Jinny, and they'll figure out who killed Eleanor and throw them in jail and, I promise, we'll be okay."

She wiped at her nose. "I just miss her."

"Me too. So much." I nestled into the pillow next to her and together, we cried.

I sat up. Mikki was gone and I was still on her bed, the quilt rumpled beneath me. The sky was purple gray and half a moon squinted into the window from between two clouds. Time had felt so strange this week, ballooning and shrinking from hour to hour. I spotted a clock on the wall—still late afternoon.

I crept back into my room and looked around, taking in the details, all things that Eleanor, once a living, breathing, red-blooded girl, had chosen, given places of honor in her bedroom. A Frida Kahlo portrait watched me coolly from above the door. Had Eleanor truly planned to move to Mexico, or was it a harmless fantasy? It felt so campy and farfetched. As ridiculous as my best friend turning up dead on the roof of her own company headquarters. The teenage girl who'd picked out this cloud-covered comforter never saw it coming.

My eyes fell on her yearbooks on one end of her bookshelf: thin, stapled ones in grade school and then shiny hardcovers in high school. I pulled out the last paperback one; growing up she'd gone to school with Ted and Cameron, if I remembered correctly, and I was curious to see them all as kids. But when I pulled it out, it wasn't junior high, as I'd expected: Hillside Elementary School was splattered across the cardstock cover. But the year was just a year before high school, and Eleanor was in . . .

Right, the two skipped grades.

Suddenly I was sick of being alone. *Why come all the way up here to hide in our respective corners?* I went out into the hall and paused at the top of the stairs, facing a window that overlooked the back patio. The pool. That fucking pool.

It'd all been innocent. We were so young, drunk on our youth and promise, rising stars about to set the world on fire. We'd proposed toast after toast, clinking our shot glasses together heartily, sampling different bottles from Gary's vast booze collection, aged Macallan and Hendrick's Gin and a weird, licoricey Hungarian liqueur, its bottle the shape of a cartoon bomb. And that's what we were—bombed.

I gazed down, as if this were a play, as if I could travel back in time and watch from up here. My eyes rolled across the girls below: Eleanor in her mother's silk robe, me lining up Solo cups on a side table, Mikki in a crop top and jean shorts, fiddling with the music. And Jinny: skinny, relaxed, with huge wire-rim glasses and a patch shaved from her black hair above one ear.

Her backstory was the stuff of legend: Jinny, the story went, had hopped a train north to escape from her family, squashed in a trailer home in Appalachia. She'd stopped in New York but hated the vibes there, so she continued north, settling somewhere outside Boston. She was a few years older than us, and Eleanor had met her during her high school years. We rule-following Harvard students all had girl crushes on her—we were honored when she chose to hang around after making a delivery, shooting the shit and enjoying her wares with us. She'd dropped out of high school the moment she turned eighteen, had lived on the streets when she and her crust-punk boyfriend had split, and there was an aura of danger around her, a thrilling rebellious streak. She lived somewhere between Cambridge and Beverly—we were never sure where, and it probably changed by the week—so it was a no-brainer to hit her up while the three of us were in Eleanor's hometown.

We'd all been giddy that night—it was finally warm and graduation was a few weeks away, and Eleanor had just scored her investment meeting to get Gleam off the ground. In fact, it was a celebration: Eleanor's parents were out of town, so we'd have a secret party, not telling anyone or posting on social media so that our other friends wouldn't feel left out.

In my mind, the little figures on the patio milled around: Booze was everywhere, splashing into cups with pours of Sprite or Diet Coke. Coke, real coke, from Jinny's backpack, little lines Mikki expertly arranged on the patio table. Tabs of Molly, of course, and some ketamine, though I was too scared to touch it. Jinny had had a little of everything, and she was rolling, seemed genuinely happy to be there with us.

We were playing music from somebody's phone, dancing next to the swimming pool. I could feel it all: the dizzying hum of the season's first cicadas, wafts of lilac eddying around, a few fireflies strobing in the lawn. Mikki cueing "Empire State of Mind" on her iPhone and clapping in delight as Eleanor stood to shout-sing along: *"Let's hear it for Neeew Yooork . . . "*

Someone had had the great idea of going for a swim. And Eleanor said it was fine, as long as we left everything how we found it. So we'd peeled the pool cover back halfway, folded it on itself, then stripped to our underwear and jumped in. Diving and doing handstands and dunking each other, so full of life and liquor. Jinny's eyeliner bled down her cheeks. I had the dizzy notion we were all best friends that night, Jinny was one of us, although we only saw her every few months, although she knew much more about our lives than we did hers.

I watched as the imaginary Hana below me had another idea, the decision that would change the course of our lives. *Pizza.* I'd wanted frozen pizza, volunteered to make it, climbed out of the pool shrieking about the cold. I'd closed the patio doors behind me and stumbled to the basement, holding on to shelves and things to keep from falling as I made my way to the chest freezer in the back. And I'd found a box, pepperonis and sausages and tiny squares of red and green peppers glistening on the front, and hugged it to my chest idiotically before beginning the climb back upstairs.

The lights in the kitchen had been on, and using up my full, drunken concentration I'd found a pan, sliced at the pizza's plastic covering—*careful, careful with the knife,* I told myself. The other three were still outside, music blasting. I managed to get the pizza onto the cookie sheet and slide it into the oven without burning myself, and I'd celebrated that small victory for a moment before realizing I hadn't turned it on.

I was still fumbling around the kitchen when someone banged against the glass door, and I screamed and dropped the Coke and rum I'd been clutching. Then Mikki threw open the sliding door and stepped inside, tripping over the base.

The next part was hazy, the timeline unclear.

Jinny fell, Eleanor cried, slurring and sobbing as she stumbled inside. They were dripping everywhere, trembling from the wetness and the terror. Jinny had slipped and hit her head on her way into the pool, they said again, and they'd tried to get her out but she'd gotten herself tangled in the pool cover, fighting them off as they tried to yank her out. And then she'd gone limp. By the time they'd pulled her onto the cold cement, she was already gone, already cold, already dead.

If I'd been out there . . . well, we'd never know. But it was easy to imagine things would have turned out differently. I'd have noticed her more quickly, coordinated our rescue effort. I'd have run inside and dialed 911. But even then, standing just inside the sliding doors, drunk and damp and high, I'd done nothing.

I've thought about it a lot since then. Perhaps I didn't protest because my inebriated mind was performing some unspoken calculations. Four drunk women, three of them white. The cops who'd come knocking if we dialed those three numbers.

All at once, as I stood in front of the second-story window, sparkly static whooshed in front of my eyes, and my hands and feet screamed out with fizzy tingling. Holding on to the wall for support, I shuffled back into Eleanor's room, closed the door, and sank to the floor.

My eyes fell on her grade-school yearbook, still leaning out from the shelf. It snapped into place, like popping a single bit of bubble wrap. Eleanor's *Gleam On* article, the one we'd worked so hard on together, me pushing for more details until it was just right: The Herd's origin story, how she'd hated this junior-high-only Adventure Camp, ropes courses under the male gaze, the long yarn from that to New York's premier all-female coworking space and community. But if she hadn't gone to middle school . . . ?

Would Mikki know what to make of this? It was probably nothing, some simple explanation; Eleanor had gone to camp in grade school, maybe, and she'd moved the story up by a few years to make it more relatable, fudged the dates. I wandered the house, peering in on seating areas scattered every which way. Again, it struck me how cavernous this mansion seemed, how easy it was to lose a person, tangled in the neon-blue tarp stretched like skin over the pool outside. Mikki was nowhere to be found and this just compounded my confusion, a general sense of disorientation, of reality crumbling off in tiny flakes.

I almost walked directly into Karen, who was coming out of the basement, carrying wine.

"I—I wanted to see if you needed help with dinner or anything."

She looked alarmed. "It's not even five yet," she replied.

"Oh. I . . . I fell asleep."

She inched toward the kitchen. "Well, speaking of five o'clock, I was just going to open this nice Merlot blend. Can I get you some?"

She chattered nervously as she battled with a corkscrew, and I took in the scene: two empty bottles lined up by the sink, a lipstick-stained glass she'd pulled over next to her. While we visitors had retreated to our quarters, Karen had been drinking. Before today, even at fancy restaurants, I'd never seen her finish a glass.

She carried over two hearty pours and I clinked hers before taking a sip. Her small-talk soliloquy made me nervous; normally Gary was the talker. Finally she ran out of steam and fell silent.

"Can I ask you something?" I asked. "About Eleanor, I mean." I looked down at the wine, gave it a little spin.

"Of course."

"She skipped seventh and eighth grade, right?"

"That's right, yeah. The school psychologist thought she'd be fine jumping *three* years ahead, but we thought that was a bit much."

"Right." I took another sip. "But she seemed okay with two?"

"Oh, she thrived." Her voice cracked. "She seemed so relieved to be challenged, to not be sitting in class bored out of her skull. That boredom was much harder for her, being so far ahead of the other students. She'd grasp a concept in two seconds and then the class would spend two weeks on it."

"For sure. That must've been awful." I tapped a nail against the glass, listened to the chime. "How did you know it was bothering her? Was she acting out, or . . ."

"It wasn't good for anybody. She was always . . . almost too smart for her own good, I'd say." She grimaced. "Certainly smarter than the rest of us here, that much was clear."

There was discomfort in this, pain in the jokey self-deprecation. Sober, she might have been able to cover it up, but I saw it in the way she recovered, curled herself over her glass.

"This is gonna sound random, but did she ever go to an adventure camp? Like in the summer, before the school year?"

She swallowed and looked up; her eyes made it clear she had no idea what I was talking about. "A *what* camp? Adventure? That sounds like Eleanor's nightmare."

"Okay. So she didn't . . ." I wrapped my fingers around the glass's spine. "It's just weird, because when she announced she was starting the Herd, she wrote this essay. And . . . maybe she was just remembering it wrong, or conflating it with something else, but . . ."

I saw Karen's eyes, white and round as two sand dollars, and stopped. It was that *Oh crap* look, equal parts bewildered and defensive.

"I'm getting all mixed up," she announced, touching her temple. "I haven't been eating much and then I just went ahead and opened this wine because it's what we do when Eleanor's here for the holidays, and usually Gary or someone will say, 'Hey, it's five o'clock somewhere!' and so I just . . . I thought . . ." Abruptly she pushed both palms onto her face and I watched in alarm as her shoulders shook, her crying somehow both huge and tiny. After a moment I scraped back my chair and put my hand on her back, rubbing gingerly, but she didn't seem to notice.

"Do you want me to find Gary?"

She shook her head, her hands moving with her face.

"Do you want . . . should I help you upstairs, do you want to lie down?" This she ignored, too, and I thought suddenly of my mom, what she'd definitely want in that moment: "Would you like to be left alone?"

A little sobbing noise slipped through her fingers and she nodded. I thought about attempting a hug and instead gave her shoulder a final pat, then headed back upstairs, dread building in my lungs with every step.

I'd seen Karen cry like that exactly once before. When I woke up in Eleanor's bed almost a decade ago, I'd been so hungover my skin hurt, my eyeballs, my bone marrow, every cubic inch of me. I'd lain still while my sludgy brain tried to figure out how much of the night before was a nightmare, a bad dream.

None of it, it turned out. It was all real, too real. In the late hours of May 7, while Jinny's body leaked blood onto the patio, we rising stars had listened to Eleanor, cocaine coursing through our veins, alcohol gnawing away at our brain cells. We faced her, crying as she decided we couldn't handle this now, her parents would know what to do, we should move the body inside and then deal with it in the morning, when we were clearer, when her parents could help.

I'd watched, trying not to scream, as Eleanor and Mikki carried Jinny inside and laid her on her back. We'd turned off the lights and huddled together on Eleanor's bed, afraid to be alone. As we shivered in the dark, Eleanor told us again why this was for the best—graduation was around the corner, we had illegal substances in our systems, it would be clear we were breaking the law, our futures could be ruined. Plus we'd already moved the body, and there was no guarantee anyone would believe that it was an accident.

Then Mikki had begun to freak out, her chest heaving, *I can't breathe, I can't breathe, I can't breathe.* And Eleanor had run her fingers through Mikki's hair and said we would get it all straightened out in the morning.

We'd woken to the sound of Karen's screams. They'd gotten Eleanor's voicemails, begging them to hurry home, but we'd slept through their calls back. Eleanor had explained everything, all three of us sobbing with high-pitched coyote sounds, and Karen had cried silently, shoulders shaking, just like she had a minute ago.

Gary asked about Jinny's age, several times, confirmed that she was older than us. Nailed down exactly who this woman was, what we knew about her, who might come looking. It later dawned on me that he was doing the math: a stranger, a homeless, vagrant drug dealer, careful not to set down roots nor leave a trace. Now, it occurred to me that he'd be found responsible alongside us, since there'd been a minor—Eleanor, secretly twenty—drinking in his home.

He'd looked each of us in the eyes, speaking kindly, carefully: *And you're positive you didn't tell anyone about this trip. That no one knows you're here.* We'd all nodded, sniffling like toddlers.

Then you drive back now. You say you never left campus, had a quiet night in. Work on your story on the drive home, get it straight, repeat it until you can say what happened down to the tiniest detail. From this moment on we never, ever mention that girl again.

I reached for the old-fashioned knob on Eleanor's door and locked myself inside. It was dark, abruptly, like a riptide had yanked down the sun. So Eleanor had lied—convincingly, to my face—about the

Herd's origin story. *But why?* Had something else happened around that time that made her long for a no-boys-allowed club, but she fictionalized it for the *Gleam On* blog? I tried calling Mikki, listening hard in case I could hear the ring—no luck. *Hmm.* Karen wasn't about to tell me, but Cameron or Ted might know something, a secret or story squirreled away from their shared childhood.

I grabbed my purse and headed downstairs. As I turned into the hall, I paused in front of the door to the den. It was closed, Katie shut up on the other side of it. Her words still stung, her defensive flailing, but I felt a sudden, sisterly urge to tell her about the weirdness with Karen and about Eleanor's odd fake Adventure Camp story. Katie was smart, her brain making pinging, Christmas-light connections I'd never spot on my own, so maybe she'd have some insights. Actually, she'd been researching that damn book—maybe she knew something I didn't.

I knocked, softly and then three crisp thumps. The old door was closed but not latched, so my last bang sent it swinging inward. I caught the knob in my hand, apologizing as some of the room came into view, and then froze. There was movement, a scramble, and then four eyes stared back at me, wide as raccoons'. The rest of the scene sorted itself out around them: Katie and Ted were on the pull-out couch, her with one end of a sheet pulled up to her heart, Ted with another end strewn over his lap.

The spell broke and with a little shake of my head, I turned away. "Oh my God, I'm sorry, the door wasn't latched."

More rustling as they presumably flung clothes on. "Hana, is everything okay? What are you . . ."

I peered out into the hallway, but mentally I kept hinging back and forth between them: Katie . . . and Ted. Ted . . . and Katie. This felt unfathomable, like learning your coworker met your childhood friend while backpacking across Nepal.

"Sorry. I was just—I don't know where anyone is, and I was

gonna walk over to Cameron's. Just wanted to let you know. Is he . . ." The awkwardness plumed, filling up the room like smoke. "Ted, is he home, do you know?"

"Uhhh . . . I think so. Try his cottage first." His voice ached with embarrassment.

I pulled the door closed, tugging too long in an unsuccessful bid to get it to latch. Then, face burning, I yanked my coat from the hall closet. A hunter-green backpack on the floor caught my eye; it wasn't mine or Mikki's, and it hadn't been here before. Something of Eleanor's, pulled out by Gary? The top gaped a bit, and I couldn't help myself—I nosed it open and pulled out the manila folder inside.

My chest froze: The first page was a printout of a Click profile, annotated in small, spiky handwriting. *Eleanor.* I turned the page: bank statements, Eleanor's account number printed at the top, all slightly askew like someone had snapped surreptitious photos of the originals. Sprinkled with dots and arrows and question marks. Nausea mushroomed in my belly as I continued flipping through: a copy of a scratched-out Post-it, a meaningless code in what looked to be Eleanor's handwriting. Then a confusing block of numbers and text, and I had to follow the scribbled annotations for a few pages before I realized this was Eleanor's browser history, filched from the router.

The router. The knapsack, rugged-looking yet expensive, was obviously Ted's. *Why on earth had he been stalking her? And where had he gotten all this? Had he broken into her home,* or—the thought like a flashbulb—*Eleanor's office at the Herd?*

I glanced back down the hallway, where Ted and Katie were still closed up in the den. *She was safe with him, right? Where the hell was Mikki—where was everybody?* I slipped the folder back into the bag, zipped up my coat, and hurried out into the tundra.

CHAPTER 19

════════

Katie

Hana rattled the doorknob for three excruciating seconds, four, pulling at the door and twisting hard as I squeezed my eyes closed and silently begged her to stop. Finally, she did, and we listened as she moved farther down the hall.

"Sooo . . . that was awkward," Ted announced, correctly.

I cupped my hands around the lower half of my face, then glanced at him. "Really? Because that was part of an elaborate ploy to indulge my exhibitionism." He looked at me with enough alarm that I flopped back on the bed. "I'm *kidding*. Haven't you noticed by now that I make stupid jokes when I'm uncomfortable? Because holy hell, am I uncomfortable."

"You and me and her both." He zipped his jeans and sat back on the bed, springs creaking. "What do you think that was all about? I thought you two weren't talking."

"We weren't. I have no idea." Already, her intrusion felt removed, like a scene that should've been cut from a movie. Everything about today had had a sad, cinematic, dreamy quality to it, come to think of it. The huge mustard-yellow house that looked exactly like I'd pictured it. The thin hallways and rattling windows and multiple fireplaces, all the architectural details I'd walked past on a self-guided tour, running the pads of my fingers over every surface. There wasn't a speck of dust here, not anywhere.

Earlier today I'd spotted a lineup of photo albums in a seating area near the front door. Sitting cross-legged on the floor, I'd pulled one out and opened it, gluey pages sticking as I dragged them across the binder rings. Eleanor in first grade—too far back. I tried another where Eleanor was a little older, skinny and shiny-haired with a mouthful of braces. I found the right era, bell-bottomed jeans and neon tube tops, but I never did find the exact shot I'd seen in the Facebook group, the one on the page with the zigzagging blue glue behind it.

Surreal, that was the word for today. An entire lifetime had passed since we'd left Penn Station, and it wasn't even dinnertime. It was instantly clear our visit was a bad idea; Gary could hardly speak and Karen kept babbling, high-pitched and taut. After poking around in their photo albums, I'd come upon the grieving couple drinking wine in the kitchen and felt an instant urge to apologize—here I was, a stranger wandering their home as they tried to mourn their freshly killed daughter. Gary looked up and his expression told me he was thinking the same thing—what the hell was I doing there?— but Karen had waved me over and fetched a glass for me.

They'd asked me questions, politely pushing over follow-up after follow-up like a long line of dominoes. I told them about my free-lance work, living in Michigan for a year, attempting to join the Herd. They asked about my book project, about the fake-news fac-tory in Iron River, and my chest seized up as I mumbled something about still nailing down a new angle since the research hadn't gone as planned. I was cagey but they barely seemed to notice, each wrapped in their own cocoon of grief.

And then Ted had walked in, cherry-nosed, and explained that the snowblower's shear pins had needed replacing mid-job, but luckily his dad had a set back in their garage, which was all to say that their drive was snow-free and the snowblower was in better condition than when he'd taken it out of the Walshes' garage. They'd listened blankly and then murmured their thanks, and Ted had noticed my *save-me* glance.

"Ted, I was actually hoping you could show me how to do something on my laptop," I said, "for an interactive story I'm writing? I could use your help."

I'd started to rise and Gary picked up the cue, announcing he was going to head to the basement to watch the Patriots game. Exchanging looks, we'd all left Karen with her back to us, staring out at the darkening patio. One sconce was like a spotlight on the snow-covered pool.

It was a bit of a blur after that—in the den, Ted had remarked, *Oh, I love this room,* and I'd pushed the door closed without really thinking, and then I'd sat on the foldout bed and asked how he was doing, and he said he'd been unable to sleep last night, thinking about Eleanor, and I agreed and started to cry and said we never should have come, never should have imposed on Gary and Karen, and he'd gently wiped a tear from my cheek and said that he, for one, was glad I was there, and then he let his hand rest against my jaw and then my palm went to his chest and then, and then, and then.

And then Hana burst in, and now she was gone, and the room had that dizzying, whiplash quality, gears switched so suddenly and so entirely. Right when things were about to get good, to be honest. When Ted and I had probably both been wondering who was going to float the idea of obtaining a condom first.

Now I just felt confused. Something had happened, something

had nudged Hana out of her fury storm and back into speaking-with-me territory.

"I'm gonna try calling Hana. We were fighting, like, two seconds ago, so she must've come in here for a reason." I patted at the bedding around me in search of my phone. "Siblings are the worst."

"They are." He leaned against the sofa's back and rubbed his beard. "They're, like, the only people you can take your stress out on. And we're all pretty upset right now. Cameron was just yelling at me about me not paying off a parking ticket in person for him or something."

"A parking ticket? *Definitely* not your problem. Anyway, this is different. Hana's right—I did something pretty shitty. Oh, here it is." Finally I spotted the screen's glossy blackness on the hardwood floor. I called her, then dropped the phone back onto my lap. "Straight to voicemail. I hope she's okay." I gazed out the window, where old-fashioned streetlamps cast golden, bell jar–shaped glows. "I wonder why she's going to see Cameron. She probably wasn't getting any attention here."

He raised his eyebrows. "Getting any attention?"

"You saw how Gary and Karen were being."

He nodded. "What were you two fighting about?"

I took a deep breath. "Like I said, it was my fault, she wasn't being . . . overbearing, or anything." And then I told him, how I'd been grabbing furiously for something else to write about. I recounted how panicked I'd felt, how I would've said anything to make the nightmare end—the furious agent, the advance I couldn't repay—and it was only after the words had left my lips that I realized what I'd done. How a book was all I'd ever wanted, ever since I was a little girl in Michigan, filling notebooks with stories and using markers to make fake picture books, writing "author" on every line that asked what I wanted to be when I grew up. And how it'd all fallen apart now—how my idiotic agent had told the wrong person, turned Eleanor's death into a public spectacle. I stared at my hands as I spoke, methodically dragging my thumbnail across each cuticle, and when I finished speaking and looked up, Ted had uncrossed his legs. Subtly, like a wilting flower, he was leaning away now.

"Why couldn't you just write the book about the fake-news people?"

It was the same question Erin had asked a couple weeks ago, and even she had sounded less judgmental, more curious. What a mess I'd made.

"I'd rather not talk about it."

He frowned, nodded slowly. "But, like . . . was it worth it? Selling out your friend so you could keep the book deal?"

My whole face contorted around my eyebrows: "I just said it was shitty. I feel awful."

"Right. I just . . . Eleanor was probably going through a lot and didn't need her friend sticking her under a microscope. I bet she could tell, and that it sucked."

I stared at him, my eyes and mouth both o's. He looked around the room, anywhere but at me, and shrugged. "I'm just saying."

Tears surged down my cheeks. "Are you saying it's my fault she tried to leave? That she got killed?"

He reared away from me, like I was an unexploded grenade. "No. Shit, don't cry. I'm just, I dunno. I feel bad for Eleanor. She was my friend. *Hey.*" He pulled me into a hug and I cried on his shoulder for a moment. "We're all tense. Let's breathe."

"I'm gonna try calling Hana again," I announced, turning away. I accidentally opened my phone's photos app, and it gave me an idea. "Hey, have you seen this before?"

He grabbed it and looked close, the image I'd copied from the Antiherd, tween Eleanor in her low-slung jeans and corset top. "Ha, where did you find this?" He grinned. "It's in one of our photo albums at home. Cameron used to tease her about it."

Cameron. The air in the room felt different, quivering, a sudden drop in cabin pressure. I fished around for a red herring: "It showed up on a memorial site today. I've been seeing what fans are posting online."

"Yeah, that was probably him." A wistful chuckle. "She was a firecracker."

I grabbed my phone back and gazed at it. This little Eleanor—Ted had known her as a tiny thing, had probably biked around the neighborhood with her, played night games in the dark. I'd met her when she was just a teenager and she'd awed me then, brilliance blazing like a blast of heat. And if Ted was right, I'd played a part in snuffing it out. I'd made her feel like she was in a fishbowl, turned the Herd into a crucible. Suddenly I was crying again, wet lines streaming from my eyes and nose.

"I think I wanna be alone," I managed.

"You sure?"

"I'm sure."

He pulled the door closed behind him and it didn't latch, swung open a second later, so I could hear him clomp down the hallway, rustle for his bag and coat, and slip out into the night. I lay still for a while, humiliation and fury beating around me like a huge heart. Because he was right: I'd tried to sell out Eleanor, one of my best friends, to save my own ass. Chasing wildly after prestige, after my Big Fancy Publishing Deal, somehow caring more about impressing my agent than about my actual friends. All because I was a fucking unethical moron during my year in Michigan.

For a moment, it'd all seemed too good to be true: After a few weeks of playing nurse to Mom, feeling lonely and useless, I'd spun my sad move to Kalamazoo into gold. My article on nearby Northern Sky Labs, pitched on a whim after someone from high school mentioned she knew the CEO, had gone viral; Erin wanted to represent me, a bona fide publisher wanted to make me an author. Now, finally, I had something new to focus on, something to give my life structure and meaning, something solid and impressive to tell my former high school classmates when I bumped into them at the drugstore. It would be great, because it had to be.

And at first, it was. The CEO, a charismatic fortysomething named Bill, was an ideal antihero: witty, outrageous, totally unapologetic in his pursuit of profit. His little brother, Ben, was CTO, and though he lacked Bill's charm, he seemed to be the more sympathetic of the two, glad to be making Scrooge McDuck levels of wealth for the first time in his life, but tormented by the implications of their creation. Bill's taciturn wife handled the bookkeeping, and she made my life easy—scheduling interviews, ushering me into investor meetings, inviting me along on extracurricular activities, fishing trips and boating days and picnics and ATV outings, the kind of scenes she correctly assumed I'd need to add some color to the narrative. She was small and striking, brilliant in an unsung, under-the-radar way, married to her high school sweetheart and quietly fulfilling about four hundred roles.

And we became friends. How could we not? I was so lonely, not eager to leave their small headquarters and see Mom in her frailty, and so she and I stayed late some nights, or even drove together to her pinewood home, sipping beer and chatting. She wanted to know everything about New York, every detail, and then in gummy tones I told her how good she had it—this husband, this house, this unexpected windfall, making money from the social-media scramble without having to compete in the twenty-four-hour beauty pageant herself.

And we were deep into one such conversation early in the fall, sitting on her plump, floral-patterned sofa, on a Monday night when her husband, Bill, and brother-in-law, Ben, were down in Chicago for an expo. I'd brought over some brandy and we were talking about high school, comparing our experiences—her with twenty-eight other kids in her graduating class, Bill among them, and me just an hour away with close to two hundred classmates. And how we'd both found others to serve as armor: her BMOC boyfriend, now husband. And my sister and her cool friends at Harvard, the ones who loved when I visited, who saw past my bad skin and braces and made me feel less invisible.

"But everyone who meets you sees you," Chris said, slurring a bit. "You can't . . . you're unmissable."

I smiled, then looked away. "Except I feel like nobody really misses me right now." I finished my glass, the golden liquid no longer burning. "I miss other people, but they don't miss me."

Half the brandy was gone. Chris topped off our glasses.

I took another swallow. "There's no way I can drive home now," I said, my concern like something scampering off into the woods.

She looked at me a long time. She had the widest brown eyes, a smattering of freckles. The thickest, most beautiful hair.

Her voice a whisper: "That's okay."

She took my glass and set it on the coffee table. The world had that wobbling, churning quality, a vortex tugging at the corners of my vision. I reached forward and watched, heart pounding, as my fingertips slid up her thigh, around her hip, slowing at her waist just as the other hand reached her cheek.

When I woke up the next morning, I was in love with her. I stared at her hair, wheat-colored in the window's winter light, and tried not to audibly giggle. *That's* what that feeling had been, all along. When I kept thinking of her, whatever quiet but hilarious comment she'd make about a situation. How I kept relating things to her, to things she'd said, so that more than once, Mom had said, *Wow, you two certainly have grown close.* It hadn't even occurred to me to touch her, and now that I had, it was all I wanted to do.

So I did. Twice more that day, neither of us sure what we were doing, kissing and giggling—her sweet-smelling hair, her soft neck, her knees. A dreamy week of work, every glance between us like a cymbal crash, smiling into the oatmeal I cooked for Mom in bulk. Then Bill went hunting again, set up camp in the woods, and I drove the hour to Chris's home after Mom went to sleep, heat building in my hips as I wove through country roads. I fell asleep in her arms, and in the morning she roused me with the subtlest strokes, her fingers skimming inside my elbows, my wrists, my palms, my hip crease.

"I like all your inner corners," she whispered, and I'd reached for her jaw and kissed her, hard.

I can see it exactly as Bill saw it: a few feet above and away from my body, as if our consciousnesses melded. Sheets tangled at the foot of the bed. Knotted limbs, subtle movement, knees like pyramids and a round flash of buttocks. Chris's voice like a whimper, as if she were in pain. It's odd, how similar the sounds we make are when we're hurt or turned on. Vulnerable, in both cases.

It was a moment before Chris noticed Bill glowering at the door, and she gasped and stiffened, then pushed me away with both hands. He flicked on the lights and leaned against the door.

What are you . . . what the . . . how could . . . His hand found his left shoulder, then his eyes followed, confused, as if something odd were happening there. And then, with the sudden jolt of someone in a dunk tank, he collapsed.

Oh God—just remembering it sent fresh horror through me. I'd moved quickly, sprinting across the room and checking for a pulse, screaming for Chris to call 911 as I lined up my palms on his rib cage and pushed, rhythmically, everything I'd learned years before in a training course flooding back to me. Chris rushed back in, shrieking her address into the phone, and draped a blanket over me as I beat, beat, beat his heart from the outside in. Chris asked if I was getting tired but I ignored her—I was afraid that if I stopped, his death would be my fault, and so I didn't let up, not even to dress. I remember the wail of distant sirens, red and blue flares silhouetting the trees, all of it growing, intensifying along with the mounting knowledge that they'd be here soon, that my metronomic compressions were a countdown, my ticking death clock. Bangs at the front door and Chris, bawling, took off in her robe, and then a bright, flapping wave of humiliation as the EMTs burst into the room. It was like being in a dream, that moment when you look down and realize you're not wearing anything.

Chris vaulted into the ambulance and they left me behind. I sat at the kitchen table and stared out at the woods outside. There were a few deer out there, a clump of does and fawns, clomping around majestically. A pack of coyotes had been picking them off one by one that season; hunters were complaining that their weekend excursions had been fruitless. A doe swung her head my way and stared. Judgmentally, I thought. Finally I gathered my things and drove home, careful not to wake Mom in the early-morning light.

Bill was fine after triple bypass surgery. I knew this because Chris texted me back exactly once, before my texts stopped going through, before calls went straight to voicemail, before Chris disappeared from my social networks and my life, one big Block. "Bill is okay. I'm sorry but I can't talk."

Bill didn't contact my editor or the nearest major newspaper or threaten me or do any of the things I'd envisioned as I cried in my childhood bedroom; instead, he, his brother, and all other Northern Sky Labs employees just refused to speak to me from that day forward. It was a brilliant, passive checkmate: The book was ruined. Chris was cut off from me like a limb. And it hurt like a sickness: all the nerve endings in my head and neck and chest, crying out like a choir, *ow, ow, ow*. I didn't have enough material to write the book, and even thinking of trying made me nauseous. I stayed cooped up inside for my last six weeks at Mom's, watching movies with her at night. She didn't ask about the book, why I was no longer out reporting, and I was grateful I didn't have to lie.

I cried for a few minutes, gazing out the window onto the Walshes' snowy street. I thought about the deer again. The coyotes too—all social creatures, like us. But a herd's primary purpose is to keep the highest percentage of its members alive. Evolution doesn't care about the individual, about survival of the least-fit. We team up for the most selfish reason possible: self-preservation.

Ted had said something odd, earlier, something that was bothering me, and I waited for my pulse to slow enough that I could search for it. Something about a ticket that for some reason was Ted's problem . . . even though they lived in different cities. Cameron here in Beverly, Ted in New York.

I'd dealt with a parking ticket once, when a meter in the Bronx expired on my rental car. So I knew that you could go to New York State's janky website and pay it online. All you need is a license plate number, which I had thanks to Cameron's profile picture: tailgating at a Patriots game from the back of his SUV. I typed it into the online portal, and there it was: recorded at 11:56 p.m. on Monday, December 16. The night before the Herd's big announcement, hours after Monday Mocktails, after the last known sighting of Eleanor, a traffic cop had tucked a ticket under the windshield wiper of Cameron's black SUV. It was illegally parked in front of a fire hydrant near Watts and Varick.

A block and a half from the Herd's front entrance.

The revelation lit my body like a Lite-Brite—suddenly everything was alive, thrumming, blazing from the inside out.

"Okay," I said aloud. "Okay, okay, okay."

It took longer than I would've liked for my thoughts to organize themselves into something coherent. I whispered them aloud, as if setting them on a mental workspace:

Cameron was in town the night of the murder.

Cameron's car was found within a few hundred feet of the murder site.

Cameron had that photo of Eleanor, the one that ended up in a chatroom devoted to people's hatred for her.

I tried calling Ratliff and hung up with a groan when her voicemail clicked on. I called Hana, then Mikki, feeling the precious seconds pass as both went straight to voicemail.

Whoever was behind this—they'd done what every smart preda-tor would do. They'd separated us from the pack, nudged us into our own corners. I stood and gazed out the window toward the Cor-rigan house, the white columned one Mikki had pointed out on the drive here. But condensation coated the window, and impulsively I reached for the old-fashioned latch and the pane swung toward me with a little snap.

Silent night, dark and dampened with snow still swirling off of trees and bushes and onto the street. So quiet, peaceful even, until—

A scream. Unmistakable. Before I could think, I'd yanked on my boots and was sprinting down the driveway, the wind jabbing me through my sweater, cold lunging at my scalp and throat. I barely noticed, didn't care, as I slid on a slash of snow, skidding to my knees and then taking off again, wet moons stamped across the top of my shins.

Because I kept hearing it, over and over in my mind, as though it were still playing out, a loop broadcast across this tiny little neigh-borhood.

Because the scream.

It sounded like Hana.

PART IV

CHAPTER 20

IF STEVE WERE EVE: LANDMARK MOMENTS FROM
THE CAREER OF APPLE FOUNDER EVE JOBS

By Katie Bradley *Published to* Gleam On *June 24, 2017*

Ed. note: On June 19, a New Yorker *profile of Gleam
founder Eleanor Walsh called her "Steve Jobs if Steve were
Eve—young, pretty, and obsessed with makeup."*

1985: As Apple's retail spaces were gaining steam, Eve
Jobs remembered an especially beautiful stone sidewalk
she'd seen on a trip to Florence, Italy. She calmly <u>insisted
that her stores line their floors with authentic Pietra Ser-
ena sandstone</u> from a particular quarry in Firenzuola,
Italy. Some reasonable (male) VPs pointed out that con-
crete could mimic the stone's texture and color, but Eve

could not be swayed, citing her own exceptional taste. Due to her frivolity and poor financial instincts, she was promptly removed from the company.

2003: Eve Jobs was diagnosed with pancreatic cancer. For the following nine months, she <u>refused her clinicians' orders</u> to undergo radiation, chemotherapy, and surgery, instead pursuing such alternative therapies as juice fasts, acupuncture, herbal remedies, and veganism. She reportedly even visited a psychic. Due to her unbecoming stubbornness and silly, girlish devotion to the oft-mocked Church of Wellness, she was promptly removed from the company.

2005: Speaking of juices, Eve Jobs ordered a fruit smoothie in a Whole Foods in California, and when the elderly barista didn't make it to her specifications, she <u>flew into a rage</u>, screaming about the employee's "incompetence." The event was captured on film and ruined her career immediately. Due to her nasty, entitled disposition, she was promptly removed from the company.

2008: Apple's much-anticipated MobileMe system, meant to sync mobile devices with users' computers, <u>was a disaster from the start</u>. After a *Wall Street Journal* <u>article</u> tore it to pieces, Eve called a town hall meeting on Apple's campus. With shrillness, an ugly shade of lipstick, and tremendous hate in her heart, she <u>publicly berated the team for more than thirty minutes, noting, "You should hate each other for having let each other down."</u> Due to her out-of-control temperament, she was promptly removed from the company.

2010: At a conference, Eve Jobs for the first time presented <u>a tablet called "the iPad."</u> The announcement was met with shock, disgust, and mockery thanks to the name's obvious ties with female menstruation. The product launch was quickly canceled, and due to Eve's poor judgment and female sexual organs, she was promptly removed from the company.

CHAPTER 21

Hana

Cold had descended on everything again, bitter wind and puffs of feathery snow rolling across the street like tumbleweeds. The road hadn't been plowed yet, so I walked carefully along a track carved by car tires. My toes felt frozen inside my winter boots, and I couldn't tell if moisture had seeped through or just coldness.

Katie . . . and Ted. Ted . . . and Katie. When . . . what? I knew she'd met him the night he'd come to reset the router—the night before our Christmas Lights outing, which felt like a century ago—but she hadn't mentioned him since. *So what the hell was* that? Yes, people seek comfort in others in grief. Yes, some people turn to sex the way others (e.g., Karen) turn to alcohol. But I couldn't stem the outrage: It wasn't even six o'clock, their friend had been found dead less than three days ago, and those two couldn't keep their hands off each other?

A car flashed its high beams and I shuffled onto the slush-covered curb. There were no sidewalks here, just hulking old mansions with neat front lawns abutting the street. I hurried the last few yards and turned into the Corrigans' driveway. Icicle lights hung from the roof, in front of the pillars, but all of the windows were dark. I curved around to the brick-and-white cottage out back and rang the doorbell. Finally the door swung open, belching heat into the night.

"Hi." His hair was back in a little ponytail, his cheeks flushed.

"Hey, Cameron." I stuck my hands in my pockets. "Can I come in?"

He held the door open and I took a few steps forward before another voice made me jump.

"Hiii, Hana!" Mikki, leaning back from the living room sofa at the end of the hall, her voice a singsong. "What's up?"

"Oh, hey! Didn't know you were over here!" Cameron followed me down the hallway. I'd matched Mikki's cheery tone, but something was off about this whole diorama. And not just the mess, although that was apparent: the movie cliché of a thirtysomething's bachelor pad, with dishes piled in the sink, mounds of dirty laundry dotting the hallway, and several bags of snacks yawning open on the coffee table.

"Just needed a break from Gary and Karen," she said. "Er, I guess I should say I wanted to give *them* a break from *me*. They seem exhausted."

"Totally."

"You want a soda?" Cameron called from the kitchen.

"Got anything stronger?" I asked, then cringed as he said no: *former addict, zero substances, that's right.* "Whatever you've got is fine." I dropped into a recliner and turned to Mikki: "I was thinking the same thing. About Gary and Karen? They were so insistent about us coming but looked like they regretted it immediately."

"Yeah, they're not doing great." Cameron handed me a Sprite and then crashed onto the couch, and as he did I watched Mikki's eyes float to the floor under the coffee table. I followed her gaze and saw it—a little purple cotton bralette, the kind flat-chested Mikki favored. I looked up at her and for a second, we were like bad actors in a telenovela: My expression read *WTF*, Mikki stared at Cameron with desperate, *help-me* eyes, and Cameron looked back at her in confusion, his brows and head slightly askew.

It went through me like a gunshot, and for a second I considered pretending I hadn't seen anything. Instead I laughed and said, "Didn't realize this trip was gonna be such a fuckfest." It felt good, the brashness. I saw why Katie must like it.

Cameron coughed. "No, we were just—"

"Cameron, stop," Mikki said. "Yeah, we have been . . . hanging out, when we see each other. For a few months. Sorry I didn't mention it, but I know you . . ."

She hesitated and I thought she was about to say *have a crush on Cameron*, which would of course require that I kill myself or her or all three of us on the spot. Cameron looked at her curiously and she continued, "You have a lot of loyalty toward Eleanor and might think it was weird I was hooking up with her ex."

"Huh." I leaned into the seat's leather back. I knew this changed something, the social web I'd mentally spun around Eleanor, but I wasn't yet sure how. Katie and Ted, Mikki and Cameron—I'd somehow become a fifth wheel. "Did Eleanor know?"

"No way. She'd be weird about it." Mikki shrugged. "I didn't want to make her jealous or anything. Cam and I just . . . hit it off, that's all."

Would *Eleanor have been jealous?* She never mentioned Cameron. "When?"

"I went down to visit Ted in October," Cameron said, gesturing with his can. "We ran into each other." They didn't exchange looks, besotted or otherwise. None of this felt particularly romantic.

"And it's been on since then?"

"No, we haven't—"

"We've barely seen each other since then," Mikki finished. "Sorry to . . . keep a secret, or whatever. But."

"It's fine." I took a long sip of pop. The revelation was like a branding iron on my chest, and I fought not to let it show. "Hey, you know what's weird? I just walked in on Ted and Katie hooking up."

"Just now?" Mikki yelped, at the same time Cameron said, "Wait, Ted and who?"

"Yeah, just now. With my sister. I thought they'd barely said two words to each other."

"Whoa." Mikki shook her head, amazed. "Okay, now your fuck-fest comment makes more sense. Were they embarrassed?"

"They hadn't closed the stupid door properly. We were all equally mortified." I started to giggle and it turned into a choking noise.

"Aw, Hana." Mikki shot me a sympathetic look. "I keep doing that. Starting to feel normal and then bursting into tears, because, shit." I nodded, pulled myself together. "So you're done being mad at Katie?"

"Well, I'm still mad, obviously, but I wanted to talk to her be-cause . . ." I strained to remember—my memories were floating around like snowflakes, Ted's creepy stalker file, Karen robotically pouring wine. Then I remembered: "I found out the strangest thing about Eleanor. It all started 'cause I spotted her yearbooks, and it reminded me that she skipped over seventh and eighth grade. . . ."

I recounted the story, my gaze bouncing between the hallway, the ceiling, my Sprite, before settling back on Mikki just as I fin-ished. I leaned forward. "What, what is it?"

She opened her mouth, then stopped herself with a little snap of laughter. "I haven't told anyone this and I can't believe you're the first to catch it," she said. "None of that happened to Eleanor—it happened to me. In middle school. And I told her about it at some point, maybe like sophomore year, and then she brought it up years later when she was starting the Herd." She swept her hair together, then tugged it over her shoulder. "She asked if she could, quote, 'borrow' it, because it worked so well with the brand narrative. But she also said the post and press release and everything else were already written and approved and about to go up." She looked away. "It kinda felt like she was *announcing*, not asking. Letting me know as a courtesy, like, 'Oh, by the way.'"

The hairs along my biceps and back were standing tall, buzzing beneath my sweater. "And you didn't . . . have a discussion or tell her you felt uncomfortable?"

She shook her head.

"That's fucked up," Cameron contributed.

Mikki was gazing out the window, her expression inscrutable, so I fumbled on: "Did she ever do anything else like that to you?"

"She was pretty bratty when she was little," Cameron offered. "Pissed a lot of people off. Would just break your toy or smash your sand castle for no reason."

"Jesus, maybe don't speak ill of the dead, Cameron." Mikki tucked her feet beneath her.

I pointed with my can. "Her parents said she was just really bored. And that it got better after she skipped grades."

"Yeah, maybe. She fell in with the cool crowd in high school," Cameron said.

"And stopped smashing sand castles?" Mikki finished.

"And started dating you," I added. "The first time." He winced a little and I noticed it, pressed at it like a crack in a pane, some small and childish part of me perhaps eager to volley back the hurt: "Why did you and Eleanor break up? The first time?"

He flicked his eyes toward Mikki, then ran his fingers over his jaw. "Oh, you know. I remembered what freshman year of college was like. I thought she should be free to explore."

Liar. Covering his mouth, avoiding our eyes—he hadn't magnanimously set Eleanor free, and I knew it. Of *course* she'd told us about her ex, how she'd waited until her last week at home to tell him it was over.

And then they'd given it another go our last year at Harvard; as Eleanor told it, *it just happened* while she was home for the summer. But she had seemed increasingly frustrated with Cameron that time around: rolling her eyes when they were together, complaining about him when they were apart. From what we could tell, raw animal attraction had brought them together again, but practicality—her big plans for Gleam, excitement from early investors, her shiny new life in New York City in stark contrast to Cameron's life in Beverly—had pushed them apart for good.

"Can we talk about something else?" Mikki pulled her hands inside her sleeves.

"Right. Sorry." I shook my head. "That was . . . a weird thing to bring up."

We gulped at our drinks for a few seconds. The moment grew almost unbearable.

"It's weird she married Daniel," Mikki announced. Cameron and I reared back, and she shrugged. "I mean, I was never allowed to say it. But he's weird. He always gave me the creeps."

I gawped at her. "Well you certainly haven't mentioned *that* before."

"No, he's just . . ." She shrugged. "He was so perfect. And boring. Aren't boring people usually the ones who turn out to be psychopaths? I mean, I've seen a lot of *Criminal Minds*." Cameron looked up from his phone sharply and we both stared at Mikki for a moment before she added, "The *show*."

I shook my head. Did Mikki really not see how generous Daniel had been in keeping the blackmail a secret? How he'd protected us out of his love for Eleanor? "He worshiped her. I don't think he even wanted to open up their marriage, but he did it for her."

"And you buy that? You don't think he resented her?" Mikki tucked her hair behind her ear. "I always thought it was weird she didn't have any pictures of him in her office."

"No, she had that photo of them on vacation. And that same picture was the background on her phone."

"Was it? Huh." Cameron looked around, then leaned askew to slip his own cell back into his pocket.

The doorbell chimed, making all of us jump. Cameron rose and clomped down the hall.

"It's some girl," he called, and then we heard dead bolts unlocking, the door opening with a swoosh.

With my head cocked, I could just make her out: "Is Hana here?"

"Katie?" I yelled, struggling to get out of the La-Z-Boy. I hurried down the hallway with Mikki right behind me.

"Hana!" Her relief confused me; she pushed past Cameron and grabbed for me. "Oh my God. It must have been a coyote or something."

"What's going on? Why aren't you wearing a coat?"

"I need to talk to you." She lifted her brow and leaned forward. "Confidentially. Like, now."

"Wait, where's Ted?" Mikki grabbed the front door Cameron was attempting to close and peered out. More snow was falling, thick, wet flakes.

"I thought he came back here. But I need to—" Katie's eyes did something desperate, an ocular *ahem*.

"When did Ted leave?" Mikki pushed the door closed, then wrapped her arms around her chest.

"I don't know, ten minutes ago?" Katie jerked a thumb toward the columned main house. "Is he in there?"

"I'll check." Cameron pulled his coat from a peg and scooped keys off a hook. "He can't have gone far."

"Wait—we should—" Katie's shoulders slumped as he pulled the door closed. She turned back to us. "I just learned something crazy. Cameron was *there*. His car was parked a block from the Herd on that Monday—the night Eleanor was killed."

"What?" Mikki took a step toward her. "Why?"

"I don't know, but he's been trying to hide it. Which seems pretty freaking suspicious." Her teeth began to chatter. "And there's something else. I think he was posting in the Antiherd. That hate group? He put up an old photo of her and wrote some other . . . awful things."

Headlights crashed through the nearest window, blinding us. We all turned, squinting, in time to see Cameron's SUV tearing out of the driveway, wriggling in the snow through a wild three-point turn. It gunned down the street, kicking up a rooster tail of snow and slush, then whipped around a corner as its back wheels spun out of control. And then Cameron disappeared from sight.

CHAPTER 22

Katie

Mikki spoke first: "Did he just make a run for it?"

"Maybe he's looking for Ted?" Hana said, and then she looked around as if she, too, was shocked by how stupid it sounded.

"Why did he leave, what happened before I got here?" They looked back at me with doll eyes. I flung out my hands. "*Something* had to make him take off in a blizzard."

"He was looking at his phone right before you rang the doorbell," Hana said, scrunching her mouth. "But I didn't see what was on it."

"We should call Ratliff. Right?" I listened hard, expecting some- one to confirm, and then realized—no, I was waiting for Hana to jump in, to handle things. Like she had the night of the Herd event. "I'll do it." My voice was clear and steady. I was proud of myself for exactly 0.3 seconds. "Fuck, I didn't bring my phone."

"I've got it," Hana said, hurrying back into the living room. We

heard her voice, high and official-sounding, from what I assumed
was the living room: "It's Hana Bradley—sorry to bother you so
close to the holidays. We're in Beverly with Eleanor's parents, and
her childhood friend here, we think he might have had something
to do with her death. . . ."

They spoke for a few minutes and then Hana plopped onto the
couch. "She's gonna contact the local precinct," she said. "She'll
keep us posted."

"Are they gonna put out an APB?" I demanded. Using the cop-
show term gave me a little thrill. "Because he's looking shady as
shit."

"I don't think so. She said she can't immediately put a red flag on
someone, quote, 'driving away in their own car.'"

"Well, great. We all saw how concerned they were about Eleanor, quote, 'leaving of her own accord.'" I crossed my arms and
Mikki snorted.

Hana stared into the distance for a second, then sprung up and
marched down the hall. Mikki and I followed and found Hana in
Cameron's bedroom rifling around under the mattress, running her
fingers against the box spring and then crouching to look under the
bed.

"Uh, what the fuck are you doing?" Mikki asked.

"Looking for Eleanor's phone."

"*What?*" Mikki took a few stumbling steps back.

Hana sat back on her haunches. "Her phone went missing a few
weeks ago. The same morning that graffiti appeared. They think
whoever stole it had something to do with the spray-painting."

"Why?" Mikki's eyes narrowed.

"Because the same message was spray-painted on the walls in the
San Francisco Herd and the Fort Greene worksite. Eleanor had
photos of all three on her phone, and someone sent those photos to
The Gaze. She didn't want news getting out ahead of the Titan acquisition, so I made the whole thing go away."

"The same message was at the other sites? And you kept that out of the news?" I stretched my eyebrows up and my mouth down, impressed. "Even I didn't know you're that good of a publicist."

She leaned forward onto all fours and stared under the bed. "Thing is, her *new* phone, the one she got to replace the stolen one—they said the texts and emails we got on Tuesday came from it, and that it was used to send that I'm-in-Mexico email a few days later."

We nodded.

"And tonight, I said something to Cameron about how Eleanor's lock screen was a photo of her and her husband. Which was true for ninety-nine percent of the last year—I wasn't thinking about her new phone. But when she got it a couple weeks ago, she made it one of the new Gleam backgrounds."

I glanced at Mikki to see if this was making more sense to her. Had Hana lost her mind? "Yeah, so?"

"So I said something about the background photo with Daniel, and there was this split-second where Cameron was confused. Like, 'No, that's not right.'" She stood and fluffed the pillows, checked under the unmade duvet. "Which could mean he had her latest phone. It's just a hunch. Could be nothing."

"We should slow down." Mikki wrapped her arms around her waist. "Maybe he just didn't know what picture she'd set as her background."

Near his dresser, Hana froze. "I don't want to be right either. But him being in New York, showing up on Eleanor hate sites—it doesn't look good." She went back to thumbing through socks. "Help me, would you? It could be anywhere."

On leaden legs, I approached the closet and pushed aside the sliding door. It was a damn mess, a bachelor stereotype: shirts clinging to bent wire hangers, piles of jeans toppling on the top shelf, a casserole of clothes and shoes along the floor.

"Why would he hide it here?" I asked, using one sneaker to nose through the jumble. "Why wouldn't he just destroy it?"

"No idea." Hana was on her knees, her cheek near the floor as she peered beneath the bureau. "I just feel like there's something here. Mikki . . ." She looked up. "He didn't take you in here? You hooked up in the living room, right?"

"Wait, what?" I turned so suddenly my elbow crashed into a bunch of empty hangers; they jangled as I tried to pat them into stillness.

Mikki nodded miserably, still frozen by the door. "But Cameron would never . . ."

I crossed to Hana and pressed a hand on her shoulder. "You've gotta stop. This is weird." It wasn't like Hana to be so oblivious, so unable to read the room. She stood and groped around in his book-shelf, not looking at me. "Hana."

She whipped around and her eyes were shiny with tears. "It . . . it has to be here . . ."

I pulled her into me, one hand on her back and the other on her skull. She let out a hiccuppy gasp and hugged me back.

"Jinny's mom," Mikki said quietly. She cleared her throat and said it louder: "Jinny's mom."

Who's Jinny? Hana pulled away, staring at the floor next to my feet.

"It's the only thing that makes sense," Mikki said, her voice tiny and tense. "Celia Hurst. We have to tell the cops, they have to look into her, she—"

"This isn't about Jinny." Hana turned to look at her. "It's about Cameron. I know you don't want it to be him, but it fits. And maybe, I don't know, maybe Ted was helping him or something, but it wasn't this random woman from Appalachia."

"What's going on?" I looked back and forth between them, my pulse quickening.

Hana stared at Mikki, her expression equal parts warning and terror. "Mikki, no."

Mikki gazed back, their eyes locked for what felt like hours, years, and then Mikki turned to me: "This is all our fault."

Hana's knees buckled and she sank to the floor. A ripping sensation in my chest: *What had she . . . could she . . . ?* I kneeled next to her. "Whatever it is, we'll figure it out. Just tell me what happened."

She squeezed her eyes shut. My heart beat wildly, a scared creature in a jar. I wanted to hit Pause, stop before I learned whatever awful thing I couldn't unhear. Snow drummed against the window; the lights flickered once, threatening to go out.

Mikki tiptoed over and sat near us. "We knew this woman, Jinny," she began, "and she used to sell us drugs. She went missing nine years ago, after she came up here with us. To Beverly. To the Walshes'."

And they told me, taking turns, words spilling out like wine. I pictured it as they spoke: Jinny's flail on the slippery pool tiles, blood seeping into the chlorinated water. Gary—a developer, a boss, commanding by definition—calmly instructing them to pack their things and leave.

They finished speaking and the silence hovered like low-hanging clouds. Finally, I shook my head. "And nobody tried to argue? No one called 911?"

"Eleanor told us everything would be fine, and we believed her." Mikki raised her eyebrows. "She's very convincing."

"So you just returned to school like nothing had happened?"

Hana shrugged. "It was horrible. We saw Jinny's picture on the news and everything, and all the awful pleas from her mother for anyone with information to step forward. But somehow . . . everyone assumed she'd just run away. And we were all so busy getting ready for finals. I know that sounds . . . unthinkable, but it's true."

Another long silence. Mikki flicked away a tear.

"Did you feel guilty?" I asked.

"Of course we did," Hana snapped. "We felt terrible. But what could we do? Life goes on. Life got good. We got great jobs, Gleam took off . . ." She shook her head. "And for eight years, there was nothing. And then I got the first blackmail letter." She finally finished, recounting what had really happened when she'd rushed to Daniel's apartment on Saturday. How she'd taken Eleanor's final blackmail letter home with her and watched it burn to ash, the December 31 deadline at the bottom blazing white and then crumbling into gray.

I crossed my arms. "Isn't there a paper trail? Connecting you to the blackmail?"

Mikki shook her head. "We all got Bitcoin accounts. It was surprisingly easy."

"Jesus." I rubbed my brow. "But now Eleanor is about to miss a payment."

Hana nodded. "I don't know what'll happen on the first, but it can't be good."

Something clicked, one of life's minor mysteries: This was why, after graduation, Hana had dropped everything and moved to L.A. Like Eleanor, like Dad, she'd tried to run.

Mikki cleared her throat. "Cameron told me something. Right when—after we hooked up. You know how guys get. All vulnerable." She squeezed her eyes shut. "He said he knew about Jinny. All these years. From Gary. I don't know why or how, but he did."

"Jesus," Hana said.

"But I don't think he'd tell me that if he was the one blackmailing us." She wiped a tear, smearing it across her cheek. "I told him I didn't want to talk about it. But he said that last year, he started sort of obsessing over Jinny's mom. She's still looking for her daughter, which is incredibly sad. And she's not doing all that well, she's struggled with addiction; maybe that made Cameron see her as a kindred spirit."

Hana's eyes widened and Mikki looked at her. "He didn't contact her or anything. I don't even think he talked to Ted about it. But I guess at Christmas last year, Cameron cornered Eleanor and told her he thought she should come clean. For Jinny's mom's sake. And she was like, 'Fuck no, and if you say a word to anyone, I'll turn on you so fast. I'll say you were entirely responsible for Jinny's death, and people will believe me.'"

"*Eleanor* said that? She threatened Cameron?" I shook my head, amazed.

Hana rubbed her temples. "I believe it. She could be . . . ruthless. It's part of her brand."

Mikki nodded. "And then this year, around Thanksgiving, apparently Eleanor told her family about the Herd buyout, and word got around to the Corrigans. And Cameron's first thought—it sounds so noble, I don't know if he's full of shit, but this is what he told me—his first thought was, 'If Eleanor's about to become filthy rich, she has to set up a fund in Jinny's name.' Somehow help the family that'd fallen apart after we took her away." When Mikki looked up tears varnished her eyes, but her voice remained steady. "That's as far as he got when you came by."

"So you had no idea he was in New York the night Eleanor . . . went missing?" *Killed, murdered, stabbed to death*—words I couldn't utter right now. She shook her head.

Hana wound her hands together. "I saw him the next day." Mikki and I uttered shocked, guttural noises. "The day after Eleanor disappeared, I mean. Wednesday. I went over to Eleanor's apartment—I told myself it was just to look for clues, but I was looking for blackmail notes, anything that would tie us to Jinny. I hoped she'd been smart enough to destroy them, but I had to check."

I watched her cry, feeling my impression of her shifting like tectonic plates inside my skull. I'd flitted through the week with nothing but a passing, *What's Hana hiding?* This—this was a Mr. Hyde side I never wanted to meet.

"And Cameron showed up at Eleanor's apartment," she went on, her voice small. "I let him inside. He said he'd just gotten into town and I . . . I'm an idiot, I believed him. He said he was there to help, but I thought he'd come to beat up Daniel or something—he was surprised when Daniel wasn't home. But maybe that wasn't it at all. Maybe he was trying to . . . I don't know, remove some evidence or something."

"Let's back this up," I said. The facts were poking out at odd angles, a tent frame I couldn't snap into shape. "We know Cameron was in town on Monday. The night Eleanor was killed. And he was still there on Wednesday, when you saw him at Eleanor's apartment."

Hana looked up. "Maybe when Eleanor finally scheduled the big announcement about Titan, he decided to drive down to see her. Make his final plea."

"But you really think he would hurt her?" Mikki rocked forward, snuffling. "Maybe we're looking at this wrong. Maybe—maybe he did reach out to Jinny's mom, maybe he said something that made her want to confront Eleanor. Maybe he learned she was gonna try to hurt Eleanor, and he came down to protect her."

"Hello?" Ted's voice boomed down the hall.

We froze and stared at one another, like naughty pets caught red-handed.

"Cameron?" Ted appeared in the doorway and I blushed at the sight of him.

"Ted, hi!" Hana swept us all into the hallway, casual and smooth. "We were just about to head back over to the Walshes'."

"Is Cameron here?" Ted craned his neck to look behind us.

I spotted an opening: "No, he said he was gonna go looking for you. Have you heard from him?"

Hana had nonchalantly led us back to the doorway. Ted shook his head.

"I texted him earlier, right after—when I got back from Mr. and Mrs. Walsh's." His ears reddened. Right after we'd been walked in on mid-hookup, right after he'd called me selfish and I'd told him to leave. "Cam didn't reply, but I was down in the basement with the game on so I don't know if it went through. I just came upstairs to get a beer and saw that his car was gone, but all his lights were on. I figured he went out and I was just gonna shut 'em off."

"And then you saw all our coats here," Mikki finished.

He was looking at his phone, Hana had said, *right before you rang the doorbell.* "What'd you say to Cameron?" I asked. "When you texted?"

He shrunk a bit, frowned. "Nothing important. Hey, so where's Cameron? And what are you guys still doing here?"

"What'd you say in your text?" I squared my chin at him. "Was it about me?"

"What? No."

I took a step forward. "Were you in a rush to tell him what a bitch I am? For trying to write about Eleanor?" I knew it wasn't the case, wasn't in character for him at all, but I could see how uncomfortable I was making him. That mounting eagerness to set the record straight. "How her death is basically my fault?"

"No! Jesus! You think I think that?" He shook his head. "I asked him about that old photo of Eleanor. Okay? Like, 'Hey, have you been posting this online?' I thought it was kind of a shitty thing to do when she hated that photo. I don't even know if he saw it—he didn't reply."

Of course. Cameron had received that text and put two and two together, spotted the walls closing in.

I can't imagine what face we were all making, but his glance shot between us. "What, what is it?"

"We're heading back to the Walshes'," I said, before anyone could break in. *We think your brother's a killer* was not a conversation I felt prepped for; Mikki seemed reticent to accept it as a possibility, and typically Hana was conscientious to a fault . . . but tonight we were all loose cannons. "Why don't you keep trying

Cameron? It's coming down hard out there—he really shouldn't be driving."

Ted continued to frown, but he nodded as we gathered our things. He flicked off the lights and walked outside with us, then hooked toward the main house with an awkward wave. The snow felt heavy on my cheeks and eyelashes and the crown of my head, like small, cold loogies. Everything still felt very wrong. Where was Cameron?

Gary and Karen, at least, were in the kitchen, sliding vegetables and salmon fillets into the oven.

"Well, there you all are!" Gary said, trying to sound jolly, but his face fell when he saw our expressions. "What is it?"

I cleared my throat. "Something weird is going on," I said. "We were over at Cameron's and he . . . took off."

Karen set down her knife. "He what?"

"He grabbed his keys and ran out. Really gunned it," Hana said.

"In these conditions?" Karen brought a hand to her mouth. "That's dangerous!"

"We called Detective Ratliff because we realized some weird things about him. About"—I sucked in a breath—"about what he was doing the night Eleanor died, and why he didn't tell anyone he was in New York."

"You're kidding," Gary gasped. Karen moaned and reached for him.

"Why don't we all sit down," Hana said. Rustling and squeaking as everyone yanked back kitchen chairs.

Again, I felt the instinct to pull back and let Hana do the talking, but instead I walked them through it: The strange posts in the Anti-herd. The parking ticket the night of the crime. How he'd just grabbed his car keys and sped off mid-conversation, which was not exactly the behavior of an innocent man. Karen and Gary kept nodding blankly, their eyes dull as the room filled with the smell of root vegetables and fish.

"Let's not jump to any conclusions," Gary said when I'd finished.

"Does anyone smell burning?" Karen added, pushing her chair out noisily. We watched, stiff as ice sculptures, as she slid the trays out of the oven and swiped her potholder at the smoke. Gary rose and began pulling plates from a cabinet; without speaking, and with all the ease of a bunch of robots, we set the table, spooned things onto serving trays, found our seats again.

"Let's say grace," Gary said, and Hana, Mikki, and I exchanged frantic looks as the Walshes bowed their heads: *Bless us, O Lord, and these thy gifts . . .*

We passed the pepper. We remarked on the garlicky pistachio breading patted onto the salmon's side. The Walshes asked about our New Year's Eve plans and we answered, in turn. The three of us kept catching one another's glances as our forks clanged against our plates. We were Norman Rockwell's most fucked-up tableau yet: two healthy, round-faced parents, three beautiful young women, eating off pretty patterned china while the snow throbbed outside.

Gary half-stood to pour more wine into my goblet and Karen grabbed at the water glass he'd nearly tipped, and I felt a rush of cold, bracing as menthol: Behold these sweet, straitlaced Baby Boomers who'd opened their home to me. Who'd opened their home to Eleanor and her friends, too, and then somehow made it all go away when things fell apart. Did they see Jinny's face every night? Was the guilt gnawing at them from inside?

"So, I think we're gonna head back to New York first thing tomorrow," Hana said, when we'd all given up pretending to eat, food flaked apart and pushed around our plates. "We'll connect with the detectives there, and . . . get out of your hair."

One would expect them to insist having us here was no trouble, even out of knee-jerk Catholic guilt. Instead they stared. Our facades were collapsing, solid outsides thawing and crumbling apart from head to toe.

"Cameron's a good kid," Gary announced, and we all turned to him. Mikki started to cry. "He's a good kid."

"Thank you so much for letting us be here," Hana concluded.

Karen nodded slowly. "It's been a long day. I'm going to head to bed. Gary, let's go."

"We'll take care of cleaning up," I added, rising to pile dishes.

Karen stared at me, then nodded. She and Gary shuffled away.

"What the fuck was *that*," Hana hissed, once they were out of earshot.

"I thought that dinner was never going to end," I said. "Clearly they cannot handle the idea of Cameron having anything to do with Eleanor's death."

"They're close—he's basically their surrogate son." Mikki turned on the faucet and stuck a plate under the tap. Her tone confused me—was she still defending him? "They *really* don't want it to be him."

"Here's what I don't understand," I said. "Obviously I barely know Cameron, way less than you two. But if he was driving down to New York to talk to Eleanor, why would he bring a scalpel? Or whatever sharp tool?"

"I don't know." Hana shook her head sadly. "We don't know what she said, what went down. I don't think it was planned, I really don't."

"But what about the graffiti?" Mikki added. "And this stolen phone? The original one, from back before—before any of this."

I took this one. "I don't think it was related. Some people really did just hate her. And the Herd. All of it." I sighed. "Some people are just shitty."

Hana dropped a fistful of silverware into the dishwasher. "Another thing I don't understand: He knew she was trying to get a fake passport. He suspected she was getting ready to make a run for it." She repositioned a spatula. "If he thought she was about to disappear, wouldn't that be a pretty good outcome for him? She would leave town, she couldn't pin Jinny's death on him, he could even turn us all in and start that . . . *memorial fund*, if that's what he wanted."

I set a stack of serving dishes on the counter. "Could be. Or maybe he was lying about wanting to help Jinny's family. For all we know, maybe he was helping Eleanor disappear. Driving down to personally deliver her starter kit for a new life."

"Well, let's hope they find him and he can tell us himself," Hana said.

I leaned against the counter. Mikki was going to town with the pull-out faucet, fire-hosing dishes with total concentration.

"You know, if he does, you might have to face charges in relation to Jinny," I said. "There's no statute of limitations on this stuff."

"We know." Mikki nodded at the backsplash. Her face looked miserable, but her shoulders softened, like frozen meat defrosting.

"I miss Eleanor," I said. Even if she was ruthless; even if she'd threatened Cameron, and Mikki and Hana before him, in order to keep Jinny's death a secret. She'd inspired us, made us feel sparkling and special and proud. That was a gift, even if it came with a lifetime of impersonating goodness, of being an impostor. Eleanor, unlike the rest of us mortals, didn't give a shit what others thought, and for that we were all more than willing to adore her.

"I miss her too," Mikki murmured, and Hana echoed her. I looked around and saw that they meant it, that their sorrow matched mine, and somehow this helped. Cleaning up her parents' kitchen on Christmas Eve Eve, we all took on a third of the grief.

Mikki looped the dishtowel on its hook and walked upstairs. Staring at the sparkling kitchen, I registered that cottony end-of-day fatigue, more drained than sleepy, as if my body were eager to let today end.

"I'm going to go too," I announced, then headed down the hall. But once I'd gotten ready for bed, I crept upstairs and knocked on

Hana's door. I found her and Mikki sitting on the floor, old books—children's classics and Gloria Steinem and yearbooks—scattered around them.

I sat cross-legged and picked up a yearbook. Eleanor's senior year, her photo bright-eyed and lovely. Below it, her chosen quote was from (who else?) Frida Kahlo: "I often have more sympathy for carpenters, cobblers, etc., than for that whole stupid, supposedly civilized herd of windbags known as *cultivated people.*"

"I wonder if she felt like she created a monster," I mused. "Like, she wanted to build this feminist utopia, and then she accidentally made this—this *thing* that was even more bougie and see-and-be-seen than the boys' club bullshit she was trying to get away from. 'Windbags.'" I swiveled the book toward Hana and Mikki and pointed at the quote. "I was a tech reporter—Titan is run by Silicon Valley bros. So for them, acquiring a feminist company like the Herd would be a great PR move. But for Eleanor, for her original vision . . ."

Mikki looked up. "I bet an acquisition like that opens you up to scrutiny. Maybe she felt like someone was close to figuring out what happened in college, and that's why she had to get away."

It struck me: I'd been investigating Eleanor myself, and I'd had *no clue.* This sparked in my chest a flicker of something bright: absurdity? Humiliation? Laughter, even?

Hana leaned back. "We're going to talk to Stephanie when she gets back from India. At the very least, they're delaying the acquisition, she said. Maybe she can talk to Titan about increasing diversity and expanding their scholarship program and stuff."

"Good idea," I said. "I know Titan uses diversity consultants."

She grinned. "You know more about this stuff than we do. You should talk to Stephanie with us."

"I'd like that."

Mikki pulled the yearbook off my lap and smiled at Eleanor's headshot. "This is what she looked like when we met. The day we moved into the dorms." She tapped the page. "I thought she was *so* grown-up. So beautiful and articulate and smart—you, too, Hana. I couldn't believe you two wanted to hang out with me."

I gave her arm a gentle punch. "That's funny, 'cause when I first got to know you and Eleanor, I had the same thought. Only about *you*. I was this dorky teenager and for some reason you let me hang around."

"That's honestly how I felt—here I was this weird kid from North Carolina who grew up splitting Hamburger Helper with my four siblings. But then"—her lips cracked into the tiniest smile— "Eleanor *liked* me. Took me under her wing. You, too, Hana. I was like—I dunno. Your arty friend. Some hipster flair."

"Hey, you weren't just . . . a token." Hana frowned and I wondered if she and I were thinking the same thing: a bit odd for Hana to have to reassure blond-haired, blue-eyed Mikki here.

"No, I loved it." The yearbook's slick pages hissed softly as she flipped through them. "It didn't even bother me when Eleanor would occasionally, like, ask me to put her name on an attendance sheet for her or look over her stats homework. Which meant . . . finishing it."

I reared my chin back. "Really?"

She shrugged. "I was the outsider, and she was so casual about it. I kind of figured . . . I guess this is how it works in the real world? If I want to run in these circles? Which I really, really did."

Hana and I exchanged a look over Mikki's hunched shoulders. *She* felt like an outsider?

"I'm sorry you felt that way," Hana finally said. "You know we love you."

"If anything, I've always been jealous of how you can march to the beat of your own drum," I added.

Hana nodded. "You don't need anyone's approval, and meanwhile I'm constantly trying to talk people into loving me."

"Same here," I said. "Only I'm trying to . . . impress them into loving me." I rubbed my palm against Mikki's back and she jumped, then looked up and gave us both a small smile.

"Thanks. Sometimes I convince myself I'm the only one who feels like she's faking it."

"Sweetie. Not at all." Hana crawled forward and hugged her, and I wrapped my arms around both of them.

"Thanks, Bradleys," Mikki said, giggling and sniffling as we let her go. "You two are all right."

"More than all right," I replied. "We're all fucking badasses."

"It's true." She wiped both eyes and exhaled, *whew*. "Okay, I'm going to sleep."

We bid her good night and then I pulled out another book: *A Wrinkle in Time*, plus all its sequels behind it.

"Katie?" Hana looked at me intently. "Why were you trying to write a book about Eleanor?"

I leaned on my palm and looked out the window, where everything was as round and gray and marshmallow-soft as everything else. "I didn't even want to write it," I said softly. "But I couldn't write *Infopocalypse*. I was backed into a corner and scrambling for a way to not ruin my career."

I looked down at the yellowed paperback in my hands. There was a broad-winged Pegasus on it, and below it the face of a glowering red-eyed man.

"What happened in Michigan?"

"I'm so ashamed, Hana," I said, my voice breaking. "I wish I could take it all back." And then I told her, in fits and starts as gray-white swirls rolled past the window, as if the Walshes' estate were actually on the moon or in a cloud or at the bottom of the ocean, wherever we'd found ourselves.

"I'm sorry," I finished. "I fucked up over and over. I don't even know what to say for myself."

"Aw, Katie. I'm sorry too," she said. "I'm sorry I was mean on the train. And for all the times I made you feel less-than. I want to do better." She gave me a hug. It felt like an ending, a coda, and so I left her with Eleanor's books spread out around her like ripples in a pond.

In the morning, I woke to Hana banging on the door.

"They spotted Cameron," she called. "We need to move."

CHAPTER 23

===

Hana

I packed my things in a haze, concentrating hard on the fabric under my fingers, folding clothes into small, neat rectangles and smoothing them into my suitcase. I popped into Katie's room and helped her strip the bed and heave the mattress back inside the sofa's belly. We dropped her sheets in the laundry room, and suddenly it was like we'd never been here, like this was all a dream.

Ratliff's voicemail had run through me like ice: A search of the automatically catalogued license plates stacked up at the US Customs and Border Protection in Derby, Vermont, showed Cameron had driven into Canada around 9 p.m. last night. He'd used a fake passport and had a huge lead on us. Finally, she believed us. If Eleanor showed us anything, it's that innocent people don't try to run. Ratliff was coordinating a search with local precincts, and she was eager to have us back in New York.

Not eager enough to send a police escort, however. The Amtrak was sold-out, of course—all twelve trains left in the day were full, even the one that got in at 2:30 a.m. So instead we killed time at a diner, then clambered onto a low-cost "express bus," which was neither express nor, it turned out, low-cost when you bought the last three available tickets a few hours before its departure. We stood waiting in the cold parking lot, stomping our feet to stay warm while Mikki cried on and off, and I stupidly remarked that at least we'd be able to sit together, since we were first in line.

"There's something else I didn't tell you," Mikki said at one point, her voice rickety, her hands tucked into her armpits. "Cameron told me that Eleanor broke up with him *right* before that weekend in Beverly. The one with Jinny. He said she basically hung up the phone from setting up her investor pitches and called him to break things off. But she told him she wanted to be the one to tell her parents, since they were gonna be heartbroken, so he shouldn't tell anyone just yet. I guess he was super, super hurt."

"Yikes." My nose scrunched in sympathy. "I remember us asking where he was that night, why he couldn't come party with us, and she just said he was busy. I thought they broke up a week or two later." I could imagine how Cameron must've heard it: *I need a fancy New York boyfriend to go with my fancy new life. You're not good enough for me.*

"I know," Mikki said. "He's been carrying that around for nine years. When he told me, he just seemed hurt, but maybe he was . . . angry too."

A beat. "So we really think Cameron did this?" Katie looked back and forth at us, her eyes wide, like Cosmo when he wants to be fed.

Mikki erupted into tears and I rubbed her back. "Yeah. We do."

The bus croaked to a stop in front of us. Mikki slumped in a window seat and I took the one next to her. I dozed off, then awoke in Jersey, and across the Hudson, the Manhattan skyline was glittering and two-dimensional, like a vast cardboard set piece studded with bluish lights. The Empire State Building was green and red, which made me sad. Christmas comes but once a year, and future ones would forever be a reminder of today, painful echoes.

The bus dumped us on Seventh Avenue and we blinked under the bright streetlamps, as we milled around in the cold.

"So do we just go home?" Katie asked.

"I'm not ready to be alone," I said.

Katie nodded. "Alone on Christmas Eve—it's just too much. I know we're not about to salvage the holiday, but I'd be down to order takeout and zone out to some bad TV."

"We could still try for Italian," I suggested. "Our original plan from last week. Mikki, can we come over?" She shrugged and said sure.

The local Italian joints were closed (fair) so we settled on Chinese, piling onto the order potstickers and crab rangoon, hoping to drown our feelings in oil and salt. Mikki queued up *This Is Spinal Tap* without running it by us, which seemed odd, but soon I was distracted by its rat-a-tat rhythm, lazy off-the-cuff conversations in thick British accents, and then the concert scenes, so loud and triumphantly silly.

A particularly deafening *shrawww* of electric guitar roused Katie, who'd fallen asleep.

"Whew, guys, I gotta go home," she announced, giving her head a little shake. "We should do something tomorrow, even if it's just another dumb movie marathon. We shouldn't be alone." She waved from the door, and Mikki stood to lock the dead bolt behind her.

I twirled cold Lo Mein noodles around a fork as Mikki settled back and hit Play. The last few days had been awful, but there was something gentle thrumming underneath the horror: answers, a cessation, the promise that, in time, we could grieve and heal and move on. My eyes jumped to a screen on the coffee table, suddenly lit.

"Is that yours?" I nodded toward it, then saw that Mikki was on her own cell. "Dummy left her phone. Wonder when she'll notice."

"Good old Katie," Mikki replied, then yawned.

I slid my own phone from my purse and checked my email. Among the holiday promotions, one from Daniel:

Hana: Hopefully you're not checking emails on xmas eve. Karen said you guys headed back today and that she and Gary are waiting for Cameron to be found. I'm doing okay. I'm taking it an hour at a time. It hasn't sunk in yet that we know the bastard who did this. The detective said they found a lot of activity from him in Eleanor hate groups. I guess he never got over the rejection and blamed her for his wasted life. Makes me sick to think that he was at our wedding.

I shook my head involuntarily. Spinal Tap was wandering through a basement in search of the stage door; Mikki was tapping out a text.

Anyway, when you're back on the grid, I want your take on this: I found it in a box of old books in one of the closets in the foyer. (I've been tearing the apartment apart looking for clues.) I don't know what to make of it... are we concerned about her mental health? Pathological lying, etc.? I don't want to embarrass her but have been trying to think why E would've kept it, and since you were around back then, I thought you might have some idea. LMK when you get a chance. -D

I opened the attachment: a photograph of a sheet of paper, slightly off-kilter, the type a tiny bit blurred. A printed-out letter with

December 18, 2016, at the top, Eleanor's address below it, "sent via certified mail." I zoomed in:

To Whom It May Concern:

It has come to my attention that your newly announced company, The Herd, is substantially similar to my own business plan for The In, an all-female coworking space. Specifically, the aesthetics, company branding, and corporate model of The Herd are nearly identical to the corresponding details outlined in my business plan for The In.

I am the proprietor of all copyright within my business plan for The In, an all-female coworking space (the "Work"). I had reserved all rights in the Work, which was first published on May 21, 2010. You neither requested nor received permission to use my Work, therefore your unauthorized copying and use of my Work constitutes copyright infringement in violation of the United States copyright laws.

I hereby demand that you, within 30 days of this letter, immediately and permanently cease and desist the use of my Work. If you do not cease and desist within the above stated time period, I will be forced to take appropriate legal action against you and will seek all available damages and remedies.

Sincerely,
Mikki Danziger

A snowplow rumbled in the distance. I looked up at Mikki slowly, my heart beating louder than the drums and bass now shooting out of her TV. She scrolled at her screen, scratched her nose, oblivious to the baffling news I held in my hands.

Eleanor with her cute camp origin story. The one she'd casually filched from her friend. I could remember the moment Eleanor described to me her groundbreaking idea for an all-female coworking space: her eyes sparkling, voice bouncing with excitement, *Oh you* have *to move here to help me start it,* her words tumbling out faster and faster and faster—

"Mikki, what is this?" I handed her my phone and watched her eyes slide across the screen. A flash of fear in her eyes, and then a watercolor wash of pink seeped into her nose, her chin, her neck.

"Well, *that's* humiliating," she said, handing it back. Her chuckle was laced with pain. "You know what's funny? I was so worried about the cops finding that. I practically tore apart her office looking for it. And I even sent Cameron—I had no idea what he'd done, obviously, but once he told me he was in town—I had him go look for it at Eleanor's apartment. I thought it would look so bad for me, make me look guilty when I'm not. But now that I see it . . ." She puffed her lips, looked away. "It's stupid. A kid with an account on Legal-Documents-R-Us."

I paused the movie, then touched her forearm. "But what is it? What's the In?"

A surge of wind against the windows; she whipped her head toward the hallway.

"Let's table it," she said, her voice wafer-thin.

"I want to know. I'm here for you."

She sniffed. "It's stupid. In school, I took this Start-Up R&D class Eleanor had taken the semester before—it's where she came up with the bones of Gleam. The capstone project was to make an entire business plan for a start-up, and . . ." She looked up, blinked. "I came up with the Herd."

"What?"

"I hadn't actually copyrighted it or anything—it was a class assignment. But I was really proud of it. Coworking spaces were just becoming a thing, and I had the idea of making it a social club, too, for all the weird, smart, misfit women like me." A dark smile. "I think I wanted to manufacture the experience of falling in with someone like Eleanor. Like I had, freshman year. That's why I called it the In—like, the in-crowd."

This was too strange—it was swooping around the room too fast for me to catch it. I leaned forward. "And Eleanor saw it?"

"The whole thing. She had a copy. Saw me working on it and volunteered to give me feedback." She shrugged. "And then everything happened with Gleam. I forgot all about the In; I was working nonstop to get everything for Gleam designed and launched. In fact, I barely touched my art supplies for two years. And—sidebar—she could have, at any point, made me a full-time employee and given me insurance and PTO days and stuff. You, too, Hana. But no, I was a contractor, slaving away for her. Doing so much for Eleanor for pitiful project fees that I couldn't even take on lucrative work. And unlike you, I have student loans. And now, credit card debt. It never crossed your and Eleanor's minds to ask if I could swing the expensive dinners and cocktails and trips with you. You have no idea what that's like."

Something shot up through me, bile or a burp or years and years of suppressed guilt.

"God, can you imagine?" she went on. "'Sorry, I can't afford the thirty-eight dollar brunch, I'll stop at a falafel truck and meet you afterward'—humiliating. Being friends with you two is nothing if not keeping up appearances."

"Mikki, we didn't know. We should have known. I'm sorry. I'm so, so sorry."

"I know." A long, choking breath. "I should have just . . . figured it out on my own. But I was happy you two were so successful. I was overjoyed when Gleam blew up." She streaked her sleeve against her nose again. "I'll never forget the day she called me in to see her—she was running Gleam out of the Cave, ironically—and cheerfully announced she was going to launch a second company, and I'd be in charge of all the visuals. It was wild: She sat there, smiling, and told me all about the Herd. Basically repeated my whole pitch deck back to me all these years later. I kept waiting for her to acknowledge that, like it was a weird joke, but she never did."

This couldn't be. This *couldn't* be. I played it in my mind again: Eleanor excitedly telling me about the Herd, making me swear I wouldn't tell anyone, even whipping out her phone to record me stating my name and giving a verbal NDA.

But no—Mikki wasn't rewriting history. Deep down I knew it, knew her words were true. Guilt grabbed at me, clawing at my chest.

"So I gathered up all my courage and sent the cease-and-desist letter. Certified mail. I was on pins and needles, waiting for her to acknowledge it, and she just . . . never did."

"Why didn't you just *ask* her? Call her out in person?"

"I did, finally. Weeks later. And she said . . . she said if I tried to tell people that, she'd tell people about Jinny."

She broke down in sobs and I shook my head.

"I pushed her." The silence bloomed, echoed around her living room.

"You what?"

"I pushed Jinny. Playfully, when we were out by the pool. Eleanor saw what happened and . . . and pointed out that no one could prove it was an accident, that it was best that no one know. But then it finally came out, years later: *If you say I stole the Herd, I'll tell people you pushed Jinny.* A stalemate."

Shock burst out of me like laughter, like a cough. My hands, in the prayer position, pressed against my mouth.

"Why didn't you talk to me?"

"I tried," she said. "But every time I mentioned Eleanor's name, your face lit up like a Christmas tree. You were so enamored of her—you didn't want to see."

"Oof," I said. All this time, I'd been envious of Mikki for seeming so carefree and unencumbered. I'd thought her and Eleanor's relationship was uncomplicated, pure. Regret widened in me like a yawn.

And then it occurred to me, the unthinkable, the other half of the horrific Eleanor-Mikki equation. *She couldn't . . . ?*

As if she'd heard my thoughts: "Anyway, I obviously had my feelings hurt, but I would never hurt Eleanor. I miss her. Despite everything, I loved her so much."

I felt the wheels turning. "So did Cameron . . . I assumed he just hated her because she rejected him all those years ago. But did he also know about this? About what she was doing to you?"

She chewed on her lip, then nodded. "He was the only person I told. He was, like, the one person who didn't see Eleanor with this huge halo around her—he believed me." She nodded again. "He encouraged me to stand up for myself. But I didn't. It kills me to think that I . . . that he . . ."

"Oh, Mikki." I pulled her into a hug and felt her shake against my collarbone. I smoothed a hand over her hair. "It's okay. It's over now."

"I feel awful," she croaked.

I swallowed. "Did Cameron tell you anything? Did you know?"

"I didn't know anything." She pulled away to wipe her nose. Eyes, nose, cheeks—all poinsettia red. "I had no idea he was in town. Or, Jesus, that he stabbed her and left her on the roof. I didn't hear from him until Wednesday—the day after we realized she was missing—and he told me he'd come down to try to help." A rickety sigh. "Like I said, I asked him to look for the cease-and-desist letter. I wasn't thinking straight; I was worried they'd suspect me. Until last night, I had no idea the killer was actually him. And now he's . . ."

She groaned and rubbed her palms over her blotchy face, then stood. "I really want to go to bed, if that's okay," she said.

"Of course. We'll do something tomorrow, if you're up for it." I slid my arms into my coat and followed her to the door.

She unlocked the dead bolt and I turned to look her in the eye. "Mikki, I'm really sorry. I want you to be able to talk to me about anything and I'm just really sorry you felt like you couldn't."

She sniffled. "Thanks." I hugged her and it was an odd, uneven hug, me in my hat and unzipped parka, her bony and birdlike under my arms. Then I trudged downstairs and spotted a yellow taxi cruising past. I lifted my arm—what luck, spotting one on Christmas Eve—and in it I rolled north into Queens, Manhattan's skyline glittering to my left.

Gary was calling, his face popping up in a goofy photo I'd taken at a Harvard football game all those years ago. The cabbie peered at me in the rearview mirror as I fumbled to answer.

"They found him, Hana," he said as soon as I picked up, his voice pulsing with hysterics. "In a motel a few hours outside Montreal. He used the fake passport to get a room at a seedy motel and they found him almost dead with a needle sticking out of his arm, they say he'd—he was—"

"Gary. It's okay. Just breathe." A sob welled up in my throat and I swallowed hard. "Let's slow down. Where are you?"

"We're at home. That Ratcliff woman called us. They're rushing Cameron to a hospital right now."

A sheet of snow slid off a tree, pounced on the taxi's roof. "But he's okay?"

"She said he's stable. That's all they know." He stuttered for a second. "She said it was a huge amount of heroin. A suicide attempt."

"But he's stable. She said he's stable."

"But they don't know if he'll be able to talk. To tell us what—what really happened to Eleanor."

"It's okay. It's okay."

I wasn't sure what to make of any of this, and I imagined Gary didn't either. He sounded terrified for Cameron—his surrogate kid, the son he never had—but did he still believe Cameron was innocent?

"He had—" He paused and moaned, a sound so sad tears poured down my own cheeks. It took him a few tries to get it out. "He had Eleanor's laptop with him. And her phone."

"Oh, Gary. I'm so sorry." I let him cry for a moment. I was touched that he called me, but also surprised. "What can I do? Do you want me to come back up to Beverly?"

"No. I just . . . I thought all of you should know. Mikki too."

Oh God—not after the night Mikki had. I'd let the poor thing sleep. "She's in bed but I'll let her know tomorrow. Can you keep me updated on any news?"

"I will. I will."

"Okay. Take care of yourself. Karen too."

"I will."

I hung up and the driver turned the music back up.

"It will be a white Christmas, ma'am," he said.

I didn't reply.

CHAPTER 24

===

Katie

I rounded the corner just in time to see a cab drifting away from Mikki's building and sighed. Now that I'd likely missed the last bus—I couldn't confirm without the use of my damn phone, presumably still on Mikki's coffee table—all I wanted was a direct ride home. Soon I'd be standing in Mikki's Wi-Fi and summoning a car. Hopefully she hadn't fallen asleep. Did her buzzer even work? My last resort would involve flinging snowballs at her window.

I went to town on the buzzer, pushing it to the beat of Jingle Bells, imagining I could hear it in the cold, still night. Finally Mikki's voice crackled through: "Hello?"

"It's Katie! Thank God you're up."

"Your phone, right? I can bring it down."

I hopped from one foot to the other. "Actually, can I come up and use the bathroom?" *And wait for my car from the warmth of your living room?*

Another beat, then the shriek as she buzzed me in. I hurried up the cracked marble steps, past red and green garland, paper candy canes, and snowman cutouts. Mikki looked harried as she answered the door, still clad in sweats, her hair pulled back in a scrunchie.

"My precious," I murmured as I scooped up my phone. There was a small glass pipe next to it, the weed inside still smoking.

"You want?" she said.

I shook my head. Pot made me paranoid—she knew that. "No, thanks. When did Hana leave?"

"Just a few minutes ago." She rubbed her eyes. "I was just gonna finish the movie and crash."

"Okay. I'll be right back." I headed toward the bathroom. The hallway was covered with framed paintings she'd brought back from a three-week stint in Vietnam: nudes on uneven sheets of bamboo paper, a few black strokes intimating the female form. I mistook her bedroom door for the bathroom before continuing down the hall.

On the walk back, I peered back into her room. I was drawn to the massive workspace hulking in the corner, covered in haphazard piles and a bulky ceramic lamp. An orange trapezoid of light from the fire escape fell on it squarely, like a spotlight. Without turning on the light, I tiptoed through the space between her closet and bed and leaned down to look.

The collages. *I've been doing these large-scale works and then taking photos of them and working* those *into my collages,* she'd said in the bathroom of the Herd, topless and powerful, all those weeks ago. There were no final products here, but I spotted a few usable chunks of photos: a mouse spray-painted on the sidewalk, the photo of it cut into the shape of a cat, and a female reproductive system, ovaries and Fallopian tubes and everything, stenciled on what looked like aluminum siding, carved into the shape of California.

The word HERE written in fat white bubble letters, so familiar I could swear I'd seen them before, with the final *E* crossed out in a careful red X, the photo then cut into a bird's silhouette.

Fringing the gray-white desktop were little scraps of photos in odd, puzzle-piece shapes, the literal cutting-room floor. The leftovers, the negative space from whatever she carved out. I picked up a chunk, smooth along one side and carefully sliced along the others, curvy and sawtooth in spots. I tilted it into the light, wriggled it to lose the glare. Mauve with delicate white pinstripes. The Gleam Room.

Large-scale works. I remembered the first time I'd entered that room, almost too entranced by the array of pretty Gleam products to notice it. UGLY CUNTS. *But there was no way Mikki . . . why would she . . .*

The overhead light switched on like a migraine, like a seizure, and I whirled around. Mikki stood in the doorframe.

"Baby girl," she said, her lips curled into something between a smirk and a grimace. "Are you creeping on my desk?" She took a few steps forward and paused by her open closet door. She leaned against it, and the hanging organizer stuffed with cocktail jewelry and feathers and beads slid along the wood.

My brain was doing something frantic—*the graffiti, the tagging, what does it mean that she did that*—while my torso took over with something much more primal: fear. "I just wanted to see the collages you've been talking about!" I stretched my mouth into a smile, groped around for a joke: "Figured I'd give it the ol' *collage* try!"

She smiled. "Why were you in the dark?"

"I—I didn't want you to think I was snooping. Which I totally am." I realized I was still clutching the pinstripe photo and casually dropped it on the desk behind me.

"Well, what do you think?" She crossed her arms. "I've been wanting to talk to you about the collection for a while."

"I'd love to see a finished one. Where are those?"

"What were you looking at?" She crossed the few feet between us and I flinched; she reached past my hip and picked up the picture scrap of the Herd's Gleam Room wall. Without looking up: "You recognize this, don't you?"

"I'm not sure. Hey, I should get going." I shifted my weight and she looked at me, her thin frame somehow formidable.

"You recognize this, I can tell." She dropped the scrap on the bed and its soft landing made me think of a snowflake.

I shrugged, channeling all my energy into seeming casual. "I know I know it, but I can't place it. Is it the Herd?"

"Ding-ding-ding!" She aimed a finger-gun my way. "That's exactly where it's from."

"I love that you worked it into your art!" I gave my shoulders a cheery shake. "Your beautiful aesthetic is all over the Herd, on every square inch—and your package design, obviously, on the products in the Gleam Room." Why was my heart pounding, jittering my entire torso? Mikki still hadn't said or done anything nefarious. But there was something I was so close to seeing, a revelation hovering on the tip of my tongue. "And now you've worked it into your own art. It's like a hall of mirrors!" I thought crazily of the foyer in Eleanor and Daniel's townhouse, the big mirror-fronted closet doors. A million Mikkis, Hanas, and me's fading out into the distance.

"I guess you could say that."

"Were you just getting the striped wall here?" I asked, my fingers sweeping toward the image. "Or were you actually capturing the graffiti? That would be very . . . avant-garde." *Because there's no way you could've done it,* I tried to beam from my brain to hers. *You would never antagonize Eleanor like that.*

"Don't tell anyone, but I was actually pretty proud of how I pulled it all off." She leaned against the wall. "I knew Eleanor wouldn't like it, but I didn't think it would really throw her off her game. She hates the word so much. *Cunt.* Why give it all that power? It's just a word. Don't be cunty."

I grinned conspiratorially, as if all of this were logical—nay, brilliant. "I love that. Reclaiming the word. Did you spray-paint it yourself?"

"In the West Village, yeah. It was easy; there were security cameras in the elevator, but not the stairs. Obviously I wasn't in San Francisco or Fort Greene—I had friends do it there. I was hoping to have a whole collection of collages done by the end of the year. And I figured out the name for it: It'll be WOMEN, but with the W in white and 'OMEN' in red." She flourished her palm, as if seeing it on a wall.

"Great title. Very ominous."

She nodded. "It was gonna be a representation of just how fucked women are in society. It's like, women unfairly can't own up to their shit because they're punished so harshly for not being perfect. Men can fuck up and move on, but not women. If you're a woman, you're always one mistake away from being worthless again. You go through life waiting for everything to be taken away, bending over backward trying to prove your worth, driving yourself crazy trying to get everyone to like and respect you. We do it in jobs, we even do it in our extracurricular lives—fuck, look at the Herd, women begging for the opportunity to spend three hundred dollars a month on a membership to a female-only space where you're *still* expected to dress up and put on makeup and smile and mingle, and you have to slit your wrists if you smear your lipstick or say the wrong thing or fart in the bathroom." Her voice was rising, growing, hurtling out like a mushroom cloud. "And the one way to win, the one fucking way to be a woman and do well in this world is to stomp on other women's backs. Like Eleanor did to me."

My voice was a small and shaky Chihuahua: "What did Eleanor do?"

She ignored me, stared thoughtfully at the photo scrap on the bed. "I thought she'd eventually see WOMEN, but she never got the chance. And now I'm not sure I can ever show it. It was just art, but I don't want to be accused of murder. I mean, the whole thing was fucked once some rando stole her phone and tried to spread photos of our work—that was never my intention."

"The police thought it was all linked," I said. "The graffiti, the stolen phone, and then the murder." On journalist autopilot, I was keeping the conversation flowing, but my brain kept replaying Mikki's mysterious rant: *How had Eleanor stomped on Mikki's back?*

"I had nothing to do with that. Her phone probably fell out of her bag in a cab, and then some asshole accessed the photos and tried to make a buck." She shrugged. "I was glad that didn't happen. I wanted my collages to be the first time people saw it."

"So the police were wrong. None of it was connected."

"Guess not. The graffiti was me. The phone was a petty thief. And the murder . . ." She looked away, blinking back tears. "Just Cameron confronting Eleanor about what she did to Jinny." She shook her head. "He must have known she was about ready to leave. It's all so . . . wrong. She *almost* got away with running off to Mexico. He *almost* got away with killing her. What the fuck was his plan with the body? Just leave it on the roof forever and hope no one ever noticed him driving in and out of Manhattan? It's all so . . . messy. So deluded."

A tear slid down her cheek and I took a step toward her. "Mikki, I haven't told you how sorry I am. About everything, but especially about Cameron. I barely knew him, obviously, and I had no idea you two were so close. It's . . . a lot." I reached my arms out for a hug and her shoulders jumped reflexively, one hand jerking toward the big orange lamp on her desk. I looked at it and her fingers retreated; stiffly, she let me hug her.

"I'm gonna go call a car, okay?" I said, and she stared blankly for a moment before nodding. She didn't move, so I turned toward the door. A few steps later my eyes fell on the craft organizer hanging from her closet door. I saw them all clustered in one pocket, like a deadly bouquet—shiny and sharp, the same tool I'd often seen in her overstuffed backpack on account of all the careful photo cutting she was doing. My chest turned to cold steel, and before I knew what I was doing, I reached out and touched the cap of one, the X-Acto knife's blade glistening below it.

"Oh my God," I said. "It was never a scalpel."

Behind me, a heavy scraping sound. "You don't understand. If you'd been there you'd understand."

Scorching heat on the back of my head, then a plummeting sensation. My legs gave out and the floor rammed my kneecaps.

I twisted around and Mikki was murky, swirling, something huge in her hands, round and orange as a pumpkin. I was moving in slow motion, my head drifting backward like I was doing a trust fall.

"I didn't know it was in my hand," she was saying. "We were the last ones there, and—and she'd told me about the acquisition and I couldn't *stand* it any longer, I said, 'You know you stole the idea from me.' And she said, 'But Mikki, it doesn't matter. Because I'm the founder, and you're not.'"

Falling, falling, downward, downward, down. My tongue and lips and teeth collaborated, just for a moment: "Fuck you."

"It was an instinct, it was like in krav maga. Like I was trying to block a blow. I shot my hand forward and it wasn't until—I didn't realize until . . ."

Another sunburst as I crashed to the floor, wooden slats bouncing against my skull. A momentary humming noise, and then, finally, blackness.

CHAPTER 25

———

Hana

Mannheim Steamroller blasted through the taxi's speakers, each synthesized note like a personal jackhammer to my brain. It'd been four or five years since Cameron came out of rehab, a posh treatment center in Arizona, and as far as we knew, he hadn't touched an opioid since. The news wobbled through my torso, prickling with pressure.

Had Daniel heard the news? I reread his email to me, the one with Mikki's pathetic cease-and-desist letter. How hugely, devastatingly sad. Overlooked by her group of friends, betrayed by her best friend, and now abandoned by her secret lover, who crossed a border to try to kill himself in peace.

I spotted a new email from a publicist friend, one I'd worked with years before: "So sorry to hear the news about your friend Eleanor. Let us know when the memorial service will be. You've probably already seen this, but I just saw it on Twitter—thought you'd want a heads-up."

She'd linked to a trashy gossip site that made *The Gaze* look like the *Times*. I followed the link, then felt a blast of heady nausea: EXCLUSIVE VIDEO: SEE THE EXACT MOMENT ELEANOR WALSH'S BODY WAS FOUND.

It started automatically—a cell-phone video, shaky and pulsing in and out of focus. Three figures in a bright window. *Us.* That Friday night, as a drum corps chopped the air on the street below, someone in a nearby building had lifted his lens and focused on the three women—Katie, Mikki, me—silhouetted across the way. The video zoomed in and I watched, rapt, as this small outline of me lifted her phone and pressed it against the glass, then said something, then tapped at the phone. Katie responded, and then the miniature me whirled around and disappeared into the light.

I'm gonna see if I can get it from the roof, I'd said, clomping toward the staircase. And that was where my perspective, my eyes on the two women in the window, faded out.

But now, on my phone's greasy screen, I could see it all. I could see how Mikki's hand shot to her mouth, how her shoulders tensed before she turned around and took a few furtive steps after me. How Katie had kept her forehead near the window's coolness, delighted, enchanted, distracted, while Mikki shifted on the balls of her feet, staring toward the staircase, both hands clenched near her mouth.

And then the camera canted upward, dizzily, too zoomed-in for a huge maneuver, and found me picking my way across the roof.

Fingers shaking, I closed the video and called Mikki. Straight to voicemail. To the right, a sign rolled past the window: LAST EXIT BEFORE TOLL.

"Take the exit!" I yelled, so loud it spooked even me. "We're going back to Greenpoint."

———

I thrust a fistful of bills at the driver and hurtled up Mikki's stoop. I leaned on the buzzer the way a bored cabbie leans on the horn: absurdly, forlornly, relentlessly.

"Jesus! Who is it?"

"It's Hana. Let me up."

"I was sleeping. Did you forget something too?"

"Let me up."

"What are you doing here?"

"Mikki, I know you knew Eleanor was on the roof." I leaned into the speaker, listened to her Darth Vader breath. "Why are you covering for Cameron?"

Sobs, splintered and crackly through the intercom. "Just let me go to sleep, Hana. Just let me be."

"Let me up or I'm calling Ratliff."

More crying, and then next to me, so loudly I jumped, the *screeeeeeh* of the door unlocking.

Mikki peeled the door open gingerly. A dim lamp cast shadows into the corners, and everything else—the hallway, the TV, the air around us—was waiting and dark. She had a hoodie on over her pajamas, and her eyes were swollen and squinty, two pale pieces of puffed rice.

"Mikki, it's okay."

She stuffed her hands into the front pocket of her sweatshirt and flopped onto the couch. On the coffee table, a lighter, pipe, and small mess of weed sat in a jumbled pile.

I perched on the sofa. "Just talk to me! I don't want to get you in trouble. I wanna help you."

She took a long, unsteady breath. "How did you know?"

I held out my phone. "This video. I saw how you didn't want me up on the roof."

Wind yanked at the windows as she watched it. Finally she pressed the screen against her knee and closed her eyes. "I didn't do it."

"But you knew she was there."

"Can we talk about this tomorrow?"

"Mikki."

She swiped at a tear. "I don't know why I helped him."

I waited. Her heater clanged, as if it, too, were growing impatient.

"He called and told me what he'd done." She dragged her sleeve against her nose. "He said he was going to turn off the lights and lock all the doors. And that he'd go into the janitor's closet and get out all the cleaning supplies, not let the blood get onto anything it could stain. I said I'd be right there."

Say no to Cameron, Mikki, I pleaded silently, like she could change how the story ended. *Tell Cameron to fuck off.* "Why?"

She turned. "Why, what?"

"Why did you go to him?"

Mikki frowned. "I don't know. He knew about the Jinny situation, obviously. And we were—we talked every single day. When we saw each other, it was . . . electric. We never talked about trying to turn it into a real relationship or anything, but . . ." She shrugged. "Love makes you do crazy things."

She wiped both eyes at once, then looked at the tears glistening on her index fingers. "When I got there, Cameron was calm. He'd been thinking. He said we couldn't take her out of the building, because someone would see us carrying her. It was the beginning of that cold snap, so he had the idea of hiding her on the roof until we could come back in the middle of the night and get rid of her."

Something surged up my throat, acidic and foul, but I kept listening.

"He carried her upstairs and left her behind the stack of lawn chairs. I helped him clean. He kept saying we just needed to buy enough time that no one would look there until a bunch of other people had passed the spot. But of course, there was still the issue of everyone looking for her. She had that presentation the next day."

I gripped my fists under my chin, thumbs digging into my windpipe. *No, no, no, no.* Mikki's face softened. "But Cameron had an idea. Apparently she'd come to him with questions about getting a fake passport. So he knew she was hiding something too. We got out her phone, and it's turned on by face recognition, right? So Cameron ran back to the roof and, and held it up to unlock it." Her eyebrows flashed. "We were shocked to find all this stuff about moving to Mexico. It felt like a gift from God. If we could just make her seem alive while people noticed that, we'd be in the clear."

She was quiet long enough that I cleared my throat. Mikki had accessed all of Eleanor's plans for escaping to Mexico—this was unfathomable, but it was my one shot, my chance to ask what I couldn't ask Eleanor herself. "Did she say why she wanted to leave? Was it the blackmail—she thought she was close to being ratted out?"

Mikki stared at me, her eyes stony but small muscles contracting around her nose and mouth.

"I don't know. She didn't say. I don't know why Eleanor did anything she did." Mikki spoke faster now, like she was eager to get the rest over with. "You know how this ends. Cameron sent out a few emails and texts from her phone the next day. And then when it was clear you and Katie were onto her, had figured out her Mexico plans, Cameron sent that final email from her laptop. We still had no plan for the body, though. Our luck was up on the security cameras: I asked a lot of questions and learned they were back up and running."

"Oh, Mikki." The air around us was charged, staticky with the knowledge that this was the very last time things would be okay. Could she feel it too?

"Then once you found her, I was taking it an hour at a time. And I was grieving—it was almost like I'd convinced myself she really *was* in Mexico, before that. When the Walshes invited us to Beverly for Christmas, I thought getting away from New York could be good—plus I could check on Cameron, make sure he was solid. But seeing Gary and Karen was awful. I don't know what I was thinking. I *wasn't* thinking."

We sat like that for a second. The heater hissed.

"You need to tell Ratliff," I said. "I'll come with you—we'll tell them everything. It won't be so bad if you're cooperative, if you're a witness for the prosecution." With a prickle of fear, I realized she'd slipped my phone from her lap down under her thigh, out of reach.

"But Cameron's gone—there's no way for me to prove it was him. There's no point." I thought I heard a thunk from the hallway and we both glanced that way. It was too cold and too late and too dark; the night was careening away from me.

I leaned forward. "Mikki, they found Cameron. In Canada. Gary just called me."

"No."

"It's true. He's in custody."

Another thunk and I sat up, twisting my trunk, then turned back in time to see Mikki's hand emerging from the pocket of her hoodie.

Her movement was so swift, so precise, it was as if she'd been practicing for this moment. A little "hah!" escaped from her lungs as her arm shot forward, then hard pressure on my lower-right ribs. My chin swung down to take it in: The entire blade swallowed by the flesh below my bra. Blood oozing out around it like wine soaking into a tablecloth. I thought, oddly, of Mom, the cancer in her breast, scalpels rooting around for the poisoned tissue.

A second passed, then another, and then, with the brutality of a stampede, sudden, epic pain. The last thing I noticed was Mikki's knuckles, still wrapped around the X-Acto knife's handle.

CHAPTER 26

Katie

An earthquake.

I kept my eyes closed because the earth was shaking, tectonic plates shifting, and I couldn't let the ceiling fall in on me, or slip into a crevasse and let the ground swallow me whole. I squeezed them shut and then had an idea:

Open them.

The earth wasn't shaking: I was. I was in the fetal position and my hands in front of my face were an odd color, orangey white. I couldn't get a good look because they were quivering, and my head, too, my vision, nothing but shakes.

I tried to loll my head back and something burned the back of my skull, a branding iron, and through my shuddering jaw I moaned. I tried to sit up, failed. Banged my cheek back down on the iron below me.

Iron—iron bars, below and in front of me. I looked beyond them and made out a wall of brick a few feet away, spotlit in the dark by the same orange glow. My logic kicked in, stitched the world together: I was outside in the freezing cold, without a jacket. I was . . . it came together, a pouncing revelation, I was on Mikki's fire escape, the one I'd seen in her bedroom, dumped and left to die. *Why was I out here? Why did my head . . . she'd hit me, right?* I tried moving my neck again and found the white-hot patch.

I had to think. Thinking was hard, slow, thick, thoughts like crankcase oil in a freezing cold engine. The first order of business was warming up. I needed to get inside. I ordered my hands to collect under me and was alarmed when they only half obliged. I wrenched open my chattering jaw and tried to scream, but what came out was a dry rasp, a white cloud, there and then gone. My heat—warmth from the inside, from my lungs, I needed to conserve it.

Roll call: Knees? Present. I awkwardly army crawled across the cold iron until my shoulder hit the window. I tried to look inside: darkness, the door between her bedroom and hallway closed. I rocked away and then slammed against the glass, once, twice, explosions of pain and the knowledge this would never work—it wouldn't open it, wouldn't attract attention, nobody would hear it in the cold with their windows sealed so tight, if only it were summer, in summer people are—

Focus. I was four floors up. Too many to jump, and in this state, my arms and legs shaking so violently I couldn't see straight, I wouldn't make it down three ladders. I wanted to cry, to scream, let the shaking overcome me and roll me right off the side.

One floor: I only had to go one floor to be on someone else's fire escape. I closed my eyes for a moment, listening to my own gasping breath, to the pounding of blood in my ears. I heard distant Christmas music, the honk of a horn. I said a silent prayer, and then I moved.

I made it down two rungs before my hands, stiff like Barbie's, failed me and I fell hard onto my tailbone. The impact jolted me but didn't hurt, and in a faraway, filmy way I knew this wasn't good, this indicated something bad. I stared at the stars overhead, a few visible even here in our huge city, with all its light pollution and pollution-pollution and people, people are garbage, there's so much garbage in the city streets, it flies up from the sidewalk and smacks into you when you—

A strange scraping sound. "Are you okay?" It was a girl's voice, a kid or maybe a teenager, and it took me a moment to realize that since it was a question, I was supposed to answer.

"Eeugh." I wasn't sure what I meant, but that's what came out. I heard her gasp and step away from the window and I started to cry, *please don't leave me, please stay and—*

"Yes, hello, there's a woman on our fire escape, it appears she fell coming down and she's not wearing a coat, she's shaking pretty violently, she could be—ma'am, are you drunk? Are you okay?" It was a woman's voice, an adult, and she appeared above me with a phone pressed to her ear, and I pointed a shaking hand at the back of my head, sucked cold air into my lungs, and said the one word I'd been unable to utter for months: "Help."

The woman and her daughter brought me inside and spread me on the floor with a blanket over my body and a pillow under my head. The shaking intensified as heat worked its way back into my limbs, firecrackers from the inside, heat and light. My brain still felt sludgy, logy, slow. I heard sirens warbling through the night and for the first time in months, I didn't tense, didn't summon Chris and with her a rushing meteor of shame and heartbreak. I was grateful for them. Eager to get to the hospital. Then I could tell—

The EMTs arrived and none of them would listen, none could hear what I was trying to tell them. I kept pointing at the ceiling and they kept tucking my hand back under the blanket. Finally I sat up and touched the back of my head, the wound there, flinching.

"Mikki, upstairs, the apartment right above this one—she did this," I said. "You need to get her now—I think she killed my friend."

But EMTs aren't cops and so they told me they'd send the nearest squad car, and it arrived, lights flashing, right as they were lifting me in a gurney into the back of the ambulance. They'd strapped me down and had just slammed the doors when there was more commotion, shouting, walkie-talkies crunching and snapping and medics hustling back outside. The woman from upstairs was going to ride with me—my angel, her name was Sue, I never did see her again—and she saw the alarm in my face and said she'd try to figure out what was going on.

The ambulance door flew open and they were lifting a second body into it, a stranger, who the hell was this? I watched as the body, unfamiliar, foreign, was locked into place next to me.

And then it was like the big twist in a movie, the huge reveal, the unfathomable surprise, the bombshell that leaves you almost *elated* with its unexpectedness, how everything you thought you knew was wrong.

It wasn't just a body. It was Hana.

CHAPTER 27

Hana

In my mind, Katie had gotten older just three times in her life, time standing still and then bounding forward in great leaps: once while I was a teenager in California, another while she was in college at NYU, and then finally while she was in Kalamazoo helping Mom. During those periods, the Disney-like spell had lifted, months could pass, and when I saw her again she looked different, older, more mature. The rest of the time, everything about her stayed the same, as if the ravages of radiation and worry and other things that left us pockmarked with each passing day didn't apply to her.

But watching her sleep on this hospital bed, I realized that again, her peaceful face had changed. Overnight, perhaps, or else I hadn't been paying attention, hadn't looked at her hard enough. Her skin was still smooth and perfect, but she wasn't the teenage-ish little sister I'd been projecting onto her.

I couldn't help it—I smoothed a hand along her hairline, and she stirred.

"I'm so glad you're awake!"

She looked at me blankly, then around the room, and I listened as the beeping on a monitor ticked up in tempo with her heart.

"It's okay, Katie. It's okay." I patted her shin. "You had a concussion and some frostbite, but you're okay."

"You're okay?"

I smiled. "You saved my life." She frowned and shook her head in confusion, then gasped and reached for her head. "Ooh, you've got a massive contusion there," I said, for some reason echoing the doctor's words. "It's where you were hit."

"By Mikki."

"That's right."

"Where is she?"

"In a holding cell. She was arrested." I lifted my shirt to show her the bandage below my bra. "After she gave me this."

"I thought you were dead."

"Oh, sweetie." I grabbed her hand. "You were hit on the head, hard, and passed out—they think for at least twenty minutes. And for most of that you were outside without a coat, so your core body temperature was dropping. They said it's totally normal for you to be confused today."

She narrowed her eyes at me. "But you were in the ambulance."

"I was." I took a breath. "I went back to Mikki's apartment to ask her about something. She told me you'd already left, but in reality you were just passed out and she'd pushed you onto the fire escape—presumably until she could get rid of me." I brought my other hand to hers, clutched it between my palms. There were bandages on her fingertips where the cold had seeped inside. "But you came to and you got help. It's incredible, I don't know how you made it down without killing yourself. But when the neighbors called the ambulance, you made them call the police too. For Mikki." I shook my head. "If they'd arrived even a few minutes later, I don't know what would've happened. I'd just confronted Mikki and she—she got out—"

"The X-Acto knife! Not a scalpel!"

"Exactly!" We nodded at each other.

Tears welled and I looked away, pretended I was telling someone else's story. "She just missed puncturing my lung, apparently, and had taken a few steps back like she was trying to figure out what to do now, when the cops arrived. They banged on the door right behind me and I started yelling for help and trying to undo the locks and let them in. The good news is: A woman screaming for help is probable cause to enter a home."

I was trying to sound cheerful and it of course fell flat. Katie looked horrified. "Why did Mikki do that?"

"There's a lot we don't know. But it sounds like she made a full confession. For killing Eleanor."

She thought about this, then nodded. "How long have we been here?"

"Well, it's almost seven, so . . . a while." I tugged at a curl and looked away. "Mom's on her way here now. She's supposed to land around noon."

"Okay." She creased her brow. "So it's Christmas?"

"That's right. Merry Christmas, Katie."

"Why did you . . ." The heart-rate monitor hit the gas again, *beep! beep! beep!* "Why did you go back to Mikki's?"

I told her about the cease-and-desist Daniel had uncovered—how Mikki had explained it away, swearing she knew nothing about Cameron, and sent me off into the night still convinced of her innocence. And then I told her about the cell-phone video, which I now knew was from a random dude who worked at a start-up across the street; he'd begun taping the drum line, same as us, and then noticed the lineup of women across from him. He'd had no idea what he'd captured until Eleanor's death became public earlier this week. (And, with true entrepreneurial initiative, he'd sold the clip to the highest bidder instead of handing it over to the police.)

"It was clear she knew Eleanor's body was on the roof, so I wanted to know why she was covering for him," I said. "And she told me she'd gone over to the Herd and helped him hide the body. It was when I told her Cameron was alive and in custody that she snapped." I sighed. "I didn't mention that he was unconscious and at death's door. She must've taken that to mean he was going to start talking—the jig was up. She had the blade in her hand—told the cops it was a reflex."

"How *is* Cameron?"

"He's doing well—he's fully conscious and cooperating with au-thorities," I said. "Ratliff called a little while ago and said he'd given a full confession with the hope of a lighter sentence." It was now obvious that everything Mikki had told me last night—the desper-ate scramble to hide a body and clean up the evidence—was true. The critical difference, which Ratliff expected cell-phone records to corroborate, was that it'd been *Mikki* who'd been alone with Elea-nor in her last moments, and Cameron who'd swooped in to help.

I smiled and gave Katie's hair a little pat. "Anyway, you saved my life. You're the reason they got me in an ambulance in time."

"I thought I was gonna die," she replied.

A knock on the doorframe—I stood and greeted Ratliff and Her-rera.

"Sorry for—er, thanks for coming on Christmas," I said. Not apologizing for things that weren't my fault: an early New Year's resolution.

"I'm Jewish, so." Ratliff's lips flickered in and out of a smile. She turned to Katie. "How are you feeling?"

"Merry and bright," she deadpanned.

Ratliff clasped her hands together. "Well, we're glad you're safe and grateful for your bravery."

Katie pulled herself up into a sitting position, then yelped; I hadn't mentioned the bruised tailbone. "I want to know what's going on with Mikki."

"Ms. Danziger is in a holding cell in the station. We'll be interviewing her later today."

"Did Mikki say anything?" Katie asked.

Ratliff shifted her weight. "She did some talking last night. She'll have a court-appointed lawyer this afternoon. But we have a pretty complete picture from Mr. Corrigan already. He's been moved to a hospital in Cambridge."

"Cameron, right?" Katie broke in.

Ratliff assented, and I added: "Ted's fine. He's still at his parents'. Gary and Karen talked to him this morning."

"That's good." Katie swallowed.

Herrera turned to me suddenly. "Hana, can we talk to you in the hall?"

I glanced at Katie, whose eyes flashed in alarm, but I smiled soothingly. "We'll be right back."

In the cold, blue-white hallway, we formed a triangle. I gazed at them calmly as my heart thwacked in my chest. My heartbeat was a drum in my ears, pulsing over what was about to come out of their mouths: the blackmail, Jinny's mom. Jinny's cold, slight body. The tangled cover on the Walshes' pool. The Walshes themselves, watching stone-eyed as we'd backed out of their driveway with a secret the size of a hurricane in our chests.

"We'll be reopening a cold case on account of something Ms. Danziger told us," Ratliff said. "From May 2010."

Breathe. Breathe. Breathe. Eye muscles relaxed, shoulders down.

"She indicated that she and Ms. Walsh had been involved in the incidental death of a young woman in the Boston area. A missing-persons case."

What had Cameron told them? And Daniel—the blackmail note he never should have seen? I pursed my brows. "From 2010. When we were at Harvard?"

"That's right." She stared at me, then leaned forward. "A young woman went missing in the Boston area. Virginia Hurst. Did you know anything about that?"

I angled my head. "That sounds familiar. It was all over the news, and obviously it's scary when a young woman goes missing in your area. But I haven't thought about it in . . . gosh, almost ten years."

My pulse was louder now, an ocean, miniature hearts beating in my neck and feet and fingertips.

Her gaze softened. "I'm so sorry to tell you this, and of course we'll have to investigate the claims. But Mikki told us that this young woman died in a drowning accident at Ms. Walsh's home that night."

I took a step back, brought my hand to my heart. This was good— now the panic could seep out as shock. "No. No way."

"We've contacted the original detectives on the case. They're pulling the files. It's not—we're not sure about it yet, but it seems to fit. I wanted you to know before we release any information. If it checks out, obviously we'll be informing the family."

The family—Celia Hurst, the Tennessee-bound mom, broken with grief and dropping blackmail letters in the post. *Would Ratliff mention the blackmail? Did she still not know about it? Surely the sender wouldn't mention it: her extortion, her grand payouts.*

"I can't believe this. A drowning accident?" My thumb found my lips. "That was . . . senior year. Eleanor had a little apartment on Mass Ave. How did somebody drown?"

"At her family home," Herrera broke in. "In Beverly."

My eyebrows shot up. "In Beverly? Where we just were?" *They have a pool,* I almost spit out, then stopped myself. "Did she say what happened?" Lying to cops—this was a battle with my instincts, with everything I'd picked up as I'd moved through the world. Eyes down, voice calm, be respectful, tell the truth. Hands where we can see 'em.

"We'll know more soon. It seems there was an accidental drowning and then Mr. Corrigan helped dispose of the body."

Cameron? This time the astonishment on my face was real. The lie buzzed in my mind like the Operation game, *burrrrhhh*: Nine years ago, Gary and Karen had sent us on our way, Karen's head bowed, Gary's chin lifted, and taken care of the body themselves. *Why lie? What had Cameron told them? More important, why was Mikki protecting me?* Suddenly tears coated my eyes and I let the big feeling, relief and horror and guilt and panic, shoot out in ugly sobs.

Herrera took a step back, but Ratliff placed her fingers on my forearm. "This must be difficult to hear. We know you three were very close," she said. "Now we're asking you, informally—is there *anything* you want to tell us?"

I kept crying in lieu of answering. A nurse pushed a new mom in a wheelchair past. I glanced down in time to see the newborn huddled against her chest, its cheek a flash of shiny pink.

Finally I shook my head. "Thanks for telling me."

"All right." Ratliff planted her hands on her hips. "We'll be in touch about having you come in for formal statements. You can go back to your sister now." A soft smile. "She needs you."

The second I stepped into Katie's hospital room and pressed the door closed behind me, I began to shake, huge full-body tremors as if my body temp were plummeting.

"What is it?" Katie called, trying to sit up again.

I crossed to her bed and perched on the edge. Took her hand again, pressed it between both palms. In a whisper: "Mikki told them about Jinny."

"No. Oh my God. No. I can't lose y—"

I shushed her. "She didn't mention me. Or Gary and Karen.

She's taking the entire fall." I swallowed hard, felt my hands still quivering around Katie's. "Except Cameron. She brought him into it. I don't know why."

She leaned forward and murmured, "But won't he tell the truth?"

I sighed. "I don't know. We all loved Gary and Karen. Maybe they had a pact—protect the Walshes above all else." I dabbed my sleeve against my tears. "They've been through enough—and they're about to have their dead daughter's name raked through the mud. They protected us. Why send them to jail now?"

"But what about Cameron?"

"It's his choice."

She thought about it. "Won't they know from the blackmail payouts?"

"Mikki didn't mention that either. If Daniel doesn't tell them about the one letter he saw, then . . . I don't think anyone will know." I swallowed. "I mean, if Jinny finally gets justice, I think that'll be the end of it. I don't see why her mother would keep blackmailing us."

She gazed at me for a moment, then looked away.

"Katie?"

"Uh-huh?"

My voice was so quiet it wafted like candle smoke: "You can't tell anyone about Jinny."

She stared out the window, at the naked branch bowing in the wind. Finally she turned to me. "Who's Jinny?"

CHAPTER 28

Katie

The press had a field day, of course, but Hana handled it all with aplomb; it was the week between Christmas and New Year's, that dark week when no one's paying much attention to the news anyway, so it all blew over surprisingly quickly. The Herd was set to reopen January 21, after Martin Luther King Jr. Day, with Stephanie (finally back from Goa) as acting CEO and a search underway for a new leadership team. And the Fort Greene construction and Titan acquisition were soldiering on, on delayed schedules; Hana mentioned that a conference room in the Fort Greene Herd would be named after Eleanor, which, 'kay.

After rehearsing her speech with Mom and me, Hana told Stephanie she'd stay through February to help with the reopening, and then she'd drop the Herd as a client—but she'd remain a member,

she kept saying, and she was happy to help them find new representation. Stephanie, Hana reported afterward, said supportive things
and seemed unsurprised.

Stephanie also let me know that my application would be processed in time for the Herd's reopening. I laughed when I saw the
email—in all the drama, I'd almost forgotten that my membership
was still pending. I thanked her but said I wouldn't be joining.
There were other coworking spaces, other networking opportuni-
ties, other places where passionate women and marginalized genders could come together, and if there weren't, maybe someday
we'd make one.

Hana got Mom an Airbnb in her building, and I think all three
of us were surprised by how well it went; Hana and I felt lazy and
heartsick and Mom filled the caretaker role, heating up canned
soup and picking up supplies at a bodega, a word she never tired of
saying aloud, in her Midwestern accent, bo-day-gah. I realized that,
in all the years since we'd grown up, Hana and Mom had really only
seen each other in Kalamazoo, in the high-stakes crucible of holiday dinners and the awful period when Mom was starting treatment.
Mom still criticized Hana (Don't you ever clean inside here? she'd
hollered once, her head stuck inside Hana's microwave, and for a
split second Hana's face revealed a desire to turn the appliance on),
but my sister seemed much more eager to laugh, change the subject, and move on these days. As if she no longer needed Mom's
elusive approval. Here, with our own quarters to which to retreat,
we all seemed okay.

Some nights I dreamed of the moment I lost consciousness just
inside Mikki's bedroom door. I couldn't remember it, but in the
dream I sensed a swirling Jacuzzi of searing pain and confusion,
and then the light changing from blue-gray to yellow-white. From
there, the dream always skated off somewhere that only made sense
in REM logic: me naked in Chris's bedroom and the ambulance
making all that noise and light, or me wearing a snowsuit and play-

ing with school-age Hana in the woods beyond our home in Kalamazoo, or me showing up for my interview at the Herd, my very
first day, realizing at the last second that I was supposed to wear
heels, only I'd forgotten and pulled on boots.

Other nights, I had stress dreams about officers in SWAT gear
busting into Hana's apartment, slipping handcuffs around her wrists
and ushering her out into the night. I'd kept mum about the Jinny
stuff, now pinned entirely on Eleanor, Mikki, and Cameron—but
someone would crack, Cameron would talk while he awaited trial
as a cooperating witness, right? Hana's arrest felt nightmarishly inevitable. But she didn't mention it or seem especially worried. Finally I asked her point-blank, and she insisted she was safe.

"But I hope they find Jinny," she said seriously, smoothing my
hair. "This has been hanging over me for so long and now that it's
over, I realize what an idiot I was for not dealing with it sooner."

"Are you going to tell them about Gary and Karen?" I asked.

She held my gaze, then looked askance. "You don't understand
how important they are to me. And to Mikki. And to Cameron."

I nodded and vowed to never ask about it again.

It seemed Mikki's gamble had worked: She claimed that she
had, rather improbably, committed involuntary manslaughter not
once but twice, and that twice her buddy Cameron had made the
whole thing go away. In lieu of Mikki's mug shot, a beautiful headshot from the Herd's website accompanied the story in newspapers,
online, and on the nightly news. It was how she liked to think of
herself looking: chin set, hair a wild blond mane, freckles blaring,
sapphire eyes staring directly into the camera with a lioness's intensity.

My literary agent, Erin, emailed when the news about Eleanor and
Mikki broke and asked if we could talk sometime in the New Year.
I'd figured out what I'd tell her and felt surprisingly Zen about the

whole thing. Then Gary and Karen surprised me by emailing me their exclusive blessing to write Eleanor's biography, or perhaps to write *their* story (*We don't know how these things work but a woman from Hachette keeps leaving voicemails*), as long as they had final approval. Which meant, I presumed, no mention of Jinny or Mikki or maybe even Cameron.

Then, on New Year's Eve, my phone rang. I don't normally pick up calls from unknown numbers, but this was a local landline, and curiosity got the better of me.

A recording clunked on: "This call will be monitored and recorded. You have a collect call from . . . Mikki Danziger." Hearing her voice made me jump. ". . . an inmate at Bedford Hills Correctional Facility. If you would like to accept this collect call, please press one."

I was a human whirlwind, somehow whipping out a digital recorder, accepting the call, and putting her on speakerphone all in one scrambling swoop.

"Mikki?"

A rush of static. "Katie? Is that you?"

"Oh my God. Can you hear me?"

"I can hear you. Thanks for picking up."

I sat there, staring at the phone. *Was this real?* "The blisters on my fingers and ears from the frostbite are finally healing—thanks for asking."

"I'm sorry. I am. For everything."

"Are you?"

"I am." Her voice trembled. "I can't tell you how sorry I am. And how awful I feel. I'm not a bad person, Katie, and I want to make it up to you and Hana and, and everyone. That's why . . . that's why *I'm* here." The emphasis was subtle, too subtle for the recording to catch, but I heard it: *I'm locked up alone, without Hana, without the Walshes, without the guilty people I could've implicated. I'm taking the fall.*

"I don't know what to say, Mikki." *Thank you* wasn't right. Something crested and plunged in me, this unbearable sadness.

"I wish I could say more. But—but I won't. And I'm sorry. And I have a question."

"What's that?"

Sine waves of static as she breathed in and out. "There's another woman here, she was a sex worker who shot and killed her pimp—and a journalist is talking to her about her life story, she's gonna do, like, an as-told-to memoir. With both their names on it."

I frowned. "Okay."

"And I've had all these requests from journalists, which I'm ignoring. But I thought maybe you'd want us to do one together. Since you're the only one I'd trust with it. And I know you still want to write a book."

In Cold Blood popped into my head—my very own true-crime thriller. Only I was a character, I was the one with a blow to the skull at the climax. Before I could stop it, my brain started spitting out lines of description, the way I'd describe the scene as I awoke on the fire escape, shaking like a jackhammer. The instant flow was at once intriguing and sickening.

"I don't know, Mikki. That's a—that's a crazy thing to ask."

"I couldn't make any money from it, obviously. But just think about it, okay?" she said. "Talk to your agent. It'd be . . . cathartic for me. And good for you. It's the least I could do."

"It really is," I replied, but the snap was out of my voice. An automated voice told me to load more time onto the call, and I hung up, blinking into my cold, dark room.

That evening, I arrived at Hana's a little after six, carrying a cake I'd made from a mix and nearly dropping it as I squatted to scratch Cosmo's ears. Hana had replaced the usual bell on his collar with a little disco ball, and I told him he looked very festive.

The plan was to ring in the New Year with a quiet night at Hana's place; we were making spicy fish tacos for us and Mom. The recipe was one of our more successful endeavors from that sleepy period right after I'd moved back, which felt like years ago, now. Hana and I clattered around her kitchen, discussing food-prep logistics and sipping old-fashioneds I'd made.

Finally, I took a deep breath. "I have an announcement."

"Oh?"

"I'm going to write *Infopocalypse*. I mean, if they'll still let me."

"*Really.*" Hana leaned against the kitchen island.

I nodded. "It's what I committed to doing. And I'm going to make it part memoir and talk about how lonely and miserable I really was while I reported it, but how on social media I made it look like everything was great. The book's going to be about fake-news culture as a whole—including in our personal lives. Curation, editing, thinking our actual realities, our *selves*, aren't enough."

"Wow." Hana nodded slowly. "I love it. Why the change of heart?"

I shrugged. "I kept telling myself the reason I didn't want to write it was that I didn't have enough material, after all my interview subjects stonewalled me. But that's not it—I was just ashamed. I cared so much what everyone thought and how, like, all these randos from high school who seemed vaguely impressed that I was writing a book were going to think I was a loser. So dumb." Cosmo slinked by and I bowed to stroke his back. "I want to channel some Eleanor energy. She didn't give a flying fuck what anyone thought of her. But . . . but in my own, non-destructive way." I hated the way Eleanor had trampled on Mikki and other women—much as I disliked peering at this side of her, I knew it was as real as the Eleanor I knew and the "Teleanor" she showed the world. But it wasn't how I'd do things. I'd remember her magnificence, the power of her confidence and bubbling laughter and ability to make you feel inspired, capable, invincible . . . and I'd find my own way to give zero fucks. *Without* destroying those around me.

Hana smiled and made vague congratulations. I pulled a cutting board out from under the sink and pressed it on the counter. "There's another thing."

Hana's face was in the fridge, lit up by its yellow bulb. "Oh yeah?"

"Remember how, right after I got home from the hospital, I had you share the time and transaction number of your last Bitcoin payment?"

She slid the vegetable drawer open and lifted a fat purple cabbage. "Yep?"

"I . . . I know a little bit about how cryptocurrency works. There's, like, a massive ledger showing every transaction—anonymously, of course." I'd dipped my toe into cryptocurrency reporting back at *Rocket*; I knew how to sift through the blockchain and triangulate a particular transaction. "And I figured something out."

Hana closed the fridge door slowly and turned to me. She gripped the cabbage with both hands and frowned. Surely she'd also noticed today was the deadline of that final demand. Surely she, too, was wondering what'd happen at midnight.

"Hana, there were only two payers," I said. She blinked and I repeated myself: "Two wallets—two accounts—transferred funds to the blackmailer. Not three. Ten thousand dollars near the end of every quarter."

In her eyes, understanding caught on like kindling set aflame. She placed the vegetable on the counter.

"It was Mikki," she said, "all along. She told me. She told me how deep into debt she'd fallen, how she'd do anything to keep up. Oh my God." Her fingers found her temple. "She showed up in Eleanor's office and told us she'd gotten a letter, too, but of course it was her. She said it had to be Jinny's mom. Because of the Tennessee postmark, and because her mom supposedly had looked at

Mikki on LinkedIn or something. We never doubted her." What came out was a laugh, barking and strained.

"Yeah, apparently it's really easy to find a service to print and mail stuff for you. Without leaving a trace." No one else had thought to Google it. No one else had thought to question Mikki.

Hana shook her head. "Wow. So it's really over."

"It's over." I sighed. "Can I ask you something?"

"Yes. But the offer expires with 2019."

"Turns into a pumpkin at midnight—got it." I pulled a knife from the block. "Do you think Eleanor was really going to leave? Run off to Mexico?"

She held the cabbage under the tap, then gave it a shake. "I think she just liked knowing she could. That she could drop everything and be out of here in a minute. And I think the blackmail had something to do with that. She realized this horrible accident from her past was going to keep following her."

"God, the irony: Mikki didn't actually want word to get out either. She just wanted money."

"And they both started feeling suffocated by the masks they were wearing." She pointed at me. "Exactly like you're going to talk about in your book. I love this new direction so much. It's the kind of messaging we *actually* need."

I didn't tell her about Gary and Karen's offer or about Mikki's proposition. They were frozen assets, useless to me for now. Instead I asked when Mom would come by for dinner ("any minute now") and she asked, absentmindedly, what Mom had done for New Year's last year.

"She went to Aunt Emmy's." I frowned at the limes in front of me, debating which way to slice them first. "I can't remember if she had more people over or if it was just them."

Hana turned on a burner, then the vent hood. She had to yell to be heard over it. "Remember when Mom and Dad had that big

New Year's party?" she called. "And they invited my band teacher, Mr. Zimmerman, and he got kind of drunk?"

I laughed, piling lime wedges in a bowl. "Did you talk to Dad today?"

She looked at me over her shoulder. "Have I talked to Dad all year?"

I pulled tortillas from their wrapper and padded over to the stove. "I haven't either. But maybe we should text him." She didn't reply and I swallowed. "What's your thing with him?"

She flipped two tilapia fillets and then shut off the fan. Instantly, the room felt calmer. "Did you know Dad had to talk Mom into adopting me?" She half laughed. "Apparently that's very rare. Usually the woman wants to adopt and the man is like, 'Hell no, I'm not raising someone else's spawn.' Some BS caveman stuff. But they both wanted kids, and they weren't having any luck, and Dad was sick of trying, apparently. Enter: me."

The fillets frizzled on the pan, growing hazy in the smoke the fan was no longer inhaling. "And then I was three when Mom found out she was pregnant. I've probably made this up, but I could swear I remember her telling me, pointing at her belly and just leaving me mystified."

She nudged the fish with a spatula. "And then I was at peak bitchiness when they split. Of course I wanted to go live with Dad in Los Angeles. California over Kalamazoo? When you're fourteen? No-brainer."

"But you *left* me," I said, like the ten-year-old I'd been at the time. "It was bad enough that he abandoned us. Then you left too."

"Ohh, Katie." She put down the utensil and pulled me into a hug. "I'm so sorry. Fourteen-year-olds are stupid." She smoothed my hair. "I guess I thought you'd be okay, because you and Mom were so close."

"But you're my *sister*."

"I know. That's why I had to move to New York. I realized what an idiot I'd been. Well, that and Eleanor begged me to come help her launch the Herd." She suddenly noticed the tilapia was leaking smoke and switched the vent back on. "Whoops."

"Blackened tilapia is totally a thing. Cajun."

She smiled. "Now, should we—"

I took her by surprise with another hug, and I heard her little giggle/sob near my shoulder. She pulled away and we were both laugh-crying. There was a sharp knock at the door, followed by the doorbell, and we both wiped our eyes, breathed deep.

"What are we gonna do, Katie?" Hana rubbed at her nose.

"I don't know," I admitted. "But at least we're together."

Mom fell asleep on the loveseat a little after eleven, and Hana and I stayed up, squished next to each other on the couch, sharing a faux-fur blanket and attacking the funfetti cake whole with our forks. Hana kept finding YouTube copies of old Christmas specials we'd taped off TV and watched every year as kids: *Frosty the Snowman*, *Garfield*, this odd Claymation California Raisins special (*Now that's some branded content*, I'd remarked). My phone buzzed on the cushion next to me—a text from Ted, the first time I'd heard from him since Beverly. I had a vague sense he was still in Massachusetts, ahead of Eleanor's funeral. I'd see him then, red-eyed and somber, but I hadn't dared to hope I'd get together with him socially again.

"Here's to a happier 2020," it read. "Meeting you was a bright spot in an otherwise shit year."

I smiled, flicked through a few funny things I could write back. Instead: "Likewise. And happy new year. ☺"

I checked the time. "Quick, Hana! We're going to miss the ball dropping!"

She switched over to live TV, plosive and blaring, and I shook

Mom awake as Hana dashed into the kitchen to open a bottle of Champagne. We counted down together, time moving backward for once, backward to when we were carefree little kids, arranging benches in the snow for elaborate games of make-believe. We hit zero and cheered, clinking our glasses and smiling at one another, and Hana's and my phones blooped with a text from Daniel: "HNY!" I volleyed the well wishes back. He was with his parents tonight, Hana had mentioned, and doing fine.

"Mom, what does 'auld lang syne' mean again?" I asked, because it's one of those unspoken, knee-jerk family traditions, like Hana pointing and saying, *That's Jean Shepherd, he wrote the book* during his featured-extra moment in *A Christmas Story.*

Mom grinned. "To times long past!"

To auld lang syne. To clever little Eleanor and her neighbor Cameron, biking back and forth between their grand front doors. To gawky teenage Mikki, thrilled to be part of a crowd, one of the girls, for the first time in her life. To Hana and me, stealing cheese cubes and red-spangled sugar cookies from the table and sitting under the Christmas tree, watching Mom and Dad's glamorous New Year's Eve party, observing all the adults in their blouses and dresses and jackets and confidence, such grown-ups with their glasses of foamy Champagne.

Hana refilled all of our flutes, slender cups of kindness yet, and we clinked them together one more time.

Karen sat in the kitchen, a fluffy white robe tied around her, practical cork-bottomed slippers on her feet. It was March, but frost still licked the windows and coated the grass beyond the patio and pool. She and Gary had just returned from two weeks in Saint Martin, hot, sunny days at the pool or on the beach or on one of their two balconies, watching the sun rise and then set, over and over.

It'd been Gary's idea, a way to relax and reconnect after the hellishness of the holiday season. Her beautiful daughter's funeral, the saddest day of her life. The sudden loss of their best friends, the Corrigans down the street—a For Sale sign had just appeared in front of their white-columned mansion, mercifully. The weird, tense weeks when detectives kept popping by the house, asking more and more questions about a weekend in 2010 that Gary and Karen couldn't possibly remember. Neither of them kept diaries or hung on to their old agenda books. But clearly the police were taking seriously the awful rantings of Eleanor's killer. Karen went to check the weather on Gary's laptop one day and found "posthumous trial" at the top of his recent Google searches, and she'd rushed to the toilet and thrown up on the spot: The idea was just too awful, Eleanor's ghost being tried for some ghastly crime. But she'd never mentioned it to Gary, and eventually, the visits from detectives had stopped.

The sun wouldn't set for a few more hours, but it seemed late enough to treat herself to a glass of wine. She rifled through the fridge and cabinets and, finding none there, opened the door to the basement and flipped on the light. She hated going down here, past the refurbished part, the leather sofa and enormous TV—hated pushing through the folding doors into the dank, cold section where bald lightbulbs hung, their pull cords swaying. She especially hated passing the spot, now a jumbled four-shelf storage unit, where the chest freezer once sat. She hurried past it, reaching the rack of dusty bottles, and selected a 2015 Cab Sauv from Sonoma Valley. She tugged on the string near her head, flicking off the light, and turned to leave. Then she locked eyes with a face staring out from the storage rack.

She screamed and dropped the bottle, wine splashing onto her slippers and spreading out along the cement floor. Flailing around, she found and yanked the bulb's cord again, bathing the area in light. She stepped forward, her pulse pounding, and squinted, but she couldn't figure out what object on the shelf—books, ski gear, boxes, old magazines, a bin of gently used gift bags and crumpled bows—had looked to her like a face. On the ground, the blob of wine lapped at a nearby box, and she hurried back upstairs to grab paper towels from the kitchen.

As she ripped the roll from the wall, her memory betrayed her, cueing up the one thing she begged it nightly not to show her: that beautiful black-haired girl, a chunk of her hair sheared down to fuzz, her smooth skin frosted over like it was dusted in flour, resting calmly in the chest freezer while Gary ordered Eleanor away, yammering about all the ways you can identify a body: clothes, teeth, marks, fingers. He ranted and muttered and slammed the freezer door closed as Karen's mind homed in on the smallest detail, one that worked its way into her dreams even now—the girl's beautiful nails, ebony speckled with tiny white stars. How rich the black looked against her delicate, milky fingers. Gary had walked in small circles, repeating the words, turning them into a mantra: *clothesteethmarksfingers. Clothesteethmarksfingers.* Like a puzzle he had to solve.

And he had, somehow, though he'd never told Karen how. He and Cameron had handled it one night, a night Gary assumed she'd slept through, and in the morning, to be kind, she played along. Cameron had never been the same after that, poor thing—missing work, moving from painkillers to heroin, his life like a car speeding off a cliff. All for Eleanor. All for their luminous little girl. All for Eleanor, dead at thirty.

She'd never told Gary her horrible secret. There was no point, not by the time they got home and found the body in the breakfast nook, just inside the patio doors. She heard the girls' story, looked at the missed calls and voicemails on Gary's phone until she'd nailed down their timeline, figured out exactly when Mikki, Hana, and Eleanor had given up and called it a night. But Karen knew how long it took for rigor mortis to set in, for a soft body to grow stiff; she was, after all, a nurse, familiar with this odd biological detail. And their story didn't check out. The pale neck Karen thrust her fingers against to feel for a pulse—still supple. The body they carried into the basement once the girls had packed their things and left—not nearly stiff enough. Karen knew her daughter and her friends weren't lying; there was no doubt in their hungover minds that this black-haired girl was dead by the time they went upstairs. What good would it have done to correct them, after the fact?

Karen forced herself back into the basement. Shit—her slippers had tracked wine out onto the carpet, ruby footsteps that looked just like blood. She gasped as she took it all in: jagged red ovals alternating their way past the sofa and up the stairs, out to the light, out to freedom.

She walked to the edge of the puddle, which had formed the shape of a kidney, of a baby in the fetal position. Slowly she sank to her knees, watching the wine seep into her robe. She walked her hands out in front of her, barely noticing the shards of glass cutting into her palms. She lowered her body down onto its side, her head resting on her forearm, and as the bare bulb droned overhead, she wept.

ACKNOWLEDGMENTS

First and foremost, I'm so grateful to you, the reader. You walked around in my brain and let my words leave little fingerprints on your mind, and for an author there's truly nothing more incredible. Of all the books in the world (and all the things you could do with your time), you chose to read this novel, and that means more to me than I can say. I hope something in it felt true to you. Thank you, thank you, thank you.

I'm grateful to my brilliant and kind big sister, Julia, who proved to me that sisters can also be best friends and who let me build snow forts and create elaborate worlds of make-believe with her when we were kids. Thanks for being supportive and insightful, always. I'm the luckiest.

I don't know what I'd do without my intrepid first readers, Megan Brown and Leah Konen, who provided swift and thoughtful notes when the first draft was so rough, you could light a match against it. (That honestly might've been the manuscript's fate if it weren't for you two.) I can't thank you enough for your time, help, and support. Massive thanks, too, to early readers Jennifer Keishin Armstrong, Erin DeYoung, Alanna Greco, and Jinny VanZanten for your generosity and insight. I'm so lucky to have each and every one of you in my life, and not just because you're all incredible wordsmiths.

In fact, I'm unspeakably fortunate to be surrounded by amazing women (and super-healthy female friendships) in New York City, Milwaukee, and beyond. Lianna Bishop, Blaire Briody, Kate Dietrick, Katherine Pettit, Abbi Libers, Kate Lord, Anna Maltby, Erin Pastrana, Katie Scott, Nicole Stahl, Jen Weber, and others (you know who you are)—I just love you so damn much.

I still kind of wake up expecting to learn there's been some mistake and the legendary Alexandra Machinist is *not*, in fact, my literary agent—but then you show up for me in ways I couldn't imagine and make even my most outlandish dreams come true. I'm honored to work with such a kind, down-to-earth, outrageously talented badass. That's true of the entire ICM family, including Ruth Landry and Josie Freedman: You are so startlingly brilliant and good at your jobs and also such great people; I'd hate you if I didn't adore you so much.

Speaking of unstoppable women, there aren't words for how grateful I am to my editor, Hilary Rubin Teeman, who knew what an *Andrea Bartz Thriller* [hand flourish] should look like well before I did. It is truly a pleasure writing for you and soaking up your genius. Thanks so much to the wonderful Angeline Rodriguez—what a privilege (and a treat!) to work with you. Sarah Breivogel puts every other publicist on the planet (<<not an exaggeration) to shame and should know that my biggest mood swing in this entire process involved learning I was moving to a new imprint with, I assumed, a different PR team ☹ and then discovering we would be working together again! ☺☺☺ I can't thank you, as well as the entire terrific team at Ballantine, enough. That includes the designers, copyeditors, proofreaders, production editors, and every other

unsung hero who helped turn this Word document into a book. Special shout-out to the person who has to make smiley faces show up here. I don't know you but I love you. ☺

I've been so fortunate to meet many warm, generous, empathetic, and talented fellow authors over the last couple of years. Huge thanks to Megan Collins (*The Winter Sister*), Kate Hope Day (*If, Then*), Angie Kim (*Miracle Creek*), Julie Langsdorf (*White Elephant*), Nicole Mabry (*Past This Point*), Daniela Petrova (*Her Daughter's Mother*), Julia Phillips (*Disappearing Earth*), Melissa Rivero (*The Affairs of the Falcóns*) and the whole DA gang for your encouragement, camaraderie, and kindness throughout this nutty process. (Reader, do yourself a favor and buy their amazing novels!)

A billion thank-yous to the social justice warriors and intersectional feminists fighting to make the world a kinder, fairer place for women and other marginalized groups. It's a scary time to be a woman and an even scarier time to be rising up and battling inequality and injustice. We see you.

Last but certainly not least, thank you to my parents, grandparents, and entire extended family—your support and encouragement mean the world to me. I love you.

ABOUT THE AUTHOR

ANDREA BARTZ is a Brooklyn-based journalist and author of *The Lost Night*. Her work has appeared in *The Wall Street Journal, Marie Claire, Vogue, Cosmopolitan, Women's Health, Martha Stewart Living, Redbook, Elle,* and many other outlets, and she's held editorial positions at *Glamour, Psychology Today,* and *Self,* among other titles.